Fits
Like
a
Rubber
Dress

Fits Like a Rubber Dress

a novel

Roxane Ward

SIMON & PIERRE
A MEMBER OF THE DUNDURN GROUP
TORONTO · OXFORD

Editor: Marc Côté
Copyeditor: Barry Jowett
Printer: Transcontinental Printing Inc.

Canadian Cataloguing in Publication Data
Ward, Roxane
Fits like a rubber dress

ISBN 0-88924-284-4

I. Title
PS8595.A767F57 1999   C813'.54   C99-930510-7
PR9199.3.W359F57 1999

1   2   3   4   5   03   02   01   00   99

THE CANADA COUNCIL | LE CONSEIL DES ARTS
FOR THE ARTS | DU CANADA
SINCE 1957 | DEPUIS 1957

We acknowledge the support of the **Canada Council for the Arts** for our publishing program. We also acknowledge the support of the **Ontario Arts Council** and the **Book Publishing Industry Development Program** of the **Department of Canadian Heritage.**

Care has been taken to trace the ownership of copyright material used in this book. The author and the publisher welcome any information enabling them to rectify any references or credit in subsequent editions.

Printed and bound in Canada.

Printed on recycled paper.

Set in Goudy
Designed by Scott Reid

Simon & Pierre
8 Market Street
Suite 200
Toronto, Canada
M5E 1M6

Simon & Pierre
73 Lime Walk
Headington, Oxford,
England
OX3 7AD

Simon & Pierre
2250 Military Road
Tonawanda NY
U.S.A 14150

For Robert Bouvier

La terre est bleue comme une orange
Paul Eluard (1895–1952)

The earth is blue as an orange

One

Indigo thought of urine as she poured samples of the yellow soda into small white paper cups. The label boasted ONE PERCENT REAL FRUIT JUICE. Ninety-eight percent gnat pee and a dash of beetle spit, she thought, smiling for the first time since she pulled herself out of bed wondering what kind of God would make her work on Sunday morning. It must be especially hard to collect the pee of gnats.

She'd been aiming for perky, but settled for civil with a segue to cheerful later on. She'd been out till after two.

She needed coffee. And now she was forced to wear orange: a pleated skirt and sweater, with *Squeeze* scrawled across her chest in bold white script. The orange was making her nauseous and she wondered how the sum of her life choices could have landed her here, at the first annual Run for the Arts, in what looked like a cheerleader's outfit, to pass out samples of pop with a man dressed as a lemon.

"Indigo Blackwell in orange. Sounds like a bruise, but you look fab. How goes the battle, baby?"

"Hey Tim. Not bad. Almost all set up. And I feel like a bruise. Too much wine, too little sleep. Can you believe this stuff is caffeine-free? They think that's a good thing. You know, you really do look hilarious."

Tim Keeler was Indigo's best friend — or at least that's what they called it as kids, when the distinction seemed important. His face peered out of a giant pocked lemon that began in a softened point above his head and came to a close around his thighs. Yellow arms and legs sprang from a substantial plastic girth and he waddled forward, squeezing the air in a feigned attack on her breasts.

"I was born for this part. Have you had a squeeze today? No, too subtle. HAVE YOU HAD A SQUEEZE TODAY. See, I'm terrific. Beautiful women beware of large charming lemons. I come to squeeze your —"

"Don't go there," said Indigo quickly. "Don't even think about it. We talked about this." His face took on a look of exaggerated hurt and Indigo smiled. "Listen to me," she said. "Behave for once in your life. You promised."

"Ow. Someone hasn't been getting any. Where'd you and Sam end up last night, anyway?"

"He stayed in. Nicole and I went to Side Effects, then to the Lounge. Didn't stay long but I'm feeling fragile. So be gentle with me."

The run began and ended at Berczy Park, a gesture of green on the verge of Toronto's downtown core, across from two cement, angular theatres. The Council needed a site that signalled the arts, but nothing too grubby — the run was black tie. The theatres across from the park lay claim to ballet and most of the opera, plays and the occasional dignified concert. An appropriate choice for the upscale arts enthusiast.

This morning, traffic was cordoned off and runners were spread on the still-damp grass, stretching, preventing aftershock. They stood out in bow ties and dickeys, nylon and mesh. Large red numbers pinned to the front of their shirts.

Indigo thought she could also pick out the mere spectators from the writers and artists in line for grants but disdainful of the need to be present, on display, while mostly corporate Canadians braced the National Council for the Arts.

The artists looked earnest or bored.

They were the ones in mostly black — bored. Ripped jeans and T-shirts. Painted leather jackets. Slim young men with powerful hands and (she embellished) dirty nails. A few shaved heads.

The Birkenstock set — earnest. Women in loose-fitting clothes, with beaded earrings and thick wool socks, unshaven armpits. Grey ponytails coaxed from thinning hair. Turquoise rings and silver bolo ties. Denim shirts.

There were celebrities, of course. Some cultish, a few larger than life — past recipients, waving (some enthusiastically, others demurely) from the top of the funding food chain. Inspiration to the up-and-comings, proof the system works.

Canadian culture, live at Berczy Park.

Indigo and Tim were positioned near the fountain, under a wide yellow banner with thick orange script: *Have a Squeeze!*

She tried to ignore it and poured, organizing the samples into stripes of orange and lemon soda, three cups wide, twelve cups deep. This amused her for the moment, suited the haze of her morning-after brain. And she preferred it to Tim's job — to mingle with a tray of mini-drinks and coupons. The ever-social, always lascivious Tim-child. Always a favourite, as long as he kept his hands off her girlfriends. And any future daughters.

Her thoughts were paddling in the tiny pools of liquid when the last of the more ominous clouds drifted east, finally, and the sun appeared, making the yellow and orange less obtrusive. Not grey day colours, she thought. Advertising colours. Promotional colours. Take-one-free-and-buy-more-later colours. Colours that needed a backdrop of sun to maintain the illusion, make her feel less out of place.

There weren't many takers, but it was still a bit early for pop. And cold, although it could have been worse. It had been a vicious spring so far: dark brown and bleak, with flurries of snow instead of rain; a topic of much bitter complaint among strangers. At least now there was green on the trees, red and yellow tulips in the dirt. At last.

She was contemplating a slightly more aggressive tack when a man approached, attractive in a dirty sort of way, looking somewhat peaked himself — pale and disheveled — although it might have been affected. He reeked of stale beer.

"Thirsty?" She gestured to the cups.

He downed a lemon, an orange and three more lemons. "I'll have a Bloody Mary. Please."

Indigo smiled. "Sorry. Red would clash. We're a fashion conscious bunch. Appearances, you know."

He stared at her, then said — "I noticed the rows. But I thought you were bored. Or maybe just anal." She saw that his eyes looked vaguely out of focus; the whites were tinged with red.

"Bang on. You've won your fill of samples and a squeeze from Mr. Lemon. Hey Tim, you're back. That was fast."

"They like me. They really like me. Peter — what are you doing here? I didn't think you did morning. Or is it still last night?"

"Something like that." The man shrugged and raised his eyebrows, smirking. "Jesus, Tim. You look totally fucking ridiculous. I hope you're getting paid well — you'll never get laid in that."

"I am, and I couldn't if I wanted to," said Tim, placing his yellow hand flat on his yellow chest and burping. "Can't even take a leak without more initiative than I've probably ever had." He turned to look at Indigo. "Refill please, my lovely." Then back to Peter. "You two know each other?"

Peter Dumas was a writer, buoyed by the success of his first play, contemplating a second, much in demand at parties.

"Indigo writes too," said Tim.

"Not like that," she said, embarrassed. "Corporate stuff. You know, PR. Press releases, newsletters, that sort of thing. Government briefs."

"Now there's a frightening thought," said Peter. "Jockeys or boxers?"

She was feeling better. "G-strings. They passed a bill, it's law."

A bang and the crowd cheered. The runners ran west for half a block, then north, with several of the fastest sprinting ahead of the pack. It was warmer now, and samples of Squeeze were in demand.

As they watched Tim wedge his way into a group of mostly women, Peter announced that he was off in search of something with a bite. "Something I can relate to," he said. "Something alcoholic. Like me. But I'll settle for coffee." He pulled out a pair of mirrored sunglasses, shook his hair and put them on.

As he left he blew her a kiss.

When Tim came back, Indigo said — "So what did you do last night?"

"Not a thing. Left work at midnight, it was slow. Went home. Crashed."

"That doesn't sound like you." Indigo had begun to fill the tray with samples, lemon on the left, orange to the right, as Tim stood by and watched.

"Yeah, well. Went out Friday, got home Saturday afternoon."

"That's more like it. Where'd you go?"

"Some warehouse near the lake. With busloads of pretty young things. Nubiles. All dancing. If you can call it dancing. It's more like the physical version of a great long *Om*. Very higher plain stuff." As he said the word "*Om*" he raised his arms, pressing yellow thumbs to yellow forefingers.

"And there's no sex," said Indigo.

"Touching is of a non-sexual nature only. We may be strangers but we all *care* about each other. Deeply. Except the crystal heads but they're another trip. It's profound." He paused and she saw that he was smirking. "It really turns me on."

"You don't change," said Indigo.

"Yeah yeah. Deep down I'm a very shallow person."

"You know, I've never been to a rave."

"I do know. I keep telling you to come, check out the vibe."

"I'm too old to trade stickers."

"Do some *e*, then we'll see who's old. Me, I like the glow sticks. And the glitter. My goddamn sheets are covered in glitter."

"Forever young."

"It's the great contradiction of raves," said Tim. "The old feel young — unless they haven't consumed enough drugs, in which case they feel very very old. The superficial feel enlightened. And it's all just a great capitalist plot cloaked in anti-establishment glitter. You gotta love the irony."

She looked at his face, which had taken on a lemon glow, and said — "You didn't just think of that."

"Okay, I read it in *The Globe*. So sue me for sounding intelligent."

Indigo laughed, shaking her head. They'd known each other much too long. "Does your friend go to raves? That guy, Peter?"

"Peter? No, Peter's a boozecan man. Prefers his nights less wholesome."

"I thought he seemed nice."

"No kidding. Nice?"

"Sure, why not? He's funny."

"He's okay. I guess. I wouldn't use the word *nice*."

"How do you know him?"

"Comes to Vox," said Tim. "Shows up before last call, half cut. Wants to know who's going where. Says he was born in a boozecan, that's why he likes them. One time he made up a whole thing around it. Said there was something wrong with his mother's milk so they improvised, gave him a White Russian, made him a bed under the pool table — where I know for a fact he's been since. He's a lousy drunk, not your type at all. Definitely not your type. Gets obnoxious. Says he sleeps all day and lives all night. I don't know when he writes." As he picked up the tray, he added — "Why, you want to fool around?"

"That's your style. I just said he was nice." And then — "Don't stare at me like that. Sam and I are fine."

A few minutes later he was back. "Look who's here. We're gonna be on TV."

"Not me," said Indigo. "Isn't that right Nicole? You said you'd shoot Tim and the banner, leave me out of it. You promised."

"Did I? Funny, seems to have slipped my mind. I must have been drunk. Now I'm hungover and it's all your fault. Besides, we have at least twenty minutes to kill before the winners come running triumphantly down the chute. Why waste it when we can have a Squeeze with you. Just do whatever it is you're doing, and I'll do my thing here. Be happy darling, I'll make you a star."

Nicole Turner worked for the ever-hip COOL-TV and its affiliate, MEGA Music. And, as a friend, she was apparently determined to make Indigo's humiliation in orange complete.

"I look like hell in orange."

"Everybody looks like hell in orange. Two minutes."

Indigo dredged up what she hoped was a sunny guise. The surprise made her anxious, but she didn't have the energy to follow through with any substantial feeling of panic. Crouching down, she found her purse under the table, ran her fingers through her hair and applied a fresh coat of lipstick; she stood up too fast and felt a wave of regret for that one last glass of wine.

On a personal level, she counted on being upstaged by Tim. But they'd be live on MEGA Music, and maybe again on the news at six. And despite her objections, the part of her that worked for Pinnacle Public Relations knew that it was something of a coup to get Squeeze on the air at all.

She admired Nicole. She wasn't jealous, although she could imagine herself in what seemed like an utterly glam existence. But despite the fact that Nicole had what most people would consider an excessive combination of brains, looks, money and men, Indigo didn't secretly — or even openly — covet her life, which made their friendship uncomplicated.

For one thing, Indigo felt awkward on camera, like she had a fleck of broccoli persistently stuck in her teeth. And she liked being married in spite of current weirdness. Sam's growing irritability was the motivation for what she called her flee-the-country fantasies, but she figured marriage was like that. If they couldn't get past it, she'd find herself a nice little flat with a skylight and a deck, reinvent herself as someone else. Maybe someone with a dog.

But that was probably braver than she felt.

Sam was obsessed with his book, writing nights and weekends, working freelance when he could. So she made allowances. Tried not to think about the way his hands used to feel on her body, or the time they had sex on the roof of their house. Instead, she went out with the girls. Or Tim. And hoped he'd finish soon.

Nicole was single and a magnet for men (like puppies are for women). She was tall, thin and voluptuous, with broad shoulders and dark eyes; one boyfriend called them bottomless, then unfathomable and near the end, opaque. A recent convert to blond, the change had the effect of turning up her volume. She seemed even more confident, in control. According to Nicole, the key to getting what you want is knowing what to ask for. "You've got to speak up," she'd say. "Expect good things. The universe provides."

Indigo didn't feel quite so together. She wanted to embrace the idea that positive thoughts bring positive things, partly for herself and partly to please Nicole. And her mother. But she found it hard to commit. It was in her nature to dwell a little too long in the darkness; she was used to it and the fear was comforting in an odd, self-defeating sort of way.

Fits Like a Rubber Dress   13

If you asked her husband, he'd say she was lovely. (Although if Indigo asked, his face would probably twitch, then he'd sigh and shake his head, tell her to stop being insecure, it's unattractive.) He'd describe her hair, the way it fell in tangled curls down her back, how it wasn't really brown or blond or red, more like waves of all three, thanks to indecisive highlights. He'd mention green eyes that gave away more than she intended. Slender legs and fingers. Winter skin year round.

If you asked her, she'd say that her face was asymmetrical, that her eyes were too small, her nose a bit too long and her ass a size too large, not to mention her feet. But she wasn't blindly critical. And she didn't think she focused on her flaws so much as acknowledged them. She'd always assumed that if she thought too well of herself — well, that was vanity. And that was bad. And then her friends would have to knock her down. They'd be practically obligated.

It was better to do it herself.

Coffee in hand, Peter Dumas wandered back to the booth as Nicole scanned the crowd. "You're exactly what I'm looking for," she said, when Tim introduced them. "Perfect."

Peter nodded. "It's a gift."

As they got ready to start the interview, three teenage boys positioned themselves in the background, where they figured they'd be on TV. One had *anarchy* sprayed in red across his T-shirt, and spikes of purple hair screaming down the back of his otherwise bald skull. Two wore dog collars. All had tattoos, ripped army fatigues and mean black boots. And while the red light was on, each wore a faultless expression of apathy — for the viewers at home.

"It's been billed as the first annual Run for the Arts," began Nicole. "But people here are calling it the Fleeting Culture Marathon. As many of you know, funding for the arts has long been the target of government cutbacks. According to the National Council, next year's budget has been slashed to one tenth of what it was only five years ago. It's no accident that I'm standing here in front of the Squeeze soft drink booth. The National Council has felt the squeeze, and it's been putting the squeeze on artists. But today, the arts community has gone to the public. Right now, more than 3,000 Canadians are running up Yonge Street. They'll run down Rosedale Valley Road to Bayview, south to Front and west to Church — for a total of 10 kilometres and an estimated pot of $90,000. The money will go toward grants for Canadian playwrights and novelists, painters, sculptors, poets and filmmakers. People like Peter Dumas — a writer whose first play, *To hell with you too*, earned him a much coveted Canadian Theatre Award, but has yet to make him a cent.

"Thanks for joining us Peter. What do you think about the Council's decision to raise funds directly from the public?"

He grinned. "I think it sucks, Nicole. But there's no choice. If it were up to the feds, only the wealthy could afford to be artists. The point — and to my mind, the problem — is that this kind of elitism leads to crap. Homogenized output. Give the masses a chance to create and you'll get vastly different perspectives. Tarnished ones, perhaps. Ugly ones. Even disgusting ones. Especially disgusting ones. But no less valid and a lot more interesting."

"So you're saying it's on purpose, the arts are under siege."

"Intent or ignorance, who cares? The point is — we've had enough."

"Given the unfortunate reality, then, do you agree this Run is a good thing?"

"Sure. As good as any. You said the Council expects to raise less than a hundred thousand bucks. What's that? Twenty grants ... thirty? A clink in the old tin cup. But, who knows? Maybe a few more people will take an interest and we'll put some pressure on the folk who sign the cheques. Can you say democracy?"

"I think I can, Peter. But what do you say to critics who think artists should be doing exactly what they're doing today. Raising their own money — taking care of business, as it were."

"I say they don't know what the hell they're talking about. I say we'll end up with nothing but commercial pap. Art as production for people who don't like a ripple in their waters. Tepid bath water from people who couldn't find a boundary let alone test one."

"Maybe so, but can you say democracy?" And then, looking directly into the camera — "In a few minutes, victory lane and a chat with the director of the National Council for the Arts. Back to you, Jim."

Indigo wasn't sure what she thought about subsidies, or if she especially cared. Would she fund the arts over daycare? Or was the question irrelevant, a non sequitur designed to inspire guilt among those who believe in something as obviously frivolous as Toronto's artistic community?

She'd been to an opening recently, courtesy Nicole, at a gallery she and Sam called the Firetrap, a warehouse loft accessible only via two flights of kindling. The artist — a short, squattish-looking man in his 50s — had mounted an exhibit of about a dozen works, each using dolls to make a Statement About War. Born in Dresden but raised in Montreal, he'd only just begun to attack his mother's waistline when Hitler turned on Poland. But, like so many Germans, he spent his adult life distracted — albeit not tortured — by an enduring legacy of death.

Chubby pink dolls were photographed in colour. Plastic babies being brutalized by mannequins clothed in military garb. Neutral faces, oblivious. Cherubs splashed red with paint. Some with streaks of grey, black tears. The photos were shellacked on board and mounted on grainy black-and-white photos of German soldiers marching.

Sam hated it, said its main message was, "Look at me — aren't I angry and clever." Indigo liked it, but not very much and not for the obvious reasons. It seemed too easy, like a rehash of yesterday's news. She was really just impressed that someone was focused enough to create an existence that let them do this sort of thing for a living.

Indigo would have liked to be an artist. She'd certainly like someone to give her the money to live what she imagined to be an artist's life. She'd never wear orange — and at next year's run, she wouldn't have to feel so *not creative*. She'd rent a studio, or build one in the basement. Sculpting appealed, or multi-media. She'd already tried photography, but couldn't get used to the lag between taking and seeing the pictures. She had no illusions about her writing. It was adequate, but it didn't share her darkness. And where's the joy in that?

Indigo decided not to fret it, not today. She had a dull creeping pain behind her eyes that was, at this very moment, a threat to her cheery outlook. She remembered Nicole giving her hell at the Lounge. They'd been sitting on the blue velvet couch near the pool table, well after one. Drinks in hand, dueling chatter.

Nicole said she gave too much energy to negative thoughts. Or, technically speaking, that she made herself nuts. And Nicole ought to know. Years of on-again off-again therapy made her a quality barstool shrink. Late last night, she decided that Indigo gave herself much too hard a time, that she was analytical verging on obsessive and, most important, she should be having a lot more fun.

"You're a sweetie, but you think way too much," said Nicole, jabbing the air with her sharply pointed finger (which Indigo grabbed and returned to its lap). "So you're job's a drag. You and a hundred million other people. That's why they call it work. And your husband's off in space. Men'll do that. He'll come back — and when he does, get him to bring you a present. Something expensive. What you need is less angst and another glass of wine."

After the race, Indigo went to get her car, while Tim rolled the banner and stacked the empty cases of Squeeze. They loaded the coolers in the trunk.

"I can't believe it's only noon," said Indigo. "I feel like we've been here all day."

"And I've had to take a piss for hours. Oh yeah — you want to come for drinks later? Patio season has now officially begun. We'll be on the roof at Babel, ducking UV deathrays."

"Sounds like fun, but I'll pass. Sam said he'd take the afternoon off. I'd rather have sex. You want a ride?"

Tim looked thoughtful. "Yeah, me too. But thanks, I have my bike. Give me a sec to change and you can have the suit." He grabbed his clothes from under the table. "Back in a flash."

Indigo's street was lined with elms and maples — stark brown in winter, like the city, aroused in spring and lush by July, a tunnel of dark green. The houses were mostly Victorian, old and narrow, brick with pointed roofs and wooden porches.

Theirs was actually theirs, thanks to some help from Indigo's mother. It was a mess when they bought it, a dive with beautiful bones, and they'd spent the past four years fixing it up.

Outside, the trim and porch were faded Wedgwood blue, peeling in spots, which stopped in a line down the centre of the house and changed to white. Semi-detached — she'd always thought of it as such an odd expression. Optimistic, since the house was, in reality, very much attached to the one next door.

On the other side, a cement path offered the illusion of distance. Barely wide enough for one, it seemed longer than it was and gave an impression of permanent dampness. When she could, she avoided it. She wasn't completely neurotic, tried not to make it an issue. But it made her feel claustrophobic to have brick walls less than a foot from either shoulder. Irrational, like they were closing in to crush her, which of course made her think of Batman and Robin and big round saw blades that always seemed to head for someone's crotch.

They didn't have a driveway and, as usual, there was no place to park on the street. Indigo was abnormally patient, and wondered if she was weary or simply resigned, finally, to the price one paid to live downtown. She drove around the block twice, without swearing, then found a space in front of her house. A minor miracle. She made up her mind to invite Sam to join her in bed, for the paper and a snooze, to see if her luck would hold.

Inside, Indigo was greeted by the perfumed rush of dried eucalyptus. And silence. She looked upstairs in the general direction of Sam's office but failed, like always, to notice the withering fern in the window, now almost dead from neglect.

"Hello ...?" No answer. Shit.

She stood listening for noise and then, satisfied that no one else was in the house, walked down the hall and into the kitchen. There was a note on the fridge: *Indi, Something came up. Home by dinner, maybe sooner. Apologies for this aft. Love S.* She poured herself a glass of milk and sat at the table.

She could meet Tim and his friends, but that would require energy. She'd have to change and get there, and then she'd have to be sociable, perhaps even lively. She could make a sandwich and sit in the yard — more reasonable but uninspired. Still she didn't move. Instead she sat for several minutes in a kind of numbed-out, final-remains-of-a-hangover-sleepy-stupor, until her brain registered the flashing green words. Sam must have used the microwave to heat up that leftover curried chicken, then taken it out part way, impatient to wait an extra few seconds. PRESS ... START ... PRESS ... START ... PRESS ... START ...

Indigo walked back down the hall and up the stairs. They creaked and she imagined that at 29, her body was beginning to argue back. She liked her bed unmade and sunk gratefully into the blue satin folds of her duvet, leaving a pile of orange on the floor beside the closet.

The distant growl of a motorcycle emphasized the thick cool silence of the house. She considered reading and picked a book up off the pile on the night stand, looked at the jacket, let it fall to the covers beside her.

In sleep it is opening night.

Indigo stands at the door, red lips beckoning a sea of basic black. The lights in the ballroom are dim, the crowd unreasonably beautiful. The audience swells around the bar, thirsty for its first collective drink, parched from the violent ache of the film. Hushed tones broken by a deep, throaty laugh, then chatter. Shock giving way to the need for expression. The chosen few — critics, friends and the self-described elite, party-queens bursting with opinion.

Reporters arrive and she is grateful. *They came.* Cameras slung around necks and hoisted on shoulders. Indigo leads the way, down a long black tunnel. Her palms begin to sweat; she mustn't keep the director waiting. Whispers in the dark. Mediocre. Violent with no socially redeeming qualities. Words of white light flash on the walls and she fights a rising panic. Trite. Vapid. Two thumbs down. At the end of the tunnel — a room, impossibly bright. The reporters are seated in rows of wooden chairs, waiting. Indigo is standing at the podium. She begins to speak and remembers that she is the director. The words on the wall were a eulogy, offered in advance like the reading of a palm.

Indigo looks up. The ceiling is made of mirror, flecked with shards of pink light. She is naked. But the reporters don't see her. They look at their watches, wondering when the director will arrive, and whether they should teach him a lesson — disappear. "We don't have to take this," says one, possibly their leader. "We have the power."

"But I'm here," she cries, chasing them back through the tunnel. "I'm here."

At the party, people are eating hors d'oeuvres, oblivious. "Spicy, but no real taste," says one. "How fitting."

Naked except for a pair of black patent pumps, skinny belt and small matching purse, Indigo is standing on the bar, searching the crowd for reporters. People are snickering, sliding furtive looks, refusing to meet her eyes. With one arm, she tries to cover both breasts, to stave off what she thinks is a final humiliation; she uses the bag to hide her crotch.

The cameras arrive, but only to record her nightmare. They are hostile, like the searing white light of an interrogation. She jumps down and twists her ankle, aware that every ungainly second is being captured on tape. She runs but the pack follows, through a lobby of marble, gold and mirror, through revolving glass doors and into the grey cement night.

Fits Like a Rubber Dress 19

Indigo waited until nine o'clock before deciding on Indian take-out. Fire-spitting food. She ordered chicken tikka, naan and two servings of raita; she liked to roll the meat into torn pieces of the soft round bread, add fried onions and lettuce and dip it all into the cool yogurt and cucumber soup.

Earlier, when she woke up and the house was still silent, she'd tried to read — a book her mom gave her on becoming master of her own happy universe. But it demanded concentration and the more she lay there the more annoyed she felt, until she couldn't stand to be still.

Sam was going to make things up to her today. They were going to hang out, have fun, take their clothes off. It was his idea. She knew she was blowing things out of proportion; she could feel the anxiety welling up like the air in a balloon that was going to burst and scare the shit out of everyone.

They had a date for Tim's party on Friday; she tried to focus on that.

It was almost four o'clock. She got dressed and went to the kitchen, opened the sliding glass door and surveyed the backyard. It needed work, but she wasn't in the mood. She tilted her head to the sky and screamed *fuck*, just once — but long and loud. The neighbourhood quivered and she smiled, went inside and washed the kitchen floor.

"Where were you?" She didn't mean the words to sound so harsh.

"I blew it again, didn't I? I'm a jerk. But wait till you hear what I did."

Indigo clicked off the news but stayed seated, curled at the end of the sofa. The living room was dark and Sam stood in the doorway, still holding his battered leather case. He was backlit by the light from the foyer — practically glowing, she thought, annoyed that she'd been forgotten so completely. He smelled of smoke.

"This guy at work hooked me up with this other guy, a friend of his, and we finally managed to connect. An acquaintance, really, not a friend. Anyway, the guy at work's gay, but he's had one partner for a bunch of years, plus he's kind of low key. But he introduced me to Graham, who's into the scene and willing to talk about it. With me. For my character. You know — Gus — the childhood friend of my protagonist who turns out to be gay and living this complicated double life. I told you about him."

"Yeah, but you should have called. Last I heard we were having dinner." She was powerless to stop the words, but they made her wince. Justified or not, she was sensitive to the whole wife thing. She'd vowed as a teenager never to get married. And then, when she changed her mind, she promised never to become one of those movie-of-the-week wives who spend their time tallying the slights made against them by some basically decent guy who never seems to win.

"I know and I'm sorry." Still wearing his jacket, Sam turned on the lamp beside the couch and flopped beside her, resting his case between his feet. "Really. I'll make it up. Tomorrow night. You and me. Dinner, wine. We'll go to Mildred Pierce." He gave her a smile, then frowned.

"Mildred Pierce, huh. Maybe I can forgive you. Did you eat?"

"I had a bite with Graham," he said, reaching into the case for his notebook. "But I didn't tell you the best part. We talked all afternoon — really detailed, down and dirty stuff — then he took me to a club, the Caboose. You should see this place, but of course you can't. No girls allowed." He started flipping through the pages, then stopped. "I had a fort like that once, but no one ever came in leather shorts."

"That's really bad," said Indigo, letting herself smile just a little. "God, you're wired. Want a glass of wine or —"

"Wait. I have to get this down." He'd already started writing.

Indigo leaned back and watched his face. She loved Sam's face, his small blue eyes and delicate cheekbones, the hint of a cleft in his chin, even the frown that had started to plow above his eyes when he was thinking.

She waited and tried again. "You want a drink?"

"No." He closed his notebook, then opened it and wrote a few more words. "What's that? No, not for me. Thanks. I'm going to work for a couple hours." He put his hand on her knee. "You don't mind, do you?"

When he retreated to his office, Indigo turned the TV back on and blipped up and down the channels, not stopping or even really watching, but soothed by the mess of noise and images.

Pacing for the sedentary.

She'd been hoping for a chance to talk; she felt like shit. Despairing — that was a good word, but probably over the top. It was good that she had a day to tone down the drama. Why inflict her stuff on Sam. She was feeling sorry for herself. Nothing more to it than that. She had her health and her teeth, a home, insurance for the car. Husband, friends, family. She'd never gone hungry a day in her life, never broke a bone. She was lucky, very lucky.

So now she felt depressed and guilty.

She wasn't tired but she wanted the day to be over. So she went up to bed and lay in the dark, watching the shadows, fantasizing about the things she'd never done — or to put a more positive spin on it — things she'd like to try.

Maybe she should take up pottery. Or acting. Do stained glass, like her mother. Have a kid or make jewellery; that'd be cool. Something substantial. She could learn to scuba dive, but she'd need a no-shark guarantee. Forge large metal sculptures. Skydive. Do horny things in discreetly public places.

On the other hand, she'd always wanted to run away to Key West and live a tanned, bohemian existence. But it might not be as much fun without free love and, either way, Key West didn't seem like a place that agreed with marriage. You never know, she thought. A back-up fantasy. She was too old to be a model, wear shocking clothes, take drugs with rock stars. And probably not pretty enough. Too old. Shit. "How can I be too old, I've never been outrageous."

Indigo put a pillow on her head to muffle the sound of her brain.

Two

A few minutes before the alarm was set to go off, Indigo moved closer to Sam and pressed herself behind him, her hand deep in the covers.

"Roll over," she whispered, "on your back."

He groaned. "But I'm sleeping."

"That's okay," she said.

He kept his eyes closed as she lowered herself on top of him, barely conscious except for his hands which held her hips, easing then pulling her down. A small connection, over in a moment, an emotional snack.

Later that morning, Indigo got a promotion. She was sitting on the employee side of Walter Green's brand new walnut desk, thinking it could double as a coffin and wondering if it was true that some guy in Texas had himself buried in a pink Eldorado convertible.

"Congratulations," said Wally. "You are the new supervisor in charge of three accounts — Squeeze, Mighty Muffler and The Beef People. You'll continue to write the Shipping Container News. And you'll probably do some writing — backgrounders, briefs, that sort of thing — for an account we won last week, a new toxic waste management company called Wish It Away. We'll talk about that later. You'll get a 1.5% increase effective immediately, and a review at the end of the year." He stood up and shook her hand across the desk. "Well done, Indi. We're all very pleased with your work."

"Thanks Wally." She tried to sound grateful and she was. But she was distracted by a hot air balloon shaped like a beer can, hovering outside in the distance, over Wally's left shoulder. A quick calculation and she figured she'd be looking at an extra twenty-three bucks a cheque, before taxes. And, of course, the prestige. Now that she was in charge someone else could wear the skirt.

"By the way," said Wally. "Sheila called in sick. Would you mind writing a press release? We're doing a cooking demo at the restaurant in the Plaza, to promote Fiorio cookware. You know the stuff — very chic, very expensive. We've got that celebrity cooking lady, I can never remember her name, it's in the file. We'll need to invite the media — tell them lunch and drinks are free. Follow the last release, just plug in the new details. And jazz it up a little, would you?"

He handed her a thick yellow folder. "Sure Wally. No problem."

Back in her office, Indigo watched the balloon until it drifted into the suburbs. Her assistant, Marcie, poked her head around the door. "I just heard the news," she said. "Congrats. You want to do lunch later? You know, to celebrate?"

"Can't, but thanks. Errands to run," she lied.

Marcie was an intern, hired for the summer to experience the glamour of public relations. A second-year journalism student, she was apparently also the only person in the office who watched Sunday morning rock videos. "Saw you on MEGA Music," she said, when Indigo appeared a few minutes later with a list of things to do that afternoon. Before Indigo left for lunch, she liked to make sure Marcie was clear on what was needed when — in case she was hit by a bus or needed to flee to New York on the spur of the moment.

"You looked so cute, like a little doll," said Marcie. "And all those gorgeous men. You must have had a blast."

"I felt like Cheerleader Barbie," said Indigo. "But if you really think it's cool, we'll get you out there the next time." As she turned to leave, she said — "I'll be back a little late. Two or two-thirty. Don't wait up."

Outside, it was one of those end-of-April days that make Canadians feel grateful. A blend of light and warmth and breeze so perfect, so fleeting, that Indigo couldn't help being reminded of those other darker, colder months that seem to crowd summer into a few short weeks. She walked east, out of the core and over to Berczy Park, stopping on the way to buy all three daily papers, a bottle of juice and a bag of yellow popcorn.

After yesterday's hordes, the park seemed empty — and surprisingly clean. She sat on the grass in the shade of a tree near the fountain, kicked off her shoes and pulled a notebook out of her purse.

She hadn't been planning to look for a job, hadn't even thought of it until she got the promotion. Maybe she was losing her grip; this did not seem like a rational response to a raise, however measly. Suddenly that morning, it felt like time for something else — a new job, or maybe a new career. A change. Something more substantial than a haircut and less extreme than a divorce. Indigo had no clear strategy, which she decided was a good thing, just a kind of restless discontent. The best approach was to be open to the possibilities.

Before looking in the paper, she ripped the bag of popcorn open with her teeth and made a list she was sure would bear no resemblance to the actual job market. She didn't seem to like public relations, couldn't remember if she ever really had. But it might just be boredom. If pressed, she'd have to admit that she didn't care if people drank Squeeze or plain old not-for-profit tap water. She didn't give a damn if a single person used Fiorio pots and pans, or if the shipping container industry gained awareness. She was trying to cut down on red meat and, as for Wish It Away, well ...

I'm turning into a shrew, she thought. Marcie would love my job, a lot of people would, and I put up with it. Who do I think I am?

Indigo lay back on the grass and decided that the sky looked optimistic through the leaves.

Maybe I could work for some fabulously exotic country, she thought. Promote tourism to Canadians. Europe would be nice, maybe France or Spain. I could test the hotels and cafés, become something of an expert on wine tours.

She'd have liked to work for a theatre, one of those smaller, riskier ones — except of course they have no cash.

Or the film festival; she could do PR. In her dreams maybe — and even then, there'd be a hundred people in line for the job, all more qualified, more colourful, and willing to do it out of the goodness of their hearts (and for connections).

Or better, she could promote the actual movies, wear funky clothes, go to parties, meet celebrities. Would she be happy then? The perks would be a distraction, but it's hard to say. If she had a good time, it might be enough. She might not notice that she was spending her energy at the tail end of other peoples' projects, never doing something of her own. (It could even be satisfying, in a supportive, almost wifely kind of way.) Then again, she might not care.

Indigo was sitting up now, getting ready to face the want ads, tossing popped kernels of corn to a squirrel too timid to leave the shelter of the trees.

Maybe she should make a drastic change. She'd read an article somewhere that said hardly anybody sticks to one career forever, not any more. What about publishing? She could start as a reader, make some use of that degree in English. And if she were good, who knows? She might move up from there, be a star.

She could become a travel agent or better, a stewardess, visit the world — they get free flights.

Or maybe Tim could get her a job at Vox, as a waitress or a bartender. She could become one of those urban butterflies who know all the good boozecans and never wake up before noon.

Encouraged, Indigo brushed the crumbs off her hands and opened a paper. She read the comics and her horoscope, then Sam's, and turned to the classifieds.

Exotic Dancers Wanted.

For the first time, she understood that she was going to die. She'd known it before, of course, since she was 8 and her grandfather died of a heart attack. He passed on, they said — and she remembered that, at the time, it sounded kind of nice. But she'd never really processed the thought, at least not in relation to herself; she'd always been looking forward, from the vantage of the young. *When I'm 16 I'll drive. When I'm 18 I'll go to university. Career on track by 25. Kids by 33.*

But now she was compelled to look in the other direction. *If I wanted to dance naked in front of smarmy businessmen for money, I should have done it when I liked my breasts. Before I was 25. Did I ever like my breasts? It doesn't matter, because now I'm too old.*

Not that she wanted to be a stripper (or as Tim would say, a peeler). She didn't. And besides, Sam would have a fit. But she hated the idea — and, in fact, the reality — that it was too late.

Three papers later, Indigo had a renewed (if somewhat naive) sense of the possibilities, and a resolve to develop the "unsinkable attitude that would keep her job dreams afloat." She was going to start by applying for a PR position with Canada's largest (and, she suspected unfairly, only major) film distribution company. She'd follow that with the airlines, then the art gallery, all the key publishing houses and COOL-TV. She'd have to remember to call Nicole.

None had ads in the paper, but everything she saw seemed too corporate or boring or underpaid or demeaning. Or she wasn't qualified. Besides, once a job was advertised, everyone would know about it. She wanted better odds.

She bummed a cigarette from the man selling hot dogs, accepted a light and sat back down on the grass. She rarely smoked unless she'd been drinking. But she was feeling gritty, and it seemed like an appropriate homage to the concept of her own mortality.

Afterwards, conscious of the taste of burnt popcorn, she stuffed the papers into a garbage can and checked her watch. Two o'clock. Time to go back to work or come up with a good excuse not to. A forgotten doctor's appointment; maybe pills were the answer. Or a shrink — someone who could tell her why a person so seemingly on top of things could feel so ungrateful. A trip to the gym might lift her spirits; she should join one. Or better, go to a movie; something violent and frightening to shock things into perspective.

She was still toying with excuses as she put her purse in the bottom drawer of her desk and sat down to contemplate cookware.

Three

It was six o'clock. Indigo ran her hand over the bar, noticing again how nice it was; the pitted surface was actually smooth to the touch, and the burnished copper brought out the brilliant red of their wine. Sam said it did the same for the red in her hair and she thought the evening had potential after all.

The restaurant was in an old film studio — in a semi-industrial area west of downtown, near Little Portugal. The room itself was cavernous, walls painted to look like cracked marble, embellished with waves of fabric and massive iron chandeliers. Arrangements of dried flowers made wild with dolls, oversized cutlery and preserved harvest vegetables, all painted gold.

"I like the research," said Sam. He'd been out all afternoon, exploring the model for his fictional neighbourhood, roaming the streets, taking notes and sketching houses. "People believe me when I say I'm writing a book, so then I know I am. And the process of getting to know the characters, where they were born, who their parents were —"

"How they lost their virginity," said Indigo.

"What's frustrating is that some days, like today, the writing part is so bloody hard. Or hard and bloody, that's how it feels. Excruciating."

"I thought you were doing research," said Indigo.

"As a last resort. When I'm like this I'm crazy. I keep jumping up to make coffee, or get another cup of coffee. Or I realize there's no coffee, so I go to the store. Then I stop at the bakery for an espresso and I take my notebook to trick myself into believing that I'm being productive when I'm really just whistling down any old mindless thing that occurs to me. Bits of conversation or decor, the mood of the waiters, the look of a building across the street. The writing's tough but the procrastination — and the guilt — is a hundred times worse. Excruciating. Did I already say that? Some writer, can't even come up with a new adjective for pain."

Standing, Indigo nudged her body between Sam's knees and pulled his thighs around her hips. Sam was not a man who gave in to anxiety often. His desire to be what he thought of as a real writer, a man's writer, like Hemingway or Miller, was as potent as the longing he'd once felt to be a reporter, a foreign correspondent or political satirist, something masculine and worthy. Something to tell the old bastard.

"You'll be fine tomorrow," she said. "Remember last time. You got all worked up, said you'd never write again. Went to bed all defeated, then what happened? Huh? You worked it out, figured out your next plot point, or whatever it was you were stuck on. By the time I got up you'd been at it for hours. So, think positive — it'll happen again tomorrow." She kissed him on the mouth and wondered if the gesture was meant to please herself.

"With my luck it will," he said. "I'm covering a computer show for *All Business Magazine*. Have to be there first thing. But hey, it's money."

"And it isn't politics." She slid back up on her stool.

"Amen to that."

Until a few months ago, Sam was what he privately (only half-jokingly) called a newspaper man. A reporter, covering business and technology, plus the odd sweeping disaster. It was a job he loved until the paper was sold and his new boss hired people of her own, and sent him reeling into City Hall.

To be fair, he did make an effort. He gave the new post just enough time to confirm that his life would be shorter if he had to spend it listening to — and worse, spreading the crap of — local politicians.

He spent a month submerged in stinking, petty squabbles. Until the day, in fact until the moment, that a particular meeting erupted. It's a matter of public record: one elected official called another elected official a slut; others were body parts; a few were bodily functions.

Sam walked out of the meeting, away from City Hall, down Yonge Street and straight into the office of his boss, where he asked for a transfer. At which point, his boss leaned back in her ivory leather chair, crossed right panted leg over left and reminded him of the modest, limited-time-offer severance package, created to "smooth the transition into the future." Of course, they'd be happy to consider any freelance ideas he might have.

And so he quit to write his novel. The one he'd been kicking around in his head since college. The one he considered a work-in-progress, despite the fact that he'd written just one page. It was a good page, if he said so himself.

As Sam finished his drink and ordered another, Indigo wondered if he missed the old job. He was the kind of writer who talked about his work but didn't show it, at least until he had a draft, not even to his wife. It had to be lonely.

"In any case," he said. "Enough about me. What's new with Indigo Blackwell? What's been going on with you?"

Indigo reached for her glass. "Let's see." A sip of wine. "Yesterday I did my cheerleader impression on MEGA Music. This morning I got a promotion and a raise. And this afternoon I started looking for a job. You know, this really is a good Cabernet. We should try to remember the name."

"You're looking for a job? No kidding — did I miss something?"

"No, not really. Maybe. I don't know, it feels like time." A waiter appeared then, and led them to the back of the restaurant, to a table for two against the wall.

Has he missed anything? We've disconnected, she thought. Hardly see each other ... rarely touch ... talk at the surface. *Stop exaggerating.* She interpreted a sudden rush of guilt as a flush of affection and softened. It's indulgent to get all gloomy. She hadn't even decided if this was a real or invented crisis, hadn't said a thing to him and yet here she was, annoyed that he didn't know exactly what she was feeling. She really should play fair.

Watching Sam examine the wine list, she wondered if the image she had of him was anything like the one he had of himself, and how close either was to the truth. Does anyone ever know anyone, really? A glass of wine and boom, residual drama. She held her fingers over the flame that poked from a small blue glass on the table, to confirm that it was hot.

They chose a bottle of the same Cabernet and appetizers instead of two main courses. It was the way Indigo liked to order — small portions of things they could eat with their hands.

"Yesterday was awful," she said, then stopped as the waiter appeared with their wine. He uncorked the bottle and poured an inch in the large round goblet. This part annoyed her, but Sam wouldn't do it. Taking a sip when there's only a sip in the glass felt awkward. The glass almost swallowed her face. The waiter and Sam were staring. What the hell did they expect to see? Did anyone order the house wine and send it back because it didn't resonate, or have a scintillating enough personality?

"That's nice," she said and smiled as the waiter filled Sam's glass, then hers.

As he walked away, Indigo said — "It was humiliating. Standing there like a piece of orange fluff, flaunting a not-so-subtle invitation to squeeze my breasts."

"And? Did anyone try?" Sam took a somewhat proprietary view of her parts.

"Of course not. But there I was, passing out free pop to a bunch of artists and writers ... people who make a difference ... who figure things out ... who get the joke and then let the rest of us in on it ... or not."

"I think you have a skewed impression of artists," said Sam. "What makes you think that everyone looking for a grant has something to say, or the talent to say it?"

"At least they want to do something important, comment on

the state of the universe or whatever it is they're obsessed by. What bothers me is that I was embarrassed and that's so arrogant."

"I don't understand, why arrogant?" asked Sam, leaning back as the waiter delivered their chevre on vine leaves and strips of roasted pepper, and some grilled calamari.

"Thank you," said Indigo. And then — "If I'm ashamed of what I do, doesn't it stand to reason that I look down on everyone else who does it? I never thought of myself as an elitist, but that's the implication."

"You're out of your mind," said Sam, squeezing lemon on the squid before taking a piece with his fingers and popping it into his mouth. "You beat yourself over the head with every stupid little thing — for no reason. Maybe this isn't what you want to do. But you have no reason to feel like you're some kind of terrible person just because you'd rather be doing something else. The thing is, you have no reason to be embarrassed in the first place. Okay, except for the orange suit, but that's just fun —"

"And that's where I ended up this morning," said Indigo. "Thinking that I have nothing to be ashamed of, so don't tell me I'm out of my mind. If the problem isn't what I do, maybe it's who I do it for. It's weird. These days, I feel like I spend all my time on things that mean nothing, but it isn't even true."

As Indigo talked, Sam spread a piece of toasted pita with some chevre.

"Look at The Beef People. Red meat doesn't do a thing for me." She leaned forward on her arms. "If anything, it makes me kind of sluggish. But it's important to the farmers raising cattle, the economy and in a bunch of other ways I never thought of. Like fur. I hate the idea of dead things, especially dead cute things. But there's a whole culture suffering up there in the cold because people like me decided it's distasteful to wrap ourselves in dead animals, like they're some kind of trophy you get for having money." She stopped for a bite of chevre. "Life gets complicated when you understand that everything you do has an impact."

"It's called cause and effect."

"I know what it's called," she said.

"So what's the downside of changing jobs?" Sam was eating most of their dinner while Indigo talked. "It sounds like a simple decision, promotion or not. You don't want to be there, so leave."

It was the kind of night that drew people out of hiding: warm enough to shed the extra layers, show a little skin, begin forgetting. It's a national strategy, a party trick of sorts — to forget the brown slush/yellow snow/black ice. By summer, Canadians (at least those truly urban Canadians who consider flagging a cab their winter sport) have erased the cold from their psyches, like women erase the pain of childbirth. They know it unhinged them, but it seems so long ago.

Indigo was a little drunk, considerably more cheerful, and frisky. "Kiss me," she said. "A good one." They were walking — partly because of the night, but also because Sam refused to pay a mechanic for things he could fix himself. The car was currently prostrate in front of their house, waiting for a filter.

They were about to turn onto Queen Street.

Sam put his case down and came toward her, arms outstretched as though he planned to fold her into them, then pecked her on the cheek.

"You smell great," she said, as he took her hand and tried to tow her up the street. "Handsome. Like a first date. Or maybe it's lust. I always get those mixed up."

Sam laughed and she thought her life was back to normal, if only for the night. "Let's do it in someone's backyard," she said, wondering how she'd react if he ever agreed.

"Sorry sweet cheeks, you'll have to settle for home. I haven't had enough to drink for that. But if I'm feeling wild, who knows? Maybe we'll leave the light on."

"You remember when we did it on the roof?" she asked.

"An incredibly stupid thing to do."

"Why? No one could see us."

"Indigo, we could have been killed."

It was almost eight o'clock and there was cause for celebration: the switch to daylight savings, sixty minutes more each day. It was a gift, the moment at which the summer lay ahead, basking in its own potential. Not to put too fine a point on it, but this was the blessed event they'd been waiting for — and the street was alive, born again, squealing through its open windows.

Sam watched where they were going and manoeuvred them east, around people bumming change, buskers, bars and madness. Indigo followed, taking it in, her chatter keeping pace.

"I should get my belly button pierced," she said. A man whose fleshy arms were crossed and resting on his bloated gut stood leaning in the open door of Much Too Cool For You Tattoos. He stared with a force that made her feel awkward — if only for a second — in her short black skirt and chunky heels.

"Why would you want to do that?" asked Sam.

"It's sexy."

"Do you think so?"

"Don't you?"

"Not really."

"I think it looks dangerous. Like the woman's not afraid. She's unpredictable, maybe a bit unstable. Men love that. For sure it's sexy."

"So do it," said Sam.

"Maybe. I don't know. I just thought of it now. You don't like it?"

"It doesn't matter — whatever you think."

"I know a girl who wears a crystal tear drop," she said. "It looks great with a tan and one of those short T-shirts. And Leslie — you remember — that woman who works with Nicole? She has her bits pierced, three times I think, wears little silver hoops. Says when she got it done she couldn't work for days. She was so horny she couldn't sit down."

"Is that all you think about?"

Indigo hesitated. "No. Not always." It occurred to her that he was right. Instead of thinking about sex — sex in general, and the more specific questions of why she and Sam weren't having sex, and how she could arrange it so she did have sex more often — she should be thinking about how to re-prioritize, make it less important to her life. There was only one problem: why would she want to do that? "You know you like me this way," she tried. "At least you do when you're not so absorbed, don't be so righteous. Besides, it's a funny story. You can use it in your book." She could tell he was only half paying attention; he'd be able to repeat the words back if she made a fuss and said he wasn't listening, but his head was somewhere else. Probably on the car.

The tone of the city changed as it rose from Queen to Bloor Street. There was still an air of dissent — rebellion barely contained, creatively channelled. But the *fuck you* mood of defiance became the more polite passive resistance. In fairness, aggression is not the overriding frame of mind on Queen Street West, but it is a dominant posture. They were in the Annex now; jeans were still ripped, but black was fading into khaki; there were fewer micro minis, no more plastic pants, and an increasing number of long, Indian cotton skirts.

They were almost home. Dusk had conceded to darkness and the street lights gave the night a vaguely metallic feel.

As they approached the corner, a man waiting for the light turned to face them, as people instinctively do when they're being watched. Indigo was looking at his arms; she liked arms and his were smooth and tanned already, muscular without being bulky, palpably bare. She didn't notice the connection he had with Sam and wondered why the stranger seemed ready to greet them; her own face betrayed a flicker of confusion as Sam dropped her hand and extended his own, grinning.

"Graham. I was just thinking about you. This is Indigo, my wife. Indi — Graham Proulx. Listen, I want to thank you again for last night. It was really helpful. Not to mention a blast."

"Nice to meet you," said Indigo.

"Sure," said Graham, barely glancing at her. With designer features that included a square jaw, cool grey eyes and a mouth set almost in a smirk, he could have been a model. He already had the pose.

Indigo felt oddly shy looking at him. It occurred to her that she should have been at least slightly irritated when Sam suggested they go for a beer. The romantic part of their evening was being put aside in favour of an hour with Adonis. But she thought he was beautiful and agreed, without shooting even a lightly pained look in Sam's direction.

They chose a nearby patio — busy for a Monday night, although the restaurant itself was deserted.

Almost immediately, Indigo was put off by how the waitress favoured Graham. An amazon with fresh cleavage and a sense of anarchistic fashion, she was just the type to make Indigo feel inferior. But Graham didn't seem to notice and, whether it was a defence mechanism created from necessity, having gone through life snapping heads, or because he simply didn't dwell on women, Indigo was pleased.

So there, she thought, suddenly grateful for Sam. Solid, intelligent Sam. Handsome but not earth-pulling magnetically handsome Sam.

Indigo ordered coffee. Decaf, since caffeine after dinner tended to jolt her awake around four. And that was the time when she felt the most alone, barely rational, afraid of things she'd normally laugh at, or at least dismiss as futile.

Graham ordered gin and tonic. Sam chose the same.

"Gin?" There was surprise in Indigo's voice.

"For a change," he said. "Aren't I allowed?"

"Don't ask me," she said and forced a laugh. "I'm not your mother." Still, she thought it was strange. He rarely drank hard liquor.

While they waited for their drinks, Graham reached into the pocket of his pants and pulled out a battered pack of Camels. He tapped the pack on the table to dislodge a cigarette, then tapped the end of the cigarette — also on the table — before putting it between his lips, striking a match and inhaling deeply, all while keeping his eyes narrowed on Indigo.

"We're the lepers of the decade," he said, clenching the drag in his lungs. "Smokers, I mean, not fags. We might as well eat our young for all the grief they give us." He exhaled with a slow, deliberate force. "But they can all go straight to hell as far as I'm concerned. Fucking fascists." He looked back at Sam, then grinned in a way that made Indigo think his edge had been performance. "It's enough to make a person bitter," he said, suddenly fey. "But I'm not bitter, am I Sammy?"

She found his hands fascinating — huge and manicured, with what looked like a coat of clear nail polish. He wore silver rings on several fingers. Simple bands, rough-hewn, one with turquoise inlay, nothing gaudy. An expensive-looking watch. He played with his cigarette, rolling it between his fingers and then pretending to singe the hairs on his forearm. She realized she was staring and feigned a sudden interest in the street, but she needn't have bothered. Graham had begun a running commentary, subtext from the night before. Sam was leaning forward, engrossed.

"You remember Darrell?"

"Which one was he?"

"He came in just before you left. Cute in a trashy sort of way. Kind of hairy. He was wearing that red fishnet T-shirt. Black leather pants, no underwear."

"Okay, I know who you mean."

"Well, he's just like the guy in your book. When he's out with the boys he's really out with the boys, if you know what I'm saying. The rest of the time he's in. Has a wife and a couple of kids. Sells mutual funds or whatever, works for one of the banks. Spends most of his life in drag — Bay Street drag." Graham laughed. "Get it? Bay Street drag? You can go ahead and use that."

"It's the quiet ones you've got to watch out for," said Indigo.

Graham ignored her. "I ran into him during the day once and he was like this mild little guy, totally straight. Probably has a Wagoneer with wood panelling on the sides, a townhouse in the burbs and one of those lawn mowers that buzz your charlie as you drive around the yard." He still didn't look at Indigo, but she thought he was conscious of her presence — conscious of not bringing her into the conversation, of changing the dynamic so that he and Sam were two and she was one. "But we hung out a couple of times," he said. "And trust me, he's an animal."

"I wonder if his wife knows," said Sam.

"I doubt it," said Graham. "And it's gotta be stressful. Keeping track of the lies, changing in bathrooms. I don't know how he does it."

Indigo waited until Graham took a breath and jumped in. "How's Gus going to deal with it?" She felt the need to gain some ground, prove that she and Sam were close. "In the end, I mean. Have you decided which way he'll go?"

"I'm not sure yet," said Sam, sitting back in his seat but still looking at Graham. "His father's like mine but Italian, some kind of mobster. Authoritarian, oppressive, never satisfied. So Gus isn't just afraid of losing his wife and kids; he doesn't want to tell his old man. Ever. He's pretty sure his dad would have him killed. I'm still thinking about whether to work in a homophobic boss, but it might be too much. He's already being blackmailed — by his sister, no less. Poor bastard."

After three gin and tonics, Sam was drunk and Indigo wanted to leave. They asked for the bill and Graham reached for his wallet. "Keep your pants on," said Sam.

Graham laughed. "Only if you insist. But I'll get you back on Friday."

"What's Friday?" asked Indigo. "Don't forget Tim's party."

"Shit," said Sam. "I completely forgot. Graham's taking me to a new club. Doesn't even have a name it's so subversive. Just the kind of thing I need."

"Don't sweat it Sammy. Another time."

"No, I want to be at the opening. I can meet you there later. Not a problem."

Indigo's jaw tightened as she took her purse from the back of the chair. "I have to go to the washroom, I'll see you outside. If you're gone, it was nice meeting you." She reached over the table to shake Graham's hand, and left.

Walking home, Indigo did what she always did when she was angry — retreated into silence and created a physical distance between them. She kept her head turned away, sought details in the darkened lawns and homes and distracted herself by keeping him out of her line of sight.

It was a defence she'd learned as a child. Her father's ranting never went anywhere, had more to do with him than her, and left little room for rebuttal. So it was better to make believe he wasn't there. It worked for a while too, until puberty made her stubborn like him and she couldn't keep her mouth shut. It's too bad she couldn't fight as well with Sam — or with anyone else. Most of the time she acted like a wimp.

Tonight, she wanted to put off what she knew would be her own insipid response. Their fights always started this way, indifference on one side triggering an emotional outburst on the other. It was usually something small that Indigo let fester while Sam moved on to other thoughts. He knew she'd bring it up eventually and, in the meantime, he'd be thinking about Graham or *All Business Magazine* or the fact that he was almost 35 and lagging.

Of course, the very fact that he seemed unaffected, not to mention uninterested in whatever it was consuming Indigo, goaded her into an increasing state of distress. So by the time she did mention it, her voice was pinched in the back of her throat and she wanted to yell or cry or both. Then she'd feel like she was too whiny or needy and really, it shouldn't be a big deal if he cancelled their date and went out with Graham, even though he'd been holding Tim's party up for weeks as a night she could look forward to — *So don't bug me now, 'kay sweetie? I need to work.*

Tonight she was determined to change the pattern, keep the advantage. She was more angry than hurt, so there was none of the usual sting, no tears to hold back, surprisingly little anguish.

Indigo could see the silhouette of a couple on their porch, watching and waiting, spending time like it was money, on a moment of peace. She could hear the sporadic shouts of some kind of game, points won or lost, probably in the schoolyard. The click of her heels confirmed the silence between them but neither seemed willing to break it.

"What does Graham do?" she asked finally, bending down to

pick up her shoes while Sam aimed his key at the lock. He seemed to be having some trouble.

"He's an escort," he said, flinging open the door and then having to lurch after it so it didn't bang the heater. "Fucking thing." He dropped his case and kicked his shoes into the corner.

"What do you mean, an escort?" she asked. "A prostitute? Or no, I guess he'd be a hustler, wouldn't he? Is that what he is, some kind of hustler?"

Indigo followed him into the kitchen, leaning at the door while he opened a bottle of beer, watching him take out a package of ham, fold a piece into his mouth and toss the rest back in the fridge unsealed. He squeezed past her into the hall.

"I hate it when you don't answer me," she said, trailing him into the living room. She had to control her tone. Her strength lay in the irritation creeping like fingers up the back of her neck, and the fact that she was sober. She had to remember that she'd been passed over again and she was pissed. Forget she was offended or vulnerable, or any of those cream-puff emotions that turn perfectly good outrage into weepy histrionics.

"Fine. He has sex with people for money. But there's more to it than that, and he prefers *escort*. Satisfied?"

"What is your problem?" she asked. "Why are you being so rude?" Curiosity made her forget that she'd planned to speak her mind, then calmly go to bed. "How old is he?"

"I don't know, 24 ... 25."

"How does someone like that become a prostitute? Hustler. Whatever. I mean, he's like so beautiful."

Sam's tone softened. "I asked him, but I didn't get the story. At least not all of it. He doesn't think I've earned it. He says he's always been promiscuous — or as he puts it, a slut. Loves to party ... likes the attention." Sam paused as though he was trying to come up with the formula that would explain Graham's existence. "He has no education, grade ten I think he said, not that he's stupid. He actually seems wise, sometimes, in a street kind of way — but maybe not. Maybe it's just because he's jaded."

"He's got a real hardness to him," said Indigo.

"I think most of that was for your benefit. He's usually a lot more charming."

"Oh. So is it me or my kind?"

"I don't know, I still haven't figured him out ... which is why I'm going Friday."

Friday. Indigo hesitated, wondering what to say that wouldn't sound feeble. "That's not fair," she tried. That wasn't it.

Sam picked up the remote. "You're not going to cry are you?"

"No, I'm not going to cry." When he drank too much he was volatile, but he usually swung from buoyant to melancholy. Tonight he was boorish. It was a side she rarely saw. "I can't believe you're doing this again though," she said. "You've been ignoring me for weeks, telling me to be patient, that you'd come to Tim's party. No work in the morning or any other lame excuse. Everyone's been asking about you. I can't believe you're blowing me off so you can spend an evening with some guy you just met, when he offered to let you reschedule. That's so fucking insensitive."

The last three words piled on top of each other in a strangled heap.

"I can't talk to you if you're going to cry." Sam clicked on the television.

"Don't do this." She walked over to the set and turned it off, wiping her eyes with the back of her hand.

He glared at her from the couch. "Why don't you get the hell out of the way." Indigo froze. "Just because you're not doing anything that matters, it doesn't mean I can't. I'm sick to death of not living up to your expectations — I don't have time for this bullshit. So I'm letting you down once and for all, right now, with a great big fucking thump. We never go out and we won't for a while. Our sex life is going to continue to suck and I'm not going bring you a bouquet of fucking flowers any time soon. Get it through your head and back off." He was still pointing the remote.

Before she walked out of the room, Indigo clicked on the television and turned the volume up so he had to raise his voice. "Look, I'm sorry." Her hand was sweating slightly as she gripped the banister and began to climb the stairs. "It's been a long day," he called. "I didn't mean it." As his voice grew louder, the energy drained from the words. "Come back. Let's talk ... Indigo? I'll try not to be such a shit. Just cut me some slack, okay?"

She found her nightie and put it on in case he came in later, lay down and closed her eyes to his existence.

Four

I ndigo lay awake for a long time with her arm draped over her face, but even without visual contact, the grey of the morning had seeped into her outlook. The medley of rain and wind beating on large, heavy trees made her think of endless days up north — an only child, trapped in a silent, angry cottage, baking cookies with her mother to mask the unmistakable smell of divorce.

(Afterwards, when it was final and her mother wanted to know how she *felt*, Indigo tossed off a series of unflattering, quickly drawn sketches of her father. Her favourite, the one she presented first, was him at the dinner table, with a bright red face and a straight purple line for the mouth. She called it *The Last Summer*.)

A fog seemed to have settled under her skin, and she wondered if she could fend off the morning by refusing to participate. Fifteen years ago, she'd have come up with a story of night shivers and trips to the bathroom. And if she performed well, she might have been allowed to stay home, reading and watching television on the couch, with a blanket and pillows and a bottle of flat ginger ale. Could it really be fifteen years? Indigo sighed and sat up, surrendering to the first of many things she wasn't in the mood to do.

She stared at Sam to rekindle the anger dampened by sleep. His mouth hung open and his lips were caked with a thin line of white. He'll be thirsty, she thought idly, moving through the room, gathering clothes for work and then closing the door behind her. Everything done softly, quietly, so as not to disturb the husband — the man asleep on the far side of the bed, half covered, still wearing his watch.

Her concern was less Sam's rest than her own desire to be gone when he woke. No, if she wanted to get back into it, she would have banged her way down the hall, leaving the bedroom door open while she showered and dried her hair. She'd have dressed beside the bed, making sure to put on a pair of heels before walking out of the room and down the stairs. She'd have put the dishes away while she waited for coffee, come back up to the bedroom for jewellery, opened the curtains and then, when he couldn't possibly still be asleep, said with some irritation — "Don't you have to get up?"

But she didn't do any of these things. Instead, she dressed in the bathroom, put her makeup on downstairs and found a copy of her latest résumé. As a small consolation, she did bang the front door closed behind her, knowing that if the gesture went unnoticed, the alarm clock was pushed well back on her night table, turned accidentally to loud and set to blast Sam awake in about ten minutes.

By the time she got off the subway, Indigo had settled into her mood. She stopped at a coffee shop, where she sat in the window drinking café au lait, intending to look at her résumé but absorbed by the people outside getting wet. The rain had stepped up its assault, battering the morning with thick, fleshy drops that slapped against the pavement.

A small, expensively dressed man swore at a taxi when it turned too close to the curb, spraying his slacks with dirty water.

The wind twisted up between the buildings, and a woman waiting for the streetcar had to keep turning her back to it, one hand clutching her skirt, the other gripping an umbrella — holding it at the top of its stem, pulling it close to her head in an effort not to lose it. Indigo ordered a second cup of coffee just to see if the woman could find her token and close the umbrella without letting go of her skirt. But when the moment arrived, she felt an unexpected twinge of empathy and was pleased to see the woman board the car, frazzled but her dignity intact.

Indigo decided that people were simply unwilling to embrace the gloom of this fine morning. That was the problem. The men half ran, dodging puddles and crossing against the light. The women seemed more stoic; they walked, but they tended to squint their eyes and hunch their shoulders, as if they were waiting for some kind of blow.

Indigo found a strange sort of pleasure in the fact that her nylons and shoes were damp, in the smell of wet clothes and hair and cement.

She'd always associated the smell of rain on cement with the city, but once — when she and Sam were in Costa Rica — she smelled the same thing driving in the mountains, where the only cement was the road. She might not have noticed — the sight of the rain forest overpowered any other sense — but she happened to close her eyes, tired after a night of margarita-fuelled merengue.

She was so shocked that she made Sam stop the car. And when he closed his eyes he was hit by it too, that familiar city smell, except that in the mountains it was crisper. And they both laughed, which they did a lot in Costa Rica, since it was their honeymoon and, as the brochures for marriage all say, the world reeked of promise.

But today was not a day to think of honeymoons.

The office was quiet, not because it lacked activity, but because the rain seemed to muffle everything, from the traffic six floors down to simple conversation. Sound waves dulled by a wash of greys and browns.

The day turned out to be surprisingly uncomplicated. Wally was in New York, Marcie called in sick and Indigo's most pressing task was a newsletter due next week. Each time the phone rang, she thought it might be Sam and then, when it wasn't, told herself that of course he couldn't call from the conference. Jerk.

Nicole's voicemail said she was out of the studio all day, but — *please ... leave ... a message.* Indigo waited until lunch and called her mother.

"Hi Alice. It's me — favourite daughter."

"Hi honey. I'm on my way to a meeting, but I was going to call you later. Can you come for dinner? I have news. Wait, hang on." Indigo could hear her mother's assistant, forming a question in that slow meandering way she had, and Alice jumping over top — "Yes, I told you. That one, the vermilion. What's the price on that? We'll need a lot, find out what's available. If there's enough I'll take the sample with me." Then, as she talked back into the phone. "Sorry sweetie, it's been one of those days. Are you still there?" An interior decorator, Alice was ankle deep in swatches for the lobby of a new hotel.

"What kind of news?" asked Indigo. She held her toasted bagel with peanut butter and jam carefully, balanced on her thumb and middle finger.

"Good news," said Alice. "What? No, I need it now. I have to leave. Call them back, tell them it's important." Alice sighed loudly into the phone.

"Tell me. I need good news," said Indigo.

"Why — what's wrong? Is everything all right?"

"I'm kidding. It's nothing, just the rain. What's the news?"

"Tonight. Listen honey, I have to run."

"Okay. Around six. Can I bring anything?"

"Nope, just you. And Sam, if he wants."

"I'm pretty sure he's busy."

"Okay then. Love you."

Indigo stared past the screen of her computer at the building next door. The darkness of the day made it easy to see inside the offices. One floor down, a man was sitting at his desk, talking to a woman in the doorway. He was wearing the requisite white shirt — already rolled at the sleeves — and it occurred to Indigo that he was probably pierced underneath. In complicated places. He might be a Darrell, wearing fishnet at night, or under his slacks. Or he might be one of Graham's clients. She had the sudden feeling that everyone else kept secret, wild lives tucked neatly behind their achromatic surfaces; that the most unobtrusive people hid the most exciting things under bland little smiles.

The man had a plant in his window and she wondered if it was one of those plastic benjaminas that she always took for real.

When the woman disappeared, he swivelled his chair to look outside, leaned back and clasped his hands behind his head. His gaze fell somewhere to the right — on someone else, or maybe nothing. Indigo thought he sighed as he reached for his mug, took a sip and cupped it in his hands. Something the woman said, or perhaps the effects of the rain.

She chose the rain and thought of Alice.

Good news. Maybe that's why Indigo felt dull: she needed some news. The promotion barely had an impact. It was sort of like local news, she thought. Boy bites dog. Film at eleven. She needed something bigger. Dress rehearsal's over. Life starts here. Party in the streets.

Indigo drifted through the morning sitting at her desk, poised over the initial draft of the newsletter, red marker in hand, looking busy but lost in speculation, again, wondering what it would take to make her feel less flat.

She was in PR. Surely she could invent some news.

A lottery win would be terrific, difficult to make happen, but she wrote BUY LOTTERY TICKET in her daytimer.

She could become a celebrity. That would be news. She'd have to do something sensational, of course — but what? She didn't have a stomach for the tabloids, so it would have to be something worthy, something philanthropic, which meant she'd need cash. She underlined BUY LOTTERY TICKET with three bold strokes of blue and added an S.

An affair would be news, give her something to moon over. A bit of attention. And exercise, which she could use. And it's not like she'd suffer any huge consequence, even if she did get caught. She supposed Sam would be pissed (he'd better be fuming). But nobody'd send her back to her village, make her mother pay a cow. In any case, why make things worse? She almost liked her current role as good guy (not that she'd admit it); woman wronged and all of that.

None of her ideas fell within the breadth of plausibility and Indigo realized that a new job was probably the biggest news she could expect any time soon. Suddenly petulant, she pulled her résumé out of her purse and stared at it before accepting the fact that this was not the time to summon even a small amount of enthusiasm — and deciding not to care. Instead, she wandered down the hall in search of yet another cup of coffee.

Alice lived a few blocks away from Indigo, in a red brick house with a pointed roof and a window shaped like an eye. The window was in the attic, once Indigo's bedroom, now a workroom, filled with paints and tools and crafts, including — at the moment — a partially finished stained-glass window.

Indigo's dresser and bed had been pushed to the side, but they were there. Reminders of her childhood. And sometimes, even now, she liked to stay, sleep beneath the same pink blanket from her teens, if Sam was out of town and she was nervous.

Downstairs, perched in a corner of the living room, was what Indigo had always thought of as an ostrich, forged in metal, the colour of soil or darkly stained wood floors. Henry was at least five feet tall and skinny, with roughly defined features and a long, narrow beak. Alice had fallen in love with him years ago, around the time she left her husband, bought a house and began to understand what people meant by better days.

Alice thrived in the untethered joy of divorce, albeit quietly. (She didn't want it to seem like too much fun to Indigo, who was still a child and might get the wrong impression.) She looked better, felt somehow lighter, tended to laugh and bring home treats.

She told Indigo that, while standing in the gallery resting her hand on Henry's cold, non-biodegradable backside, she became convinced that *this* was a lasting kind of love. Freshly unmarried, she was still trained to consider her husband's opinion — and in this case, the fact that he'd have hated it. As she savoured the thought, she wrote a cheque large enough to set off a sizable tantrum, had he known, and loaded the bird into a cab.

For years, Henry had occupied the same favoured corner of the living room. And for years, Indigo had thought of him with intense, not quite rational affection.

Beneath Henry's warm metal gaze sat Alice, brochures spread around her like homework, and Nancy the cat, crouched at the edge of the table on what appeared to be a map. The other cat, Sid, was out on the porch when Indigo got there, staring at the door. As he marched down the hall and into the kitchen, Alice said — "He wants you to think he's hard-done-by, but he's only been out ten minutes. And it was his idea."

"Not with a belly like that," said Indigo, lifted by the smell of burning incense. "So what's the good news?" She and Alice shared an inability to co-exist with secrets.

"It's Bali," she said. "Come see. I'm going to Indonesia." Alice looked almost girlish in a pair of faded jeans and T-shirt, hair tucked smooth behind her ears.

"No kidding. I've always wanted to go there," said Indigo. "When do you leave?"

"Second week in October, I think. For twelve weeks."

"Twelve weeks," said Indigo, sounding less than pleased and not completely sure why. "That's three months."

Alice laughed. "Who says you're lousy at math? But look at this — while I'm there I'm going to take a painting workshop. It's led by a Toronto artist who used to live there, sort of like a tour. She takes ten of us, and we travel around painting different parts of Bali — and other islands too, I think — getting lessons as we go. Her name's Marta."

Indigo sank to the couch beside her mother and picked up a somewhat startled Nancy, who struggled briefly, then fled to a chair across the room. "What about work?"

"I'm taking a leave. The hotel has to be done by August. We're just finishing up that house in Forest Hill. And I have two other projects — one that'll wrap in July, the other in early September. I've built in a month after that to be sure."

"What about Brian? Is he going with you?" Brian was Brian McFarlane, Alice's live-in love of close to fifteen years.

"Not for the painting," said Alice. "He'll come after. The timing's great. He's shooting a movie in Vancouver, October to Christmas. Then when he's done he'll join me. We'll putz around for a month or so, get reacquainted."

Alice and Brian shared a relationship Indigo envied, but couldn't quite imagine. They led independent lives that connected whenever. And yet, they were still sentimental in a way that made Indigo wistful; they liked to hang out alone on a Saturday night, making dinner, watching movies, holding hands. *She'd even caught them necking.* And yet, in spite of how close they were, they seemed to avoid anything that even faintly resembled Indigo's own brand of upheaval; neither appeared to be bothered by anything the other did or might choose to do, although Indigo thought there must be a limit, a line they didn't cross.

Brian was a cameraman. If he had to go away for eight or ten weeks to shoot a movie, it was as simple as — "Have a nice time honey. Try to remember to eat well." (Alice called everyone honey.) No wrenching goodbyes or jealous apprehension. Calls once or twice a week were fine.

Indigo would have loved to be like Alice, less fearful of the worst she could imagine. And, in fact, she spent a ridiculous amount of time trying to feel less insecure — making an effort to ignore Sam when he wasn't around and wouldn't know the difference. Pretending she was fine with things she wasn't. But she was cautious. An unnaturally calm surface was bound to result in some kind of turmoil underneath. An ulcer maybe, or an aneurysm.

She picked up a brochure and looked at the cover: a soft-brown girl, with a woman's eyes and painted lips. She wore a red and gold crown and matching neckpiece, and stood — arms bent one up and one down in right and left turn signals — surrounded by a circle of men, barely clothed, linked like a chain in the grass.

"Do you know where you'll go? When Brian gets there, I mean."

"It's loose, but we've talked about Thailand and Malaysia. Australia's an option. Isn't this great?"

Indigo nodded, certain that it was indeed great. "It's amazing," she said. She was almost 30 after all, intelligent, mature in moderation and capable of relinquishing her mother for at least a few months. "But I can't believe you'll be gone so long. I want lots of post cards. And an itinerary — in case you refuse to leave. I'll have to come and find you."

"Then maybe we'll keep you there," said Alice. "We'll buy a tiny hotel, maybe on an island. Amuse ourselves by asking the tourists how cold it is at home." She rested her hand on Indigo's thigh. "There's tea in the pot," she said. "Want some? It's peppermint. I can make something else."

"Peppermint's good," said Indigo. "When was Tim in Bali — two years ago, maybe three?"

"Something like that," said Alice, standing up.

Tim Keeler had become an honourary member of the household almost as soon as they'd moved in. He and Indigo both sat in the second last row of Mr. Pasquale's Grade 7 class and, since they were both Ks (before she married Sam she was Indigo Keating), they were often thrown together. Plus he lived a few doors down. Tim's father had cancer, which was eating at his brain and making him angry. The stress had pulled his mother so taut that her eyes bugged out of her head, or so he insisted. His older brother was too absorbed in his teens to pay attention. Tim made a point of being scarce.

Alice paused in the doorway. "I was thinking about him this morning. Remember how different he seemed when he got back? Said Thailand was his favourite place in the world."

As her mother made tea, Indigo browsed through the various booklets, remembering that Tim liked Bali for the women, who "weren't as much work" as the ones he went out with at home. Women no older than these, probably, who gave him body massages and handjobs and any kind of sex he wanted — if he was in the mood, which of course he usually was. Groups of naked young women fawning over his own equally bare body, hung loosely over a towel in some back room, content from beer and coconut curries, and enough sex to wonder how he would pay for what was surely becoming a massive karmic debt.

"I can't figure out how I got so lucky," he said to Indigo, when he dragged himself away, finally, sated and broke. "I've been checked out for all kinds of things — AIDS, VD, PMS. Malaria, parasites, flatulence. The whole nine yards. I'm one lucky tart."

Picking up a map, Indigo called to the kitchen — "Am I looking after the house?"

"I hope so," said Alice. She was walking slowly down the hall, balancing a plate of cheese and apple on the mugs.

Indigo stood up to help her. "Should I bring the cats to my place?"

"They're used to the street, so it might be better if they stay. I don't know, it's up to you. If you don't feel like stopping by every day, bring them home — but they might end up back here. I read about a cat who was taken to a farm somewhere, something like a hundred miles out of the city. He went missing and everyone thought he was gone. But he showed up two weeks later, at his old house, exhausted and thin, his fur all —"

"Did they make him go back to the farm?"

"No, they kept him. I think you'd have to, after that, poor old thing. Can you imagine?"

"I bet the owners felt awful." Indigo looked at Nancy, who was sitting on an open brochure. "You know, I still feel bad about that frog," she said. "The one who lived under water. You remember? What was his name?"

"Steve, but you were just a kid."

"Not really. I got him the year we bought this house, so I was — what, 12? I remember coming home on a Sunday night — I must have been at dad's — and he was dead. Face down in dirty water. I hadn't cleaned his bowl in ages ... and I think I forgot to feed him. Starved the little guy to death."

Indigo pictured Steve floating at the surface, surrounded by white strings of scum and his own poop, and forced herself to recall other awful things she'd done.

Like the time Alice wanted to show her off at Brian's oldest daughter's wedding, but she went camping with her boyfriend instead. Alice encouraged her to make the responsible decision — "But it's your choice," she said. "Do what you think is best." So Indigo grabbed her bikini and a pair of cut-offs, kissed Alice goodbye, then felt guilty about it, off and on, for — what was it now — thirteen years.

Or the time her dad's new wife called to say that she'd hurt her father's feelings, not that he'd tell her himself. She was 14 and angry; they'd been fighting. She couldn't remember the exact words, but *cold-hearted son-of-a-bitch* was in there somewhere, and *delusional;* Indigo couldn't help smiling — she'd been proud of that one. Regardless, it was tame compared to the fights that followed — until a few years ago, when he moved to Ottawa and Indigo discovered that distance made the heart, if not a whole lot fonder, less inclined to irritability.

Indigo phoned Sam after dinner. She hadn't called him earlier, on purpose, and now she was feeling anxious, wondering if he was home, if he was pissed or apologetic — if he was working or waiting or none of the above.

He answered part way through the first ring. "It's me," she said.

"Indi, where are you?"

"At Alice's."

"Why didn't you call?"

"I don't know."

"Listen, I'm sorry. For what I said —"

"Whatever. I don't want to think about it now. I'll be home in a while." She hung up quickly, afraid of softening, of not turning the words over in her head enough times to fully grasp their meaning.

Was she being unreasonable? That's what it came down to. Was it fair of Sam to absolve himself of all things concerning her while he lived his book? Was she allowed to at least resent it, or did she have to become an Alice? *That's fine honey, whatever works for you.* This was obviously a major character defect. She was selfish and demanding and there ought to be a way to change things like that. A method more effective than pretending she didn't feel the way she did.

Leaving her mother's, Indigo turned right toward Bloor instead of her usual left. It was a roundabout route, but the side streets looked dark and soulless in the rain and she was scared to walk past the school yard. Funny to be afraid of teenagers smoking pot in the doorways, to be that far removed already.

A thought occurred to her. She had to find a way to make her own life so interesting that she'd no longer feel threatened by anything Sam did or didn't do. His actions, attentions, whether they even stayed together, would shrink to the point that, while distracting in the moment, had no particular lasting impact. She'd move on, have a different life. With someone else, or not. So what?

Walking toward the lights, she played with the word *matters*. She had to agree with him — she wasn't doing anything meaningful, not really.

It was clearly a personal thing. She needed to find something she could feel strongly about, and then make it an obsession. No. Passion was a much better word. She'd make it a passion.

It didn't have to be brain surgery. She didn't have to run off and become a human rights activist or chain herself to seals — although a tad less self-absorption might offer its own brand of relief. It needn't have an impact beyond her own circle of people. Motherhood would count, if she was that way inclined, which she didn't think she was but might be. She'd been wrong about herself before.

Sam was waiting in the living room. "Hey," he said, standing up.

"Hey." She put her umbrella near the rad to dry.

"What took you so long? Nicole called."

"Did she? When?"

"A few minutes ago, she was on her way out. She said she'd call you tomorrow."

Sam followed Indigo down the hall and into the kitchen, then stood watching from the door as she popped two aspirin in her mouth, and swallowed them down with juice. "Can we talk?" he asked.

"Sure. How was the conference?"

"Boring, fine. I pitched an angle this afternoon, it's a go. Relatively painless. So far." He paused. "That's not what I meant."

"I know but there's nothing to say." Indigo turned on the tap and began washing the few stray glasses in the sink. "You're sick of me pushing you to do things, and I'm sick of having to beg for every little crumb of attention." She paused. "Are you still going out on Friday?"

"Yeah, but I thought we could —"

"Then I don't think this is a good night to get into it. I really wanted you to come to Tim's party. So I'm pissed and a little hurt, but it's not fatal. So don't start on me about expectations."

"I wasn't. You're right. I'm sorry. I've been —"

"Look, I'm in a bad mood. Okay? This really isn't the time for *mea culpas*. I'll go to the party on my own. I don't want you to come and leave early, that'll be worse. But it's not that big a deal, okay? Can we drop it?"

She felt defeated as she walked back down the hall and into the living room. They sat on the couch, not quite touching, flipping channels before settling on what appeared to be porn for the animal kingdom.

Indigo was particularly intrigued by the rhinos, which spend up to a month in violent foreplay. She felt a stir in her lower stomach when she found out that flamingos do it with as many as twenty friends watching. And by the time the orangutans started to frolic in the trees, Indigo felt like she was looking through her mother's bedroom window all over again. And she was grinning. As a pair of bald eagles fell from the sky, talons locked either in panic or embrace (who could tell?), she felt Sam move close beside her.

"I really am sorry," he said softly, melodically, brushing his lips against her ear, then pressing soft, open kisses on her neck.

She thought about resisting.

"You have nothing to worry about," he whispered, sliding his hand beneath her skirt. "You're beautiful."

Being indignant.

"Sexy."

Telling him no.

"Things will get better."

That he can't act like a shit and expect to make everything all right —

"I'll be nicer, I promise."

— with sex.

"It'll be all right. You'll see."

She opened her legs a little wider. His fingers reached inside her panties and she abandoned any remaining will to the sensation creeping up her spine and scalp, and to the warmth of his breath on her thighs.

Nicole called just before noon the next day.

"Indi — big news."

"It's been that kind of week. I have some too, so does Alice. You go first."

"I'm in love."

"That's not news."

"Yes it is. This is huge. Wait till you meet him, he's so fucking hot. What's yours?"

"I had sex." Indigo drew the outline of a large X on her pad, and began to colour it in with red.

"Congratulations. With Sam?"

"Of course with Sam. Let's have a drink after work."

"Sorry, no can do. I'm meeting Simon. I have to see him to tell him I don't want to see him any more. I considered his machine, but it seems so — well, mechanical."

Indigo stopped colouring. Simon was Nicole's most recent regular bedmate. "Wow, you're dumping Simon. You must like this one. What about tomorrow?"

"Can't. I have a date."

"With your new man? What's his name?"

"Spider. Who else would it be?"

"Is that a trick question?"

"Funny," said Nicole.

Indigo paused. "Spider's not a name, it's an insect."

"Actually, it's not. It's an arachnid. Same as scorpions."

"Sounds delightful. Is he coming to Tim's party?"

"Yeah — you're going to die when you meet him."

"Why, is he poisonous?"

"You're just full of them today, aren't you? Is Sam coming?"

"No and he's a jerk. But it's a long story, I'll tell you when I see you."

"Okay. Alice. What's up? I only have a minute."

"She's going to Bali — deserting me for three whole months. Can you believe it? She's taking a leave of absence."

"That's so cool. When?"

"October. So tell me about this bug of yours."

"He's not a bug, he's a drummer. You know the band Cringe?

Very talented. Very cute. And deep. Get this — he's got a Buddha tattooed on his shoulder. It's right over this really cool scar that he says he got playing badminton, so when he flexes his muscle, the Buddha winks. I'll get him to show you at the party."

Indigo was silent.

"I'm kidding," said Nicole, laughing. "I was saving that one up, I knew you'd fall for it. He's a great guy, you'll see."

"At least your sense of humour hasn't gone to hell, not yet. But for crying out loud, Nic. You're supposed to sleep with musicians, that's all. You know the N-word. Narcissism. They're pretty in bed, but they get ugly fast. You're not supposed to fall for them. I mean, let's not forget Marcel —"

"Yeah yeah, too late." Nicole lowered her voice to a whisper. "You're going to think this is weird, but I love his balls. He has these unbelievably beautiful balls. And his mouth, wait till you see his mouth. I'm hooked." She sighed. "Anyway, you worry too much. Listen — I gotta go, he's here. We're taping an interview. God, he's gorgeous. I'll call you later. Bye."

Indigo stared at the phone, thinking she'd just been at the receiving end of too much information. But if Nicole couldn't see Simon any more because of Spider, this was real. Or at least, as real as Nicole got. Simon had only been in the picture, what — two months, maybe three. He was a bicycle courier. It was never love, but Nicole had a thing for endurance.

It had been almost a year since she narrowed herself down to just one man, and that only lasted a month. With Basil, a dancer from *Cats* who ultimately ran off with his Mephistopheles. She also had a thing for flexibility.

Most of the time, Nicole touted the benefits of an open relationship. "Why be jealous," she'd say, trying to convince Indigo that hers was really the mature way to exist. "Just because your lover has sex with someone else, it doesn't mean you suck in bed. There's no need to take it personally. And it's easier not to if you're schtupping some guy you met at the beach." That was in her lifeguard phase. She also had a thing for youth.

After work, Indigo went in search of something wild to wear on Friday. Something red or vinyl, or — more likely — basic black, as long as it was short enough and shapely. Something to gently goad Sam. Or no, who was she trying to kid? Something to drive Sam out of his mind.

Five

Indigo's pre-party ritual included a glass of ice cold wine and music, something lively, to put her in a mood to play. Freshly showered, shaved and scented, she passed back and forth in front of Sam's closed office door, from the bathroom to the bedroom and back, several times, wearing a black lace bra and thong, thinking it was a shame that he was too involved to notice.

The panties were a touch usually reserved for their dates, and she'd been known to flip up her skirt and show him — if she thought no one else was looking. Tonight they were part of what she referred to as self-psychology: an attempt to manipulate her own emotions, to feel great about herself so she wouldn't have a couple of drinks and get all wistful because it wasn't the night she planned.

Her shopping expedition had produced another short black dress to add to her collection of short black dresses. It was sexy in a subtle way — made from a stretch fabric that hugged her breasts and brushed against her thighs as she walked — but it was less daring than she wanted to go, if only for one wayward moment.

Both clerks had insisted that the black vinyl pants looked *stunning*. They were glossy and tight, with a wide belt that began below her navel. But she didn't have the guts to wear them, told herself they'd be too hot. Instead, she splurged on a brave new lipstick. *Fall from grace red.*

Sam was just turning off his computer when she went in to say goodbye. "You leaving?" he asked. "Wish Tim happy birthday for me."

"I will. When are you going out?"

"Soon." He looked at his watch and said — "Shit, it's after nine. I'd better get moving."

"What are you wearing?"

Sam looked at her with what she took as a flash of contempt, although more likely irritation. "How do I know? I'll decide when I open the closet. Why do you waste time thinking about stupid things like that? It's irrelevant."

"Forget it," she said. "I don't know why you have to be like that. I was just asking. It's called small talk." She paused, then added — "It's a technique for avoiding conversation, when you think about it. I thought you'd have liked that."

Sam didn't bother to respond. He'd already turned away, his attention lost to the papers on his desk; he began organizing piles and mumbling the odd comment to himself, to show that she should leave.

She stood in the doorway. "Let's try this again," she sighed. "Do I look okay?"

"Yeah fine," he said, still focused on his desk.

Fine, she thought. Don't be so enthusiastic. "That's it?"

"You look great. Is that what you want me to say?" He exhaled loudly as he turned to face her, avoiding the dress, on purpose maybe, to be obtuse. She wished she never asked.

"Whatever," she said, pulling his door closed hard behind her, thinking that even simple talks with Sam had a way of sliding backwards.

Walking down the street, it occurred to her that if she was hit by a truck tonight, those would be the last words they ever spoke to each other. She rewound the conversation and played it again without the sound. The words were light blue, a cool colour, bouncing back and forth between them before losing their energy and turning black, then dripping to the floor and spreading like an ink stain.

Just another mess.

She was still dwelling on Sam when she realized how tight her neck and shoulders felt, and noticed her purse bouncing fast against her hip. She slowed her pace and her breathing, sucking in the cool, dark air and trying to force a change of mood.

Focus on the details, she thought. Bicycles chained to a black iron fence. Calm down. The smell of watered dirt. Pink flamingos. Waist high statue of the Virgin. Beneath a streetlight, tulips going mad before they died, red petals open in a rude, silent scream, black tongue. Indigo laughed.

A block from the subway, she hailed a cab — and wished right away that she hadn't. It was rank with body odour, stale cigarettes, fast food past its prime. She considered getting out, but the driver smiled and said hello; he looked eager, sitting with his back straight, slightly forward in his seat, both hands gripping the wheel.

"Richmond and Peter," she said, rolling down her window, trying to touch as little of the stained cloth seat as possible. "I'm in kind of a hurry."

The party was at Side Effects, in a private lounge overlooking the crowded bar below. Indigo climbed the stairs slowly, letting the noise sink into her pores. A final boost to her senses. Music, people shouting, laughter. The clink of glass on glass from the bar. As she stepped into the party, she spotted some people from Vox, and — was that Tim's brother, Matt? She thought he was still in L.A.

When their father died, Matt took off for California, leaving Tim to care for his mother. For the first six months she cried and Tim, who was not yet 13, was convinced she was trying to kill herself. As far as he could tell she didn't sleep, or eat anything other than frozen Cornish pasties; she just sat in his father's chair drinking heavy English beer and getting fat, in a dirty flowered house dress.

It was around then that he asked if he could come and live with Alice and Indigo — "You know, if anything bad happens."

They said of course he could.

Two years later, when Tim's mother had recovered enough to become an only slightly pudgy workaholic, Matt returned home long enough to let her fund his MBA. As a parting gesture, he allowed her to buy him an expensive summer suit, then fled.

"I hope he never comes back," said Tim, at the time. "Good riddance. How big you think those earthquakes get?"

Tim was standing near the window and Indigo watched him lean forward, whisper something into the ear of a small, titian-haired woman, then wave his beer in the air and yell — "Happy birthday to me, baby!" The woman laughed and Indigo started to ease her way in their direction, pulling his present out of her purse. He must have started early.

"Indigo. My love. You're looking hot, as always." He took a swig from the bottle and gave her a cool, slightly wet kiss that she could taste. "Indi, this is Darcey Alexander, my new friend. Darcey, this is Indigo Blackwell, my oldest friend in the world. "Indigo, can you stand it? I'm 30. That's dead in dog years."

"You're still a baby," she said, holding up his present. It was wrapped in orange paper, with clowns and balloon letters that said, *It's your special day!*

"Sure. But I meant time as in years — which my mother insists are running out, by the way — not maturity." He lifted the present out of her hand. "You didn't have to do this, but I knew you would. Let's get you a drink."

At the bar, Tim called, "Bartender, a drink for the lady," then turned to Indigo. "I love saying that."

The bartender gave her a wry smile, and said — "What can I do you for? We're serving champagne by the glass, special, in honour of creeping old age. Isn't that right Tim?"

Tim smiled back and gave him the finger.

"Sounds great," she said. And then to Tim — "Did I see Matt?"

"Yeah. He's in town for a week or so, on business."

"What's he doing? I haven't seen him in years, not since we were kids."

"Outshining me, as usual. He's a bigwig at some computer animation company, here to scout the local talent. Hollywood all the way, right down to his red silk shorts. We're all so proud."

"Come on, he's your only brother. It's nice that he came. What did he bring for your birthday?"

"An electronic organizer. What every busy bartender needs."

"Don't be like that. You know he loves you —"

"Sure," said Tim, "in his own competitive, ego-driven way."

"Okay, you win. So look on the bright side. He'll go home soon, then we can trash him. It'll be fun, just like old times. Is Darcey your date?"

"Nope. Flying solo. Too many possibilities. I met her at work, through Cybill. You know, the one with the great big —"

"— I know who you mean —"

"— heart." Tim smirked. "That great big heart with all it's great, big, beautiful padding." He opened his mouth and raised his eyebrows, as though he was shocked by his own insolence, then slapped his hand to one of his cheeks. "Cute though, isn't she? I'm going to ask her out." Grinning, he pulled a torn piece of paper from his pants. "I already got her number," he said. "Before I've had too much birthday cheer."

"Smart move," said Indigo. "This time put names — and a brief description, if you can get away with it. You know, like small, reddish-brown hair, pretty face."

"You think she has radish hair?"

"Red, you goof."

He took her hand and kissed it. "You take such good care of me."

"I know and don't forget it. So what are you waiting for? Open it."

Tim was ripping apart the paper when Indigo felt a pair of hot hands press against her waist on either side, then slide down toward her hips. She turned quickly, thinking without really thinking that it might be Sam, and saw the face of Peter Dumas, up close, his chin almost resting on her shoulder. She must have looked shocked because he relaxed his grip and said — "I was just having a squeeze. But I guess it's your night off."

"You guessed right," she said, stepping away from his hands. "How's it going?"

Tim was still focused on his present. "Hey man, glad you could make it."

"Best of the season," said Peter.

Tim threw the wrapping on the floor. "Indi — this is fantastic," he said, holding up a silver bracelet, hand carved with what looked like modern hieroglyphs. Spirals, wavy lines and number signs, etched in the metal and blackened with oxide. "I'm serious, thanks. It's the bomb." He leaned over and kissed her cheek, moving his wrist from side to side. "Fits great."

"That's a pretty awesome piece."

Indigo hadn't noticed the man standing next to Peter. He was young, barely in his 20s, she thought. The quintessential bad boy — skinny with black jeans and a black shirt, translucent skin and bangs that hung in his eyes.

"I like it," she said, thinking *that was clever*. As she took a sip of champagne, Indigo pulled in her stomach, stood straighter; she stopped short of tossing back her hair.

"This is Jon DeGroot," said Peter. "Remember the name, he's a budding *artiste*, very talented. Jon — Indigo and Tim, the man of the moment."

"Hey," said Tim, spotting a group of women in the doorway, looking for someone they might recognize. "Excuse me a sec, would you? Duty calls."

"What kind of art do you make?" asked Indigo.

"All kinds," said Peter, adding a flourish of formality. "He's a student at the prestigious, almighty and all-powerful Art and Design Institute of Canada, known to those in the know as ADIC."

She made a point of turning to Peter. "Really? That's interesting. What does he take there?"

Jon laughed and she noticed that he was even more attractive with a little less intent. "I just finished my second year," he said. "But I'm still experimenting."

"Sounds exciting — hurling paint balls, sketching nudes, that sort of thing?"

"Something like that," he said. "What do you do?"

Indigo looked at Peter, who smiled and kept his mouth shut. "I work for a public relations agency. But I'm ready to try something else."

"I didn't know that," said Peter. "What?"

"Not sure yet. Got any ideas?"

"Of course," he said. "You could work for me."

"You don't have any money."

"Who said anything about money? Do it for love. Come on, be my groupie. I have new play — set to go in the fall, I think. It's being workshopped as we speak. You can come every night, hang around backstage. It'll be fun."

"As challenging as that sounds, I'll pass. Although I'd like to see the play." She was looking at the silver pendant that hung from a black leather string tied taut around Jon's neck, a single open eye. "That's nice."

"It's a symbol for the conscious mind," said Jon. "A friend made it."

"Sounds ambitious," said Indigo. "Having a conscious mind, I mean — the pendant's nice too. I always wanted to make jewellery." She paused for a sip of champagne, then said — "Come to think of it, doesn't ADIC have a night program? I seem to remember a catalogue."

"Sure," said Jon. "I hear it's pretty good."

"There you go. Maybe I'll reinvent myself as a jewellery artist. Sell my work at one-of-a-kind stores — or on Queen Street, in the summer anyway. Sounds like a peaceful existence."

"Is that what you want?" asked Jon. "A peaceful existence?"

"Hard to say, I don't think I've ever had one. On paper maybe, but not in my head. I tend to make things difficult. Have you?"

"No, but I don't want one. I like things difficult."

"Certain things," said Peter, adopting the tone of someone who's sure he understands life's more subtle nuances. "Not everything. When I have an argument, I want it to be difficult — and I want to be difficult. The first time I make love to a woman, it should be difficult to achieve and then easy to accomplish. Fluid. If we're in a relationship, on the other hand, you — as the woman — must maintain a certain degree of difficulty all the time, or I'll lose interest and walk all over you. But when I need a drink, like now, it should be easy. Pure and simple. No effort required." He turned toward the bar. "I'll get you both one while I'm there."

"You don't have to do that," said Indigo. "Why should the woman waste her energy pretending to be difficult? That's not fair."

"It's okay," he said, taking a few steps and turning back. "I can afford it. They gave me a grant — one of the perks of an award. And to paraphrase just about everyone who has ever lived on earth or elsewhere, who said life is fair?"

Indigo was talking to Tim's brother when she saw Nicole waving at her from the other side of the room. "My alter ego," she said, glad for a reason to flee.

Matt was filling her in on what he called his latest personal highlights — how they made him the youngest vice-president in the history of his company, about his divorce, the affair he had with his assistant (of course he did, she thought), and his (positively enlightened) conclusion that all women are looking for their fathers. "At least, that's what my therapist says. And he knows what he's talking about." All that and he hadn't recognized her until she said who she was — but then again, why should he? He was still an idiot and she was 14 the last time they saw each other. And even then, Tim spent a lot more time at her house than she ever did at his.

Nicole was like a spotlight. She stood in the doorway, beaming in a white satin T-shirt, cropped to reveal a pair of lips drawn in ink around her navel, a white vinyl skirt and go-go boots (still an important retro essential for the fashionably inclined). The lips on her stomach were violet and pouting, just like her own, almost swollen, outlined with thick silver strokes.

"Hey sweetie," she said, kissing Indigo on both cheeks and then the mouth, playfully, in a surge of patchouli. "This is Spider."

"How's it going," he said, more as a greeting than a question.

"Hey. I've heard a lot about you," said Indigo, thinking that wasn't strictly true — that she assumed a lot about him, probably unfairly, based on the fact that he was in a successful band (she checked), that he had tight drumming arms and thick, yellow hair that fell to his shoulders, hoops in his ears and rings on most of his fingers. That and he was chiseled, with soft blue eyes and creases where he laughed. Much too pretty to be safe.

"Scary thought," he said.

"No, nothing bad. Not yet anyway, there's time."

"We almost didn't make it," said Nicole.

"Throws of passion and all of that?" asked Indigo, instantly wishing she hadn't.

"Good guess, but no. Spider made this unbelievable dinner — coq au vin, with fresh bread and salad and wine. He has a bread maker. We oinked out and fell asleep on the couch. When I woke up I was being drawn upon."

"I noticed the lips. Nice touch," she said, feeling guilty.

She'd been expecting someone closer to the bass player Nicole went out with a few years ago — pasty skin, big hair and bigger ego. Pants so tight you could see the outline of what appeared to be an exceedingly average penis. But this guy seemed relatively normal. Too much of a rock star for her taste. Perfect for Nicole. And the man could cook.

"You know, I almost bought some pants in that material," she said, running her hand down the side of Nicole's skirt. "Only I couldn't do it. Too much gut, no glory."

"I don't believe you," said Nicole. "You're like a string. We'll get you into this some time, go out on the town. Spider honey, will you get us a beer? Or better — is that champagne? — I'll have one of those."

"Whatever you say, Nicky."

They both watched him walk to the bar. People stared openly, women mostly, and Indigo wondered if they knew who he was, or if he looked like he should be someone famous. "Nicky," she said. "No one gets away with that. Must be love. So why the name Spider? What's that all about?"

"Stupid kid thing. Grade 6. Tried to impress a girl. Ate a spider. Puked all over the grass. Isn't he just too adorable?"

"I guess." Indigo turned to face Nicole, who was still looking past her at Spider. "You know me. Even before Sam I had a rule: never date a guy prettier than you are. They have too many options, end up messing with your head."

Nicole laughed. "I remember."

"Not that you have to worry about that," said Indigo, looking at Nicole's long, pale legs. "You look fabulous."

"No wonder I like you," said Nicole. "You say the nicest things. I feel fabulous. You know, I really think this could be the one."

"Isn't it a little soon to tell? How long have you known him, a week?"

"Six glorious days. Haven't you ever heard of love at first sight?"

"About a hundred times, all from you. Does he tour a lot?"

"Sometimes. He's got a new CD so they'll be going on the road soon, I think. I'm dreading it."

"And you're not going to see anyone else?"

"No way — and it's going to be a killer. But on the bright side, we get to make up for lost time. We've already started."

"With protection?"

"Of course with protection. What a question."

"Every time?"

"Yes, every time. You're worse than my mother."

"How is your mother? I haven't seen her in ages."

"Out there as ever. She's planning a trip to Rio next month, to some kind of spa where they supposedly do top quality work for about half the price. Daddy's all for it, so she's planning an overhaul. Face lift, upper and lower lids and a boob job. Maybe a tummy tuck, I can't keep track. She keeps changing her mind, adding more to the menu."

"I don't know why she thinks she needs it."

"I do, but I'll save you the sordid details — for now. It'll take a while, and here's my love bunny." Nicole smiled at Spider, opened her eyes wide and said in a little girl's voice — "Did you miss me?"

Indigo decided this was a good time to freshen her drink.

In fact, she'd already consumed enough champagne to ensure a headache of epic proportions. The bubbles made her feel giddy and cheerful and she flitted about, laughing, flirting, chatting with the already perfect girls fixing their faces in the can.

The great thing about parties was that they were busy and unfocused enough to obscure the passing of time. Or maybe that was the alcohol.

She'd been bothered, recently, by an impatience that crept into almost everything else she did. She'd be dying to see a certain movie, look forward to it and then, part way through, try to see her watch in the glare from the screen. Concerts and plays had much the same effect. As soon as a book got interesting, she'd start reading faster, skimming over words and scanning paragraphs, trying to make it a thing she'd done instead of something to enjoy. And if the realization weren't enough, she was also certain she'd grow old mourning the lost time, wishing she hadn't skipped over so much pleasure.

She wished it already.

To grow old may be a curse, but as selfish as it was, she had to admit that she took comfort in the fact that it was everyone's curse, something to be accepted gracefully. To grow old having led a wasted, uneventful existence — there was no comfort in that, no acceptance, no excuse and no one else to blame.

Toward the end of the night, Indigo saw Jon DeGroot standing by himself, leaning on the ledge of a window, looking at her. She went over.

"Taking a break from the lovers?" he asked.

"They're leaving. How did you know?"

"I like to watch."

"Sounds intriguing. What have you seen tonight?"

"A lot of things. You mostly."

"What do you mean, me?" She wouldn't have thought that she made an impression.

"Well," he said, "from what I can see, you've been getting chattier with each glass of champagne. But that's no revelation. Women are like that. It'd be worse if you were doing coke. You've been up and down all night, laughing and making jokes one minute, sober the next, mostly between conversations. You don't like to watch the lovers all over each other; you turn away when it gets even slightly intense, scan the crowd, find someone else to talk to."

He spoke matter of factly, like he was explaining who the killer was and how she did it. "Where's your husband?"

"You sound like you should be taking psychology, not art."

"If I'm good I'll draw from both."

"I guess, but it's weird — you know, to be watched. Should I be uncomfortable or flattered? And why aren't you busy chatting people up? There seems to be an abundance of great looking young women around tonight. You're missing out."

"Why not be both. Flattered and uncomfortable. It's an exciting combination, don't you think? And why don't you answer my question?"

"Oh, Sam. He's at a gay bar with some young hustler," she said, hoping to throw Jon over the side, even a little, for a moment.

"Interesting marriage."

"Not really," said Indigo, looking out the window at the tangle of people and cars on the street. "No — strike that. That's not fair." She sighed, aware that she was about to give too much away. Again. "He's doing research. For a novel he's writing. So the reality's not as shocking."

"I wasn't shocked," said Jon. "Is that why you want to quit your job? Need some excitement in your life?"

"Somebody give the man a talk show. You have all the answers, don't you?"

"Not really," he said. "I don't know how you got a name like Indigo. You can tell me that."

"Oh," she said. "Hippie stuff. My parents met in the '60s. My mom went to ADIC, like you. She's an interior decorator.

Anyhow, when she got pregnant, she kept having the same dream, that her insides were all this incredible iridescent blue colour, right up to her tongue — and I was swimming around in it. She thought it was a sign. Indigo's one of the seven chakras, if you know about things like that. In any case, they smoked a lot of pot in those days. You should have seen how happy she was when I married Sam Blackwell. Loved the whole blue-black thing. She's kind of funny that way, whimsical. I don't think my dad liked the name too much, but he went along. Probably the last time he ever did." She drained her glass. "Ask me something else."

Jon stared at her face, apparently thinking, then said — "Why do you want to quit your job? Let's go there. What are you looking for?"

Before Indigo could answer, Peter Dumas lurched forward, throwing his arm around her neck and hanging on for balance.

"Listen," he said, as she ducked slightly and slid out of his grasp. "Bar's closing. Come home with me. We'll have a party. I'll show you my etchings." He fell back a step as he laughed at his own feeble attempt at a joke, then bumped into the wall and stayed there, frowning as he tried to lock his gaze on Indigo.

"Thanks, but I'm a married woman," she said, wondering how he managed to get so incredibly drunk so fast. He seemed fine when he got there.

"Tell me. Are you wearing underwear?" he asked, staring at the place between her legs.

She raised her eyebrows in what was meant to be a disapproving look, but he didn't seem to notice. "Time for me to go," she said. "It's been — uh, strange. Goodnight Peter. Nice meeting you Jon."

"I'm leaving too," said Jon. "I'll help you find a cab."

On the street, he said — "It's early. Let's go someplace."

Indigo looked at the line of waiting taxis. "I don't know. I should be getting home."

"Half an hour," he said. "A friend of mine has a club. It's around the corner. Come on, it's a cool place. You'll like it."

"I think I've had enough to drink."

"So have something else. They have everything. Espresso. Mineral water. A line. A joint. Whatever you need."

"Espresso?" she asked, thinking Sam wouldn't be home yet anyway. "They really have that? Cappuccino too?"

The club was just off Richmond on a side street, down several steps, through a locked steel door and three solid bouncers. Some boozecans made Indigo think of mini city states. Excessive rules — no standing in the hall, only one person in the washroom at a time, ten dollar minimum — enforced with the relish of people determined to maintain their own little fiefdoms of power. This was different. The bouncers were friendly for starters, better looking and not so imposing. They wore baggy pants and racing shirts, wrap-around sunglasses pushed to the top of their heads and small, wireless headsets.

Indigo followed Jon to the far side of the room. The bars were only just beginning to close, so the club was almost empty. It was large and well-equipped, with a pool table and couches on the side nearest the door, a dance floor in the middle and a bar on the right, surrounded by a cluster of tables and chairs. At the back, a riser was set up with instruments, although there was still no sign of a band. "I'll be right back," said Jon. "Cappuccino?"

"Sure, that's fine."

When he sat down, she said — "I'll tell you what I want. When I'm an old woman, I want to be able to look back at my life and say, 'That was fucking amazing.' Look at all that stuff I did, all that cool and crazy shit. Then when I'm really old — when all I do is drool into my lap and there's no present or future left, to speak of, then at least I'll have a smile on my face because the past, my own past, will be a never-ending video. Forget that you need someone else just to go to the bathroom, let alone bathe or dress yourself. Or that you have no idea who all these people are who come and ask you questions. Just rewind the tape. Ignore that last bit altogether. Re-live the part where you seduced the guide at Machu Picchu. Or he seduced you. Whatever." She licked an overhanging crest of foam from the edge of her cup. "The problem is, I don't know how to get there. I can't even think about last week without regret. Thanks for the cappuccino."

"Really? I find that hard to believe. What do you regret?"

"I don't know," she said. "Spending time on stupid things. Never going any place exotic, like on safari or to the South Seas or, I don't know, trekking through Europe. Not doing something I can be proud of, that I find valuable — or even inherently interesting. I look at someone like you. You're setting yourself up to try things, meet different kinds of people. You'll have a podium, so you must have a point of view, things you want to say."

She was leaning on the table, cupping her chin in the palm of her hand. "Sam says I assume too much, that I have — what did he call it? — a skewed impression of artists. Maybe he's right, I don't know." She leaned back in her seat. "So what kind of work do you do, anyway?"

"I'm majoring in sculpture. But like I said, I'm experimenting."

"Cool," she said. "Maybe that's what I'm doing." She took another sip of foam, looking past him at a couple playing pool. The club was filling up and she was impressed by the crowd. Urban casual, too above it all to pose. Nobody tough or out of control. No kids or drunks. Not yet.

"Maybe I'm having my mid-life crisis," she said. "Early. Maybe it's because at some level I know I have to, so I can stop wasting time. You know — figure it all out, change my life. I can't believe I'm telling you this."

"If you like artists so much, why not be one?"

"Too old. No talent."

"Oh right, you're like, what — 30?"

"Twenty-nine."

"Then by all means face facts. Life's over for you sister."

"Okay, so I'm not that old," she said, smiling at the fact that he thought she was young, thinking she was way too old for him. "I still have no talent. Couldn't draw to save my soul, which means I can't paint — or carve anything that looks like anything else."

"How do you know? Besides, talent can be learned. To some degree. So you're not a realist. Or even a painter. So you're lousy. So what? Who gives a shit? Maybe there's something else you can do. Something abstract. Or jewellery. You said you wanted to try, take a class. Do something to resolve this crisis of yours. If you're into it, come by this weekend. It's the student open house. Check it out."

"Have you got something in it?" she asked.

"A couple of pieces."

"What are they?"

"Hard to explain. A sculpture and a video installation — but that's all I'm going to say. Stop by, see for yourself. I'll be there both days."

Indigo had just turned off the bedroom light when she heard Sam's key in the lock. She'd already forced herself to swallow two aspirin and about a gallon of water, to neutralize the excess. She thought of getting up and making tea, chatting a while and going to bed together, making love. But she resisted the urge. It was late and she was rooted to the bed, already on the edge of sleep. Besides, chances are it wouldn't unfold that way. Why spoil the evening now, when she was starting to see some potential.

Six

Saturday began as a day of caution. Indigo made the scrambled eggs, toast and coffee. Sam made the bacon, just the way she liked it, extra crisp. Conversation over breakfast was polite, limited to whether they enjoyed themselves the night before (they had), whether Sam found the experience useful (absolutely), and whether he'd had enough to eat (couldn't force another bite, but thanks).

She didn't mention Jon DeGroot.

They took their coffee into the yard, where they passed sections of the paper back and forth in a good-natured, some might say intimate manner, the way couples are supposed to while they still like each other's company.

"Did you read about the drunk who pulled into the gas station?" asked Sam.

"No. What happened?"

"Listen to this. The guy gets out of his car, staggers over to a couple of cops that pull in behind him, leans into their window and says — *Fill 'er up*. True story."

"That's funny," said Indigo, allowing a small, brief smile. And after a pause — "This sounds good. Potato salad with sun-dried tomatoes and balsamic vinaigrette. Maybe I'll make it tonight."

"Why don't we barbecue?" said Sam. "You can do those ribs? Choke a few arteries, let 'em know who's boss. I love those ribs."

And so the conversation went until the news had been consumed and they seemed to regain at least a basic sense of equilibrium.

Sam hadn't been in bed when she woke up. She found him on the couch, snoring softly on his side, cushion on his head, empty wineglass on the floor beside him — on top of his notepad.

Quietly, without rustling pages or letting glass clink against the floor, she slid out the pad and started reading.

Naked butt in line. First weird thing. Right there in front of me. Less than a foot from my dick. She looked to see if Sam was still asleep, then continued, stepping out of what she thought would be his range of sight.

Pale moons rising over leather chaps. Not bad. Use that. G-string up the crack. Gross. Why gross? Doorman flirted. Huge. Hairy. Effeminate. Asked where I wanted it. Meant the stamp. Red triangle. Rubbed my palm with his middle finger. Murals on the walls inside: Men in leather caps. Harnesses. Bending over. Different looking dicks. All big, of course. Have to call them dicks. Or cocks. Not a scene for penises. Too soft. Willies. Ha ha.

Reading his notes, Indigo remembered Sam telling her about an ex-girlfriend who'd once interrupted a perfectly good blowjob by grasping him in both her hands and addressing the head directly, calling it her little one-eyed milkman. He said he laughed so hard his erection withered instantly, then he started choking. They didn't go out much after that.

Sam left a few blank lines before starting again. *Man with orange hair at coat check. Waist like a girl. Took off his clothes, all but socks and Docs. Clothes in Miracle Mart bag. Gave to coat check boy. Bent over, money in his sock, ass in our direction. On purpose? Dialogue, courtesy Graham: Why's it the ugly ones who want to prance around naked? You could see the bones in the guy's butt. Give us a break. Felt sorry for him after that, almost. Watched him take a breath, stick out freckled ribs, make an entrance. Looked sad. And vulnerable, or maybe that was me. Can't be legal.*

Sam stirred and she put the pad on the table quickly, but he only rolled over. She stood still for a moment, until she heard the familiar light wheeze of his snore, then slipped to the kitchen for a jug of water — which she put on the windowsill — and went quietly back to his notes.

Music a pulse like electricity. Graham guided. Heart beat adjusted to bass line. Bartender light brown. No hair. Almost pretty. Gold bikini briefs. Stars on nipples. Even the bottles were phallic. Indi would have loved it. (That's so sweet, she thought. He mentioned me.) *Go-go dancers. Hung in cages. Transvestites. Short silver skirts. Hard womanly bodies. Naked people in crowd. Trying hard to look casual. Afraid of cigarettes. The fringe become the masses. Moral majority? Good fun, boring or an outrage. Depending on your point of view. Because it all comes down to sex.*

The writing got smaller and closer together, but Indigo managed to read most of it before he woke up. She wished she could have been there; she liked truly outrageous behaviour, in theory at least, since she couldn't remember the last time she'd actually seen any.

She looked at the back of Sam's head and felt what she considered an absurd, adrenaline-fuelled desire to kiss him (because the notes were thoughtful and candid and made her like him better than she had lately) — or maybe smack him (because he'd probably get up and hide everything). Who knew that being a sneak had such a rush. Or that it could provide such an education.

More dialogue, courtesy Graham: Try it. Check your clothes. Get a feel for the place. Let the place get a feel for me you mean. No way. You're such a square. Maybe. Can't imagine anything that would make me want to be the only one naked at a party. Not when everyone else is a guy that's for sure. Sounds like something you wake up from in a sweat. In these dreams of yours are you aroused? Forget it I'm straight. Give me a kiss. Come on, just one kiss. I have nothing against guys liking guys. It's not my thing, okay? Don't be so touchy. It makes your story less convincing.

After several drinks, Sam had grown accustomed to the idea that men were hitting on him — and accepted the fact that in some small way he flirted back.

He and Graham had run into someone named Marion, who was at least 50, short and round and bald. Graham had introduced Sam — *He's not queer, poor fuck. He's a writer* — then taken the man to a corner, slid a hand in his pants and kissed him. This was apparently how he bought cocaine.

According to the notes, Sam *couldn't bear the look on the little man's face. Flushed. Excited. Submissive. Which may have been the point.*

Sam had joined them in the bathroom for a line. (As far Indigo knew he'd only done it once before, at a party with her — said it kept him awake but not much else.) *More dialogue, courtesy me in the john: I thought it shrivelled your dick. Why, you planning to use yours? Ha ha.*

After the bar they'd gone back to Marion's condo, where they did more coke and Sam asked *personal questions.*

Unfortunately, that was as far as she got when Sam sat up and found her watering the plants.

After breakfast, he had to finish his piece for the magazine, so Indigo said she'd go for a walk, see if the lilacs were out, stop in at her mother's. She'd pick up some groceries later, be home around six.

Standing across from the college, she wondered if it was strange to come alone, somehow pathetic.

She remembered being 11 or 12, hanging around one of those mini carnivals that came to the mall from time to time, running to the store to buy pop or Creamsicles for the boys at the Polar Express. Young men, really, at least 17 and, in retrospect, quite horrible — skinny, with oily jeans and bad skin, stringy hair.

They gave her free rides and she thought they liked her. But then their girlfriends-of-the-week arrived with breasts and cigarettes, and they all had a good laugh at the kid running errands, so clearly infatuated.

Indigo thought about calling Nicole, but decided against it. Nicole would think the attraction was — well, carnal, like it always was with her. Surely this was innocent. Indigo wanted to see what the next wave of artists was up to, what was considered avant garde, how talented Jon was. She was hoping to get a feel for the place, then maybe take a class.

Okay, so maybe there was a tiny bit of lust. A speck of lust. No, not even a speck. An atom. A nearly invisible particle of lust. Nothing she'd act on, nothing serious.

Nicole would spot it in a second.

Inside, the smell of popcorn suggested film or video to the left and down the stairs, so she stuffed five dollars into the donation box, accepted an official show pin, headed right and through the doors.

She wanted to wander alone for a while, unacknowledged.

In the basement were the workshops, unnaturally clean. Tools were hung, floors swept and everything in place, but the order couldn't hide a sense of noise and grime, physical effort.

She pictured herself working alongside intense young men and women — with saws and files and sandpaper, vices and drills, welding masks and torches — wiping a streak of black on her face with her sleeve.

She already had two favourite pieces.

A wooden coffee table, painstakingly crafted, polished and buffed to perfection, with a rambling poem to the artist's dog burned roughly into its surface. The second was a brown metal stool made to look like a tree, cast and then soldered together, with branches for legs and a slice of bark for the seat, curved to hold an ass.

Students seemed to like contradiction, she thought. Or maybe the point wasn't that they liked it. Maybe they simply noticed, felt compelled to point it out.

In the photography department, someone with the androgynous name of B. Kind offered a series that, at first glance, appeared to be black and white photos from the early 1900s, hand tinted. One, two or three ladies at a time, poised in modest dresses, long and white, cut high on the neck. Ladies on a picnic blanket, in front of the gnarled trunk of an elm or, in one picture, sitting in a small metal boat, holding a parasol for shade while a man — the only man in the series — rowed, his back to the camera.

On the other side of the room, a woman in black said to her equally black-clad companion — "Positively retro, very five-minutes-ago."

Indigo's eyes were drawn to the hand-painted colours: a turquoise sash, emerald leaves, a violet parasol.

Looking closer, she thought something about the women

looked modern — their expressions, if that was possible — and decided they were simulations, taken recently by Miss or Mr. Kind. And then she noticed their hands, which were large — grotesque against the clothes and setting — and their makeup, pale with heavy eyes.

At the moment of recognition she gave a small, startled laugh and looked around for the woman in black, who was gone. She wondered how many people would browse past the photos, failing to notice they were all of men in drag.

Indigo was struck by how accessible everything felt. In most galleries the setting is austere. The artist has experimented, out of sight, out of mind. The process no longer exists.

The student show screamed — *This is a test.*

Each piece felt like part of the place and she found herself drifting in and out of rooms, brushing her hand along the sides of cold equipment, picturing the work in progress, thinking about all those people giving life to their ideas, exerting themselves just to see what happens.

She had an overwhelming sense that she should have been part of all this, years ago. Why didn't she think of it then? And, for someone who spends so much time picking over her own internal stuff, why wasn't she aware enough to know that she'd feel the urge to do it now? Why did it come as a shock?

Indigo decided that most of the work fell somewhere between mediocre and good. The occasional piece was awful, but these were more than overshadowed by the brilliance of a few. An oil painting, in particular — a David-like nude, larger than life, with a chainsaw for a penis, standing in front of an apple tree, surrounded by discarded, partly eaten fruit. The tree was chopped in half.

She liked her art provocative. If the message was a bit heavy handed, so be it. She preferred that to a painting whose only statement was *I am a piece of fruit on a table* — no matter how finely executed.

Jon's sculpture was in the same room as the painting and she stood looking at it for a long time, trying to reconcile the person she'd met with the work.

It was a man wearing a business suit, cast in bronze, except that his left arm had been torn off at the shoulder; the hand still clutched a flower. The man was holding the appendage in his right hand, extending it, still sleeved, in some kind of offering.

The style wasn't as perfectly real as the painting, but she thought it might be intentional; the roughness seemed to make it somehow darker.

The man's face was distorted, a combination of restrained pain and something else, she wasn't sure what. Maybe pleasure. Or she could be reading too much into it. The piece was titled *Tiger Lily*.

Jon was downstairs — beyond the popcorn machine in a large, dimly lit auditorium. The room was filled with holograms and video installations, the floor crisscrossed with lengths of wire held in place with gaffer tape. He was sitting in a corner with a girl, but when he saw Indigo, he got up and came over alone.

"Hey," he said, kissing her first on one cheek, then the other. It was the kind of intimate affectation that comes when two still-for-the-most-part-strangers have recently shared a late and drunken night. "Just get here?"

"No, a couple hours ago. I've seen the rest."

"Cool. What did you think?"

"A million things. I liked your man, he's weird."

"Weird. Thanks. I think he's weird too. Listen — when you're done looking around, let's grab a coffee or somethin'."

"Sure, sounds good. Which one's yours?"

He led her to a life-size cardboard cutout of a man and woman necking. He'd positioned them under a wooden arch, so he could hang thought bubbles over their heads, the way they do in comic books. The difference was that each cardboard bubble was rigged around its own video monitor, which gave the impression of seeing their silent, inner thoughts in motion.

Jon pressed a button and both videos began simultaneously. The only audio was the occasional murmur of pleasure and the quiet slurp of people very much into a kiss.

The man's thoughts were brightly lit.

He and the woman are walking in a field, holding hands. The woman's hair is in a ponytail. A sheep dog runs toward them. The man bends over to pick up a stick, throws it for the dog. The scene shifts and they're in bed under a huge white duvet. Breasts full screen — large nipples, half hard. There's orange juice on the nightstand and a daisy in a vase. The dog is watching from the door. Now they're on the steps of a church, in full wedding regalia. Breasts again, full screen. The man walks in the back door of what must be his house, puts his briefcase on the floor. The woman is washing dishes, her hands submerged in a sink overflowing with bubbles. He kisses her on the cheek and then the neck. There's a high chair at the table. She unties her apron. Breasts again.

The woman's thoughts were bathed in yellows and reds.

Her hair hangs to her shoulders, straight and polished to a shine. She's wearing a silver bikini, black stiletto boots and bikers' cap. She holds a whip. The man is crouching. He's wearing a dog collar and leash, which she also holds. She takes off her top and allows him to massage oil on her stomach and breasts, which are strategically hidden from view. She commands him to crawl to the bedroom. He's tied up, helpless. She sits on him and bites his hairless chest and shoulders, leaving marks. And then he's at the stove, cooking a meal, with the added protection of a small frilly apron. She's lying on her stomach on a large island counter, painting her nails red, drinking champagne, watching.

Indigo stood with her hands in front of her chest, twisting the ring on her left hand. She could feel the back of her neck start to prickle by the end, although she recognized that the video itself was fairly tame — that it provoked explicit thoughts, while showing very little. Only breasts.

"Well," said Jon. "What's the verdict?"

"I think my husband would agree with you. He says men aren't the ones obsessed with sex, it's really us." As she said the words, she pictured Jon naked and tied to her bed — then wondered if she'd be able to carry it off, or want to.

"And what do you think?" he asked.

She pulled her eyes away from his mouth and took a breath, looking past him at the doorway. "I'm not sure I'd want it in my living room. The bedroom maybe." She hoped he couldn't see that she was flushed.

"No, I mean about sex."

I'm in favour of it, she thought, but said — "I don't know. In a perfect world, I suppose partners would always agree on how much, how far, how faithful — unless they love a good fight, in which case the world's already perfect, don't you think? Are they really a couple?"

"Yeah. The girl's in my class and that's her boyfriend. I was talking to her when you came in. Over there. In the corner, the one with the crew cut."

"You're kidding right?"

"The wig was part of the trip."

"What a difference," said Indigo, wondering where she could buy some shiny black hair. "Did she like it?"

"It was unbelievable," he said. "She's normally this subdued little thing, nice looking but kind of mousy, not a lot to say unless she knows you. But give the girl a wig and a whip and she's ready to rule. Her boyfriend can thank me — or not. Either way, I think he's in for a ride."

Half an hour later, they were sitting on a bench across the street. It was warm but windy, and Indigo's hair kept blowing in her mouth. She found an elastic in her purse to tie it back, took her sweater off and folded it beside her.

"So. How you feeling?" asked Jon. "None the worse for wear?"

"Not bad, considering. A little slow. You?"

"I feel great. Did you beat him home?"

"Barely. Heard him come in, but I didn't get up. Too tired."

"See. No worries."

"No, but I feel kind of guilty." She turned slightly to face him. "Not because we went out after — that's no big deal. But I didn't mention it. I don't know why." She took a sip of her pop. Not Squeeze, she was boycotting Squeeze in retaliation for the orange suit. "Not that I have to tell him every single thing," she said.

"I'm sure he doesn't tell you every single thing," said Jon. "So don't waste your guilt. Save it up. Use it all in one shot, some day when you feel like you just gotta be bad."

"That's backwards. It doesn't make any sense," she said, not sure that she'd enjoy the chance to be consciously wicked, but not ruling it out. "I like it."

For a moment they were quiet, Indigo watching the school, Jon staring at her profile. "I hate to admit it," she said. "I think I was feeling jealous." She noticed his gaze and turned to face him, thinking she might feel less examined if she met his eyes head on. "Last night, I mean. Left out, like Sam gets to do all the good stuff when I want to be the one checking out weird new clubs. God, I sound like such a spoiled brat. In any case, I got over it. Thanks to you. I'm glad I came along."

"Don't thank me, I had a blast. You really suck at pool."

"That's not fair," she said, pretending to be indignant. She pinched his arm but not too hard. "I wasn't that bad. By the end."

He leaned away in mock defence. "Oh right. If you mean you weren't bouncing balls off the table any more, okay, I'll give you that."

"So I don't spend my time in pool halls," she said. "Some of us work for a living, you know. We don't all get to play as much as you."

Someone across the street shouted, "I'll see you at the Cameron," and Indigo's gaze shifted back to the people in front the school — students mostly — talking, smoking cigarettes, sitting on the sidewalk.

"Why did you tear off his arm?" she asked.

Jon smiled and touched her shoulder. "I have a thing for grand gestures." He motioned his head toward the garbage can, aiming his bottle. "Think I can make it?"

"If you say so."

He stood still for a moment, concentrating, then lobbed the bottle in an upward arc. It hit the edge of the can and bounced sideways, landing under a tree that grew half-heartedly in a large, cement box.

"There's a whole story behind the guy," said Jon, retrieving the bottle and dunking it into the can. "It's pretty stupid."

"Tell me."

Sitting down, he turned sideways so his leg was bent, part way on the seat. She was conscious of his hand behind her neck.

"His name's Hank and he's a loser," said Jon. "He has a lowlife job in a cubbyhole someplace where people yell at him and he has to work late every night while everyone else gets the glory."

"I love a cheerful beginning," said Indigo.

"Wait, it gets better. The only good thing in Hank's life is Lily, a nurses' aid he met at the hospital — ingrown toenail, very painful. He's wild for this chick so he sucks up his courage and asks her out, and to his complete amazement, she says yes. So they go on a date, then a few more. He buys her a bunch of things he can't afford and finally, she agrees to marry him."

"Sounds like love," said Indigo.

"Yep. He's got it bad. Anyhow, the guys from his office take him out to celebrate since they know he's a pathetic loser and doesn't have any friends, and they figure it'll make him do even more of their work. They take him to a strip joint where the featured act is — guess who? — Lily. In a hot little nurse's number with white stockings and garters and a cap, even though real nurses don't seem to wear caps any more. I wonder why."

Jon paused to wave at a man across the street who'd caught his eye, then continued. "One of my professors," he said. "Where was I? Oh yeah. Miss Lily. So Hank doesn't let anything slip to the guys but he can hardly bear to watch. So after the show he makes up some excuse, says he's not feeling well or something, and waits for her. Tells her he loves her and all is forgiven, but she laughs. Says she was just going out with him to get back at her real boyfriend, the chief of surgery at the hospital where she works, who's taking her to Hawaii — on business, since of course he's married — and they're leaving tomorrow, as a matter of fact, right after work. He didn't really think she was serious, did he?

"So poor old Hank cries all night and even thinks about toasting himself. But instead, he decides to try one more time to win her heart. So he steals a flower from the nicest house he can find, it's supposed to be a tiger lily, and goes to the hospital, where he rips off his arm and tries to give it to her."

"That's really gross," said Indigo.

"I know. And in case you're thinking happy ending, think again. The chief of surgery does not re-attach the arm — I thought of that, but no. Too predictable.

"Instead, Lily pulls one of those disposable cameras out of her overnight bag and snaps a picture of Hank standing there holding out the arm and flower with that weird look on his face, to put in her scrapbook. She plucks the flower out of the hand, puts it in the lapel of her jacket and tells him that maybe he ought to get someone to look at that cut. That's it. He bleeds to death right there in the hall."

Indigo surprised herself by laughing. "Ever thought of writing children's books?" she asked. "I think you have a future."

"The thing is, I wasn't depressed when I thought of it, although I guess it was kinda late at night. That's when things get weird. When you can't sleep and you're pacing. Staring out the window. It just seemed funny and kinda sick. I haven't told anyone else. Let them come up with their own stories. Let them interpret the symbolism, figure out how it juxtaposes with the evolution of contemporary themes in sculpture. Whatever turns them on."

"That's it," she said. "You're having too much fun. In my next life, I'm coming back as an art student."

"Seems like a long time to wait," said Jon, standing up. "I should get going."

Indigo twisted the lid back onto her empty bottle of juice, aimed at the garbage and said — "Think I can make it?"

"If you say so," said Jon.

"No way." She walked over and dropped it in.

He gave a single short laugh and shook his head. "You're too much. If you were one of my sculptures, I'd have to call you *Dumb chick passing time until she dies*. Of course, I'd rather call you *Woman smashing glass*. Even though I probably wouldn't have to. Fuck, Indigo, take a leap. No wonder you're having a crisis."

On the way to her mother's, Indigo had what could only be described as the urges of a madwoman. She'd had them before in different forms; she couldn't go on a ferry without having the urge to jump overboard, not that she ever would, of course; when she went to the African Lion Safari, the urge to get out among the lions was so intense she had to lock the car door.

Strangely, subways were never a problem.

The desires she felt today weren't as urgent. In fact, when she thought about it, she decided they were less urges than images. Forbidden thoughts.

Walking behind a policeman, she wondered what the chain of events would be if she reached for his holster. Would she find that her hand suddenly held a gun? Its first. Would the element of surprise, which had until then worked in her favour, revert to him because of the shock of what she'd done? Would there be a secret clasp and, if there was, would he then take out his gun and shoot her? Would he shoot her in the heart, because he was young and no one had ever tried to take his gun before? Did they give you pillows in jail?

Apparently liking the game, her mind continued.

What if she took her clothes off. All of them, except her sunglasses and her shoes (because the ground was dirty). Right on Bloor Street. And then just stood, leaning on the wall. Would people pretend to ignore her, then point from a distance? If someone she knew came by, would they stop and say hello? What would they say if she told them it was performance art, only the art wasn't her but them? Would a crowd gather and, if it did, would it be populated with the kind of men who say things under their breath to women on the street? What reaction do men like that hope for anyway, by saying things women can't hear? Even if the look on their face is clearly lascivious. Do they think we're impressed, she wondered. If we can't hear them, don't they know they become yet another dimwitted man who said something unintelligible? Not that hearing the words would change that. *Hey baby, I'd like to* ... It had never even once made her want to turn around.

Indigo found her mother in the yard, painting two old wooden theatre seats, joined by a black metal frame. Alice had already coated the seats in a rich, sky blue and was using the tip of a sponge to dab on perfect tufts of cloud.

Indigo sat on the grass beside her. "So tell me again why you're running off and leaving me," she said. "You already know how to paint."

"Because I haven't touched a canvas in years, not since college — and I miss it. This is arts and crafts. It's different. And I think if I immerse myself in it, with a good instructor, I'll come home inspired, able to do better work. And I'll get to see Bali up close, in a way that I might not be able to otherwise. What else can I say?"

"That you'll miss me."

"Of course I'll miss you. Don't be silly."

Indigo ran the palm of her hand over the grass. "Can I ask you something?"

"Anything," said Alice. "You know that."

"Would you think I was crazy if I went back to school?"

"Depends. What do want to take?"

"I want to go to ADIC," she said. "Full-time."

Alice stopped painting and looked at her. "Where did this come from?"

"I hate what I do," said Indigo. "No, that's too extreme. It's just that, I'm not proud of what I do. I never think — *Hey, I'm in PR, isn't that terrific.* Some people love it. People I know love it. Not me. I made a mistake. I should be doing something else. But it has to be right this time, something good. I'm not getting any younger."

Alice rinsed the sponge in a bowl of cloudy water, then squeezed it on the grass. "You have a degree," she said. "Isn't there something you can do with that?"

"I'm thinking it'll help later. When I go to get a job. But I want to take film and video, maybe sculpture. Metal sculpture, so I can saw things and weld them together. Give the girl a torch."

She lifted herself up into a crouch and wiped her hands on the front of her jeans. "So, what do you think?"

"I think you're impulsive," said Alice. "And I guess that worries me."

"Impulsive is what people call things when they don't work out," said Indigo. "When things go well it's called spontaneous — which is a good thing. I must've read that in one of those books you gave me."

"Sure you did," said Alice, smiling. "Not bad though." She pressed the lid onto the can of paint and banged it tight with the blunt end of a butter knife. "Come on, I'm thirsty."

In the kitchen, Indigo hoisted herself onto the counter and said — "You know, your trip helped me figure things out."

Alice's voice narrowed. "How so?"

"Well, I've been moping around, focused on everything I hate about my life, but I was looking at it wrong. I thought a new job would make things better, as much as anything could — as if it was too late to change my mind. But it isn't too late, is it? You showed me that if I don't revise the plan now, it's just going to eat at me until I'm old, and I'll still have to do it then. It'll never be too late. Why not see that now and save myself some trouble, gain some time?" She gulped her lemonade, raising her hand to show she wasn't finished. "Not that I think you're old."

Alice picked up an apple, wiping it on the front of her shirt before putting it back in the bowl. "Maybe you're right. If it's really what you want to do — and I mean for sure — then I guess it doesn't hurt to apply. What did Sam say?"

"He doesn't know," said Indigo. "I wanted to win you over first. It'll give me courage when I talk to him. This is big — I'm pretty sure it falls under joint decision in the marriage rules. I'll have to convince him, that's all. But Sam's always so logical. Ends up talking me out of things and then making me think it's my own train of thought. I hate that."

Sam's response came later that evening, with a force that caught her off guard. They were sitting on opposite sides of the picnic table, still keeping some distance, waiting for the ribs.

"That's it," he said, nodding his head slowly, absorbing the thought. "That's the answer. Become what you envy." He frowned. "But how can we afford it? I'm not exactly raking in the dough."

"I've thought about that." She picked a piece of potato out of the bowl and ate it. "I don't know if I qualify for a student loan, but I can do some freelance work for Wally — if he's not mad that I quit. I can still write newsletters, proposals, whatever. And at least we own the house, that's something." She thought for a moment before adding — "I can always get a part-time job if I need to, temping or waiting tables. But that's probably harder than it looks. I don't think people give waiters enough credit. I can't believe you think it's a good idea."

The rest of the night disappeared in a wake of enthusiasm. The air was cold, but she was afraid to move indoors and lose momentum. So they put on sweaters and socks and stayed outside, sipping wine and thinking forward. Talking about the kids they'd have, later, when things were settled — not boring though, never boring. When the money was there and they'd both reached a certain place in their careers. After they'd seen the world, enjoyed some time alone. (By then she'd be barren anyway, so it was easy to make the commitment.)

Maybe they'd work on a film together one day. He could write, she'd produce — or maybe direct. They'd be collaborators. A new dimension.

Sam opened a second bottle of wine.

Of course, they'd have to be cautious, rearrange a few priorities. They were entering — no, embracing — what would surely be profound financial insecurity. The mortgage was manageable. The car was only five years old. And a holiday could wait; they'd enjoy it more later, when they felt like they deserved one.

"Would you like to be famous?" asked Sam. They were lying on two padded wooden lounge chairs pushed together like a double bed, subdued by the dark and a heavy meal, the rise and fall of traffic in the distance.

"I don't think so," she said. "I wouldn't like the scrutiny. What about you?"

"I'd hate to be signing-autographs-in-K-Mart famous," he said. "But I'd like to be quietly famous, known to people who read. *Hey, isn't that Sam Blackwell, the guy on the best seller list? He just won one of those big literary prizes, I can't remember which one. He's on the cover of this month's* Vanity Fair, *but he looks even younger in person.*"

"And handsome, don't forget handsome," said Indigo, her hand under his shirt, sharing his heat; this was the Sam she enjoyed. "But I'd hate to be so famous that someone decided to do a biography," she said. "A tell-all book with nothing to tell, how humiliating. Or worse — if they psychoanalyzed me and figured out that I'm self-focused and full of fear, that I'm not really interesting at all."

"Something else to worry about?" offered Sam.

"No. I think that's beyond even me. I mean, there's very little chance that I'll be famous. And even if I thought it was possible, I'd drive myself to the brink trying to see my life in any kind of cohesive way, as one big picture, to make sure that it reads well. What would I have to do? Start organizing food drives or causing scenes in public places? I'd have to focus all my energy inward, which means that I wouldn't end up doing anything that would make me famous. Life becomes art, but it's bad art so nobody cares."

Pressed against Sam, she thought it might be nice to make love outside in the night, her nipples at their best, hard and pointed from the cold. But the feeling passed and she didn't bring it up. If he wanted to, he'd suggest it himself, wordlessly, by turning his body to face her. She'd become much too easy. And if he wasn't in the mood, he'd turn her down and then she'd have to feel rejected.

"So tell me about last night," she said. "Did you have a good time?"

"It was crazy. You'd have liked it."

"Why's that?"

"It was all about sex. Not that I actually saw people doing it, not up close. I kind of ignored that part. But it's wild, you go to a straight club and sex is just one part of it. Usually not till later. And not right there. But here that's all it was. Sex. Without any pretenses. There were people walking around naked for cryin' out loud. It was too much."

"Sounds like fun. What about Graham, how was he?"

"Fine. Kept his clothes on, if that's what you mean. I think I amuse him."

"Does he want to convert you?"

"Of course not, he knows I'm straight." Sam took Indigo's glass out of her hand, took a drink and gave it back. His was empty. "I learned a lot about him."

"Like what?"

"Well for one thing, his parents practically fight over each other to see who can be more supportive. They don't know he's an escort, but that's because he thinks they'll worry. He said when he came out they put condoms in his Christmas stocking. They even celebrated Pride Day, in their squeaky clean suburban neighbourhood. Put a flag on the roof and everything."

Indigo thought he sounded envious.

Sam was raised on the prairies, where the skies really are big, sons really do have obligations and, if there are go-go dancing transvestites in cages, she was pretty sure he'd never seen one.

He'd spent his first years on a farm, where his father still managed thirty or so head of cattle, grew a little corn. His father was the kind of man who stayed put and expected his children to do the same. But Sam refused — wouldn't be cowed by threats, wouldn't even argue.

He always took notes when he spoke to his parents, not to keep track of things to use against them, but to remember the best lines. "It's all fodder," he said. Look at these. Pure gold. When I get published it's really going to piss them off." On the page, he'd written — *Your brother knows from responsibility ... Sissy work if you ask me, this book business ... You think you're so bloody superior, shoulda been born east ... Selfish from the day you came, squawkin' and screamin' me me me ... Save your money 'cause you're getting shite from here boy.*

Sam said that, for as long as he could remember, his father had been ferocious in the name of God. Rigid and unforgiving. Drove his family to church every Sunday, said grace before meals and punished his children heartily, quoting the Bible as he washed their mouths with Zest.

When Sam left home, he rejected his father, his past, the church. Convinced himself that none of it was relevant, not to a man who lived in downtown North America, voted left and prayed to no one.

He once told Indigo that if there was a void in his life — and he wasn't saying there was — it was the void of every human overwhelmed by the sheer chance of it all. It wasn't spiritual, at least not in a way that made him want to bow to mortals wearing robes. Sam shared what he called the historically accurate view that religion was devised to keep the masses underfoot. He, for one, did not require the threat of eternal damnation. He preferred to answer to himself.

"So what do they think he does?" asked Indigo. "If they don't know he's a prostitute."

"Get this. They think he's a make-up artist. Brings them autographed pictures. Demi Moore, Ru Paul. Who else did he say, let me think. Tom Jones. Ted Kennedy. Engelbert —"

"Not Engelbert."

"Uh huh. Told me they hang them in the rec room. Next to the macaroni art he made in kindergarten."

Indigo had trouble picturing Graham as a child. "Did you ask the question? Why does he do it?"

"Yeah, and I said it wrong. Made him mad."

"What did you say?"

"I wanted to know why he sells his body, when he has so much going for him. He took offence. Said he sells his time. Just like everyone else. Said it's like partying to pay the rent. Doesn't see anything wrong with it. And it's not like he has to fuck anyone he doesn't want to. Except you should have seen this little guy he was with last night. What a life."

"So did you stay till the bitter end?"

"Pretty much. I got some really good material. I don't know what I'm going to do with it yet, but I know it's good." He finished her wine, then said — "It's getting late."

He wasn't going to tell her any more and the moment of closeness, when they might have had sex, had gone. It occurred to Indigo that in a way, wanting sex with Sam was a habit. More a response to his lack of interest than any real desire of her own. At least that was the case tonight, with a belly full of red wine, meat and potatoes, and strawberry-rhubarb pie.

Tonight it was better to talk and be still.

Seven

Indigo chattered her way through the rest of the weekend — first to Nicole, then Tim and then her mother again, polling her friends the way she always did when there was something to decide. Indigo liked people to approve, which is why she avoided calling her father in Ottawa. She and Sam were making the trip to see him Friday; better to wait and tell him then.

On Monday, she called in sick and spent the morning across from the college, watching the scant spring crowd, choosing courses from the calendar.

She called Sam from a pay phone at the corner.

"They'll never let me in," she said.

"Why not?"

"I'm late. I should have applied in March. And I want advanced status, so I can skip first year. You think it's hopeless?" On the phone beside her was a girl, almost a woman, wearing a tight blue dress and platforms. Her notebook was open, and Indigo spotted *Dexadrine made me feel normal, not too happy*, in loopy teenage script. The girl said — "Don't you want to see me?"

At which point Sam said — "Have you talked to them?"

And Indigo said — "What?"

And the girl said — "You can't relax around *me?*"

And Sam said — "Have you talked to them?"

Indigo forced her eyes away from the girl. "No," she said. "I haven't talked to them. Not yet."

"So make an appointment, see what they say. What have you got to lose?"

"I guess you're right. Okay. Thanks."

She hung up the phone, wondering if Sam's enthusiasm was motivated, in part, by the need for more space of his own. Of course he was proud, pleased that she wanted to mould herself into someone more impressive. But that aside, school would mean less time to sweat over meaningless details. It doesn't matter, she thought. Whatever the reason, he was glad and she was grateful.

Why not make things easy for once, leave it alone?

The interview was as stressful as any new business pitch. Probably more, since she was alone and feeling naked, as though she'd planned an elaborate striptease for a lover, except that she didn't have the moves so it just seemed awkward and pathetic. Of course, she may have been projecting. There were five on the panel — three men and two women; four professors and a terse little man from admin. They sat in a line, facing her from across a row of tables, asking questions. "We don't *usually* admit people this late" said one. "Why should *you* be an exception?"

Indigo remembered talking as they nodded and wrote things down on yellow pads. Beyond that it was hard to know anything. She was flushed and grinning like a fool. But they didn't call security or demand to know who the hell she thought she was.

They just watched, nodded from time to time or pursed their lips, smiled the odd thin smile and left her lots of room to babble.

Indigo's portfolio consisted of half a dozen videos she'd worked on at Pinnacle — including a documentary to promote a summer crafts festival, and a Felini-type video on how to sell insurance. She didn't produce them herself, technically speaking, but she did help come up with the concepts, and worked with the directors. (For the interview, she puffed these responsibilities into several full writing credits, plus that of assistant producer.) Wally knew she liked that sort of thing, so he let her get involved. She hoped it was enough.

"Thank you for coming," they said, without any apparent enthusiasm, but also without disdain. Or obvious irony. "We'll be in touch."

As she loaded the car, she wished she could have known for certain. "Not that I expected to hear by now," she said to Sam. "But still. My dad's such a tight-ass, he's gonna go ballistic. Maybe I shouldn't tell him. You think I can get away with that? Until I know I'm in?" She looked back at the locked house. "Maybe I should wear a dress."

"You know you'll never last," said Sam. "You'll have a couple drinks and tell him. And if you try to keep it a secret, you'll only end up fighting with yourself and feeling bad about it later. Stop fretting."

Indigo knew he was right, but she would have preferred not to tip her hand, not until there was no room left for sabotage. Until she'd quit her job. Maybe until her second year — hell, why not graduation. "Hey dad, I just finished film school. Want to see my reel?"

Best efforts at an early start (they were on the road by three), got them to the highway in time to idle along with the rest of the Friday exodus. The 401 boiled with the fervour of city folk just recently awoke from hibernation, determined to spend every weekend moment either on the road or at the cottage. Or at someone else's cottage. Somewhere (anywhere) but home. Away from their own kitchens, beds and VCRs. Spring cleaning. Yard work. The usual bars, restaurants, people. Just away.

"Did they like your article?" asked Indigo, breaking a silence that had stretched for miles of stop and go, but mostly stop. Up ahead, they could see what looked like a tractor-trailer splayed across the right lane, shoulder and gully, and flanked with pulsing lights that caught the sun.

"What? Yeah, I think so. What the hell is going on here?" They were still within the city limits.

To their right, a sign for the zoo made Indigo try to remember the last time they'd been. Not for years. "We should go to the zoo some time," she said. "That'd be fun, don't you think? Maybe next weekend. If it's nice. See the meer cats."

Sam glanced sideways at the exit. "The last time we were there that bird stole our fries," he said, slowing to a stop, again, and rolling down his window. "That peacock. You remember? It wasn't enough we were feeding him. He wanted the whole damned box. Snatched it off the table." Glaring in the rearview mirror, Sam said — "I don't know what possessed us to do this on a Friday afternoon. It's the same every time. Somebody oughta do something about these goddamn trucks. IT'S FUCKING MADNESS." He shouted the last words out the window.

She wanted to ask him to calm down. That kind of hostility — the kind that seemed far out of proportion to the insult — had a way of sticking to her mood, subverting her entire afternoon. But she knew the one thing guaranteed to make an excited Sam even more excited was the suggestion he relax. "You're making it worse," she said, thinking for the first time that day, albeit not the first time ever, that she and Sam were failing. There was a hint of perplexion where she'd hoped for easy rapport, the affinity she had with certain friends. But she and Sam never seemed to quite understand each other, not completely.

"LET'S MOVE," he yelled, his knuckles white around the wheel.

Indigo took a breath through her nose and blew it out her mouth. "Do you really have to do this? We're stuck, so what? We're stuck. Why don't we try to make the best of it. Please? Or at least not the worst of it?" She unbuckled her seatbelt and reached behind her for the bag of fruit. "Here, have a grape."

Without looking, Sam reached his hand inside the outstretched paper bag. And then his frown dissolved and she saw that he'd relaxed his shoulders; the wheel was looser in his grip.

Just like that, she thought, he shakes the tension off like water.

Indigo looked down at Sam's legs where they emerged from khaki shorts, white and lightly hairy. She thought of touching one, resting a casual hand on his thigh. But it wouldn't seem casual, not with this much thought beforehand, so instead she took a grape between her teeth.

"Okay," said Sam. He was bobbing his head to some invisible beat. "You want cheerful. Why didn't you say so? I can do cheerful. Let's see, something happy. I think they're going to let me do another piece for *All Business*. Probably more than one. It's a supplement. Travel technology. Laptops, cellphones, pagers. Portable satellite dishes. All that stuff. It's not a done deal, but it looks good. And it pays well. A couple thousand. Maybe more."

"That's great. What about the book? How's it coming?"

"Fine. The same." Looking in his sideview mirror, Sam waited for the car on his left to pass, signalled and swung in behind it. As they picked up speed, he said — "Now we're getting somewhere."

"I think you should let me read what you've done so far," said Indigo. "I've heard a lot of writers do that. You know, show the person they're with. Their wife or whoever, their lover. At the end of the day. Whatever they've done. And then they talk about it. Have a glass of wine. Bounce ideas. Get another point of view."

"No offence," said Sam. "But I don't want another point of view."

They looked at each other for a moment, before Sam focused back on the road and Indigo turned to the landscape — a field giving way to a tall, dark stand of green. She said nothing.

"Don't take it like that. You know how I am," said Sam. "I know what I want it to be and it's not even close. Tell me this: Why would I want your opinion on something that's still in progress? I already know the problems. I can see them. I don't need another perspective. Not yet, anyway. My own gives me plenty to do."

As they sped past, Indigo tried to fix and re-fix her gaze on the perfect rows of space between each perfectly planted row of pine.

"Besides," he said. "Yours'll be important later. When I have a draft."

She knew there were people who opposed this kind of symmetrical reforestation. And she saw their point. There was beauty in the disarray — or, at least, the perceived disarray — of nature in its purest form, untouched by human intervention. (If there was such a thing, any more.) And trees in single file, even luscious trees, do tend to spoil the illusion of wilderness. Not that most people, if they thought about it, would expect real wilderness butted up to this particular highway, which sped from one major city to the next.

Fits Like a Rubber Dress   95

In any case, she couldn't help it; she'd loved the rows long before she was ever told she shouldn't, since she was a child. She liked to imagine herself running in a line between the trees, on a velvety carpet of needles, in a sheer white dress and nothing else. It had been years since she'd thought of that, and now she added a man. There should be a man there too. Not Sam — even in the fantasy, she knew that Sam would demand to know why they were there, wandering, half dressed, with no apparent purpose. It was in his nature, thought Indigo, and you can't fault a person's nature. However, since it was her fantasy, she felt entitled to leave him at home. She invited Jon instead.

After what she thought was an appropriate silence, she said — "Did you call your mom?"

"Uh huh. Last night."

"How was it?"

"Fine. We talked, said nothing. Just the way she likes it."

Indigo turned to face him. "Did she get her birthday present?"

"She said it was nice but we shouldn't have, it's far too extravagant. Like she always does. And you know she's never going to wear it. Like she never does. Not even to church. She'll fold it in tissue, put it away. I don't know why we bother."

"Because she needs pretty things, even if she doesn't know it. God, it's only a scarf. What would she do if we sent her something really good, like diamond earrings? Clip-on. I'm sure they make them, we should do it just to bug her." Indigo reached behind the seat and pulled out a box of chocolate cookies. She offered one to Sam. "Did you talk to your dad?"

Sam glanced at the box and shook his head. "She said he went into town for some part. But I know he was there. It was like, twenty to eight or something. His time. He's always home then. I'm sure he was stuck to his LA-Z-BOY, watching the weather channel."

"No. Seven-thirty's *Wheel of Fortune*. No matter what."

"I forgot. Vanna. The man's only vice."

They were quiet after that, Indigo watching the land slope by, dotted with cows and sheep and their still-teetering young, bales of wet blond hay. Sam's parents lived in a house like some of these, with a wooden barn worn grey with sun and rain, and muddy fields. It had all seemed so honest, at first, so functional. Or rather, so not dysfunctional, which seemed like it would have to be more than simply functional.

It wasn't.

When she finally met them, Indigo couldn't help thinking that Sam's parents were a parody of the hard-working farmers on television. They were hard working. That was the one undisputed cliché. But the strong, silent father spoke in short, mean sentences, glared at the people in his home as though he couldn't quite fathom how they got there, and would have liked it better if they hadn't. He growled at his wife who, after almost forty years of marriage, didn't seem to have an opinion or thought of her own. Or want one. She cooked and cleaned and spoke in whispers, deflected any attempt by Sam to steer them away from all but the safest conversations.

"Bad year for strawberries. Late summer. Then that rain."

"Old Mrs. Williams died. You remember Mrs. Williams. She was 97. In her garden one day, gone the next. Just like that."

"Have more pie, Sam. It's your favourite."

When Indigo needed excuses, it was tempting to analyze Sam. To draw the line straight from his parents to the son that avoided anything he didn't want to do, discuss or think about. The Sam who was stingy with affection. Preoccupied and cranky. Stubborn. But it was tempting as well, to see brave determination where it smelled like self-absorption, and to interpret it as a grab for the kind of success that would prove his father wrong.

Not exactly immune to analysis, Indigo tried to resist passing judgement. Except when she absolutely had to, like when the other Sam, the one who was funny and playful, even romantic, had been out of sight so long she thought she might have made him up. When she'd spent too much time alone with her own thoughts and they'd stretched so far out of shape that she had no choice. There were days when, right or wrong, she needed reason. Something to lean on, something she could hope to fix.

Just past Kingston, a green sign with white letters read: Ottawa 157 / Montreal 241.

"Let's go to Montreal," said Indigo. "Instead."

"It's going to be fine. You always get nervous and it's always fine."

"Easy for you to say. Your dad's on the other side of the country. Besides, I like Montreal. I like the culture."

Sam glanced at her, then said — "What do you mean by that? What do you mean by *culture?*"

"What do you mean, what do I mean?"

"It's something I've been thinking about. *Culture.* Not the arts, not that kind of culture, although that's part of the package. The rest of it. *Culture* culture. Quebec's always going on about it. I think that's a very cool thing. It's important to them. And it's pretty obvious. What they're talking about. Language. *Tourtière*." Sam stopped talking while he manoeuvred them around what appeared to be a gang of grannies in a motor home. The driver, whose pink sun visor made Indigo think of orthopedic shoes and death, smiled and waved. "And there's always some immigrant community that's in the news, ragging on about its culture. Again, pretty visual stuff. Religion. Food. Language. Clothing. There was all the fuss about that cop who wanted to wear his turban. You remember? A couple years ago? Anyway, that's not the point."

"What is the point?" asked Indigo. "I think he was RCMP."

"Our culture. Mine. Yours. How would you describe it?"

"Not food," said Indigo. "What did we have this week? Thai Monday. Indian Wednesday. And I had Italian for lunch yesterday. That new place I told you about, on Queen. It was good. Not expensive. We should check it out." Indigo stared at the cars. It was something she did out of habit; even though she wasn't driving, she'd find herself absorbed by the traffic up ahead. "Your parents do turkey. That's tradition. That's part of your culture. And church. You used to go to church. What were you again, Anglican?"

"Presbyterian."

Indigo frowned. "We have fondue at Christmas. What do you think that means? My mother's never made a turkey in her life. Go figure." She popped another grape in her mouth. "All these years and I never noticed. I have no cultural identity. I'm so glad we had this little talk."

Sam laughed. "I read someplace that either you're right and people like us have no culture to speak of, or we're a mix of all kinds. A party pack."

"Okay, that's better. Culture sluts. I like that. I can work with that." A boy in the back seat of a passing car caught her attention. He stuck out his tongue and Indigo smiled, blew him a kiss. "You know," she said. "Maybe this question of who-am-I-where-do-I-fit-what-am-I-doing is in fact the essence of Canadian culture. Or at least, the part that applies to us. Sorry, I'm in between cultures right now. Or no — I'm only doing sub-cultures. Corporate culture ends at five. Club culture starts at ten. We're chameleons. What do you think?"

"We don't do the night thing much."

"I know and we should. We're missing out. I hate to admit it, but I've always thought it seemed sort of glamorous. People who never see daylight. Even the drug thing. Or pardon me, drug *culture*."

Despite the opening, Sam didn't mention the cocaine. "You always —"

"Tim went to this drummers' circle the other night. A bunch of drummers all just zoning out and jamming together. Like, maybe a dozen." As she spoke, she was looking at the tractor trailers parked to the side of a truck stop, and absently thinking of donuts. "It didn't even start until the bars closed, went past five. That's when he left, but he said they were still going strong. It was a Monday night. Can you believe that? We never do anything on a Monday night. We act like we're old or something."

"Indigo, we work."

"Yeah, well. That's no excuse."

Richard Keating liked people to know that he lived on the same sparkling street as three members of the current government, two from opposition, too many doctors to count, and a tenor. (A *professional* tenor.) He lived with what Indigo called his new-and-improved wife and children, in a white house with Corinthian columns and a walkway lined with topiary.

Indigo stepped up to the double front doors and stopped, shifting the pot of orchids to the crook of her left arm. With her free right hand, she rummaged in her purse for lipstick, twisted off the cap and applied a redundant fresh coat. "I never liked topiary," she said. "It always seems embarrassing, like dogs in fussy outfits. How's my lipstick?"

"Stop fretting," said Sam, rapping the knocker three times hard in quick succession. He never used the bell, said he preferred to announce their arrival with thumps of the metal lion's head on wood, said it appealed to his sensibilities.

Her father was wearing polished shoes, grey slacks and a shirt in the blue of his eyes. His still-thick silver hair had been cut extremely short with bangs, in the manner of movie stars, certain celebrity lawyers — and evidently psychiatrists. (Indigo wondered if it made him feel superior, if he wanted to outdo his patients both in mental health and fashion.) "You made it," he said. Then louder, behind him — "Charlotte, it's them. Come out here. They brought you flowers."

Charlotte was Richard's ex-receptionist, his second wife and the mother of his boys. The Keating twins. Andrew and Ian. "Sons, thank God," to complete his perfect new existence.

Or perhaps, as Indigo thought, avenge his old one.

When she was younger, Indigo wondered what kind of bizarre aligning of the planets could have incited her parents to date, let alone have sex. *Her* parents: Alice and Mr. Keating. They seemed designed to find each other irritating. She wondered what had happened to her father — it must have been after they were married — to make him starched and humourless. (In a show of male solidarity, Sam and Tim both favoured alien abduction. "Yep," said Sam, once, when the three of them had smoked a joint. "Classic case." To which Tim nodded and replied — "You are so right on it's scary.")

For a long time she felt betrayed, childishly indignant, on behalf of both herself and Alice. But over the years, as so often is the case, she revised her opinion. She still would have given her parents an award for most unlikely couple, but she came to believe that her father felt betrayed as well. He had rigid ideas of what it meant to be a grownup. Alice not only refused to adhere, she found them hugely entertaining.

When he and Alice separated, Richard moved into a condominium — to plot his new life, thought Indigo, impressed by the sheer range of possibilities.

With a practice devoted to the rich and confused, he had no shortage of options. She imagined women — wealthy, beautiful, some quite deranged. Exotic travel. Maybe he'd take a sabbatical, move to an island, live like Leonard Cohen. Buy his own small plane, or a loft in Greenwich Village.

Indigo was disappointed when his tastes, while expensive, turned out (in her not-as-humble-as-she-liked-to-think opinion) to be obvious and dull.

First he acquired Charlotte — who was pleasant and easy to manoeuvre, attractive in the way a pattern of tiny pale flowers is attractive — and the house. He bought a cottage in the Muskokas, began a collection of *early* Victorian furniture. Indigo was fascinated; she'd never met anyone with such a loving devotion to things. He took an almost paternal pride in hand-carved walking sticks, first editions bound in leather, antique cigarette cases, art deco glass.

Aperitifs were served in the living room, where Charlotte brought trays of tiny, elaborate hors d'oeuvres.

"These pastry things are delicious," said Sam.

Indigo nodded and swallowed. "Unbelievable. You must have been at it all day, Charlotte. What a treat."

"It was no trouble," said Richard. "She likes to cook." He walked over to the buffed cherry armoire, opened one of the drawers and took out a business card. "Before I forget," he said, "I need you to do me a favour." He handed the card to Indigo. "Call this man. He needs some public relations. I said you'd fix him up."

The card read: Harvey D. Morten, The Rest is Here.

"Who is he?" asked Indigo.

"Business acquaintance, once removed. He owns an old age home in Toronto — a venture that is about to become the subject of some fairly serious allegations. To do with the level of care, mostly, although I think there may also be some financial irregularities."

"Sounds like bad news," said Indigo. "It's not really the kind of —"

"Don't be so naive," said Richard. "There are two sides to every story. Have you learned nothing?" With an exasperated sigh, he sat on his newly acquired red velvet parlour chair, circa 1880, and crossed his legs. "From what I understand, there's no real truth to any of it. However, while Mr. Morten is at the centre of the storm, as it were, he's only one of several partners, and therein lies the problem. Another partner, who I hasten to add has no real involvement in the home, is an acquaintance of mine. Someone in the public eye, who does not wish to be connected with any of this."

Indigo tried again. "What exactly do you want from me?" she asked, knowing full well, but resisting the urge to say that even if she were planning to stay at Pinnacle, which she wasn't, she'd hang glide from her office tower naked — during rush hour — before taking on one of his shady political cronies.

A comment like that might be seen as provocative.

"Use your brain, Indigo. It isn't what I want from you, it's what you can gain from them. This promises to be a high-profile case. Mr. Morten is willing to pay a good buck for some effective counsel —"

"Thanks to those financial irregularities," said Sam.

Charlotte put her hand in front of her smile, but Richard ignored him. "From what he tells me, there was one isolated case of negligence, and they fired the woman responsible. But some opportunistic lawyer jumped on it, and now a bunch of malcontents with nothing better to do than launch nuisance law suits think they're about to get rich. It's shameful. Anyway, Morten will give you details."

"If I call him," said Indigo. "Things at work are —"

"You are going to call him."

"Why, what's the big deal?" she asked. "All this to get on the good side of some politician?"

Charlotte, who'd begun passing around a plate of canapés, said — "Golf."

"No it's not about golf," snapped Richard. "That club is a goldmine. Can't even walk down the hall without bumping into someone's mid-life crisis. More bloody Porches in the parking lot ..." He stopped, tightening his gaze on Indigo. "If you must know, I need a sponsor to get full-member status in a certain club. Which I happen to want. It's very exclusive."

"Very," said Charlotte. "It's a men's club. No women allowed."

"I thought only gay bars did that," said Sam.

"Don't start with me Charlotte," said Richard, without looking at her. And then — "If I can help Morten, my associate might be willing to help me. It could be very lucrative."

Nothing made Indigo understand the futility of world peace more than a conversation with her father. She tried to block the phrase *sprung from his loins* from her thoughts, but it hovered perversely.

Her distaste must have shown because his mouth slid into a smile.

"Don't tell me you object. Are you really so provincial? Listen sweetheart, you may as well learn. It's how the world works. And by the way, I've chosen to ignore the fact that your husband seems to understand what is and isn't *de rigueur* at gay bars."

"Listen dad, it's not that I —"

The front door slammed shut.

"Hey big sister," said one of the twins, Ian, leaving his backpack on the floor and striding into the room. "Hey Sam."

Indigo gave him a hug. "I can't believe how tall you are. You used to be such a little geek."

"Not any more. Made the basketball team. Me and Andy."

"Andy and I," said Richard.

"That too. So it's goodbye to geekdom forever. Just think of us as gods."

Everyone laughed. "God's gift to egomaniacs maybe," said Indigo.

"That's okay," said Sam. "Wait till he gets to college. He'll fall for some beautiful goddess — or several — then he's in trouble. Beautiful women have a knack for deflating egos. They don't even have to try."

"Sounds like a man who speaks from experience," said Richard. "Something you'd like to share with the group?"

"Not if you plucked the hairs from the top of my toes," said Sam, and everyone laughed again.

Indigo helped herself to another piece of brie. "So where's your evil twin?" she asked. "I haven't seen you guys since Christmas."

"Should be home any sec. He's in love, it slows him down."

"What did I tell you?" said Sam. And then — "When you're 16 you think men have all the power. But you're wrong."

The remark surprised Indigo and she looked over at him, but his attention was fixed on the food. She'd always assumed he had the power, although it was hard to know when or how that happened.

In the relatively small chunk of time before dinner — which, despite the season, was not a barbecue, since Richard hated eating out of doors — Indigo and Sam managed to sidestep several arguments.

Charlotte didn't argue.

Richard didn't seem to care.

At one point, he aimed a wedge of cheese at Sam and said — "Got a job yet?"

"Always did," said Sam.

"I mean a real job, like the one with the paper. None of that namby pamby nonsense. You been looking?"

"I'm a freelance writer. Nothing namby about it."

"Another word for unemployed, that's all that is."

"No sir, it isn't. I make money, pay the mortgage."

"You get by is what you're saying. You really think that's enough? How much you pull in last year?"

They were drinking vodka and tonics with lime.

A little while later, he said to Indigo — "Your brothers are going to campaign in the next election. You could learn a thing or two from —"

At which point Charlotte said — "They haven't decided."

And Richard said — "Oh, it's been decided. They're going to

do what I tell them." He turned to Sam — "You know, Andrew's going to be a lawyer."

"Maybe," said Andrew.

"He's only 16," said Indigo. "Give the kid some time."

At which point, her father stood up to freshen his drink and said — "You're not exactly the best person to be giving advice, are you sweetheart? So why don't you just stay out of it. There's a good girl."

The more Richard drank, the more evangelical he became, taking it upon himself to elucidate the righteous path, which on this particular evening encompassed everything from the government's economic policy (an obvious no-win conversation, during which Indigo and Sam kept their mouths pressed shut), to the unkemptness of Toronto versus Ottawa (he thinks the poor shouldn't have to see so much of the rich, that it's demoralizing, although Indigo thinks that what he means is quite the opposite), to the way those goddamned greenies are to blame for the recession (by the time he tossed off this little gem, Indigo and Sam had figured out that if they didn't disagree, he'd move on to something else).

The twins had left them to it after dinner, pleading homework.

In the morning, as they all sat down to breakfast, Indigo was thinking that she might not tell him after all.

In fact, she was feeling quite pleased with herself when Richard said — "So how's that job of yours? Have they made you VP?"

"Account supervisor," she said. And then, against her better judgement — "But I have bigger news than that."

Her father put both hands flat on the table. "A promotion. Why, that's just great Indigo. Why didn't you say something sooner? We'd have chilled champagne." He looked at Sam — "I knew she'd make something of herself one of these days," then back at Indigo — "Congratulations, sweetheart. Now don't tell me you're pregnant."

"No dad, I'm not pregnant."

Charlotte smiled. "More coffee?"

"Come on Indi — spill it," said Andrew, drumming his fork on the table.

"Stop with the fork," said Richard. "I won't tell you again."

"Yeah," said Ian. "What's the news?"

Indigo looked at her father. "I've applied to go to film school," she said. "Full-time. I'm quitting my job."

Silence.

All eyes turned to Richard, who didn't say anything for what seemed like a very long time. They waited, watching, while he made a ritual of touching his napkin to his mouth, folding it neatly and placing it beside his plate.

Andrew was the first to speak. "A filmmaker," he said. "That's intense."

"I'm not in yet," said Indigo, "but I'm keeping my fingers crossed. I can hardly wait to know for sure. I'm going to take some other stuff as well. Sculpting, I think. Maybe —"

"How could you be so stupid?" Something in her father's tone made her think of cracked cement.

Indigo hesitated. She'd been hoping to deflect a fight, or at least to keep it civil. But his eyes were like hands pushing her backwards. Stay calm, she thought. Focus on the defence. "I don't think it's stupid," she offered, finally, aiming for quiet but firm, not quite managing either.

"Well you're wrong," said Richard. "This is by far the dumbest thing you've ever suggested. And we all know it has some stiff competition."

"I'm not *suggesting* anything," said Indigo. "The decision's made. All I'm waiting for is an okay from the college, then I'll tell my boss. You make it sound like I want to kill my first born or something."

"That's not the worst idea I've heard," said Richard. "Save yourself some heartache."

Indigo blanched. "I can't believe you said that."

"Neither can I," said Charlotte. "It's none of my business, but —"

"You're damn right it's none of your business," said Richard, still glaring at Indigo. "When are you going to grow up and take some responsibility for your life? Art college. What a load of crap that is. You want to express yourself, develop your creativity? Do it on your own time. You have no right to give up a good job, an earning job, an adult job —"

"I have every right," she said. "And I'd expect a little support from you. Aren't you supposed to understand this sort of thing? Isn't that what you do for a living? A little insight maybe, some empathy. Don't you encourage people to follow their dreams, do what'll make them happy?"

"I'm not being paid for empathy here. I'm your father. Happy is beside the point of this discussion. Too damn selfish, that's your problem. Immature. Doesn't even occur to you how irresponsible it is to quit a career. Become some kind of flake, like —"

Richard stopped. He was leaning forward in his chair and Indigo could see the glaze of sweat that had formed across his brow. Bad sign.

"Go ahead and say it," said Indigo. "I know what you're thinking."

"Oh really. What am I thinking?"

"You were going to say 'like Alice' — a flake like mom. Weren't you?"

"Works for me."

"Go to hell," she said.

Richard's attention snapped to Sam. "What do you think of all this?"

"She doesn't like what she's doing." Sam spoke slowly, achieving the calm that Indigo had hoped for. "It's her life. She's entitled to do something else, if that's what she wants. I'm behind her."

"Then you're a bigger bloody twit than I thought."

"Dad —" It was the twins, Andrew and Ian, in chorus.

"Never mind guys," said Indigo, standing up. "It's what I expected. Charlotte — I'm sorry to cut things short, but I think we should go. It's a long drive. Thanks for breakfast. Everything was picture perfect. As always."

She and Sam left Richard at the table with his wife and boys.

In the days that followed, silence. Richard didn't call to apologize, and neither did Indigo. But that was no surprise. Their fights had a history of resolving themselves slowly, subsiding first into a reluctant cease-fire, then a reprieve and finally, cautiously, peace.

According to Indigo, her father is overbearing, controlling and inflexible, unwilling to accept another point of view. In Richard's expert opinion — which Indigo says he brandishes unfairly — she has the unfortunate combination of poor judgement and a fierce, intractable will.

They began to disagree regularly around the time so many children and their parents do, when she was a teenager and he was anything but. Their opinions started to clash although, for the most part, the opinions themselves seemed secondary, with conflict being the point.

Over the years, she's run storming out of his house, and he's refused to speak to her for weeks. They've yelled in the yard and in front of friends. He's stopped the car and ordered her out. And she's demanded that he stop the car, and slammed the door behind her. They'd even fought when they agreed, because he was condescending (her words) or because she didn't fully understand the substance of a point (his).

With all of this in mind, Indigo prepared to wait.

Eight

"You ready?"

"Huh? Ready for what?" Sam was on his back on the sofa, balancing a bowl of tortilla chips, a second, smaller bowl of salsa and a third of sour cream, in a line down his stomach and lap, converter in hand, can of Coke against his side. He was listening rapt to the final harried pitch of an infomercial for the Improved In Your Dreams Invisible Abs Rolling Flexhibitionist Machine, which doubles as a clothes rack. If he ordered now, they'd throw in the special patented Butt Bouncing Barometer for only $19.99 — endorsed by a now-distant member of the British Royal Family.

She had to admire his dexterity.

"Dim sum. I told you. With Nicole and Spider."

"Who the hell is Spider? Not that musician. I hate Nicole's boyfriends. I hate musicians."

"You love dim sum."

"I hate dim sum. You go. There's a documentary I need to watch. On the guy who invented quick-dry cement. You have no idea how important that was."

"It's a beautiful day. We're doing music after. Soca band. It's free."

"I have work to do." He fought a smile. "I hate music."

"Get ready, we're leaving. You might want to put shorts on, it's hot."

When they got to the Pink Pearl, Nicole and Spider were already at a table by the window, drinking Tsing Dao. Spider was sitting forward in his chair; Nicole leaning back in hers. On the linen tablecloth, a teapot and four white ceramic cups, upside down.

"Sorry we're late," said Indigo. "We had to stop for cash."

"You're in time for our first tiff," said Nicole. "Isn't that right, babe."

Spider stood up to shake Sam's hand. "Hi. I'm Spider."

"Sam," said Sam.

"He asked me to meet his parents." Nicole began righting the cups. "I'm thinking it's way too soon." She paused, teapot in hand, to give Indigo a meaningful look, which entailed tipping her head forward and slightly to the side, and raising her eyebrows. "They live on a farm."

Spider said — "It's not a *farm* farm and believe me, this isn't fighting. There aren't any cows or chickens. Just dogs and cats. And a cockateel. It's not even far."

"Barbara," said Nicole. "He says the bird's name is Barbara. Isn't that just the cutest thing you ever heard? Can you see me on a farm? With Barbara? She'll probably hate me, shit on my head or something."

"I was raised on a farm," said Sam. "And that's what I'd do. If I was a bird named Barbara. Right on your fake blond head." He laughed.

Nicole ignored him.

"Sounds like fun," said Indigo, hoping they wouldn't start in front of Spider. The last time Nicole had called, she'd berated Sam (at three-martini length), pronouncing him the product of what she called his chilly, narrow childhood, and suggesting that he fuck his wife more often. It wasn't well received.

A woman appeared pushing a food trolley. She was young and pretty without any make-up, perfect black hair smoothed into a perfect black ponytail. She lifted the lid off a bamboo steamer. "Dumplings," she said, in her soft accented voice. "Shrimp or Pork."

"Both," said Nicole. "One of each."

"See that Nicky? Sounds like fun. Listen to your friend."

She shrugged. "I know, and I want to meet them. Eventually. Really, I do."

"Why not now?" Indigo speared a dumpling with her chopstick, as another young woman appeared with curried squid. "Yes please," she said, nodding. "No, just one. I think. That okay with you guys?" And then, having received the appropriate signs of approval — "What's the problem? Why don't you want to go?"

"No problem," said Nicole. "It's only been six weeks. I mean, parents. Jesus."

"So don't go," said Sam, gesturing for another two Tsing Dao. "Who cares?" What he called the minutiae of her life made him cranky.

"Don't listen to him," said Indigo. "He met Alice on what, our second date?"

"Alice is Indigo's mom," said Nicole. "She's different."

Spider said — "You know what? It doesn't matter. Do whatever you think. Really. It's not a problem. We'll go some other time."

He looked like he was telling the truth, thought Indigo. It wouldn't be a problem. She and Nicole both watched his smooth, affable mouth as it opened to accept a piece of dumpling. Sam stared out the window at the lake.

"What? It's no big deal," said Spider. "Eat."

Nicole picked up her chopsticks. "All right," she said. "You win. If it's that important. When?"

For Indigo, this kind of relationship negotiation had always been a source of intrigue. It was almost scientific. Content divided by tone, multiplied by length of time together, equals outcome. Nicole was done the moment he'd said "really."

"Next weekend, if it works for you. I thought we'd start slow, one night." He took a pull from his beer before adding — "We get to sleep in my old room."

Nicole sighed. "Wouldn't you rather go to New York?"

Nice try, thought Indigo.

"We could do that too. There's a long weekend coming up. Why not then?"

Hopeless, of course, but extra points for effort.

Nicole put her hand in his lap in surrender. "That actually works," she said. "I'm going to be there anyway, on business. You can meet me. I'll come to yours if you come to mine."

"To what, your parents?" asked Spider.

"What are you nuts? My choice of destination. New York. Believe me, you don't want to meet my parents. Not until you absolutely have to."

Indigo smiled. "It's settled."

"Thank God," said Sam, nodding to the woman bearing spring rolls. "Yeah, two of those. The suspense was killing me."

Nicole looked at him for a moment, then turned to Spider. "My meeting's on a Wednesday. If you came Wednesday night we'd have a couple extra days. It'd be like playing hooky."

"Just like old times, eh Nicole?" Even without the grudge, which Sam seemed bent on keeping, he tended to pass through phases, alternately thinking Nicole was talented, funny and sophisticated or hipper-than-thou, self-centred and a bitch. Today seemed to be the latter.

"Like you're perfect," said Nicole. "Farm boy."

"Tart. Why don't you tell him what you did at your —"

"Come on guys, play nice," said Indigo. It made her nervous when they didn't get along, especially in public. They knew too much about each other, without the responsibility of an actual close friendship — although, if pressed, she knew they'd admit to a certain, reluctant fondness. Nonetheless, they were both perfectly willing to explain the other's flaws, in detail. Even better if they had an audience. And if there was actual risk, because the person in question was more than a chance bystander, someone Sam or Nicole actually cared about impressing — well, in a prickly enough mood, that was gold.

"I wasn't that bad." Nicole shrugged. "All right, maybe I was a little wild."

"Not me," said Spider. "I was a total nerd. One of those kids who liked school. Did my homework. Got good grades. And you might as well hear it from me, I never smoked a cigarette. Took a puff, coughed my guts out, never tried again."

Sam said — "You better be careful what you say, Nicole. You'll scare him off."

"Don't think I don't know it."

"Come on," said Spider. "How bad could you have been?"

"Look. Out there," said Nicole. "Is that a boat race?"

Even Sam laughed, and Spider said — "Mission failed. Manoeuvre unsuccessful." He kissed her hand. "You can tell me. How were you so awful?"

"Whenever a person says 'you can tell me' it's pretty much guaranteed you should keep your mouth shut. Let's just say I had issues," said Nicole, "and leave it there." She looked at Sam. "Truce?"

Spider let it go and Indigo knew that, at some point, if they stayed together, Nicole would find a way to make it all a funny story.

She'd describe herself as a little Lolita, with hot pink nail polish on stubby, bitten nails. And too many boys. Or maybe she'd forget the boys and focus on the shrinks. The way she obsessively doted on her father because he was a man and didn't seem to need anyone, because he flirted with her friends and their mothers and waitresses and nannies and women in line at the bank, because more than a few made offers — like Nicole couldn't hear or wouldn't notice — and because no one seemed to think this was a problem. Most of all, it was because she wanted his attention for herself.

She'd skip the way she was mean to her mother, refusing to listen, calling her names. Or maybe she'd simply revise the parts she didn't like, invent a few new details.

She was good at make believe.

They'd all had years of expensive therapy. Her parents appeared to have settled into something that passed for love, if you didn't look too closely. She didn't hate her mother, idolize her father, or sleep with every loser she could find. They were each officially cured, she said, as close to normal as they'd ever be.

They could hear the music long before they saw the band. It was lively and persuasive and they all increased their pace. The stage was by the lake, outside and free of charge to anyone who braved the crowds.

And there were crowds.

People of all ages. All jumping up to Trinidad's own Silver Soca Daddy.

"Is anyone here from GUYANA?"

The mass let loose a small vocal surge.

"Is anyone here from VENEZUELA?"

The surge grew louder, and Indigo's chest began to tighten like a spring.

"Anyone from JAMAICA?"

Louder and tighter.

"From BARBADOS?"

Louder still and almost taut.

"Is anyone here from .... TRINIDAD?"

The crowd burst into a frenzy, including Indigo and Nicole, who were fuelled by three Tsing Dao and the sun that felt like a hot, voluptuous stare on their bodies, or at least that's how it felt to Indigo, but even she had to admit she hadn't been laid much, lately, and might be letting her libido get the most of her imagination, just this once. She and Nicole were part of the crowd: jumping up and down, waving their hands in the air.

Spider did his own, low-key version of dancing on the spot, but without the hand action. Sam weaved, slightly but unmistakably, hands in the pockets of his shorts, feet planted firmly on cement.

The music had its own smell — of coconut lotion, sweat and marijuana. There were only a few white faces, including a man dancing beside them, sipping from a silver flask. Every now and then, he'd shoot his hand in the air and yell — various intelligent-sounding lines that meant absolutely nothing out of context. His accent sounded Scottish; and, based on his permanent grin and the way his head seemed to weave on his shoulders, he'd been letting loose for quite some time. Possibly days.

His moves were beginning to slur and she could tell that he was flagging.

And still he danced. Gyrating. Twisting. Humping.

Never stopping.

It's all in the hips.

Everyone in motion.

The ones Indigo liked best were the couples, dancing — well, let's just say very close together. There was no delicate way to describe it; the men had their women turned around and bent over in what looked like simulated sex, albeit up-tempo sex with clothes between their parts. What made Indigo laugh was the look of concentration on their faces.

"Is it me or is getting hotter?" she asked, fanning herself with her hand.

Spider leaned close to her ear. "It's called wining. This, what you're doing. The swivel thing. They call it wining. You're not bad."

Nicole had moved back so her ass was pressed against him and their bodies bumped in tune. He held her by the hips. "He loves Trinidad," she said, looking up from her now coitally bowed position. "I think I know why."

Indigo looked at Sam, who shook his head and said — "Fuggedaboudit."

But he was grinning.

When the band took a break, Spider said — "What do you say kids, time for a beverage?" And then — "Met a guy in Trinidad who made the best lime daiquiris you ever tasted. He was an artist."

"That's a pretty big compliment," said Indigo.

"No, I mean he was an artist. A painter. Quite well known. Underwater landscapes mostly. He just happened to make amazing lime daiquiris."

They decided to pass on the bar near the stage, which overflowed with the sweaty, thirsty aftermath of soca — but also had a lineup. There was one further down, on the water. "You know what I like," said Sam. "No one's too old or too young. Everyone dances. Little kids, grannies. They're all right there. It's cool."

Indigo was glad that he finally liked something; he couldn't have said more than a mouthful of words since they'd left the Pink Pearl. But then again, Sam was often quiet — and if there was one thing Indigo had learned, it was that his demeanour was never a positive sign of enjoyment. Or lack thereof.

They lucked into a table at the edge of the patio, where their view of the lake was interrupted only by the flow of heavy couples in knee-length shorts, with heavy gold and heavy American drawl.

Spider said — "You don't have kids, am I right? How long you two been married?"

"Nope," said Sam. "No small humans. Not yet."

"Four years," said Indigo.

Nicole said — "I've been trying to talk her into it," when a waitress appeared with bread and introduced herself as Winsome. "Is that really your name," asked Nicole, who — assured that the girl was indeed telling the truth — waited until she'd taken their order and gone before ripping a whole-wheat bun into chunks and dropping it on the ground beyond the railing.

"Talk her into what?" asked Spider.

"Having a kid," said Nicole. "I think we're ready. If it's a girl let's call her Winsome."

Sam said — "What's it to you? I thought this might have been the one part of our lives you're not involved in."

"I guess you thought wrong." Nicole smiled sweetly. "I figure Indigo's married, she should be the one to bear the kids. I can hardly bear the thought. I want a title though, like godmother only different. Better. Fairy godmother. That'd be good. I'll bring presents, take them to their first restricted movies —"

"What's in it for her?" asked Sam. "Besides motherhood, which she can have without you."

"Presents. Like I said. And I'll pay for a baby-sitter, take her out on the town. Hell, I'd even take her on holiday. Which is more than I can say for you."

It was a conversation they'd had many times, and Indigo said — "We're negotiating."

"Yeah," said Nicole. "She wants a cleaning lady."

"Not once a month either, once a week."

"That's way out there." Spider looked back and forth between them, nodding. "You guys are tight. That's cool."

Sam said — "Two sides of a coin."

"He's right. It's like we're totally different," said Nicole. "Maybe that's why we get along so well. We complement each other. She thinks about everything and I don't think about anything at all."

"That's not true," said Indigo.

"Sure it is. You pay attention. Try to figure things out and deal with them — even if you don't have to. Aren't I right Sam? She wants to fix everything. Make life all happy and good. And aesthetically pleasing, can't forget that. It all has to match."

"Which is never going to happen," said Sam.

"Right, but you've got to give her credit for trying. Whereas I, on the other hand, have raised avoidance to an art form. One of my many talents." Nicole, who'd been aiming for the pigeons, had attracted several gulls. "Look at that fat bastard," she said. "I have to throw two at a time to give anyone else a chance." The gulls stood in a loose semicircle, watching Nicole with greedy eyes, inching closer. "Oh no you don't, you little rodents. Keep your distance."

She stood up and pretended to lunge at them, but they could see the railing. "Okay then, to heck with you." She wiped her hands on her napkin. "It's like Indigo's this weird little bird. Not a seagull. Something smaller, not so aggressive and *irritating*." She pretended to throw a piece of bread, but didn't fool them. "Yeah, but no I mean it. She's kind of gawky, not in looks. In her head. Flying off in different directions —"

"Here we go," said Indigo. "She does this all the time."

"So let me finish, I'll be quick. There's a point. She's neurotic, but not in a big way. Makes me laugh like hell. But there's something about her, I don't know what it is exactly, something innocent. Or maybe that's not the word. Naive. Idealistic. I don't know. Gentle. It's like I feel the need to protect her, make sure she's okay. Anyway, here comes the point, wait for it ... the point is, that's as maternal as I get, which is why I'm not having kids." She reached for her daiquiri. "All right, I'm done."

"I don't buy that," said Spider.

"What's not to buy?"

"I think you'd make a great mother, from what I've seen. I can't believe you wouldn't want to have kids. If the situation's right."

It occurred to Indigo that this was a test, the kind of thing Nicole did in reverse, except that he was nowhere near as subtle.

"Well, if you put it that way. I guess I can't rule it out."

Indigo, who was taking a sip of her drink, almost choked on the crushed ice. Kids had always been a non-negotiable item. Nicole had been adamant: she wasn't about to let some guy stick her with a couple of whining brats. Indigo looked at Spider, hair pulled into a thick ponytail, strong chin, lithe body. They would breed incredible offspring.

"So what'll you do?" asked Spider.

"What do you mean? When?"

"If you don't have kids. What'll you do with all that extra life?"

Nicole jumped in without a pause. "That's easy," she said, and Indigo laughed. "More of everything else. I have a great job. I've always wanted to live somewhere else, maybe a few places. Before I'm dead. See the world as a native."

"I've been thinking about that," said Spider. "Someplace smaller. Without so much concrete." He rested his arm on the back of her chair. "I've been looking around. You know, to buy something. A piece of land. Someplace tropical. Quiet. Sort of a home away from home. Pick my own fruit in the morning. Jungle on the doorstep. Costa Rica, maybe Ecuador." He laughed. "I hear the waves are bitchin' man, totally tubular. When I grow up I want to be a surfer."

"Jungle sounds good," said Nicole. "But I was thinking maybe New York. Or London. That'd be fab —"

"When do you think you'll know about the job?" asked Sam, and Indigo pinched his leg. "Ow, why'd you do that?"

Spider said — "What job?"

"That's what I'm doing in New York. I have an interview."

"That's what I thought, with who?"

"It's not a who, it's a what. WEBE-TV. I've been putting feelers out for ages, hoping to land a gig. It's sort of what I'm doing now, only better. I'd get to live in Manhattan."

"I see," said Spider.

"Uh oh," said Indigo. "That doesn't sound good."

Nicole leaned toward him. "Every woman knows that *I see* is the code for I'm upset. And it's our code. You're not supposed to use it. So tell me. What's the problem?"

"No problem," said Spider. "Let it go."

"You could come with me."

"Whatever. We can talk. Later. Let it go."

"Listen baby, it's not a for sure thing, okay? It's only my first interview, for God's sake. Even if I do get the job, which I probably won't, it'll be after at least three interviews. And even then, it's just an offer. There's no reason to think about this. We're not there yet."

Nine

Indigo was trying to decide whether to think of her new life as an alternate reality or the more exotic parallel universe.

The sliding glass doors were open, and she could smell the end of summer in the cooler evening air. She was sitting at the kitchen table, dreaming her way through the prep work for spaghetti — crushing a clove of garlic, chopping a pepper, pausing to watch one of the neighbourhood cats watching a songbird in the feeder, slicing mushrooms.

She liked the sound of alternate reality. It was decisive. An alternative. A choice as opposed to some random quirk of fate.

The boom of a thundering voice suspended her thoughts. "You're a bitch. I've said it before and I'll say it again for the whole goddamn world to hear. I MARRIED A BITCH." It was the politician next door, the one married less than a year to the woman on the news.

Indigo heard the slam of a sliding door, and then — "You think you're so smart, you bastard. IMPOTENT BASTARD. COULDN'T GET IT —"

The door opened and the man shouted — "I AM NOT IMPOTENT."

There was a pause before they both started laughing, then silence, and Indigo imagined them looking at each other with sly, suggestive smiles. "Well," the woman might have said. "Make us another drink, won't you darling?"

They were a source of fascination, fighting loud and often, throwing parties in the yard, entertaining celebrity friends. But their house was up for sale. The husband told Sam they'd built their dream home. The lot was huge, he said, nestled (and he did use the word nestled) on its own sprawling acre where the edge of the suburbs touched grassy fields and streams. For the moment.

What would they do without an audience?

Indigo watched as a jay scooped in and the songbird flitted away, wondering what had become of the cat. Perspective is everything, she thought, forgetting the momentum of her knife, which slid through an onion and into her hand.

Her eyes instantly fogged and the violence stopped her breath. But she didn't move for at least another minute, just sat there — watching blood drip from what appeared to be a nasty gash, down the lines of her palm and onto the cutting board — before lurching to the sink and holding it under the tap.

Leaning forward on the counter, Indigo wondered how she might convey the sting of onion juice in an open wound — in paint or metal or stone, or even on film. The kind of pain that makes a person lightheaded, that was making her nauseous even now, as she pressed a towel into the cut.

In fact, from the moment she ripped into the envelope, then leapt through the house waving her letter of acceptance from the school, she'd become preoccupied with precisely this kind of thought.

It had already made her days more exciting.

She'd been thinking about how to communicate the smell of oranges when she stepped onto the road without looking, and the man in the yellow Camaro — quite a handsome man as she recalled — had to slam on his brakes to avoid her. He gave her the universal what-the-hell-are-you-doing signal, raising his eyebrows, gesturing with both palms up.

But then he smiled. So she thought she was forgiven.

Changing realities gave her a sense of starting over — not, as her father said, of plummeting backward, into a second adolescence. It felt more like renewal.

She was eager to get her hands dirty, excited about the people she'd meet, the intelligent conversations she was certain she'd have over coffee with men in black jeans and T-shirts, and women with strong opinions and hair on their legs.

She wanted a sense of chaos in the order.

With an uncharacteristic lack of anxiety, Indigo had given three months notice at work, while managing to parlay her full-time job into a nice little freelance arrangement.

Nicole's parents were abroad and she spent a weekend at their cottage, swimming and picking raspberries. Winning at Scrabble. Losing at chess and Monopoly. Reading and thinking and waiting.

One afternoon, when she and Sam had the place to themselves, they had sex on the dock in daylight. (Her idea.) It wasn't very good, but she decided that the scrapes on her spine were a testament to the wonders of change. Sam still wasn't around too much, even when he was, but he seemed to like her better now that she had things on her mind.

Back at home, she practised being an art student — spent a great deal of time choosing clothes that looked old and thrown together, carried a sketchbook in her purse. Twice she made an appointment to have her navel pierced. Twice she made excuses to cancel.

Nicole surfaced part way through July, when Spider went on tour.

If a measure of success is column inches, Cringe was doing well. The new CD stood firm on top of the charts. They made the covers of *Spin* and *Rolling Stone*. And their days were turning tabloid.

The lead singer, Rock Hard, was being divorced by his wannabe actress wife, whose career had so far been limited to one music video, but who had nonetheless managed to attract a not-unimpressive amount of attention. (And a hefty bag of clippings.) Seems she was upset about a carload of women who just wouldn't go away — or, more specifically, their effect on Rock's already solid ego.

"They follow him everywhere," she said to *Probe Magazine*. "He thinks he's some kind of God or somethin'. What a bunch of f---in' hooey that is. This is a man who collects the hairs in the sink and saves 'em. Who pads his f---in' jockstrap. And these tramps have nothing better to do than follow him around. It's pathetic."

"Yeah, what's with that?" asked Indigo. "Don't they work?" She and Nicole were sitting on a patio, drinking beer and eating fries on a Sunday afternoon.

"Spider says they're taking the summer off. They're university students. He says they wanted to do something really out there, the more juvenile the better, sort of one last scream before adulthood. So they made Rock their idol, in the classic sense. They're calling it their summer of worship."

"Why don't they go to Europe like everyone else?" asked Indigo.

"I know, it seems kind of dumb to me too."

"So they're hanging out with the band then."

"Stop worrying. He's faithful." Nicole smiled at a man walking by — who took his sunglasses off, then put them back on, then pushed them on top of his head. "And if he's not he said he'd tell me. So I can make my own decision, based on all the information. Either way, it's not the most important thing."

"You're a better man than I," said Indigo.

"I can't be bothered with the bullshit, that's all. People do everything they can to make sure their partners don't fool around. And sure — that's part of it, I guess. But you can't stop them if that's what they want to do." She poured the last of her beer in her glass. "Don't look so grim. Fidelity's overrated. The important thing is respect. Tell me the truth and I'll do the same for you."

Indigo considered this morsel of insight. "When's he back?" she asked, making a mental decision to stop being such a prude.

"Three months."

"Wow. That's a long time for you."

"Tell me. I hate having no one to play with." She picked up a fry, wiped it in salt and dipped it in ketchup, then popped it in her mouth. "I've always found sex with myself kind of shallow."

Indigo laughed. "I know what you mean. How long's he been gone?"

"Two and a half weeks."

"No one else on tap?"

"Not if he keeps it in his pants. If he doesn't, all bets are off." Nicole signalled the waiter for another round of drinks. "I have a theory," she said. "Relationships are limiting at the best of times, right? Don't answer that, of course they are. So for me to survive in one, things have to be either equal or in my favour. So I'm spoiled, tough beans. It's part of my charm."

They paused to watch a dog lift his leg and pee on a bicycle chained to a tree.

"Come to think of it, there is one guy," said Nicole, "a new grip at the station. Fresh out of school, eager — with the nicest, roundest, firmest-looking butt I ever did see." She gestured as though she was grabbing two great handfuls.

"Isn't it weird?" asked Indigo, picturing a pair of butt cheeks where Nicole's hands were, floating over the table. "Sex with a much younger man, I mean. Don't you feel self-conscious?"

"Are you kidding? It's the best. Ask my mother."

Indigo couldn't help grinning. "Your mother? No way."

"I know. I couldn't believe it either. Way to go, mom. It was strictly revenge sex — daddy started it." Nicole squeezed some lime in her beer, letting the thought sink in for effect.

"Well," said Indigo. "Tell me. What happened?"

Nicole leaned forward. "It's all so daytime drama," she said. "Daddy had an affair with a woman at his health club and mother found out. So she had a fling with some kid she hired to paint the kitchen. One of the neighbour's boys, home from college no less. A pup."

"That is so cool," said Indigo. "Right back at you, dear. How did your dad find out?"

"Walked in on them. I think she planned it that way. Poor kid freaked — he was ready to jump out the window. Daddy had to convince him that the door was a smarter choice, that he'd probably break his spleen. And he wasn't going to try to kill him or anything. It was all very civilized. Daddy was upset though, didn't think she could do it. Figured he was the only one with options."

"Looks good on him then," said Indigo. "So where do things stand now?"

"I'll save you the sentimental details. It was over pretty quick." Nicole waved her hand dismissively. "They've agreed to work things out — and, to their credit, they both seem to want to. Honest and true. No more cheating. For now. And daddy gets to pay fifty grand or so for the overhaul in Rio. Not a total loss, since he'll get a smoother-looking wife — with bigger tits."

"Your mom and a college kid. That is too wild."

"I'm telling you Indi, it's highly recommended. Whoever said nothing lasts forever has never had the good fortune to fuck a nineteen-year-old boy. I wish I was going back to school. I'd have a ball."

"You'd have a collection," said Indigo. "I'd prefer to focus on the work."

"You really are a wimp, you know that? No sense of fun."

Indigo let her eyes drift to a girl unchaining the bicycle. "No sense at all, maybe."

By mid-August, Spider's absence was having a more notable effect. The letters were nice, said Nicole, but the phone sex was stale. Already. She was faithful, although she had trouble remembering why. But Indigo could see that she was suffering — clinging to her promise to prove that she could, painfully aware of things male.

"Look at his arms," she'd say, mooning at a stranger in the street. "And his legs. I love nice legs." And then, to make things more bearable, perhaps — "Spider has beautiful legs." She adopted a mantra. "To love is to suffer," she said, constantly.

"Not to love is to suffer," said Indigo. "It's the second part of the quote. Woody Allen."

"Shut up," said Nicole. "Not to love is to surge through life, bouncing into handsome, naked men. Besides, who asked you?" She was getting testy.

The party didn't make things any easier.

To make up for Sam's recent lack of effort with their friends, he suggested they host a barbecue — which they started with a fight. A disagreement, really, since Indigo wasn't inspired to carry it through.

It was six o'clock and guests were expected any minute. The house was clean, the beer cold and the food waiting — including vegetarian burgers for Tim and Darcey Alexander, who'd been together since his birthday. (Tim had actually snuck a steak as recently as a week ago, when he and Indigo had dinner. But in front of Darcey he was a new man, profoundly changed by the joys of meatless life.)

The doorbell rang as Sam was wrapping forks and knives in paper napkins. "I'll get it," he said. And then, as he left the kitchen — "Oh, I forgot. I invited Graham. You remember. Graham Proulx. He's not coming for dinner. Said he might stop by later."

Indigo remembered. Graham the escort Graham. Beautiful Graham. The one Sam kept going out with, who she'd complained about with reluctant curiosity to at least four people who'd be there tonight. She turned off the tap and yelled after him. "How could you do that without telling me?" Of course, she'd have said to forget it.

By the time he came back, Indigo had taken several deep breaths to calm herself, but she needed a vent. Why was she so angry? A hollow, shaky feeling fingered the insides of her stomach as she poured some punch for Tim, and Sam gave Darcey a beer.

They heard the screen door smack shut. "Knock knock," said Nicole, piling into the kitchen with beer, wine and half a dozen people.

"Hey," said Indigo, smiling as she pinched the back of Sam's arm, harder than she intended.

"Ow. That hurt."

"Oh. Sorry," she said, with what she hoped would pass for lightness.

When everyone else had been steered into the garden, she said to Sam — "You didn't forget to tell me. You knew I'd be pissed, and you didn't want to deal with it." She handed him a plate of cheese and crackers from the fridge. "Here, put some grapes on that. They're in the sink." As she pulled out a tray of vegetables, she added — "All I want to know is why you felt the need to invite him. You want him to meet our friends, my mother, the people you work with? I thought he was your research subject, in which case it's cruel to treat him like some kind of amusing specimen. Or are you friends. Now that you've been to a few gay bars together?"

Sam twisted the cap off a bottle of beer and took a long, thirsty drink while Indigo waited.

"What are you looking at me like that for?" he said. "So I like him. He's an interesting guy. What's the problem?"

Good question, thought Indigo. What exactly was the problem? And, not sure of the answer, she took the offensive.

"Don't make me the bad guy in this. You knew I wouldn't want him to come, so you must have some sense of the reasons. You're the one who didn't tell me — I'm just not sure if you were being a coward or manipulative. Either way it was shitty." She put a bowl of dip on the tray and handed it to Sam. "In any case, forget it. It's too late now and this is a party. I don't want to fight."

Sam kept his distance after that, chatting with the guests, waiting until she was done being annoyed — or, more specifically, until she wanted some attention. His strategy, if one could call it that, had worked. After a glass or two of wine, Indigo pulled him into the hall, grabbed him gently by his shirt.

"Kiss me," she whispered. "A good one." And he did, pushing his tongue in her mouth. He gave her that.

It took about five seconds for Nicole to spot Graham. Indigo was standing in the glow of a bamboo torch, scanning a nearby table, trying to remember where she'd left her drink. "Tell me that man isn't gay," said Nicole, grabbing her arms from behind. "The one over there with Sam. Tell me you got him for me."

"Sorry sweetie, that's Graham." Indigo was struck by how utterly decent he looked. Tanned and speckless in white, practically gleaming — without even the slightest hint of sleaze. "Come on I'll introduce you."

With an improving outlook to match her newly optimistic life, Indigo felt less inclined to compete. And she finally noticed that treating Graham as a rival was a lousy way to lessen his effect; Sam let her rant, and did exactly what he wanted anyway.

She needed another approach.

If you can't beat 'em, join 'em seemed obvious, but Indigo resisted. In her somewhat potted state, she decided it was bad enough that clichés were part of life, that everyone has to hear them over and over again until they die — not believing them at first, but eventually coming to accept their hackneyed wisdom. Wasn't it almost too much to bear that clichés tend to capture some basic truth, she thought, without having to admit that they're profound?

When you're older, the years really do go faster. Time, if it doesn't heal, at least gives you fresher wounds to lick. Money can't buy happiness. In a few years, she'd probably find herself telling some poor kid that youth was wasted on the young. They'd already pushed their way into her ears, her mouth, her thoughts — and she resented it.

As they approached, Sam said — "Good timing, girls. We're talking about your favourite subject. Sex. Oh sorry. Graham, this is Nicole. Nicole, Graham."

Graham smiled and shook their hands, said how nice it was to see Indigo again, and pulled out a pack of cigarettes. He offered one to Nicole, who accepted with a throaty thanks and what Indigo decided was a come-hither look.

Of course, Nicole knew as much about Graham as she did, making him an excellent target. They talked, they laughed, they flirted. They shared a cab. And when Nicole phoned the following afternoon, she thanked Indigo for the party — and God for making Graham gay.

It turned out that when she arrived home — alone — just after two, Spider was on her doorstep. Surprise. He had four days between shows and couldn't stand to be away another minute. "So forget dinner Tuesday," said Nicole. "No offence, but I got a better offer. I'll call you when he leaves."

Once again, Indigo had wasted energy on nothing.

Graham charmed everyone he met, and failed to do anything shocking. Indigo had vaguely hoped he'd do something to justify her pettiness — like getting drunk and coming on to her mother's boyfriend, showing up in leathers or getting bored and ripping all his clothes off. (She had a preference for the last one.) He said it was too bad Tim was straight, but that was it — an impeccable guest.

When the bleeding stopped, Indigo bandaged the side of her hand and opened a bottle of wine, finished making the sauce and sat outside.

School didn't start for a week, but already there were changes.

Sam had understood; she told him at the cottage — when they swam to the island a few hundred metres out. "My brain's always been filled with words," she said. "Conversations or my own analytical stuff, whatever. It was so dominant that everything else seemed flat. And now it's like my whole environment's expanding — there's so much more than I ever thought there was, everywhere. All I have to do is notice."

Now she sat on the ground in the middle of the yard, rubbing her cold feet on the dry but colder grass. With the setting sun reflecting yellow on the dark grey clouds, the sky looked like a painting. There was a word for that sort of thing — for the impression people get that reality mimics art instead of the other way around — but she could never remember what it was. It looked like a Turner; he was always so intensely good at light.

The barbecue next door smelled of burning meat, but there was silence.

Ten

Everything she needed to say fit on a Post-it note.

S. — Meeting Nicole for dinner. Won't be late. — I.

Once upon a time there were hugs and kisses to add, maybe a heart with an arrow. Have a nice day. But Sam never really went for that sort of thing, so Indigo stopped. It seemed sentimental, and she didn't like to be the only one.

As she stuck the note on the fridge, he came bouncing down the hall and into the kitchen.

"Good morning Mrs. Blackwell." She watched as he guzzled juice from the carton, wiped his mouth with his hand and grabbed the note off the fridge. "Glorious day, don't you think?" He pushed her against the counter, kissing the side of her face and then her neck; she could feel him hard inside in his pants.

"What are you doing up?"

"That, my lovely and patient wife, is the million dollar question."

He pulled away, grinning — like he won the lottery or Robert Lantos called, heard he was writing a book, wanted rights to the movie.

"What time did you come to bed?" she asked, suspicious.

"I don't know. Four thirty. Five. Right after I typed *The End*."

Indigo squealed and started to laugh. "You're kidding, that's fantastic. When can I read it?"

"Soon. It needs some work. I want to show a couple scenes to Graham. I'm nervous about his character, how he thinks and reacts. I want to make sure —"

"I want to read it too," she said.

"You can, just not yet. I want your opinion on a real first draft, and I still have to massage it a little." She must have looked hurt because he added — "Soon, I promise," as he grabbed her by the wrist and pulled her up the stairs.

Indigo lifted a video camera to her right eye and looked through the lens at her teacher. Press the button and shoot. His smile was fading under the pressure of eighteen students eager to sign out equipment, all clamouring to see their own point of view.

Aiming downward, she wondered if a close-up of a black floor speckled with white paint would look like something under a microscope.

It didn't.

But her shoes did look removed from her body, as though they were simply parked at the foot of her jeans. She recorded her left hand, fingers flailing then together, turned modestly away. Poised. The way hands are displayed in commercials, by women who use the right soap.

It occurred to her that she might not recognize her own hand if she saw it in a photograph, that its identifying marks were easily removed — silver and white gold rings, granite nail polish — transient memories.

Her thoughts flickered with the image of a barely remembered game show. A line of wives had to identify their husbands' bare legs from the thighs down. Could that be right? It didn't sound like any show she could think of, more like a dream.

She tried to picture Sam's penis. Would she be able to recognize it? There must be millions that lean to the left. What if it was poking through a hole, without the context of his scrubby, brown pubic hair and appendix scar, and the mole shaped like an ear?

Taking a step back from the students huddled around him, the professor looked at his watch, then lifted his voice above the din — "Okay people, time to go."

The afternoon was hers. To get to know the camera, find out if the world was different through glass. Her own world. To see if a lens was like a window, inviting her to view things from a distance, objectively, as though she was close enough to watch but not participate.

Indigo wanted to focus, so she put some money in her pocket, spare tapes in a knapsack, and everything else in her locker.

The first stop was a park not far from school, on the outskirts of Chinatown. If the rumours were true, old men and women came to the park every day at dawn, to practice Tai Chi — although presumably not in the winter. She told herself that she really should come out some time to watch. Dawn was such a pure part of the day, too bad it came so early.

Lying on her back beneath a poplar, she tried shooting the light that trickled through the leaves. She rolled onto her stomach to watch a squirrel watching her, and added her own low, rambling commentary. "My name is Indigo Blackwell and I've lived in the city forever. I come out when it's warm, and try to collect enough stories to last me the winter. If I don't, I get hungry. Usually in January. For what? I don't know. Light."

The squirrel stood still as though listening until she finished, then darted up the tree as a large black nose came into frame.

Resisting the urge to stop shooting, Indigo nudged herself back and onto her knees, staring all the while into the great wet nose of a Dane. She also resisted the urge to say something, anything, to let the dog know he was on familiar, friendly ground. He sniffed at the camera for a moment, apparently baffled, before hearing a man's voice — "Winston, come here ya big doofus, leave the lady alone," and bounding off.

Indigo wondered what people would think of her work. What

she was going to think. If it was bad art and she knew it was bad, would that make it ironic, which was good? Or was irony yesterday?

This was a problem. She didn't trust her judgement.

The professor had mentioned ants as a metaphor for the city — raised it as a bad example. *Of course*. Because they all knew that, didn't they? That had relieved her somewhat. She thought she would have known, even if he didn't say so. Hadn't she already begun her own small fight against clichés?

For her first video project, she was thinking about that game musical chairs, as a metaphor for life.

Ten people, nine chairs. The music starts and the people walk slowly, like predators, taking possession of each chair with a look, as it becomes the closest one. The music stops, everyone scrambles. The person left standing exits the frame, and a gunshot is heard. A woman in a man's suit (because the grim reaper would be ridiculous) takes away a chair. The music starts. When the last person is left, he smiles with relief. But the woman in the suit comes and takes the only chair, and the music starts again.

Indigo thought about having an announcer say something after every shot. *Overdose. Suicide. Hit and run. Decapitation.* It lacked subtlety, but maybe that was part of the point. Be outrageous. Persuade herself and others of its fabulousness, and make it so. Attitude counts.

Using the trunk of a tree as a guide, Indigo positioned the camera on a picnic table, propping it with sticks to raise the angle.

She placed herself against the tree and stood, silent, as the camera stared blankly — coldly she thought, confronting the lens with a glare before turning away, embarrassed. She didn't know what to do with her arms, whether to fold them in front or let them hang at her sides, so she put them in her pockets and wondered if she remembered to wear deodorant. Moisture was beginning to form on her neck and back, and she wanted to check — to put her finger under an arm and smell it. But she couldn't let the camera see something as base as that. Not yet.

So far it was winning.

"Okay," she said, with what she thought was too much volume. "Pet peeve."

Indigo paused.

"Cabbies. The kind who hit their brakes at the first hint of yellow, even if it's only in their mind."

Naw. Too pedestrian.

She smiled. "Niagara Falls." This was good, she was beginning to actually feel irritable. "What I want to know, is whose bright idea it was it to make the falls purple? Sure, light 'em up at night. Good plan. But purple? Fucking purple? They're not spectacular enough on their own? One of the great wonders of the world? Maybe we should add a little colour?"

She was starting to enjoy herself.

"Okay." She tried again. "Biggest fear." She winced. "Forget that. Too much to pick from. Okay, any fear. Fear of the day. But don't get all earnest on me."

Indigo paused to think it over, then yelled — "NO STOPPING. BE SPONTANEOUS." A self-conscious smile wiped away with her hand, and then — "Okay. What if I suck? What if I'm not capable of making the kind of art I like? I see myself as kind of round at the edges. A bit too soft. Yeah, but no really. The good ones are either pissed off or crazy, aren't they? Especially video artists. They seem like a pretty angry bunch." She scratched her nose, realized what she was doing, stopped and smoothed her hair, never taking her eyes away from the camera.

"Okay. So that was dumb. I've hardly seen anything, how would I know? Lydia Lunch and General Idea. But they were pissed. Okay, Lydia Lunch was pissed. Really pissed. Made me feel guilty. And I'm not a man. Or part of The Machine. Or rich." She paused. "Maybe we're all guilty."

As Indigo looked away and took a breath, she noticed a man feeding birds across the park and remembered that bent old lady in New York who died and left an apartment filled with poison bird seed; turned out that every day for years, this apparently sweet old woman had sat in Central Park, cheerfully murdering pigeons.

She turned to the camera. "Okay. So maybe there's a better way to look at this. Blunt instead of angry. To the point. Impolite for a good cause. That's different. I mean, I can be impolite. Say what I think." Pause. "Here's one ... NO CLICHÉS. I'm the producer — hell, I'm the director. And I say ... NO CLICHÉS." Indigo jabbed her finger in the air in a parody of tough, except that she couldn't stop blushing.

"See? I can do this."

She pulled her features into a sneer as she walked, in frame, to the camera, shoving her face in the lens. "Anybody got a cigarette? Wait. That's not right. Cut." She frowned, then louder — "GIMME A DAMN CIGARETTE."

Smiling, she turned the camera off.

The clouds hovered, refusing either to leave or fulfill their potential. If it rained, Indigo was prepared to wait it out in a bus shelter, where she could shoot people getting wet. But it wasn't going to rain. Her timing wasn't that good. And she assumed the gods would be unwilling to lavish her with those kind of pleasures (the perverse kind) on her first day out with a camera.

Maybe later, when she knew what the heck she was doing.

Walking south toward Queen, she aimed the lens randomly at strangers. Some stepped out of frame, a few looked away. A punk with a squeegee gave her the finger and a smile, then stuck his hand out for some change. (She gave him a dollar because of the complexity of his dye-job; his crew-cut hair was white with purple dots the size of quarters.) Most maintained their momentum, pretending not to notice. She experimented, shooting feet and then heads until she tripped over a curb, forcing an ungainly, stumbling recovery. She took it as a hint and stopped recording.

Indigo was on her way to Vox. The night before, Tim had left a message — said he needed a favour. "Don't worry though, it isn't cash."

As she passed a store of party clothes for hip young urban men, she thought of Jon DeGroot. She hadn't seen him since the spring or thought of him in days — all right, since this morning. (He'd become something of a minor obsession.)

It should have been simple to find him, but days of taking her time in the halls and drinking her coffee in front of the school yielded nothing. She could always call him; it stood to reason that struggling young artists were listed. But then, if it were easy she'd have broken down already.

She hesitated at a payphone, which was ridiculous. She already knew there were twenty-seven DeGroots in the phone book, three Js. And she already knew she wouldn't do it.

As long as she was there, Indigo fished a quarter out of her pocket and called Nicole. "Are we still on for dinner?"

"You're going to kill me. I'm tired and cranky. I want to go home to my bed. Can we do it another time? Do you mind?"

"Are you sick?"

"No, just partied out. We got home really really late, and I had to be at some schmoozefest with the mayor this morning, all perky and full of beans. So I'm ready to bite someone's —"

"What do you mean, we got home. Is Spider back?"

"For a couple days. But he's only got three more weeks on the road and then he's home. So it's almost over. You're not mad about dinner, are you?"

"No, of course not. Call me later."

Outside Vox, Indigo put a new tape in the camera, then shot her way in. The room was narrow and dark, with booths for two along the left and tables to the right. At the back, Tim was filling a tray with pints of draft. He waved as she walked toward him and it occurred to her that this might be the longest job he'd ever held.

They began university together, but he dropped out in second year, said he didn't like the library. After that, quitting became one of his defining characteristics. He tried life as a bicycle courier, but exhaust made him nauseous — and, as he said, nausea made him want to puke. He objected to the mess of drywall and the wages of a clerk. He learned to clean pools, but nobody's wife ever wanted to fuck him. And he washed windows for exactly fifteen minutes, until he composed himself enough to get off the side of the building. He went to Vancouver, but he didn't like the rain. So he came home.

"Hey you," he said. "Trying to find out what makes me the best bartender this side of, well ... this side of anyplace?" He leaned forward, spreading his hands on the bar. "Is it talent, charm, dexterity? My incredible good looks? Analyze all you want, you'll never discover my secret. No one will." He let out a demented, high-pitched cackle as a waitress took the tray.

"You're out of your mind," said Indigo.

"Then you're out of your element. Tat for tit so show me yours. Want a beer?"

"Oh, that's very mature," she said, trying not to laugh and jiggle the camera. "Whatever's on tap. But give me a sec."

She wanted to tape the artwork, see how it changed when she fed the image through a camera, then spit it out on screen.

The owner of Vox made a point of supporting local talent. He replaced the pieces often, and he'd been known to buy work he didn't have room for just to give the artist a break. This month, car parts were hung like sculptures — a generic fender and hood, two doors and the badly dented rear of a Porche, ambiguously titled *wishful thinking*.

After that she checked the washrooms, with Tim standing guard outside the men's. She shot the urinals — although he refused to pee on tape — and settled for a toilet flushing. The best graffiti was in the second stall of the women's, which Indigo captured from what she felt was the legitimate seated position. In black letters that yelled over the rose coloured background, someone had written — APATHY KILLS. And below it in red — *who cares?*

As Indigo settled herself at the bar, she decided to reserve judgement on what the camera did to point of view and, by extension, how her own observations might change when she saw parts of her life on a screen. She agreed that on the one hand, distance might bring objectivity. Not that her life needed further dissecting, God knows. But couldn't that same remote quality lead to indifference? She laughed out loud as Tim slid her beer across the bar.

Apathy kills.

"You're in a good mood," he said. "How's your life?"

"Better all the time. You?"

"Life is a beautiful thing," said Tim.

"So you're still in love then."

"Why does it have to be love?"

"I don't know. Don't you want to be in love?"

"No. Do you?"

"I'm married, I'm supposed to be in love." She thought she heard a sharpness in her voice. "But now that you mention it, I'm not even sure I know what that means. That's got to be a bad sign, don't you think? You're so quick to reject it, you tell me. What is love?"

"You're asking me? Jesus Indi, how the hell should I know? I love you."

"That's not what I'm talking about."

He paused tapping his fingers to his bottom lip, then continued. "Darcey and I connect, you know? And I think about her all the time, but she's usually naked in those thoughts and it's still new so I'm pretty sure it isn't love. Don't get me wrong — she's great. But people are always so damn hot to fall in love and I don't know if I go for that. I boycott love. I want to be infatuated. I want that feeling where you can't sit still and you just can't get enough of the person. Maybe that's love. For about ten minutes. Then it changes. Every time. Tell me it doesn't. Turns into what I can and can't do. Then the inevitable. Mortgage. Diapers. I'm too young for that shit."

"Poor baby, so many pressures," said Indigo. "Maybe you're right. But it's all fucked up. I mean, I want love. I really do. But infatuation, like the kind you said, that should be called love. It's that intense. And then that other thing, later, when you've known each other for a million years and it's all oh-so-comfy, it's not even the same beast. Or it shouldn't be. You really think it has to go to hell? Every time? No wait — don't answer that. I'd rather live in hope. Anyway. Aren't we getting just a little ahead of ourselves with Darcey?"

As he spoke, Tim caught his reflection in the mirror behind the bar and smoothed his hair. "Yeah well, maybe. It's just that we're having a great time."

"And this is a problem."

"No, you women are the problem. You just can't leave well enough alone. We're having great sex, laughing our heads off — Kama Sutra sex — and I can hardly enjoy it all because I know what's coming." He giggled. "Well, that's not exactly true, but I know she's going to want to talk soon, have the conversation. All the signs are there."

"You mean the 'where is this going' conversation?" That had always been the cue for Tim to leave.

"Do you realize how great it is to date a massage therapist?"

"I guess that would —"

"It's like totally blissed out. We're talking buck naked, oiled down. Aromatherapy, candles and the most unbelievable hands, kneading and rubbing." Tim was leaning over the bar now, touching his beer to hers. "There's even a lust combo, to put you in the mood. Get this, it's got sandalwood and patchouli, all that dippy '60s shit. So I'm thinking maybe free love wasn't just rebellion. Maybe it had some help, all that incense they were burning — *it was in the air, man.* Shit works too, makes you horny as hell. I never been so —"

"I think I get the point."

"Yeah, yeah. But that's not all. She's into this herbal healing stuff. Last week, I thought I was getting that wicked flu that's going around, and she gave me these drops. What were they? Anyway, whatever it was it worked."

"Echinacea?"

"Yeah, that's it. How'd you know?"

Putting her tray on the counter, the waitress said — "Half of the house red." Then louder, through the kitchen window — "Two Pad Thai."

Indigo said — "Alice swears by it."

"Of course she does." Tim reached for the open bottle of wine on the counter. "How is your mom? You know, I really have to get over there. It's been too —"

"So what are the signs?" asked Indigo.

"What signs?"

"You said Darcey's showing signs. What are they?"

"Oh. Last week she made lasagna, called it a special dinner to celebrate our four month anniversary." He finished pouring the wine, then said — "What the fuck is that? Four months. Gave me a card and everything. That's one for sure. And she's making plans. You know, for the future. Things we're going to do *together*."

"The nerve," said Indigo. "Making plans, what a bitch. What's she trying to nail you down for, New Year's Eve?"

"No, Halloween. And I'm not telling you any more if you're going to make fun of me. She wants us to dress up in sync and go to some party. You can come if you want, it's in a warehouse — two live bands, all you can drink."

"You're too funny. You should read some of those trashy women's magazines. They're all about you."

"What's wrong with me? I'm a good guy. Funny, great in bed."

"As opposed to funny in bed and great." Indigo drained her glass. "Let's eat something."

"It's not like I'm seeing anybody else. I just want to know I can. That if some drop dead gorgeous woman offers me a blowjob in an elevator — and she doesn't expect me to pay for it — I can accept with a clear conscience. Every man wants that. Some won't admit it, that's all."

"You're hopeless, but I love you anyway. Come on, let's have Pad Thai. Oh, and what's the favour?"

Half a block from home, Indigo began her final segment. The camera had gone from surprisingly light to surprisingly heavy and awkward. But she was starting to understand what it was like to frame the world in tiny squares.

"This is my sidewalk," she said, aiming down. "Step on a crack and break your mother's back." And then, after a pause — "Kids are such a pleasant species."

Still holding the camera, she looked both ways and crossed the street. Her arms felt tired and she wanted a nap, then a bath and dinner out, maybe Italian. But she didn't see the car and Sam was probably gone for a while; it was only five and he did mention meeting Graham, although he thought he'd be home early.

She stopped across from her favourite house, the one with a group of life-size bronze people in the window, and said — "This is where I live. I have a maid and a studio loft, and lovers who come and go at crazy hours." She laughed. "Just kidding."

Across from her own house, she said — "This is where I live with a man. Do you believe me? Truth in video, there's one for discussion. No really, cross my heart and hope to die. He's my husband, although that makes it sound like more than it is." She licked her lips. "That's not fair, now I feel guilty. Things are fine. I had sex this morning — or rather, we had sex. I have sex all the time." She took a breath. Enough of that.

"That's our maple tree," she said. "I love that tree, I'd climb it if I could. It matches the one we have in the yard. Damn. And that's our locked front door, which I can't open because my keys are in my purse — which is in my locker." Pause. "Those are the steps I'd probably sit on, waiting, if we weren't so incredibly well organized. But if I'm lucky, there's a spare out back."

Another pause. "The question is, do I feel lucky?"

With a videotape for evidence, she decided to confront her fear of the long narrow path beside the house. Halfway down, she pressed herself against one wall and pointed the lens up to a sky that was now nothing more than a sliver of grey. Brick closed in on every side like the walls of a deep well. It made her dizzy and she suddenly felt the need for open air; she managed to keep the camera rolling as she ran into the yard and stood on the grass, sucking in the space, allowing herself to be soothed by the expanse.

When she turned around, Indigo saw that the sliding glass door was open. After all that, Sam was home.

Her back hurt and she was aching for a glass of juice. But she had one more quest, perhaps the most important: a tour of the house, to see what it said about her.

Stepping into the kitchen, she was confused by what she saw. The broad shoulders of someone kneeling, a bare back pushed between Sam's knees, blond hair rising and falling in his lap. Sam's face tilted to some higher power — eyes clenched, pants around his ankles. A familiar moan, beginning softly then louder. Eyes opening and then a yell. Sam leaping out of the chair, fumbling. Bare back turning around. Graham's face — oddly satisfied, a winning smile.

She still hadn't lowered the camera.

"What the hell are you doing?" It was a strange question coming from Sam, as he hopped up and down pulling his pants up, and tucking in his shirt.

Graham seemed calm, almost cheerful. He stared into the lens as he wiped the corners of his mouth with his fingers.

When her own lips finally parted, she half expected silence — but the words shot out. "What am I doing?" She let the camera swing to her side. "What the fuck are you doing? Wait. Don't answer that." Her hand leapt up to stop him. "Don't say a word. How could I be so stupid? All this time, giving you space, waiting out your goddamn tome. I didn't even think of this. Pretty funny, huh? The joke's on me. Well you can both go straight to hell. You deserve each other."

And then she was quiet.

Everything was a blur except that first image, now branded on her brain. "How could I be so stupid," she repeated to herself, walking past them. Tears were forming puddles of black around her eyes, running down her cheeks and mixing with her saliva; she let out a sob, leaning forward into the sink.

"Indi ..." Sam hesitated, then tried — "I know what you're thinking, and you're wrong. This hasn't happened before."

"I don't believe you," she said, wiping her eyes, still facing the cupboard. As she ran the cold water, she slipped the knapsack off her shoulders and let it fall to the floor. She bent over to drink from the tap. While her body felt disoriented, her mind wanted violence in a very collected way. Nothing extreme, just an outlet for the pressure in her chest.

She turned around.

Standing near the door with an amused look on his face was Graham, and Indigo felt like a specimen — a curiosity — entertaining, but essentially unimportant. She looked at him, trying to think of something nasty to say, but she was afraid he'd laugh, so she settled for — "Are you still here?"

As he turned to go he smiled. "Nice to see you again Indigo."

She picked a glass out of the dish rack and hurled it at the wall beside the door, returned the smile as he ducked, and yelled — "Fuck you."

"Indi listen to me," said Sam. "I think you should calm down."

"You do. Well, that's very interesting. I'll take that under advisement. Sorry, advice rejected. You lose." She picked up another glass and threw it at the wall behind the table, at the same time analyzing the look on Sam's face and trying to decide if it was shock or fear, or maybe both.

"Indigo, I can explain. It didn't mean anything. Honest."

She chose a plate this time, and yelled — "No clichés. Do you hear me? Do you fucking hear me? You're a writer, can't you come up with something less banal than that?" Sam jumped into the hallway as chunks of plate bounced off the wall.

He spoke from around the corner. "I think you're overreacting."

"And I think you're a jerk." As she said the words, Indigo felt a final spasm of rage escape from her throat. More than anything else now, she wanted to sleep, to take her clothes off and huddle naked within the cool, familiar walls of her bedroom. She picked up the last glass in the rack and filled it with cranberry juice, then slid down onto the floor.

"Look," he said. "You know how insane I've been. About my goddamn tome, as you so eloquently put it."

Indigo considered resting her face against the tiles, pressed the glass to her cheek instead. "You're safe now," she said. "I'm unarmed."

She let her head fall back to the cabinet.

Sam peeked around the corner, then came in and crouched beside her. "He said I don't get it. My character's flat. He says it's obvious. I can't write about a gay man without — you know ... having ... at least ..." He sighed. "Indigo, try —"

"And you believed him. What a bunch of baloney."

"The thing is, I agree — about the character that is. He's a walking stereotype. You know, I'm pathetic. I go to a couple of clubs and write him as though that's all he is. All anonymous sex and witty repartee. It's funny, Graham set me up. He was waiting for it. He figured he'd show me that side of things and see if I had the depth to get past it. And I didn't. This was a way to fix that."

"Funny." She repeated the word. "Bloody hysterical."

Indigo looked around her at the shards. "I bet he's been feeding you the same line since moment one, and you didn't want to tell me in case you decided to go for it. Don't lie to me — am I right?"

Sam was silent.

"Don't be a coward, answer me. Am I right?"

"I don't know, maybe that's true."

"Then at the risk of repeating myself, go to hell." Indigo drank the rest of her juice in a gulp, imagining steam as the cold liquid splashed onto her very hot guts.

She left Sam sitting on the floor.

Eleven

Upstairs, Indigo was propelled by a manic urge to flee. She concentrated on the physical, stuffing clothes into a bag, followed by a credit card and passport. Just in case. As an afterthought, she added candles and a book on how to meditate, which had been sitting on her night stand, unopened, for more than a year. And a pack of over-the-counter sleeping pills.

When she came back down, Sam put his hand on her arm and said — "Don't do this. Indigo, I'm sorry. I didn't mean to hurt you."

Her own hand gripped the door. "Your dialogue needs work."

She tried to think of something else to add in parting, something clever and urbane. But nothing came, so all she said was — "Don't forget to water the plants."

Her immediate destination was as sure as the panic constricting her throat: outside, where she could breathe, where she could see the sky, where she'd have some room to think. It didn't work. She was frantic, even there, anchored only by the weight of her bag and the camera. The dusk itself was oppressive and she stood at the edge of the lawn, hyperventilating, desperate for a way to escape the confines of her body.

Later, she'd deal with her mind.

Viewing the situation through puffed eyes and a pair of dark glasses, Indigo realized that she was too embarrassed to see anyone, including her mother, and made the decision to hide for the night. She left Sam standing on the porch and, without looking back, heaved herself ahead in search of a taxi.

For the next little while, the mechanics of choosing a place to stay, getting there and signing in, required all of her resolve. She directed the cab to the grandest hotel she could think of, one with antique vases in the lobby, and rooms with a view of the city and the lake. It was swank and expensive, and she chose it without guilt. Not even a whisper. If she was going to spend the night holed up in a room feeling sorry for herself, the room should be lovely. It only seemed fair.

At one point, when she thought she was going to cry, she tricked herself out of it by closing her eyes and fixing her thoughts on the credit card. Since her own cards were at school, she'd taken one of Sam's — an extra one he got in her name, in case of emergencies. She actually smiled as she signed the blank receipt. Tonight was on him.

Inside, the room was beige and gold, with a king size bed and paintings of wildflowers — mellow blues and greens with a hint of violet. Prozac colours, she thought, for me. How thoughtful.

She dumped her things on the floor, opened the sheers and gave in, finally, to grief. Life is never what it claims to be, she thought, dropping into a chair and leaning forward, hugging her knees, letting herself steep in self-pity, the regret of ignorance lost.

What an idiot not to have suspected. She'd always seen herself as an aware sort of wife, someone who tried to know the secrets. But this — this was contrary to everything she thought of as her life.

When her sobs gave way to silence she stayed where she was, hunched forward in the chair, staring at the thick cream carpet; she was glad she didn't feel like throwing up.

It occurred to her that the appropriate response might be to go out and get even — which would mean getting drunk, then laid. She sat up and wiped her nose, but in the bathroom even she had to laugh at the thought; she looked like her face had been stung, eyes ringed with red, swollen lips, head exploding with mucus. It was very attractive.

As an alternative, she found a bottle of scotch in the minibar and used it to swallow some aspirin. She'd always hated scotch, but it fit the image she had of the evening. It was raw. She should have thought to bring some cigarettes.

After the scotch she drank the cognac. Then the vodka, mixed with a ten-dollar can of juice. And then she took her clothes off.

Standing in front of the full-length mirror in the foyer, Indigo considered videotaping herself videotaping herself naked. She wondered if she'd look back on the moment with pity or revulsion, or whether it might instead turn out to be pivotal, whether she might capture the precise second during which she got a grip.

With a resounding "screw him" she chose pivotal.

She started to smile then, but ended up pulling her lips back over her teeth and imagining her skull without the flesh. (That she pictured it so readily surprised her.) For the first time, she saw — truly saw — that her body and her life would part. One would be rubble, dust, nothing. The other memories, then nothing, unless she became famous in which case she might achieve a certain temporary immortality. It occurred to her, again for the first time, that even immortality was not, could not ever be, infinite.

Indigo sighed and sank to the floor, letting what she tried to think of as her own, small, personal, essentially meaningless tragedy once again seep into her thoughts. Another round of tears and she didn't spill a drop.

What was she supposed to do now?

And then, through the mess of her hair, she looked up.

And smiled for real.

Anything she wanted.

Indigo pulled herself onto her knees and pressed her face up close to the mirror. Too puffy for wrinkles. Determined to assess the signs, she lifted her breasts and let them fall, then twisted around to check her ass and thighs for cellulite — the dreaded C, along with cancer, colonics and cauliflower. Not as bad as she thought, but she suspected that the alcohol was creating a physiological version of Vaseline on a lens. What was she trying to prove, anyway? That it was her fault? That she wasn't too far gone, she could still find someone new?

As Nicole said, some young thing.

She drained her glass. "Someone who wants to play," she said. "I'd like that."

Time to look at herself in a new way, she thought, searching her bag for the black lace thong and stilettos. That was better. She pinched her nipples hard, contemplated going to the ice machine like that, to see if she had the nerve. Decided against it. Instead she messed her hair and pouted, tried to look kittenish, then laughed and spoiled the effect.

She watched herself take another sip of her drink, thinking she'd had just about enough alcohol for the torture she knew lay ahead. She couldn't resist.

Indigo forced herself to stand under a cold shower until her nails were blue and her teeth were bouncing together. And then she played the tape.

It was almost midnight when she phoned her mother.

"Honey, where are you? Sam called."

"Sam's a jerk. What did he say?"

"That you were mad and left. Why, what's going on? Are you okay?"

Baileys in hand, Indigo started to talk. "You know the worst part?" she asked, rhetorically, since she didn't pause long enough to let Alice get a word in. "It's been going on for months and I didn't have a clue. I hate this."

"I can't believe that," said Alice. "He says you've got it wrong."

"Don't defend him."

"I'm not, honey. I'm just saying that maybe you shouldn't jump to conclusions. That's all."

"Oh right. I should believe it was a one-time thing, in the name of *art*. I don't think so. I'm not that stupid — or maybe I am, or was, whatever. Not any more. I'm cynical as of today. Hold on."

Indigo put the phone on the bed while she slipped out of the complimentary robe and under the covers, untucking the sheets with generous kicks. "Sorry about that," she said. "You know what makes me nuts? The first time I met Graham, they were talking about some married guy who was gay and went out and screwed around all the time, and his wife never knew a thing. Shit. They were probably talking about me — just for a laugh, to see if I'd notice."

"I really think you're wrong, Indigo. Sam's not like that."

"How do you know? I don't know that and I'm his wife. Who the hell is Sam?" She sighed. "How can you live with somebody and sleep in the same bed every night and talk and even have sex once in a while, and still be total strangers? I know I sound naive, but this shouldn't be happening. Okay, so we're not all over each other like you and Brian, but we're not like you and dad were either. We have things in common, or I thought we did. We're young, getting along for the most part. I really hate this."

A few days later, Indigo was settled in her childhood room, staring out of the window shaped like an eye. It was the third week in September, a Saturday afternoon. Warm and sunny enough to drag even the most resistant out of doors, under threat of coming winter.

Across the street, a neighbour was unloading crates of purple grapes from California, hauling them off the back of a pickup truck and piling them in the driveway, then carting them into the house, one at a time.

Indigo imagined a basement filled with shelves and demijohns. And months from now, sons and wives and cousins getting together to sample this year's batch of wine. Men in the living room smoking, women cooking, children doing whatever it is that children do. Everyone eating and yelling and laughing.

She'd still barely spoken to Sam.

His logic didn't connect with what she was feeling.

"It was a mistake," he said, "but it only happened once, *I swear to God.*" And when that didn't work — "It's not as though it had an *emotional* context," followed by the slightly impatient — "For crying out loud Indi, nothing like this would *ever happen again.*" The conversation ended abruptly when he suggested she "get over it," and "stop acting like a child." What planet was he from?

She hung up, stunned, and proceeded to talk herself out of her marriage.

If she was indeed a closet puritan, then what he'd done was

unforgivable — at least in the short term. She'd need some time and space to think. Maybe a small act of revenge. If, on the other hand, she was liberal enough to accept this kind of behaviour, then why had she spent the last year fantasizing about and yet refusing to have an affair?

The truth was probably somewhere in the middle, but Indigo had begun to question more than Sam's sexual preference. She was pretty sure she'd been wrong about that, that he wasn't leading some outrageous double life. And she thought she loved him, although she recognized that in all the confusion, it was hard to separate love from a sense of attachment.

No, the thing holding her back was a sense of detachment. It made her wonder if she didn't like him less, now that he was vague most of the time, and irritable. Why bother? Sam was a lot of work and not a lot of fun. And frankly, she found herself warming to the image of life as a single student. A woman with range.

Indigo spent the next week either out or up in her room, less because she was fragile than to give her mother and Brian some privacy. She still found it hard to believe they'd be apart for months — on purpose — Brian shooting his movie on the coast, Alice painting Bali. Unless they were bored with each other.

In the same position, Indigo knew she'd be afraid. Afraid of a long, slow decline, death by distance. But her initial reaction was usually wrong when it came to things like this, not that it mattered now.

Alice and Brian would miss each other desperately, reunite for a sex- and sun-kissed month in Indonesia, then live happily ever after. Someone had to.

The morning Brian left, Alice watched his taxi pull away then came upstairs, where Indigo was sprawled on the floor drawing Sam.

"So," she said. "Are you feeling abandoned?"

"Not yet," said Indigo. "You don't leave for a week." And then, looking up — "Maybe I should go too. I like to paint." When Alice didn't smile, she said — "Just kidding. I have work to do, classes to attend, revenge to plot. Don't give me that face, I'll be fine." She smiled. "Really. Here alone in this big, old, rambling house with no one to talk to but cats."

"You could do worse," said Alice.

Indigo gave Sam a ridiculously small penis, which dangled from the opening in a pair of crotchless panties. "I have."

"Glad to see you're not bitter." She pointed at the dots on Sam's chest. "What are those?"

"Pimples. Great masses of them. They're on his bum too, but that's another picture. It's a series."

Alice frowned. "Honey —"

"It's okay, mom. Just a little harmless aggression."

"Sam called again. He's very upset. He wants to talk to you. He'd like to work things out."

"So I understand."

"And you're having none of it."

"Why, you think I should?"

"It doesn't matter what I think. But no, not necessarily. I just want to know what's going on ... how you're holding up ... what your plans are."

Indigo climbed onto the bed and put her arm around her mother's shoulder. "Put it this way: I'm safe around sharp objects, but I'm thinking a whole pile of pretty nasty things about the man I supposedly love. Some days I hate his guts. I want to step on his feet with really sharp heels. But that's not even true, so I don't know." She lay back so her head was on the wall. "I've been thinking that maybe it's time to learn that certain things are meant to last a certain amount of time and that's it. I mean, I can understand why people want more of a good thing. What I don't get, is that we seem conditioned to want more of the same whether it's any good or not. What's that about? Habit? Fear? Anyway. I don't want to think about it now, okay? In a few months. When you come home."

"All right." Alice sighed, nodding her head with slow deliberation. "I guess I can understand that. And you know you're welcome here. But don't you think you should at least talk to him, let him —"

"Okay," said Indigo. "Tomorrow. I'll tell him what a louse he is, tomorrow."

Twelve

The way Tim described it, the window in Darcey's bathroom meant he could stand in the shower, hidden by a loose lattice of branches, and look out over the street. He liked the idea that, in theory, he could lather himself while watching hot young women who haven't got a clue they're being watched.

He was annoyed that it had yet to happen; while in the shower, he claimed, he had yet to spot a woman under 80.

More than once, Indigo had endured

his dissertation on what he called the self-indulgent bliss of Darcey's bathroom. Yes, she agreed that his bathroom at home seemed like an afterthought. Or, all right, if he wanted to get creative, a drywall mausoleum at the edge of his damp basement flat. The grout was eternally mouldy and the cabinet too small for his various tonics, creams and scents. The walls were the colour of old dried blood and the overhead light fluorescent.

"I think you need help," said Indigo, once, when he asked if she thought being in love with a person's bathroom might be reason enough to move in, hypothetically speaking, of course. "You're obsessed."

The problem, which Indigo felt compelled to point out, was that Tim's bathroom looked nothing like any bathroom he'd see in a men's magazine. Even the kind of ironically urban magazine that used the down and out, drug addicted and/or out of their minds instead of professional models, to prove how funky and close to society's cool, dark underside they really really were. Really. And this, said Indigo, knowing that Tim liked to imagine his life as one extended photo shoot, displeased him.

At Darcey's, he could lock himself away, experimenting with essential oils and gels. Her theory, according to Tim, was that he felt inspired by the colours in the room. Walls painted white with just a hint of pink to give the skin a healthy glow. Framed photos of the sky, the ocean, a patch of Himalayan poppies, all blue to calm the senses. The towels were either violet — to improve creativity and heighten mental strength — or blue for those days when the violet felt oppressive. At the moment they were blue.

His own theory, shared exclusively with Indigo, was that Darcey's theory was crap. He didn't buy into what he called that airy fairy stuff. It seemed wise to let her think what she wanted, but the truth was he liked her styling products. He liked her expensive shampoo and conditioner. He liked her anti-wrinkle eye cream. He liked towels that weren't all pilled and the fact that he never had to clean the toilet. He was not a complicated man.

"I just masturbated," he said, having come to the door in Darcey's robe.

"Feel free to keep the details to yourself," said Indigo.

Most of the week Darcey worked at home, in a room draped with sheer coloured fabrics. But today was Tuesday, which meant she was at the hospital, giving massage and aromatherapy to people in palliative care. ("What, you think it's not going to happen to you?" she'd asked, when Tim had looked appalled.)

Tim had taken the subway to work for the lunch shift (even though he hated being underground). Which meant that he had to come back for his bike and, since he didn't have time to stop at home, a shower. Oh darn.

Indigo borrowed a bike from her mom and met him there.

"You know," said Tim. "I'm very good in bed. You're single now, or pretty much. Time to get back on the horse. Want to see me naked?"

"Don't flatter yourself Trigger."

He sat on the couch, crossing his feet on the coffee table. "How come we never did it, you and me?"

"Because you're a pig. Come on, get ready. We're going to be late."

It was a conversation they'd had before, never for real. They did kiss once, in high school, after smoking a pipe of hydroponic weed. But it made them both laugh, so instead of making out they ordered pizza. They never tried again.

"Help me get dressed then," said Tim.

"How old did you say you were?"

"No, really. I'm serious."

As he and Indigo surveyed the bedroom closet, Tim marveled again at the benefits of dating someone close to him in size. Darcey's jeans were tight, but she had a penchant for quality, oversized shirts. He picked the used navy cotton off the floor and dropped it in the hamper, then did something he normally laughed at: he consulted the colour wheel. Just in case.

"I think I got it. Listen to this," he said. Wearing green gives the impression of stability and good practical sense. That's like, perfect."

He was on his way to borrow money.

Indigo was there because of all those times his mother said he should be more responsible, like her. "So don't say a word about you and Sam going splitsville," he said. "I need your reputation intact."

Tim wondered aloud whether a small gift might create a benevolent atmosphere, make his mother feel charitable — and ensure the smooth transition of a thousand dollars from her account to his. But Indigo cringed and he changed his mind. All he said was — "God, a Matt move. That's really gross."

"Yep," said Indigo. "Pretty slippery." They used to say that

Matt's attitude was so greasy that his words were coated in a thick shiny film that had to be bad for the listener. As she recalled, they'd been rather pleased with themselves for that one.

It was settled then. No gift.

They decided his mother would understand; she knew that he needed a holiday. Air that didn't smell like beer, smoke or exhaust. A break from the slog of tending bar, the tedium of being the only (mostly) sober ship in a sea of drunks. And as he said to Indigo, he didn't have to mention the added benefit — that it was a nice, not-so-subtle way to remind Darcey that, as good as things were, he was an independent man, prone to wandering. *So don't go pinning your plans to my back like a sign that says kick me.*

"That's good," said Indigo. "You think of that yourself?"

"Yes, as a matter of fact, and I resent the tone of your voice. Darcey needs to know that we're just hanging out. We're not getting married. I'm never getting married."

"Come on, Darcey seems like a pretty together kind of person. You really think she'd want to marry you?"

"They all do, eventually. It's my curse. I bear it."

Tim had some vacation time coming, and he had a destination. Some friends from the west coast were planning a two week trip through the mountains, timed to coincide with the turning of the leaves. There was room for another in the tent.

But he was broke.

As a rule, Tim liked to buy things. He was in possession of two credit cards — both overwhelmed — and he'd just been turned down for a third. "I can't believe this," he'd said to Indigo, waving what amounted to a polite *you've got to be kidding* on formal bank stationery. "They should be lining up at the door to give me money. I'm totally irresponsible. They make a fortune off me." Every month, Tim spent until his cards were refused. He paid the minimum due and the maximum interest. What more could a bank want?

He ranted to Indigo so he wouldn't rant to Darcey. For maximum impact, the trip had to be a surprise.

As they unlocked their bikes, he decided that in lieu of a gift he should bring some dessert. On Sunday mornings, he and Darcey liked to sit in a tiny café on the Danforth, with their lattes and croissants, and read the paper. Tim told Indigo that, for the past few weeks, he'd been discreetly enthralled with a waitress, convinced that her friendly smile was a front for something more.

It was obvious. She wanted him. Not that he planned to ask her out. He just wanted to feel that first flush of attraction — the kind that never lasted anyway, so there was no real need to pursue it — nothing more.

And there she was, alone behind the counter looking sullen, pale bangs hanging in her eyes.

Indigo stayed by the door, feigning interest in the notice board, reading the ads for yoga, classes on how to make paper out of vacuum cleaner lint, and midwives.

"What'll you have?"

"What are you offering?"

The woman said nothing, only sighed and waited.

"How about one of those smiles of yours — you know Miss, your smile is famous. You don't think people come in for the coffee?"

She started picking at one of her cuticles. "Your girlfriend didn't go for a cornball line like that, did she? Doesn't look the type."

"Probably worse, but she loves me anyway."

"Then I'd say you're a lucky man. Yep, that's what I'd say. Lucky."

On the way outside, armed with three pieces of raspberry mousse pie, Tim said — "Did you see those nails. Chewed way down, practically bleeding. That totally grosses me out."

Tim Keeler's mother was sixty years old and she looked exactly that, although she'd been threatening a "wee nip and tuck" since her 40s. Her face was like cracked bone china; below the neck was something else. Her clothes always looked as though they were bought five pounds ago, accentuating her bold, slightly bossy style as much as her breasts. She wore long, proudly fake, red nails.

Years ago, more than a decade after her husband died of cancer, Mrs. Keeler got engaged then changed her mind. The closer she got to the day, the more she said she lived the past. Her first marriage — in Brighton, to a handsome young cabinetmaker. The voyage to Canada, from Liverpool to Montreal, five days of grey and green (they were all horribly green) on the S.S. *Atlantic*. Icebergs off the coast of Newfoundland. Two sons. Friends and parties. A thriving furniture business, original design, strictly custom work. And then the end. The tumor in his nasal passage, an especially gruesome demise.

It was all so very long ago, another life.

When she cancelled the wedding, she said — "I've been alone

too long. I'm no longer in the mood to compromise." That and she couldn't bear to move, or move him in.

These days, Mrs. Keeler bought and sold antiques. And besides a view of the water, her fully paid for condominium was an ideal place to store items she bought for the shop. She liked to live with them a while, she said, get them into her bones before she priced them. In fact, there were so many sideboards, davenports, cabinets and chairs along the walls that it looked as though someone had pushed everything back to clear space for a party, except that the rest of the floor had its own series of obstacles. Every surface overflowed with lamps and clocks, framed sepia photos of strangers. Since Indigo's last visit, the dining room table and chairs had been replaced with an oversized writing desk, complete with leather blotter, and two church benches.

"I'm so glad you could come, dear. Come in. You didn't ride your bicycles, did you? I hate the thought of you riding those things in the city. Tim, you really need a car. Tell him, Indigo. It's dangerous out there. You'll never convince me otherwise. I drive to work. I see what it's like. What do you want to drink?"

"Whatever you're having, mom. Nice table."

"Same for me, Mrs. Keeler. Thanks."

"Oh, that old thing." It was her favourite joke, an antique-sellers' joke, out of the way in the first five minutes as she poured their gin and tonics.

She raised her glass. "What shall we drink to? Are you still seeing that girl? What's her name — Dorrie? She seemed nice. You should have brought her with you."

"Darcey," said Tim, as his mother forgot the toast and took a swallow, then smiled and stroked his cheek.

"Yes, I remember. Lovely girl. We're having roast beef, is that still your favourite? And mashed potatoes. When you were small you called them smashed potatoes, do you remember that? You used to drive those little cars through your food — I think it was meant to be snow — and lick it off the wheels. Quite disgusting."

Mrs. Keeler had a demeanor that masked her intelligence. She came across as flighty, vaguely scattered, which she didn't mind a bit. She thought it gave her an advantage.

She walked over to a curved mahogany sofa near the window, sat down and patted the seat beside her. "Did I tell you I'm going to England?"

"No," said Tim. "When?"

"Next week. It's your grandmother's birthday, do you want to come?"

"How old is she?" asked Indigo.

"Ninety-three. Daft as brick, of course, but what can you expect. I don't suppose it'll be much of a holiday. A lot of people you don't know. Warm beer and drizzle. Oh well, another time." She had a way of holding up both sides of a conversation. "Have you spoken to your brother?"

"You know I haven't."

She gave him her standard look of disapproval, mouth turned down at the corners, left brow raised. It was a face that Indigo and Tim could mimic perfectly, and often had, and they both looked away to keep from laughing. "Yes, of course. You know, it wouldn't hurt to make an effort. He doesn't know what it is you think he's done —"

"He doesn't give it two seconds thought and you know it."

"You're too hard on him. Indigo knows, don't you dear? He's never done a thing to you and you act like he's some kind of traitor. All I'm saying is that I think the two of you should try to be more brotherly. Is that too much to ask?"

"England. When did you decide this?" asked Tim. He was looking past her at the sailboats in the harbour.

"Today. I was all set not to go, thought I'd send a little something from the shop. She loves anything crystal. But I had a vision. Well, not my own vision exactly, but I was stuck in traffic and all of a sudden I looked up and there it was — one of those giant advertisements — British Tours. And I thought, well, it is my old mum, daft or not. And I had the cell, so I called. Right there on the Gardiner Expressway. Are you sure you wouldn't like to come? No, that's all right. Never mind. I don't blame you." She paused for a sip of her drink. "You look thin, dear. Are you eating enough?"

"You always say that. I'm fine."

"Maybe it's the shirt, that colour doesn't suit you. Makes you look wan."

Tim waited until they'd cleared the plates to ask her. He was reasonably sure she'd say yes, but he hoped that after three gin and tonics, the compulsory speech would be brief.

"Hiking. Well, that does sound healthy — unless you meet a bear. Aren't there a lot of bears in the mountains?"

"They're more afraid of you than you are of them."

"Oh bollocks, dear, excuse my French. Have you ever seen a bear's teeth?"

"It's okay, mom. I've done this before. We take precautions — hang all the food out of reach, make noise, lay off the perfume — or no, I guess that's for the bugs. In any case, there's nothing to worry about."

"Are you going?" She turned her attention to Indigo, pen poised, chequebook on the table.

"I wish I could," said Indigo. "It'll be great. Tim really needs the break."

She looked at him, still not writing. "Right then. Do you even have a savings account?"

"Of course. It's just that it's empty. At the moment. I've had a lot of expenses."

"I see." She wrote his name and the date, and stopped. "I'm going to give you the money — it's not a loan, I don't want it back. But I want you to think about something. Promise me you will." She paused. "Promise."

"Okay, I promise. What?"

"You're getting too old for this. It's time you started developing some sort of adult existence. Act your age." She signed her name and put the pen down. "I bet you go to those things too, don't you? Don't lie to your mother. I can always tell when you're lying."

"What things?"

"I know what a rave is, don't think I don't. I keep informed. With all those doped up teenagers. Look at yourself. It's just not right. A thirty-year-old man should not be going to parties with a bunch of kids." She tore the cheque out of the book and slid it toward him.

"I don't hang out with kids, mom. Now you're being silly."

"Don't call your mother names. And what about this Darcey, is she Ms. Right? Because you don't have a lot time to waste. If she's not the one, move on. It's time to grow up and settle down. Like Indigo. Now here's a girl with a head on her shoulders. I always thought you two would end up together, I hope you don't mind my saying that, dear. Of course, your Stan's nice too."

"Mom, we're like brother and sister."

"That's exactly what I mean. You're as close as any two can be. You'd be great together."

Indigo put her hand up to her mouth and cleared her throat.

"Mom, you're embarrassing me. Look at it this way, even if she did see me that way, which I guarantee she doesn't —

"Which I promise you I don't —

"She knows everything about me. I'd never get away with anything. That's no way to start a relationship."

Indigo laughed out loud and Mrs. Keeler sighed, one of those long, deep sighs that usually meant she was close to giving up. "You were born when I was 30. And that was old. I was meant to be past that sort of thing. Matt was almost 10."

"We can't all be the same, mom. My life is fine."

"Except the part about no money."

"Except for that."

By the time Darcey called, Tim and Indigo had both fallen asleep in the glare of late night television, worn out by the kind of strenuous conversation he usually tried to ignore. He wasn't ill-equipped, just unprepared to dwell on mysteries he'd never solve. Indigo liked to do that sort of thing and, as far as Tim could see, it didn't make her happy, didn't bring her any closer to the truth. Why bother? Tim was proud of the fact that he'd travelled half the world without becoming weighted down with heavy thoughts.

But tonight he weakened.

They'd been sprawled on his futon, eating sour cream and onion chips and hopping channels. They caught the beginning of an old movie, but Indigo asked if he didn't find it sad that all those beautiful young people were either dead or in homes for old actors, unable to control their bodily functions, and did he ever smile so hard that he pictured his skull without its flesh?

So then they found a nature show, and she said wasn't it coincidental that there was a grizzly fishing for salmon after what his mother said and, since he was going camping, maybe they'd better watch and get some tips.

But the show wasn't about bears; it was about the allegedly perfect chain of life, which Indigo and Tim found suddenly depressing. As the announcer said in his standard, nature-show gravelly voice: with the exception of humans, everything is food for something else.

"Yeah right," said Tim. "So we like to think."

For salmon, life has but a single purpose. The need to carry on the line, do whatever it takes to get to the spawning ground, release the eggs, cover them with shit and die. Goal achieved.

But why? If the next generation is born for the sole purpose of ensuring the following generation, and so on, what's the point? All that trouble — fighting currents, dodging bears and fishnets. Tim was confused. If the only point is to eat, reproduce and die, so the kids can eat, reproduce and die, so their kids can eat, reproduce and die, he thought, it seems so unnecessary. The ultimate in futile.

On the other hand, if he could have faith in nothing — or, more specifically, the lack of something — his mother's argument for living a responsible life would be irrelevant. As long as he wasn't hurting anyone (which was something he tried not to do on principle), why go the pedestrian route? If his own DNA didn't have him scrounging for a mate, there must be a reason. Why pass on bad genes?

Even so, it bothered him to think that life was just a fluke, a lucky combination of gases and chemicals. It bothered his ego.

Last summer, sitting on a streetcar, Tim said he happened to read the sign in front of a church. It said: GOD IS NOT ON HOLIDAY. That sign had hung in his thoughts for months.

He knew the Bible would have something to say about this, potentially reassuring. But where to start? He couldn't possibly read the whole thing, although he did have a Bible, somewhere, stolen at the end of a drunken week in Vegas.

"You might as well give it up," said Indigo. "You're going to hell for sure."

It disturbed him, he said, to think there was no meaning to be found in human lives — not individual lives, which have varying degrees of meaning to other individuals — but in human existence? The whole decaying mess.

As they talked, he kept coming back to pleasure. As an alternative. How nice, if it were simple, he said. Get the basics taken care of, then have a good time. Forget Sodom and Gomorrah. Don't pay any attention to all that decline of civilization nonsense. Given his own peculiar time and place, he was in a rare position to make pleasure his lifetime pursuit. Why waste the opportunity?

Unless the Buddhists were right. Forget pleasure. The world isn't a playground, it's a giant bloody training centre.

Tim said afterwards that when the phone rang, he was being eaten alive by a pride of lions, who were chewing on his intestines as he barked and tried to push them back in his stomach. There were chips all over the bed.

"Hello?"

As Indigo sat up, he said — "Hey. Darcey."

And then — "No, that's okay, I'm up. What's going on?"

Indigo yawned, wondering whether she should call a cab or stay the night. She hated waking up at Tim's.

"Sure, no problem. I can water them. No, it's okay. Where you going?"

Indigo watched the expression on his face deflate.

"Really. That long." And then — "No, it's cool. It's cool. But I'm heading out west in a couple weeks, so if you're still gone ..."

If there was a God, she had a sense of humour.

Thirteen

Indigo walked slowly, bowing her head against the wind, balling her hands inside the pockets of her coat. These days her favourite place was anywhere alone, where she didn't have to find the words. Words were the mechanical side of questions, thoughts, decisions; she didn't have the energy for those.

At the corner store she noticed a man in one of the aisles, watching her over his *Auto Trader*. She took a step back, out of his line of sight, and wondered why she cared. She was distracted by the man behind the counter, the fur on the back of his hands and chunky gold signet on his pinkie. He was staring at her too, his one long eyebrow raised, and she felt a pang of confusion before realizing — "Oh. Sorry. Menthol. Small, king size. *There's* a contradiction."

"Huh?" He turned his body to the wall of cigarettes, but talked to her over his shoulder. "What's that you said?"

"Small and king size, it's ... Nothing, never mind. Any brand, I don't care. Yeah, that's fine. Whatever."

As she rummaged through a box of lighters, the man tapped his ring on the cash register. "Shouldn't think so hard," he said. "Can't be as bad as all that."

"No. I guess it isn't." She smiled vaguely in agreement although, in fact, there was nothing on her mind. Nothing beyond her desire for a cool green lighter to match the cool green letters on the pack of cigarettes. That was the strange part. She'd been moving around in a daze that seemed deliberate, as though she was looking hard at the world. But it wasn't that at all. The world barely made an impression and her thoughts were like a thousand distant voices, all chattering at once, so the effect was simply noise.

Satisfied that there were no green lighters in the box, Indigo settled for matches — a pack that offered a chance to change careers, be an electrician. And a lottery ticket. There was a lot to be said for choices.

Reluctantly, she was on her way to Sam's.

Reluctantly, because she had no desire to put all this behind them. That had been his phrase, meant to sound soothing, she was sure, but unsuccessful.

Pressing the phone against her ear, she listened to the way he said the words — quietly, with an even tone, as though he needed to keep her calm. She could tell he was trying to be patient. But he exhaled noisily, exasperated, and gave himself away. She was someone to be persuaded, like a child, made to see the logic. So when he said — "Come tonight, please, I'll make dinner, we can talk," Indigo heard — "Come so I can make you see it my way."

She said yes because she didn't have a choice. Sam was her husband. Apparently he was upset. And she promised her mother she'd talk to him, even though she'd rather ignore the whole sordid mess, at least for now.

Indigo was tired of analyzing a scene that, frankly, bore up a bit too well to analysis. It was exhausting. Was she angry because he put his penis in someone else's mouth? Because the mouth belonged to a man? Or because he turned to Graham to work out the problems in his book, when he'd barely discuss them with her? "We have issues," she thought, sarcastically, mimicking Nicole. Ones she didn't want to think too much about, but which acted like a bleating neon sign behind her eyes: *run away*.

When she finally climbed the steps and rang the bell, Sam was at the door in an instant, out of breath, holding a dishtowel, as though he'd skated down the hall. "You could have just come in," he said, brushing her cheek with his mouth as she turned her head away.

Inside, Indigo inhaled the warmth of roasting garlic. "Something smells good," she said, feeling guilty, as she perched on the couch like a guest. Through the glass-paned doors at the edge of the living room, she could see that the dining room table was set with linen and candles. He'd even decanted a bottle of wine — in a vase, but who could fault the man for trying?

The last time they saw each other, Indigo had felt too close to her own surface, as though every emotion, every thought, had singed her flesh. Today was the opposite. She was buried so far beneath herself that her skin was cold to touch. The muscles in her face felt stiff.

They started simply, pouring wine, easing in with casual questions.

School was a blast, everything she wanted, harder than she thought. Alice was fine, starting to pack for the trip. Tim was spending a lot of time with Darcey although, as usual, he wouldn't admit to anything serious. Spider was back in town. Nicole got a tattoo. Or so she says.

"You're kidding," said Sam. "Of what?"

"I haven't seen it, some kind of Celtic symbol. Life or fertility or something like that. I think. I don't know. On her shoulder." Indigo sipped her wine. "So how are things? How's the book?"

"Awful."

"I thought you were close."

"So did I. But I've hardly touched it since you left. Can't focus. It's this ... Indi, it's everything. I feel like shit. You're not here so I sit around watching bad television. Drink too much. Hardly eat. Can't sleep." He rubbed his forehead. "I've lost weight."

Indigo resisted. "You'll eat well tonight," she said. "Dinner smells great. What are we having?"

"Indigo, when are you coming home?"

"Do we have to do this now?"

Sam leaned forward, putting his glass on the table and his hand on the couch between them. "I need to know what you're thinking. I love you. You have no idea what this —"

"Okay fine," she said, a little too abruptly. "Not yet. Maybe not at all. I don't know." She looked away, then forced herself to meet his eyes. "Look. Things haven't exactly been good. Now this. I don't know if I'm coming back ... if I want to ... do this I mean ... here, with you. In any case, I'm not committing to anything. Not today, maybe not for a while." She paused. "So there it is."

Sam leaned back. "Don't you love —"

"Stop it. I know what you're trying to do and it's not going to work. I'm still unbelievably pissed. You'd be surprised how much anger I've been able to hang on to. And it feels great, better than anything else I can think of. So you're not going to goad me into some kind of weepy, blabbering state. There's more to it than love and you know it." She still had the urge to swear and call him names, but noticed that her desire to cause him physical pain had passed. The evolution of anger, she thought, gulping a mouthful of wine, as hard to sustain as anything else.

"All right," he said. "All right. We can deal with this. Take it slow. Whatever you want. But Indi, you don't understand —"

"Stop saying that, it makes me crazy when you say that. I understand perfectly. And if I do manage to block a few details, all I have to do is look at the video. It's all right there. You're the one that doesn't understand."

"Let's not fight. Please. It's not going to solve anything." The creamy texture of his voice made her feel like an animal, something he wanted to coax back into its cage. This was a mistake, she thought, reaching for her purse as the oven timer buzzed and Sam said — "The roast. I'll be right back. Dinner's ready."

To stop herself from leaving, she lit a cigarette and took two minty puffs before putting it out in the cactus, then sliding the evidence back in her purse.

End of round one.

Later, as Indigo reached across the floor for her panties, she said — "Remember, this doesn't change anything," and Sam, sitting naked on the couch, smiled and said — "Spend the night. I'll make it worth your while."

In the shrinking glow of the embers, she wondered why love felt strongest when it seemed precarious, or whether (as she suspected) that was lust, and love was something else.

She'd confused the two before, more than once. Okay, many times. There ought to be a handbook.

Indigo tried to remember the last time they'd had such energetic sex, if ever. She'd been naive to be surprised. Sam knew exactly how to weaken her resolve. Wine. Candles. Those little roast potatoes. Tears, in spite of what she said, both his and hers. And, of course, the fire. He'd fixed the chimney, finally, and bought some wood. Real wood, to appeal to her sense of smell — as well as her sense that he was trying. Fingers trailing down her arm and up her thigh. What harm could it possibly do?

"I have to go," she said. "I have an early class."

"I'll set the alarm."

"No. Thanks. I don't want to."

They said goodbye at the door, Sam's robe open in the front as he tried to keep her in a hug; Indigo anxious, waiting to pull away until it wouldn't seem deliberate.

Released into the cold night air, she walked with her hands out from her sides, letting the wind slip between her fingers. At the corner, she allowed herself to be swallowed by the busier street, by people walking in and out of bars, lingering in doorways or simply moving ahead, buffered by strangers.

As she walked with her head down, eyes on the pavement, the sounds of the street grew large and suddenly hollow — as though someone upped the volume in her ears and added reverb: the rise and fall of senseless conversation as she passed it; traffic that felt so close she might have been horizontal on the centre line; even her own breath, which sounded in her head like someone huffing into a microphone and out of amps the size of buildings.

She stood against the wall to light a cigarette, dragged on it once, then gave it to a guy bumming change.

"Hey cool. Thanks ma'am," he said.

Thanks for reminding me, she thought. Ma'am.

When she started school, she hadn't felt as old as she expected, more inconspicuous than anything, although that is one of the signs. Apparently.

She decided she was on the cusp of falling apart. Not so far gone that anyone else would notice, but far enough to spot the signs herself: the fret mark starting on her forehead, the tiny line above her mouth. When did she become a person who frowned and pursed her lips? Her romantic side wanted to believe the line had been earned giving blowjobs — at least that gave it an erotic context, life lived to the fullest, all of that. But why was that romantic? And when did she start associating blowjobs with a full life? In any case, it was probably from the way she talked, brushed her teeth, drank through straws. Could she be any more tedious? Even her wrinkles were trite.

It occurred to her, for the second time that day, that maybe she needed a shrink; she was clearly sex-addled, maybe crazed, although that might imply she was getting some. The first time was during dinner, when Sam asked the (in her mind premature) question of whether she still loved him. It was then that she realized she had absolutely no idea.

"Don't be stupid," he said. "You don't need a shrink. You're feeling a bit detached, that's understandable. But listen to me Indigo, you're one of the sanest women I know."

To which she replied — "Not detached, unhinged. What if I've been feeling crazy?" — more to see what he'd say than anything else.

Sam had paused mid-bite, looking at her with what she described in her mind as thinly disguised irritation. "Well stop," he said. "Just stop. Don't feel that way."

"What do you mean stop? What kind of answer is that? That's not an answer. You can't tell a person not to feel the way they feel."

A moment of silence then, while they both continued eating, and after which they pragmatically dropped the subject.

Indigo caught her reflection in the window of a health food store and smiled, amused by her own neurotic tendencies. At least she knew she could be ridiculous, that had to count for something.

The night before her mother's flight, Indigo stood watching her transfer piles of clothing from the closet to the suitcase, check items off a list, frown as she tossed in extra shoes then took them out.

Turning to her daughter and pointing a bottle of milk of magnesia for emphasis, Alice said — "In case you're wondering, I'm not worried about you."

"What do you mean? Why not?"

"Because you'll be fine. Some time on your own will do you good."

Indigo did not fail to notice the irony. In the past year she'd had plenty of time alone and it had made her cranky — yet her mother was right. She was, in fact, looking forward to a big empty space of time in her own house, starting immediately.

Already behind in her jewellery class, she was determined to work through the weekend, to finish cutting the silver she'd need for a small round box: her first assignment. She'd already padded the dining room table, at the end of which she clamped a piece of plywood. She'd been to the smelter, felt inspired by the sheet of sterling, exposed like a blank page or mound of clay, except that it stared back with her own muddied reflection.

But she felt it was nonetheless a mother's job to worry, so she said — "You're still supposed to worry. It's your job."

They'd both gone to the Bali orientation, met the others in the group — ten in total, mostly women, one couple, plus the artist/teacher/guide, Marta Stone. All eager, barely contained. Marta giving details: this is where we'll stay, what we'll eat, how to dress. Bring this, bring that. Everyone grinning.

They were the last to leave Marta's loft.

"Have you eaten?" Alice asked her. "We were thinking sushi."

It turned out that after the tour, Marta planned to stay in Indonesia, do some painting in the caves. There'd been talk of a show in Jakarta, in the lobby of a bank, plus she had a few commissions. She paused to pluck a stray grain of rice with her chopsticks, then popped it in her mouth. "I like a lot going on," she said. "Keeps me cheerful."

Indigo sipped at her thimble of sake. Secretly, she used to wish she was a man, albeit a man with feminine qualities (plus height, hair and a dazzling penis, but that was something else). Tonight though, sitting across from Alice and Marta, watching them and listening, she changed her mind. The opposite was just as appealing. At least.

Marta was utterly self-sufficient — defiantly so, perhaps — but also warm and sympathetic. Artistic contradictions, thought Indigo. Like Alice only more so. She was married, lived in Toronto, with extended trips abroad. Indonesia mostly, with forays to Australia, New Guinea, New Zealand. Usually alone. Protective of her right to view the world without a man. Unafraid of what she'd see or leave behind.

Fits Like a Rubber Dress   169

Predictably, Indigo felt a surge of her own independence.

So much so that on the morning Alice left, when the bags were finally closed and the limousine waiting, Indigo said without a hint of sarcasm — "Don't worry about anything here. Really. Take lots of pictures. Send me a postcard. Be careful. And have a wonderful time. This is a great thing you're doing."

At the curb, she hugged and kissed her mother one more time. "Call if you need anything. And remember, no sex with strangers. I don't care how hot it gets."

And then she was alone.

It began to storm that afternoon. Indigo sat in school, half watching as the sky grew heavy and dark, half listening to a lecture on the use of self in narrative structure. When the professor decided to end the day with videos, there was a splatter of applause. It was the class before the weekend.

Of the videos she'd seen so far, Indigo liked *The Confession*. It seemed uncanny that this piece would present itself, given recent events with Sam, until she realized that disclosure, real or contrived, was a popular theme in video.

A young man in white, sitting on a chair in front of a red background, leaning forward, hands clasped earnestly in front, brow furrowed. Talking, explaining, rationalizing. Too little detail to know exactly what he did, but enough to suspect violence, maybe because of the red.

"I didn't recognize myself," he said. "I lost control. That wasn't me. You have to understand." An all-purpose apology.

His expression said it was painful to remember, so forgive. It was an accident. It would be wrong not to forgive a man so filled with remorse. Ask any judge, remorse counts. And he'd gone further. He put his soul on videotape, to be played again and again, to show how sorry he was, forever.

His innermost thoughts. Or probably not. Pretend inner thoughts, imagined by the filmmaker — or better, a group of his friends, drinking beer, tossing together a life.

But then, there aren't any rules about truth any more than there are about love. None that stick. So who's to say that someone didn't simply set up a camera, sit on a chair and confess. The beauty of make-believe is the fact that it's a perfect disguise for real events. Flickers of reality, with no way of knowing. The same as any conversation.

Indigo scanned the class for someone who looked trustworthy. Such a subjective concept, honesty. Was the boy in the beige sweater and glasses more likely to be honest than the girl with the motorcycle helmet under her chair, or the boy with stringy black hair and a bar through his tongue? Wasn't the whole notion of an honest look misleading, white hat versus black hat, something to be cultivated or railed against but, either way, manipulated?

And how did telling the truth ever come to be associated with wide eyes and boring clothes, anyway?

Indigo turned to the back page of her notebook and wrote — *If you can't find anyone to blame, blame Hollywood. I blame Sam.*

Sam looked honest, especially when he wore his chinos. And to be fair, he probably was. As apt to tell the truth as anyone. No less honest than Indigo.

She remembered at least one recent lie, a week or so back, when she cancelled a dentist appointment. Said she had a meeting instead of the petulant truth — that she didn't feel like having her teeth cleaned, couldn't bear the thought of a paper bib or fluorescent lights or the tube that sucked saliva from her mouth.

What would they have said to that? Nothing. What could they possibly say? Nonetheless, it seemed polite to lie.

After class, since she had no umbrella, no jacket and nowhere to be in a hurry, she sat on the floor against the wall in the giant glass foyer of the college, thinking about how to develop a story on screen, whether she'd prefer to let the subject speak alone or add narration. A growl of thunder in the distance made her wonder if the cats were in or out, but she couldn't remember. So she checked her purse to make sure she had money for a cab — including a stop at the store for some logs — and began to gather her things.

Change of plans.

The silver box she had yet to begin could wait until tomorrow. This was a night to read in front of the fire, plotting her video, deciding how to use the footage of Graham and Sam. The way to make it interesting, she thought, would be to take this moment of drama, sixteen seconds to be exact — a scene that changed her life — and make it part of a different story. Truth handed out as fiction.

But as angry as she was and she was angry, did she really want revenge to that degree? Was she so thoroughly cut off from any feelings of loyalty, empathy or even love, that she wanted to humiliate him? Sam would be mortified. That and he'd never forgive her. And as for her, she'd probably never get over the guilt. The only person who could conceivably benefit was Graham, only because he seemed intelligent enough to understand that she'd have become something less in Sam's eyes. Something petty and mean. Too bad, she thought. The revenge had been fun while it lasted, if only in her mind.

As she stood up, she caught a whiff of damp hair and leather as a voice close to her ear said — "I knew I'd find you, eventually."

She hadn't thought of Jon DeGroot in — well, twenty minutes anyway.

"Hey," she said, turning around, waiting for the obvious.

"I heard you were here. I've been keeping an eye out."

"You're kidding. That's too bad." She tried to nonchalantly hang her knapsack on her shoulder, but it fought with her purse and, after struggling for a moment, she leaned it on the floor against the window. "I was hoping to surprise you. How's it going?" She folded her arms then changed her mind and let them fall, put a hand in her pocket. Her face felt hot.

"Great," said Jon, as his pager went off and he unhooked it from his jeans. "Crazy." And then, looking at the message — "Some guys have no patience."

"You want to get a coffee or something?"

"Can't," he said. "I'm late as it is. Some other time though. For sure. Soon. You coming tomorrow?"

"What's tomorrow?"

"Peter's play, Peter Dumas. Opening night."

"News to me." She paused. "You think I can still get tickets?"

"I can call him if you want — there's a party after, should be pretty good. Give me your number." He pulled a pencil out of his jacket pocket.

"This is too funny," said Indigo.

"What's that?"

"This. Me. Standing in school, giving my number to some hot young guy. I'll be necking in the stairwell yet. Forging notes from home." She watched his mouth spread into a soft pink smile and reminded herself that he was way too young. A pup. That, and she was still a married woman, strictly speaking.

"Sounds like a second chance," he said. "Fresh start, all that."

"Either that or my life is into reruns." She took the pencil out of his hand and wrote her number on his sketchpad.

He looked at it, and said — "That's not the one I have. Did you move?"

"Did I give you my number? I don't remember that." Indigo tucked a loose strand of hair behind her ear, thinking it really was too bad she looked like hell.

"Looked it up. I was gonna say hi, wish you luck. I couldn't believe you quit your job. Kept meaning to call, never did. You know how it is." He shrugged. "And here you are. Go figure. I'm inclined to think it's fate."

"A little far-fetched, but I like it. I'm house-sitting. My mom's in Bali. Painting the scenery. She left this morning."

"That's a cool thing for a mother to do. Where's Mr. Indigo?"

"I thought you were late."

"I am," he said. "But it's a mathematical fact, curiosity beats punctuality."

She smiled. "It's a long story. Mind you, it's also very entertaining — gripping even. Real edge-of-the-seat stuff. But it's just not the same crammed into twenty-five words or less. So I think you'll have to wait."

"Okay, I'm hooked. But you're right, I gotta fly." He put his hand on her arm. "I'll call you."

Twenty minutes later, as she ran from the taxi to the house, Indigo said — "Shit. The cats." Sid, looking damp and irritable, was waiting on the porch. "Sorry Sid, you big old monkey. Okay. Don't look at me like that, I said I'm sorry."

She dropped the logs beside the fireplace, threw her knapsack on a chair and went to the kitchen. "It's freezing in here, where does she keep the matches?" Sid jumped onto the counter and hovered, tail erect and quivering, while Nancy whined and pushed against her legs. "Okay," she said, reaching into the cupboard for cat food. "Yes, you're hungry. I understand that now. Food first, fire second. How insensitive of me."

It was after nine when Jon called. Indigo was lounging in front of the fire, notepad on the table, eating still partly frozen cherry cheesecake.

"I scored some tickets," he said. "They'll be at the door. For you and a guest. No charge. Oh, and Peter says hi."

"That's great," said Indigo. "Thanks."

"So what are you doing now? You want to go for a drink?"

"No, it's lousy out there. I think I'll hang in. I have a fire going —"

"Great, I'll be there in twenty minutes. Where do you live?"

She had to smile. "You mean there's something you don't know?"

"Your mother's name. Or I would have surprised you."

As she hung up the phone, Indigo leapt off the couch and ran upstairs to change, hurling her sweats into the closet, shutting the door. She brushed her teeth, put her hair in a clip, changed her mind and shook it out, then settled on a braid. Then it was back downstairs to tidy up, quickly. She laughed at herself for being nervous. "He's a friend," she said out loud, as she wiped the kitchen counter. "Too cute by half and way too young."

Ten minutes later, after arranging herself on the couch as though she'd never left it, she looked at the fire, decided it was too romantic and reached for the lamp.

She heard him running up the steps.

"You're soaked." His jacket was zipped to the neck, but it was raining hard and he didn't have an umbrella. There were tiny beads of water on his lashes.

"Hey," he said, then smiled. "Thanks for the invite. I love a woman who won't take no for an answer."

She watched while he took off his jacket and shoes, then said — "Do you drink red wine? Say yes, I think it's all I have. Unless you want some tea."

"Wine's good," he said, looking past her into the living room. "Cool. Where'd you get the bird?"

"That's Henry. My mom bought him when she left my dad decided he represented the kind of love that lasts forever so we're both kind of sentimental about him I think she got him near the market at some small gallery I don't think it's there any more it was on Wellington or Front one of those on the north side I think with exposed brick and beautiful floors she got him around the time we bought this house when I was 11 so that's God eighteen years ago how old did you say you were?" She closed her mouth to stop the words, and waited.

Jon sat on the rug in front of the fire, letting Sidney sniff his fingers. "Hey buddy. Are you ever fat. This is one big cat."

"That's Sid," said Indigo. "He likes men and that's Nancy on the couch she's kind of crazy goes psycho a couple times a day flips out all over everything including Sidney she's sweet though once she gets to know you they're almost as old as the sculpture 13 I think or maybe 14 I don't remember ancient in cat years." Her hand went up to her mouth. "Okay. I'll shut up now." She paused, not sure what to do, then laughed. "Wine."

The phone rang as she walked down the hall into the large open kitchen and dining room. "I don't know why, but I knew it was you," she said to Sam, glad for the extension. Of course it would have to be him.

"What are you doing, you want to come over?"

"No. I don't feel like getting into it." At the opposite end of the house, she could see Jon checking out the bookshelves.

"We won't, I promise. I'll leave it alone. We'll just hang out."

"I can't."

"Why, what are you doing?"

"Nothing. I don't want to, that's all." She paused long enough to tuck herself behind the counter. "Look, I don't think we should talk for a while, okay? I need some time."

"What's a while?" asked Sam.

She noticed that her hand was shaking slightly as she opened the cupboard and reached for a bottle of wine. "I don't know. A few days. A week. It's not the kind of thing you nail down. We'll talk when we talk. And if you call before I'm ready, I'll let you know." She opened a drawer and found the corkscrew.

"So now you get to decide everything."

"No. I get to decide things for me. You get to decide for you. If you don't want to talk when I call, just say so."

"You know that won't happen."

"Look Sam, I don't want to deal with this now, okay? I'll call you soon."

Silence.

"Okay?" She assumed the burning in her chest was guilt and tried to ignore it.

"Whatever." He hung up.

In the living room Jon was on the floor, roughly stroking Nancy, who seemed to be enjoying herself — rolling on her back, purring, rubbing her face against his hand.

"I can't believe she's letting you do that." Indigo poured two glasses of wine and sat on the couch. "You must have some kind of pied piper thing going on, because she never ever goes there. She hates the fire."

As Jon got up, Nancy paused for a moment, on the verge —

nose red and wet, pupils black — before tearing out of the room and down the hall.

He raised his glass. "Salute. To crazy women. I mean cats. To crazy cats."

Indigo felt oddly shy, unnerved by the intensity of Jon's grey eyes, the smoothness of his face.

"Wait," he said. "Before you start. We don't need this, do we?" He reached across her lap and turned the lamp off. "That's better. So tell me. What's going on?"

When a second bottle of wine had been opened and the conversation had shifted from Sam and Graham to the distaste of married life in general, then on to ambition, art and Alice, Indigo said — "Now it's your turn. What about you? Tell me your story."

Jon stood up and stretched. "Twenty-one," he said, walking over to the bird and pretending to choke its skinny metal neck. "But I'm wise beyond my years."

"Everyone thinks that," said Indigo. "It's hardly ever true."

Jon moved around to the back of the sculpture, letting his hand brush down its length. "Forever doesn't exist," he said. "My parents died when I was 4. They were watching television, must have been the news, when a car went out of control, crashed into the house. Right through the living room. I was asleep upstairs." His voice was even, like he'd told the story many times in the exact same words.

"God, is that true? That's terrible. I'm sorry."

"Don't be. I mean, I don't remember it or nothing. I was raised by an uncle."

"In Toronto?"

"Everywhere. He's a diplomat. Washington. England for a while. Spain. Africa." As he sat back down beside her, he said — "I never fought a bull but you should see me rumba." And then he kissed her. A kiss that made her lower belly hum, sent blurry streaks of pleasure up her neck. Her thoughts quivered. Or it might have been her inner thighs. (She imagined they were laughing.)

Indigo leaned back, overwhelmed by the faint smell of cologne and the sweetness of his mouth. His hand felt hot through her tights; everything felt hot, especially under her tights. She imagined a voice inside her head — "Excuse me. EXCUSE ME. Have you completely lost your mind?" It sounded like Sam.

"Hold on," she said, pulling away for a sip of her drink. She considered stopping, telling him she couldn't do this. But she knew that, at best, she'd manage an "I shouldn't do this," which would leave him free to convince her. And the idea of putting up even a weak protest seemed silly. Why would she want to do that?

As he pressed her into the couch, she tried to memorize the softness of his face, and the brush of his fingers as they crept beneath her shirt. Indigo's own hand slid across his shoulders and chest, cautiously at first — until she discovered the ring in his nipple — and then with the abandon of a willing sinner.

Fourteen

Indigo woke to the smell of her mother's perfume, the weight of Jon along her back and a slow, silent scream inside her head. The telephone rang — accusingly, she thought — and, as if in response, Jon began kissing her shoulder, prodding her ass with his morning hello.

"Don't you want to get that?"

She wondered if he meant the phone.

If she didn't move, maybe he'd go home and the ringing would stop.

She wasn't ready, didn't know how to

respond in the glare of the morning, whether Jon's roaming hand was a good thing; it felt like a good thing — it felt like an exceptional thing — at the moment, skimming up her thigh.

Damn. The phone had shut up, finally, but Sam hung up and called again. There was no question it was him. Indigo could feel him at the other end of the line, cursing, calling her names under the censored bleep of the ring. Or maybe that was her, chiding herself. Nobody else knew she'd slept with two men in three days, one she barely knew — who, of course, was the one behind her now, ready to make a wet spot on her mother's favourite sheets. Again.

I have no reason to feel guilty, she thought, remembering the expression on his face, hair falling forward, as he pinched her nipple in his lips. But what did reason have to do with anything, especially guilt? It was obvious: she was planning to suffer for this one. She smiled and rolled toward him, sliding down.

In that case, what the hell.

Later, after she fed the cats and flipped some eggs, turned down a final fuck on the grounds that she was late for something, kissed Jon inside the door and nonchalantly checked the street before he left, Indigo crawled back into Alice's bed. But even as she lay, intent on the details of the night — that fine, hot mouth and all that lovely smooth/hard/softness — she couldn't help but think of Sam. She put her head on Jon's pillow and thought of the hurt in Sam's voice, pulled the covers over her face and saw the look in his eyes when she told him she wasn't coming home.

This wasn't going to work.

She pulled the phone onto the bed and dialled the person most likely to applaud the unveiling of her wild side, with no success.

"Hello babies. This is Nicole. Can't come to the phone right now, so tell it to the beep. See ya later."

She hung up and tried Tim.

"Hey. Leave a message and I'll call you back."

"Hi, it's me. Hope you're not busy tonight, I need a date. I have tickets for Peter's play — don't ask — it's opening night, and the party after. I don't know what it's called or what it's about or anything, but you probably do. So call me. I'm home. At Alice's. You know what I mean. Anyway, call me."

As Indigo made the bed she thought of the word dalliance, related to dally as in wasted time — not an aspersion she tended to cast on sex. When she and Sam first met, they used to spend what seemed like days in bed. Seemed that way because they were. Days. Leaving the sheets only for replenishment. Wine and snacks. The occasional shower. Condoms.

She wondered if Jon was someone she could spend a day or two in bed with, whether the hours would dissolve or stretch on end, interminable, if there was nothing to be had but sex and conversation.

Indigo couldn't resist smiling. Her younger self might have wondered on a more ambitious scale: whether he was a man she could be in love with, if not for the rest of her life then at least a few years.

To her current self the better deal seemed like a couple days in bed — although she did recognize that current in her case meant this precise moment and that change was inevitable, perhaps even imminent, however unwelcome.

Downstairs, she sat at the dining room table, both feet pressed against the floor. The sheet of silver looked flawless, and she found the first scratch of the compass vaguely thrilling. Maybe graffiti artists felt the same way as they sprayed the first line of paint on a bare brick wall. That sense of something changed forever, of never going back.

To cut the circle for the lid she sat hunched forward, silver firm in her left hand, saw in the right, pushing the blade up and down as evenly as possible, trying not to think of Jon. When the phone rang her hand jerked forward and the saw blade snapped in half. "Shit," she said, letting the saw drop hard on the table and reaching for the phone. It was her third broken blade in an hour. "Hello."

"Baby sweet love darling." It was Tim.

"Hey, how's it going? Did you get my message?"

"I did and I'd love to."

"Great."

"One thing though."

"What's that?"

"I told Darcey she could meet us after and come to the party. You don't mind, do you? We were supposed to go out."

"No, of course, that's fine. You can have two dates. You want to just meet me there? It's at the Final Stage. The show's at eight, so about a quarter to?"

"Yeah, that's good. It's supposed to be quite the play. Real edge city."

"You know, I forgot to ask what it's called. Isn't that awful? I haven't got the tickets yet, they're at the —"

"*Bite Me.*"

"Excuse me?"

"It's called *Bite Me.*"

"Are you serious? That's too weird."

"Peter says it's some kind of S&M love story. The lead's a masochist. From what I hear, the party's gonna be crazy. You got any leather?"

"No. Do you?"

"Yeah, you remember those pants. I haven't worn them since the '80s. But anything black'll be fine."

"Cool. I can do that."

As she began filing the edges of the silver disk, Indigo tried to list every man she'd ever slept with, including the two single nighters she pretended to forget.

It worried her that although the number — fourteen — seemed respectably high, she'd never been able to maintain what she thought of as an honest sexual relationship. It had looked promising with Sam, at first. But it seemed like the closer they got in every way but sex, the further apart they were in bed.

It was never allowed to just be fun, once they were married.

And frankly, she resented his lack of imagination.

Sam had called her sex-obsessed. (He would, she thought.) She did not however agree, since at least part of her preoccupation lay beyond the act itself, in the message it delivered. Not that she didn't enjoy sex; as she tried to explain to Nicole, there was nothing more poetic than the purity of those few orgasmic seconds. And nothing more pleasurable, on so many levels, than hours on end in bed, naked in the right combination.

But to Indigo's mind, sex was also the measure of desire. A lot and it was there, none and it wasn't. As obvious as an erection in a bathing suit and just as hard to hide.

She looked at the phone, then sighed and put the saw down.

Sam answered on the second ring. "Hi," she said. "It's me."

"I called this morning. Where were you?"

"Still in bed. Listen, I'm sorry about last night, okay? I was kind of abrupt. But I meant what I said, maybe we shouldn't talk for a while. Take some time, see what happens."

"Let me get this right. You're calling to remind me that you don't want to talk to me?"

"No, I need to come and get some things. If you're going to be around later. I thought I'd pop by, use the car to get some stuff. I'll bring it back tomorrow. If that's okay with you. Unless you need it."

"Why ask? You always do exactly what you want."

She could say the same to him, she thought. "Okay. In about an hour then."

"I'll be here." His voice sounded small. "Maybe we can have a cup of coffee or something — if it's not too much to deal with."

Until that afternoon, she'd been subtle about the transfer of effects. A duffel bag filled, pocket of earrings and bracelets, half a dozen books, extra pair of shoes. Only small and immediate things, barely enough to notice they were gone.

By contrast, the suitcase at the door seemed so decisive.

"This feels like a dumb question but I have to ask," said Sam. "Does this mean we're separated?" They were sitting at the kitchen table, both with hands around their mugs of coffee.

"I don't know," she said. "Why, someone else in line? Graham maybe?"

"Don't be stupid, it's not like that. I want to know what's going on. That's all. If it's over, tell me."

"Hard to be sure."

He didn't say anything at first, just stared into the yard. And then, turning back to face her — "This is ridiculous. Indigo, I'm sorry for what I did. I mean I'm really sorry, but nothing I say seems to matter." Between them sat an open box of shortbread which he pushed toward her. "Here, I know you like these."

"No. Thanks."

"You want to know what kills me? I actually spent time thinking about how you'd react if you found out. I knew you'd be mad, but I didn't let it stop me. Hell, it barely slowed me down. I didn't think you'd ever have to know. And even if you did, I figured you'd take it — like you always take it when I do something selfish. I thought you'd yell and cry, make me promise a bunch of things. Then I'd buy you flowers or maybe something better, have sex and that'd be the end of it." He tried to smile but the corners of his mouth stayed down. "I guess I was wrong, huh?"

Shifting position, Indigo angled her body to the side and

crossed her legs away from him. She seemed to fold in on herself, the closest she could get to fetal in a chair. She spoke quietly.

"First of all, if things had been good between us, this probably never would have happened. But aside from that, how could you think this was small? It's a huge fucking betrayal. How could you not have seen that?" Leaning toward him, she picked up a piece of shortbread, turned it over in her hand, then put it down. "I keep wondering what I would have done if you told me. In advance. Would I have freaked out, tried to talk you out of it? Would I have wanted to watch? I like to think I'd have been at least a little open-minded." She sighed and leaned back. "Now, when I look at you, I keep thinking how dangerous it is to project your own thoughts onto someone to the point that you believe — I mean, you really believe — you know them. It's like a great big joke on humanity. Everyone does it. Maybe we have to. Maybe if we saw each other the way we really were, nobody'd ever get together. Laid, sure. Married, not a chance." She stood up. "Look, I'm tired. I don't want to do this."

"You have to do this. I mean, for Christ's sake, we've only —"

"I don't want to think about it, not until I've had a chance to breathe. Right now the edges of everything seem out of focus. What we talk about, how I feel, what I want. Every time I see you, we talk in circles and I end up mad or in tears and more confused than ever. Sometimes I think I should just get over it, try to do the old forgive and forget thing. Other times I can't even stand the taste of your name in my mouth." She gave him a small, weary smile and touched his hand. "Hey, that's not bad. Don't you think? Feel free to use that."

He pulled his hand away. "I can't believe this," he said. "I can't fucking believe this. You expect me to just hang around and wait. Twiddle my dick until you say we're getting divorced." And then softer, almost pleading — "At least give me a hint. Tell me if you think it's temporary. Or do I need a lawyer?"

She stood up to leave. "Do what you want."

He followed her down the hall. "What I want is my life back, which means you come home and things go back to normal, the way they were — only better. I promise they'll be better. Then I can get some work done, not to mention sleep. Then it's like you always say you want, happily ever after. End of story."

"Hope you have a second choice," she said, letting the screen door slap behind her.

At home — which her mother's house had once again become — she unpacked and lit a fire. She lay on the couch and closed her eyes, felt trapped inside her brain, got up and put some water on for tea.

Sam was right, she was being unreasonable. Maybe a contrite husband was, in fact, the best that she could hope for. What if she divorced him and ended up drifting from one bad choice to the next, each new relationship making her feel just a little more used up, a little more alone, and older — a lot older? What if leaving Sam became the regret that eclipsed all other regrets? What if she turned into a bitter old woman sitting on a park bench sucking dusty candies from the bottom of her purse and mumbling to herself about the good old days when she was married, even if her husband was, generally speaking, a cranky, self-absorbed fuckwit?

In the space of an hour, fear and blame expanded in Indigo's veins, overtaking what was left of her righteous indignation. Until she thought of the pinched cement path beside her house, the pressure of its walls and the dread that made her think of death. At least there she knew enough to run, focused on her freedom. How many times had she felt that way with Sam? Confined by his moods. Frustrated to the point of rage. Yet rooted to the bed she made.

This was her chance.

Or maybe Jon was her chance. Not that she was getting serious; she simply knew herself enough to understand that he was useful. A happy distraction.

Then again, she did marry the guy. There must have been something that made her think they could do it till death did them part. Indigo rubbed her forehead, trying to remember what it was about him, wondering why she still sometimes faked an orgasm, since he didn't seem to notice. Analysis paralysis, she thought. Maybe Nicole could recommend that shrink.

She was still obsessing when the phone rang.

"Hello?"

"Hi honey." The line echoed badly.

"Mom, it's you." At the sound of her mother's voice, Indigo started to cry.

It had stopped raining, but the street was wet and the air still damp and cold. Indigo stood inside the foyer, waiting for Tim, hoping to see Jon, hoping not to, dreading that first uncomfortable moment.

She left the car at home, in case she decided to drink. It seemed like a good idea. Drinking. As much as it took to make her cheerful, not enough to edge her into maudlin. It sounded like a plan.

A fire truck screamed by, followed by a second then a third, as a woman in a black velvet cape and leather bodysuit swept through the doors, unsmiling, boots to her thighs over fishnet, long satin gloves.

Indigo watched from a corner as people arrived in twos and threes and fours, amusing herself by inferring their intimate details.

That woman in the red coat is plotting the murder of her hairdresser, for one bad perm too many. If she gets caught she'll be acquitted. Women everywhere will rally, say she was pushed too far. And then — adjusting to the theme of the evening — that looks like a man with a fetish for neatness, someone who does it into white linen napkins folded smartly into swans. The man in the rear went out alone last night. He allowed himself to be seduced by an alien, who gave him the best fuck of his life and is, on this very night, about to lay a cross-species egg. He thinks she was from New York.

Seduced. Now there's a thought. Two people. One in control, one persuaded. Which was she? And what if Jon assumed he was going home with her tonight, what would she tell him then? It stood to reason that the remedy for emotional overload might be a little sensory deprivation. The intelligent response would be to spend some time alone. Still, if he asked nicely ...

As Tim came through the door, she spotted Jon across the street with his arm around a woman. Big blond hair above a long dark coat. "Oh, God."

She turned away quickly, forcing a smile.

"You look great," said Tim. She was wearing the requisite small black dress and heels, with seamed stockings and a short leather jacket. But her attempt seemed suddenly pale.

"You too. Come on, it's cold. Let's go in."

It was intermission before Jon spotted them — standing off to the side near a pillar, watching the slaves work the room with trays of champagne and chocolates shaped like genitalia. The slaves wore studded collars and leather harnesses, with chains across the chest. They avoided eye contact and weren't allowed to speak.

"They can't be the real thing," said Indigo, chewing the inside of her mouth. "They look too much alike, too perfect."

She and Tim were trying to decide if the barely clad men were actors. "But when you think about it, what a concept. A gorgeous naked guy to do anything you want, clean your house."

"I'll get you one for Christmas, if you're good. Do you think there's a girl version? The thought of a woman who does what you tell her, it goes against anything I've ever seen or —"

"There you are," said Jon, putting his hand on Indigo's shoulder. "Did you meet Gina?"

"I don't think so." Indigo wished the bells would ring to announce the second act, override this conversation.

Gina said — "You look familiar."

Indigo shrugged, avoiding Jon. "I don't know, maybe."

"It would have been at the student show," he said. "Gina's in my video class. She and her boyfriend were the stars of that installation I did. You remember. In any case, Gina — this is Indigo and Tim."

"So that was you," said Indigo, feeling the tension drain from her smile. "That wig was incredible." She turned to Tim — "Gina wore this cool black wig, straight to the shoulders. Very hot."

"You should give it a try sometime," said Gina. "It's like you're this whole other person. Nigel — that's my boyfriend — he says he can't believe it's the same old me. Says it's like dating some weird psycho chick who keeps showing up with different personalities. But I know he loves it. Picked this one himself." She tilted her head to the side. "Here, feel it."

"I will," said Tim, petting its length. "Wow, it's soft. You'd never know the difference."

"You pretty much have to go for the expensive ones," said Gina. "When they're cheap they look like shit. Tacky. Completely unconvincing. Like those awful toupees, the hair equivalent of white belts and polyester suits." As a slave passed, she lifted a glass of champagne from his tray, took a sip and said — "I was born to be a bitch."

"We were just talking about that," said Tim. "I think Indigo'd like a guy on his knees, washing her floors in the nude."

"I never said that."

"Oh, come on. How long have I known you?"

"Sounds good to me," said Gina. "As long as he's using his tongue."

Tim made a face. "Yuck. That's about as erotic as a smack in the head."

"Now you're catching on," said Jon, and everyone laughed as Peter slipped in beside Indigo, put his arm around her waist and licked her face.

"Hello to you," she said, wiping her cheek. "And yuck."

"Welcome to my night. I hope you like the play. I'm horny." He looked at Indigo — "You want to come backstage?"

"I don't think so."

He turned to Gina. "You?"

"Get real."

"But I'm the writer, the playwright, the man with a mind as deranged as this production, and even more fabulous. I need admirers, hangers on, an entourage. What's wrong with you people?" Peter scowled at them for a moment, then smirked. "Oh fine then. Be like that. You'll change your minds, just wait until the party. You'll be surrounded by sex. We'll all be surrounded." He winked at Indigo. "See you in the dark, my darling."

As they watched him stride away, Tim looked at Jon and said — "He seems just a tad wound up."

The decor was faux dungeon, with a maze of smaller rooms shooting off a large main chamber, and walls painted to look like damp stone blocks. The slaves had graduated from passing out drinks to other, presumably more satisfying duties. They were strung to walls and crawling on the floor, bending over to have their bottoms whipped or paddled, licking boots.

Indigo spoke in Tim's ear — "Looks like you're out of luck," she said. "They're still all guys."

The date dynamic had shifted en route. Darcey and Tim were together, and Gina's boyfriend had shown up looking sullen, upset by the garters on display beneath her very short skirt.

Jon ran his hand down Indigo's back as they waited in line at the bar. "So what do you think?"

"I don't know — amused, curious. Take your pick."

"I pick aroused," he said. "What'll you have?"

The bartender was a fat, balding man wedged into a leather corset, the flesh of his breasts tumbling over the top.

"Why do you think he does that?" she asked.

"What, pour drinks?"

She laughed. "No, wear that in public. Don't you think it's humiliating?"

Jon leaned into her ear and spoke softly — "I think that's the point."

As she looked around the room, Indigo said — "All right, here's one. Why do you think the slaves are all men?"

"He who writes the play gets to choose, I guess. We're getting a peek at Peter's inner child, and he's been a naughty naughty boy."

Exploring, they discovered a number of theme rooms: the predictable classroom, doctor's office and library, complete with ultra-strict school-marm, nurse and librarian. There was also a dentist's office, which Indigo refused to even contemplate, because — "I'm sorry Jon. There's nothing erotic about the dentist."

In the farthest room, they found Tim and Darcey watching a mini sex show, put on by a mistress and her crawling slave. "Lie on your stomach," said the woman, digging her heel into his ass, pushing him forward.

Darcey was half smiling and Indigo thought she looked mischievous, whispering in Tim's ear from time to time, sliding her fingers between the buttons of his shirt.

"Ow," he said, rubbing his chest where she twisted a piece of his flesh. "Who knew she was this impressionable."

Laughing, Darcey patted his shoulder and said — "I'm kidding, don't get your hopes up. Tell you the truth, I think it's pretty silly. I'm ready to go when you are."

Surprisingly, Jon turned to Indigo and said — "Me too. Had enough? I have a surprise for you at home."

"What kind of surprise?"

"You'll see. Come on, let's get out of here." He took her hand, but she stayed where she was, holding him back.

"Actually, no. Not tonight. I have a big day tomorrow, lots of work. I'm going to find Peter, say goodbye, head home. Another —"

"Forget tomorrow, Indigo.

"No, really. I —"

"Stop. Do not say no." He took her hand and held it to his chest. "It's time for you to loosen up, chickadee. Enjoy the moment."

Good argument, she thought. The man already knows my weak points.

Fits Like a Rubber Dress   189

They spotted Peter in one of the rooms, at the mercy of a small, clearly dangerous woman. She stood erect, a whip in one hand, the crotch of Peter's pants in the other. "I said on your knees." They decided not to disturb him.

As she followed Jon down the stairs, Indigo said — "You know, there's something I like about this place. Not that I want to be hung from pulleys or anything. I just like when people admit what turns them on, even though it seems nasty or deviant or at the very least weird to the majority. It's like most people are afraid to venture outside of this image they've created for themselves, I mean sexually. Especially in a relationship. If one partner grows or changes, or even if they stick to the same sex they've always had, and they never talk about it or push it in new directions, that's it. They're doomed to lose touch."

As they walked out onto the street, Indigo shivered and did up her coat, shoved her hands as deep into the tiny leather pockets as she could. "Never mind," she said. "It's hard to explain."

Jon whistled at a taxi, which turned off its light but didn't stop. "No, I think I understand," he said. "Your husband gets done by another guy and you're not sure you can buy his explanation. You think there's more to it. So you're going over the details, wondering if he has an actual bent or maybe just your basic, harmless homoerotic fantasy — and you can't find out because he won't cop to any of it."

As another cab pulled up, Indigo said — "That's the current example, sure. But I look back and I remember moments, a little something that really got him going — I don't know, like a scene in a movie or something — and it makes me realize that he has this whole erotic life that I'm not part of."

"And you don't have that?"

"Of course. Everyone does. But to a lesser degree. I tend to talk about it, too much according to him. I guess that's what gets me going, or one of the things — I like talking about sex. What can I tell you? So if I hold back on certain fantasies or whatever, it's because I've already said more than he wants to know. Way more."

As they drove west, past the commotion of downtown into a more deserted industrial landscape, Jon said — "So you didn't answer me before. What did you think of the scene?"

"I liked it, I guess. It was pretty cool. I don't know." She was thinking that she did like it, but she didn't know why. She had no desire for pain and less to be humiliated. She didn't want to swing a whip or give the orders. She didn't want involvement. But there was something about being in the room that made her feel, if not quite part of the action, then at least an accessory to it. Sam would have said she was being ridiculous, but she found the whole thing almost glamorous. The shiny clothes. Cinched flesh. Behaviour that was raunchy enough to frighten the masses and yet to her mind strangely dignified (if that made any sense at all and she was pretty sure it didn't). It would piss her father off, for sure; she could almost hear him ranting about the degeneration of society. She liked that too.

Indigo shifted in her seat. School hadn't become the battle with her father she expected; he called a few weeks after their fight, suspiciously calm, and said she was old enough make her own bad decisions. "I should have sent you to private school," was his final weak jab. "It'll be different with the boys."

An anxious thought flickered in her head but disappeared before she grasped it, a feeling of hollow disquiet. When her mother left, Indigo had been surprised to discover she was even less inclined to see her dad. She thought she'd need him. And sure, they spoke on the phone every now and again. But there was something about being cut off from Sam and both her parents; doing things she knew they'd disapprove of; having secrets.

She turned to Jon and said — "I think I must have voyeuristic tendencies."

He nodded, watching her face. "This was pretty tame compared to some. If you're interested, I know this woman. She throws a few parties a year. We could go some time, see what you think." He ran his hand up her thigh, curling his fingers on the flesh above her stocking. "But you'll have to dress the part."

Around the side of a darkened building, through a steel door and into a freight elevator, up several flights and down a fluorescent hallway, was the door to Jon's studio, painted yellow with a target in the middle. Red, white and black.

As he opened the door, he said — "Bull's-eye."

The room was a box, as tall as it was wide or deep. Windows waist high to the ceiling along the length of two walls. Organized clutter. To the right — under the window — a platform and a futon, books underneath. To the left, a kitchenette. In the middle, a small Mexican rug and loveseat, two wooden crates for tables. Evidence of artwork everywhere. An easel on a drop sheet. A table spread with tubes and jars of paint and brushes, spatulas and rags. At least half a dozen tool boxes. Tripod. Video camera. Sketchbooks on the dresser.

Along the left wall, masking tape held sheets of drawings and paintings, most unfinished, over what appeared to be an abstract mural. "Great place," said Indigo. "How come you're hiding the mural?"

"What? Oh, that's not anything. I got mad one day. Threw a bunch of paint. Smeared it around. Felt better." The phone rang but he didn't pick it up; instead he took his pager off his belt and tossed it in a drawer.

From the window, she could see the lights of the city centre in the distance and the darkness that spread in between. She threw her coat on the bed and rubbed her arms to shake the chill. "So where's my surprise?"

Jon laughed. "First a drink," he said. "Beer okay?"

"Sure. Anything."

He put their glasses on a crate and lit a candle, opened a small wooden box. Inside — two pills the size of aspirin. Small, round and pink, with a heart stamped into the surface.

"What's that?"

"E. Ever done it?"

"No, but Tim does. All the time. That's ecstasy, right?"

"Then I'm your first."

"Not necessarily," she said. "What does it do?"

"Everything."

She felt an odd, excited tingling and wondered how she could even think of being aroused after last night's acrobatics. "Could you be more specific?"

"I looked it up once. Ecstasy. In the dictionary. They called it the frenzy of poetic inspiration. I thought it was a good description. Of the drug, I mean. Except without the frenzy part. It's a few hours of joy, that's all. Nothing extreme or scary. No big hangover, unless you drink a lot which you won't because I don't have much to drink." He handed her a pill. "It'll make everything beautiful. You'll see."

"Sounds like an anti-depressant," she said, staring at the tablet in her palm while Jon put the other on his tongue and drank some beer.

"To say the least." When she still hesitated, he said — "Listen, don't worry. You're gonna love it. I swear. Would I do anything to hurt you?"

At that moment, with a beer in one hand and a promise in the other, it occurred to Indigo that she had absolutely no idea whether Jon would hurt her or not. She didn't think so. Not with a face like that.

For the next half hour, they sat on the loveseat and waited. Jon wanted to know about Sam. Did she plan to go back? Did she love him? Was their sex good? Difficult questions. Muddy answers. I don't know. Maybe. Sometimes.

"Have you ever been with a woman?"

"No. I've thought about it, I think probably everyone's thought about it. But no. It sounds like one of those fantasies that's better left there. What about you?"

"I've been with a number of women."

"That's not what I meant. More than one at a time?"

"Mostly in pairs." He smiled. "Never with a man. Not yet."

"So you think you're bisexual. What is it with me and the opposite sex?"

"No, just curious. I like to think I'm hard to categorize. I belong in the miscellaneous pile, straight with an asterisk, read the fine print, certain exceptions apply. I think a lot of people are like that — my God, we may be on the verge of a trend." He took her hand out of her lap and kissed it. "You know, I read someplace that a lot of babies are born both male and female. Well, maybe not a lot, but more than ever. Hermaphrodites. Because the world is a fucked up place. Because mothers sniff glue or smoke or drink. And all those toxic chemicals. In our food and water, breast milk, the air we breathe, everywhere you can possibly —"

"I sort of thought that was getting better, I don't know why. You know, overall. It's not like we're living in the dark ages. These aren't the '50s. We can see what a mess we've made in the past, so it stands to reason that we'd start taking better care of things."

"You would think that. Of course you would, you're very sweet. Deluded, but sweet. And it'd be nice if it was true. But progress is like one of those moving walkways at the airport. Once you're on you can't get off, even if you want to buy a magazine. It's like, look around. There's too many of us. And we're all taking and eating and building and throwing out and generally pissing it all away. It's all our faults —"

"Are they healthy?"

"Who?"

"The hermaphrodites."

"I think so, but it doesn't matter. The doctors go ahead lob their little things off anyway. Problem solved, or so they think. I'm not so sure. Can you really force them all to be girls, if they're born in between like that?"

"I don't know. It might be worse to have both. Can you imagine? If you happened to live in some corner of the world where a paisley shirt is enough to get a guy a beating. What a life. But you know what?" She sighed and put her hand on the crown of her head. "I think I'm starting to feel something. The top of my head feels warm."

As she stood up, a yawn floated out from her smile and carried her into a stretch. She lifted her arms above her head and twisted her back as she walked to the window, let out a small moan of pleasure.

Jon said — "It's good to stretch, I don't know why. Helps you get off."

Indigo climbed onto the sill and stood. "It's starting to rain again," she said, pressing her palms against the glass. The road seemed to shimmer in the glow from the streetlights, although it might have been her eyes. Cement had never shone like this before. It looked like water, dark and calm. Or ice.

She rolled her head from side to side, allowing the warmth to spread from the back of her scalp, down her neck and into her limbs. She imagined tiny waves of blood beneath her skin, pulsing, as her hands drifted over the softness of her own breasts, down past her sides and hips, to the curve of her thighs.

Jon was beside her, inhaling the smell of her hair, touching her back, looking past her at the sky. "We need music," he said, and she watched him climb back down to the floor. "Something not too fast, not too slow."

She made her way across the room behind him, thinking that he might just be the most beautiful man she'd ever seen. "And I need a kiss," she said. "Not too hard, not too wet. The softest kiss ever put on a pair of lips."

Afterwards, she spoke thoughtfully. "Don't you think it's weird that lips come in pairs? It seems to me that the top and bottom lip are really just two sides of the same thing. Like pants. We call them pants, even a pair of pants, when its really just one item of clothing. It makes no sense."

Jon pulled her over to the couch and onto his lap. "You're right about the pants, not the lips. With that logic, fingers would all count as one because they're joined at the bottom. Five fingers, one hand. Two lips, one mouth." He kissed the tips of her fingers, then moved to her face and her lips, the top and then the bottom.

"You win," she said. "But I think I'm thirsty. Have you got another beer?"

"That too," he said. "I have an idea."

"Tell me."

"I want to paint you."

"Now? That seems like work."

"No, I want to paint on you. We can wash it off later. Are you warm enough to be naked?"

In the corners of her eyes were trails of light, flashes of white and pink and green. A shiver leapt up and down her spine and she started to laugh. "Okay," she said. She was conscious of the music in her voice. "That sounds nice. Let's be naked."

Fifteen

The smell of bacon tugged at the lining of her stomach, dragging her up from that last, light layer of sleep. She opened her eyes, then closed them quickly. Jon was on the other side of the room, humming as he flipped what appeared to be an omelet — altogether too cheerful for someone who went to sleep as the sun began to rise.

Indigo's thoughts wandered back in pursuit of a clue to her own state of mind.

At her insistence, Jon had taken his clothes off as well, then spread a dropsheet on the floor while Indigo piled her hair on the top of her head. He turned her into a swirl of thick red and fine white stripes. The paint had been cold, the strokes of the brush a soft, reptilian tongue. And as she stood, naked in the centre of the room, she thought how liberating it was to be revealed yet unselfconscious. Unfazed by her exposed, quivering flesh.

She remembered yammering on as the thoughts leapt into her head. Women should think of their bodies as ripening, she said, instead of aging — adding that the metaphor should end before the person began to rot. On the other hand, maybe it wasn't such a good comparison.

Jon said she was beautiful, she remembered that.

And then he reached for the video camera, to prove her boldness to herself. Up close at first, standing with her back to the lens, then her front, twirling in circles. On the window sill. That was when Jon got dressed and went outside, shot her from the street. Standing in the window, arms spread. A silhouette. And before she remembered to worry, he gave her the tape. Said to put it with her jacket.

"Listen," he said. "This is important. There are things I have to show you."

He said he wanted to rescue, mend, then release her into the wilderness. Not that he had any right to interfere, but hadn't her marriage become sort of — well, institutional? He wanted to sign her out, set her free. She needed more. He could taste it in her mouth.

In the shower, they watched as the paint washed away like blood from an open wound. And then, with her hair still wet, she'd agreed. They were drinking tea, getting sleepy. Or she thinks she agreed to something. But what? She wouldn't have made any promises. Not yet.

They ate breakfast on the loveseat, Jon in a pair of shorts, Indigo in a T-shirt that said — THEY CALLED HER TEENAGE TRAMP.

"I think I'll take a cab," she said. "I can't stand the thought of wearing Saturday night clothes on a Sunday morning. It's like a sin or something, not that I pay attention to things like that. Obviously."

"Try Sunday afternoon," said Jon.

"You're kidding. Damn." She stuffed the last of her toast in her mouth as she walked to the sink. "The cats are going to be pissed. I've got to get out of here."

"So what are you going to tell him?"

"Tell who, Sam?" She found some dish soap under the counter.

"Sure. Why drag it out? If it isn't happening — and you say it isn't — end it. Sever the ties. You can't honestly want to live that kind of life, can you? Relentless domesticity."

Indigo had to laugh. "It's not as bad as all that. I don't know. I don't know what I'm going to do. Probably nothing yet." She turned on the tap. "I still feel kind of shell-shocked."

Jon stared at her from the couch. "Oh. I get it."

"What do you get?"

"Nothing. Forget it. Forget I said anything." He put his plate on the floor, still half filled with food.

"Oh come on. You're not going to get all weird on me now, are you?"

"I'm not getting weird." He paused. "You don't know what you want. I do."

"And what would that be?"

Jon leaned back, crossing his legs and putting his arm on the back of the couch. "You know damn well, Ms. Blackwell. That would be you."

"That's crazy. That's what that is. We've gone out, like twice." She paused. "Gone out. How's that for a benign little euphemism?"

"That's got nothing to do with nothing. Thing is, I know it's good. No, not good. Great. If you can't see that —" He got up and walked to the sink, putting his arms around her from behind and pressing his teeth softly into her shoulder. "Then I guess I'll have to show you."

In the bathroom, Indigo washed her face and rinsed her mouth with toothpaste. Not a complete wreck, she thought, pulling her hair into a messy bun. There was a ladder in one of her stockings and she felt a little slow, but that was just the void, empty space where one might expect a hangover.

The aftermath of ecstasy. A small price, really.

She wished she hadn't left the car at home.

As the taxi slowed to a stop in front of her house, Indigo handed the driver a ten dollar bill. She wanted to say *keep moving*, that she changed her mind, that he couldn't leave her yet. The words *get me the hell away from here* repeated themselves over and over, burrowing into her brain. Out loud, she said — "That's okay, keep the change."

The air smelled of falling leaves and mulch and, in the distance, burning wood. If the moment were different, she might have closed her eyes, raised her face to the sun and smiled, letting the heat sink into her skin. But she couldn't. Not with Sam sitting on the steps, waiting.

He watched her get out of the cab, then stood as she approached, blocking her path. "Where have you been?"

"At a friend's." She walked past him to the door.

"What friend?"

"I don't have to tell you that. What are you doing here?"

Inside, the cats pushed against her legs, bawling. "Just a minute," she said, raising her voice to shut them up. It didn't work. They ran part way down the hall toward the kitchen, then stopped, turned around to see if she was coming, yelled some more.

"I need the car," he said.

"You should have called."

"I did."

"Then you should have called again."

He shook his head. "I don't think so. Then I'd have to accept whatever bullshit line you threw me." He followed her into the kitchen. "What did you think? That I'd sit home waiting for you to grace me with a few minutes of your precious fucking time, while you're off slutting about? I want to know who you were with."

She thought for a moment, then said — "You don't know him. It's not a big deal. We're friends." And then — "I met him at Tim's birthday party. You know, the one you stood me up for. Oh sure, we became fast friends. He took me to a boozecan and everything. After the party. As a matter of fact, I got home just before you did. When was that? Gee, it must have been after four o'clock." For the sake of her advantage, she skipped the part about the student show.

"Did you sleep with him?"

"That would be none of your business."

Sam's face hardened. "You're a bitch."

Indigo reached into her purse for the car keys, then tossed them on the counter. "I guess that's it then."

He picked them up.

As he left, she called out — "You can't tell me what to do any more. Do you hear me? I don't care what you think." Holding onto the counter, she watched him in her mind as though she'd followed him out to the car. The tears finally came as he unlocked the door, got inside and drove away without a backward glance.

"You should have seen the way he looked at me," said Indigo, holding up a black leather boot. "What do you think of these."

Nicole shrugged. "They're okay. The square toe thing's kind of over though."

Indigo said — "I was wearing these black stockings, with a huge run in the thigh. It set the tone beautifully. He was disgusted and you know what? I don't care. It's like I've been released from some kind of orbit. I don't feel the pull of his judgement." She looked at the bottom of a clog, then dropped it on the ground, took her own shoe off and slipped it on. "I had a pair of these in high school," she said. And then — "You know, I'm sick to death of trying to stay on his good side."

"So what are you going to do? I know a lawyer."

Indigo put the clog back on the shelf. "I don't know. I'm not just sick of him, I'm sick of everything. I'm sick of myself."

Nicole reached for a pointed brown suede boot, then gave it to the salesman. "Seven and a half," she said. And then — "So you don't want a divorce."

"I don't know what I want," said Indigo. "I never thought I'd be the one to walk — unless I was totally sure that we couldn't work it out. But as Jon would say, why beat it to death?"

Sitting down, Nicole took off her shoes and stretched her toes. "The young stud," she said. "Been seeing a lot of him?"

"More than I should." Indigo already hated that she couldn't stop thinking about him — wondering where he was, hoping he'd call, wearing clothes with him in mind, washing her hair every damned day — not wanting to cop to any of it. "But listen, I don't want to talk about that. I almost forgot. Let's see the body art."

Nicole accepted the boots and put them on, then stood in front of the mirror. She was wearing a tight black skirt and tighter grey cardigan. Once she'd stared a while (turning to both sides, sticking her breasts out, smoothing down her sweater) she smiled and said — "That's it. They have to be mine." With the decision made, she undid the top two buttons of her sweater, then pulled it off her shoulder. Between her spine and the strap of her bra was a tree within a braided circle, in deep black ink. "It's the tree of life. Pretty cool, huh."

Indigo ran her fingers over the surface. "It's awesome," she said. "But don't you think you'll get bored of it after a while?"

"Not a chance," said Nicole, watching Indigo's reflection stare at her back. "The roots symbolize a connection with the life we're living — the earth, here and now, yada yada yada. And the branches reach out to the stars or the next life, whatever you want to believe. But in shaman cultures, trees are sacred. So it wouldn't be the physical earth at all, just levels of the dream world."

Indigo nodded slowly. "I didn't know you were into all that."

"I'm not. I just like it." As she readjusted her sweater, Nicole looked coolly at the salesman, who'd slipped in beside Indigo to watch. "I'll take those," she said. "And something to clean them with."

Indigo was still focused on the back of Nicole's sweater. "You know, that's exactly what I need." And then, when Nicole gave her the *I don't think so* look, she said — "No, I mean it. It's perfect. Did it hurt?"

"Sure. Not for long. You really think you'd want one?"

"Why not?"

"I just didn't think you would, that's all. You're so —"

"So what?"

"Indecisive. Like you said, you want everything, so you can't commit to anything. These don't rub off, you know."

"They don't? Gee, I guess I better not then. Come on Nicole, support me on this. It'd be cool, don't you think? In a place that's not so obvious. Like here, above my butt. Something in honour of change."

As they waited, Nicole spotted a matching purse. "Here, I'll take this too." Indigo, who had tried on a pair of sunglasses and was now stooped in front of the too-small/too-low mirror, trying to imagine what they'd look like without the tag hanging down her nose, said — "It's weird. I seem to be the least agitated when I'm doing something new. Does that make sense?" She gave up and put the glasses on the rack. "I don't have the answers, so I avoid the questions. Keep moving. And you know what? It makes me wonder why people spend so much time trying to deal with things in the first place. If it doesn't work, say goodbye. Do something else." As they walked out of the store, she said — "I guess I should divorce him, maybe. It might be too late. He was pretty mad when he left. He might divorce me."

"You don't seem too torn up about it," said Nicole.

"I have my moments. Not many, not yet anyway. Mostly I try to ignore it. It's the new me. I'm sick of thinking everything to death."

"Me too," said Nicole. "It's a real drag."

Indigo laughed. "Yeah right. You barely give anything a second thought. It's one of the great things about you."

"This is different," said Nicole, steering them into another boutique. "There's a skirt in here I want." And then — "Spider and I are spending tons of time together. It's going *well*."

"You sound like you're complaining."

"No. It's just that I didn't expect him to be so — I don't know, stable. I mean, he's like, in a band *and* he wants to have kids. Can you believe it? He actually said that."

"Are you into having kids?"

"It's hard to picture, isn't it? But I think you're on to something. Refuse to deal, see if it goes away. I've always been good at denial."

Indigo trailed behind Nicole, who moved along the racks, stopping to finger various items of clothing. "You know, I was at Tim's the other day, and he wanted to know if it occurred to me how rudderless we all are."

Nicole held up a slim grey skirt. "What did you say?"

"I didn't know what to say. I never thought of myself as rudderless, not like him. What's he ever wanted? Just that bar he used to talk about, the one on a beach in fantasy land."

"So where did all this come from?" asked Nicole. "Let's get real. This is Tim we're talking about." She slipped into a changeroom with the skirt.

"I know." Indigo frowned at herself in the mirror. "His mom's been on him again. Wants him to do the right thing, settle down, be a man. But that's nothing new. So it must be Darcey. Now there's a woman who's sure, don't you think?"

From behind the door, Indigo heard rustling, then Nicole's voice — "You think she wants kids?"

"I don't know. Probably not with him. I mean, come on. She seems pretty quick on the uptake. And anyway, even if she did, she wouldn't bring it up. She's way too smart for that. But you know what else he asked me?"

"What?"

"We were talking about the meaninglessness of human existence — you know, the usual stuff — and he wanted to know if I believe in God."

"Do you?"

When Nicole came out, she was wearing the skirt with her new suede boots. "The last time we had this conversation, you were having trouble with the whole suspending disbelief thing. That was a while ago."

"I told him I'd like to believe, that I hope to eventually. It's on my list of things to do." She pulled a piece of loose thread from Nicole's skirt, then added — "Sam believed in God all his life and now he doesn't. How come nobody I know believes in God? What do you think that is?"

"You'd be surprised," said Nicole. "Look around, God's making a comeback. He's da man. Or da woman. Whatever."

"And you?"

"Sure. Absolutely." She adjusted one of the mirror doors to look at her butt. "I believe."

"Since when?"

"I don't know, a while."

"You're kidding. You've become religious. Without telling me."

"I prefer spiritual," she said. "More flexibility."

Indigo flopped into one of the stuffed chairs meant no doubt to soothe impatient men. "See now, that's very cool," she said. "One day you don't, now you do. It's like, I can appreciate elements of a whole bunch of religions. The way people find God in a stone or a tree or —"

"Some brown suede boots," said Nicole.

"Sure. Why not? Brown suede boots. And I totally love that incense they burn in the swinging thing. Whatever. Oh, and the chanting. I saw this goddess ceremony on TV once, and they were chanting to Isis and I can't remember who else but it was amazing. I'd love to be part of something like that, you know? But it's always seemed to me that you can't just decide to believe; it has to be there. I'd like a pound of faith please."

Nicole looked at Indigo's reflection. "Isn't that why they call it faith? Think about it. If you did have proof, wouldn't that defeat the purpose? Where's the leap?" As she ducked into the changeroom, she said — "What does Tim think?"

"He doesn't have a clue. I don't think he's ever really thought about it. Before now I mean. It drives him nuts to plan ahead, always has. And I guess he figured that, even if he did choose to believe, he didn't have to yet — because God's a death thing, you know what I'm saying? I'm just guessing, but he probably thought that unless he was close, why worry? Maybe 30's close enough."

As Nicole paid for the skirt, she said — "Let's go find ourselves a drink. Shopping makes me thirsty. You can tell me all about your boy toy." She clasped her hands together playfully, adding emphasis with the bumping together of bags. "This is so unlike you. My baby's growing up."

Sixteen

The needle stung — not each time it pierced her flesh, over and over again a hundred times and more in quick succession — but in one expanding burn. It throbbed, which made Indigo strangely happy, made her feel intrepid. But, in fact, the physical pain was nothing compared to the agony of giving up control. Of bending forward over a chair so her skin was taut, unable to watch while a man she didn't know engraved her back with an indelible tribal design.

It was the pain of putting herself in someone else's hands completely.

Truth be known, she felt a little foolish.

The tattoo was small. Uncomplicated. A pattern within a circle, abstract, with fluid black lines ending in points, to the right of her spine above her dimple. Nowhere near as elaborate as the photos on the walls, designs that spread forcefully over backs and arms and thighs and feet and breasts and penises.

After jokes about buxom blondes on biceps, thorny roses, tiny birds and Playboy bunnies, she made an appointment with a studio that seemed to take things a tad more seriously. And then, in the time it took to get there, Indigo built what might have been a simple procedure into the launch of her new self; a symbol of her metamorphosis — from wife and woman on the cusp of upper management (or so the story had evolved) to something harder to define but better, infinitely more interesting. She was certain.

The permanence of this particular form of declaration both frightened and compelled her. She had a consultation, chose a design, asked questions.

The artist was a dream, tall and wispy, with a gentle voice and steady gaze — which she assumed spoke well of his hands. He suggested that she bring her favourite music; she wanted him to choose. Something soft with an African beat, that didn't make her want to dance. She'd bring the candles and incense.

They set a date and as she left she felt elated.

By the time she got home she was scared.

And so it went, back and forth until the day, the afternoon and then the moment.

She arrived early, sat in a chair by the door, contemplating the other part of the business, which was piercing. A poster on the wall showed a vagina strung with hoops. There were nipples, lips and tongues. Noses and eyebrows. And the one Indigo could barely keep her eyes off — a silver bar stuck straight through the head of a penis. It had to be a trick.

Upstairs, she tried to relax and be still, subdued by the roll of drums and a hint of perfumed smoke. The flame seemed to share her anxiety, fidgeting this way and that above the candle. Indigo's jaw was clenched. There were lines of expectation in her forehead. But the pain wasn't as sharp as she'd imagined and, after a while, bordered on a kind of pleasure, both exquisite and intense.

"It's the endorphins kicking in," he said. "Pretty nice, huh? Best high going."

They talked quietly, she at the mercy of his hands. About the energy that flows from the artist. The human desire for symbols.

"Tattooed a man's anus once. With flames."

Indigo thought about this for a moment before telling herself to stop; before deciding not to think about it — ever again — even though she knew full well she'd have to, now that it was there. "He was HIV?" she asked.

"Don't worry. Everything's sterile."

Looking at the wall, she found that in fact she wasn't worried, which worried her but only slightly. "My life just did a 180," she said. "But I don't just want something to symbolize that, I think in some weird way I want to prove it."

"Careful. I need you to keep still." And then — "Prove it to who?"

She smiled, noticing for the first time that she felt uncluttered, that the tension was gone from her neck. "I know I'm supposed to say myself," she said, shifting her gaze to the window. "But it wouldn't be the truth. Not the whole truth anyway. I mean, I guess it's pretty obvious."

He said something else in return, but she was barely listening.

She was focused on the sky that promised snow, caught up in her own bravado — amazed by the way she'd swerved off course, possibly out of control (it was hard for her to be objective). It was as though she was following some road farther and farther away from the person she thought of as home. It wasn't just the tattoo. She'd cut a class to be here, even though she felt behind and insecure. And she didn't tell Jon or anyone else beforehand, because that was one of the things she disliked about herself, her need to seek approval.

As the artist dabbed her wounds, she remembered there was blood. She wondered how much, feeling a ball of nausea form in her chest before telling herself to breathe, calm down, don't move. Don't dwell on what you can't see, she thought, and smiled a stoned smile of surrender.

She was floating on a tide of optimism. How lovely, those endorphins. Those pretty little points of light she imagined bouncing through her veins. Better than ecstasy; better than the frenzy of poetic inspiration.

When she called Jon, he said — "There's a party tomorrow night. I want you to come. We'll go shopping after school."

"For what?"

"I want you to wear something you never thought you'd wear, not in a million years. Something shocking."

"I don't know, Jon. I don't really —"

"Don't worry, I'll pay for it. Indigo, listen to me. I didn't want to say this on the phone, but don't you agree there's something between us, something unusual?"

"Sure, I guess. But what does —"

"Good answer. Me too. But it's time to take another step, turn up the heat. That's what it's all about. It's the reason we're together, I believe that. And you're going to have trust me — trust that I love you, but understand that I'm willing to push you, that I want to push you, hard. It's time to shake things up."

"Sounds intimidating."

"Exactly. Come on, Indigo, don't be so conservative." There was impatience in his voice. "This is what you want. Here's a chance to go to the edge, see if you like the view. It'll be great. I haven't steered you wrong yet, have I? So why the resistance? It's boring. I want to show you things, let you feel them, touch them, taste them. And I promise, it'll be fun. Completely different from anything else you've been to. Say yes."

She paused. "All right, but I'm staying home all weekend. No matter what. I have a ton of work to do."

As she hung up the phone, she said — "Damn, I forgot to tell him" — then smiled, touching her fingers to her lips. Even better, she thought, a surprise. It was hard to believe he loved her; she wondered what that meant.

Next morning, Indigo finished soldering what she hoped would be a perfect silver box. Most of the class seemed further ahead, but she tried not to panic. There was still the weekend. Barring any snags, she could do the filing and sanding on Sunday, polish it early Monday and still hand it in on time.

As she sat bent over a torch, exasperated by the effort required to get the balls of solder flowing neatly down the seams, she began to feel the clammy squeeze of too many deadlines, impossibly close together.

At lunch she sat on the floor against her locker, making a list of all the things she had to do — and when — and quietly freaking out.

In the next three weeks, she had an essay due on the relationship between cinema and social change, exams in art history, pop culture and the properties of metal, and a scene to analyze for her screenwriting class. She was also well behind in her video; the project wasn't due until Christmas, but she'd barely done a thing.

Shit.

She put her head in her hands, allowing herself a moment to be overwhelmed before insisting she pull it together. On top of the pile, she'd added a freelance job, a forty-minute speech to write on the benefits of importing toxic waste. After reminding herself that she needed the cash, she climbed off the floor and popped a couple of extra-strength aspirin, then slid back down to gape at a calendar.

Late that afternoon she bought a dress. Short black leather that from a distance could have been rubber, stretched tight around her frame. She'd lost a few pounds and what she liked to think of as her newly chiseled face, reminded her of the mannequin on display in the Leather Emporium — pouting, inviting, daring passers-by to enter the lair of the lizard. Buy and lose the fear. Seize the day.

A chunky silver zip ran from her crotch to cleavage and said without modesty, real or otherwise — *If you're not thinking about what's under this dress you're a fool. Look how close it is, how easy it could be.*

She was feeling oddly grateful for the chance to look this hot, before she was old and too far gone to care. Nicole would say she was being pessimistic. But in the tight skin of some long-dead animal, Indigo's humility gene, of all things, was over-amping and it didn't suit the look. Leather and hardware. Voluminous breasts. Sharp, dangerous heels. She shouldn't be this human underneath. She should have an edge. A streak of rage that would have made it good — powerful and life-affirming — to snap a whip on someone's ass. But instead she laughed, imagining herself as he came. A look of concern. "Did I hurt you — you okay?"

A sheep in wolf's clothing.

It was Halloween night.

By the time she got home, the street was teeming with tiny

marauders. A group of six or seven ghouls followed her up the path and to her door, waiting on the porch while she went inside in search of treats.

The only thing she could find was the jar of after-dinner mints above the stove — candies in cellophane, red and white stripes or sometimes green or clear, with the names of restaurants printed on their sides. She dumped a handful in each of the outstretched bags, then quickly closed the door and turned the light off.

There was work to be done.

Over the next two hours, Indigo had to eat, shower and transform herself — physically and psychologically — into some kind of sex goddess plaything. Adding to the drama was the need to keep the house dark and ignore the fists, tiny and otherwise, pounding on the door.

There was a message from Tim, reminding her about the party — the one he told her about, with live music and all you can drink, plus food, for twenty bucks. He said to call before nine if she wanted a ride, and left the address just in case. "I'm Thor, God of Thunder," he said. "Darcey's one of the Valkyries. You've got to see these breastplates. We're going to freeze our asses off. But hey, we look *maaahvelous.*"

It was a shame that one night had to offer so many things to do. Earlier in the week, Nicole had called to say that Spider's band was one of three set to rock a cozy club for several thousand. Indigo hated to choose — she'd have liked to bop around — but she couldn't wander the streets dressed for a fetish night. Or could she? A smile crept over her face as she stood in the shower (which they told her not to do), letting shampoo run down her back, enduring the sting of her own punctured flesh.

It was hard to know where she'd be willing to go, these days.

Jon instructed her to take a cab to his place; he bought some champagne to loosen her up and, as it also turned out, some cocaine.

"I've only done it once," she said. "Ages ago. It didn't seem to work, but the next morning — God, what a headache. I remember hiding under the covers, feeling sick and sorry for myself. Of course, it had nothing to do with the gallons of wine I seem to remember consuming; it was strictly this stuff. I think I'm immune to the good part."

Jon was leaning forward on the loveseat, left elbow resting on his knee, using his health card to chop at a small white pile of powder. Half smiling, he looked sideways from behind his bangs. "I guess we'll see."

Indigo watched as he separated two narrow lines from the pile. "Maybe it is worth another try," she said. "Why not."

He hadn't mentioned in advance what he was wearing, but (as she expected) it was black — skinny pants and a tight, spandex T-shirt, silver studded belt and the pendant he'd worn to Tim's party. She reached over and held it in the tips of her fingers, then let it fall against the hollow in his throat. "The symbol for an open mind, isn't that what you said?"

"It's the conscious mind. But I like your interpretation."

They stayed at Jon's until eleven, laughing and talking — or rather, Indigo leaping through her own warp-speed conversation, while Jon mostly listened.

Part way through he interrupted. "Listen. No, stop for a minute. Listen. I want to give you a name. An alter ego." She opened her mouth to respond but he grabbed her wrist. "No, wait. I've been thinking about this. Tonight you're Helen. Helen Bach. Do you like it?"

"Really?" Indigo thought it sounded embarrassing. "Okay. I guess. If you want. I knew a girl named Helen in high school we were in the same auto mechanics class the only two girls but then she got pregnant and we never saw her again and then I was the only girl in the class which was very cool being the only girl I mean I hardly ever had to —"

In between rounds of conversation, when Indigo paused for a sip of her drink or a breath or just because she had to stop talking, they let the music stretch their senses, making out just enough to make them both want more.

"You look so fucking good in that dress," said Jon. "Undo the zip. Let me see what's underneath."

She walked to the centre of the room, pulled the zipper down until the dress was open wide, until she stood revealed in her leopard-print bra and panty, black stockings and, as an added touch, a thin silver chain around her waist. He was smiling, and she noticed his hand on the crotch of his pants. "I think we're just about ready to go," he said. "Let's do one for the road."

"In a minute." Indigo slid the dress off her shoulders and tossed it on the couch, turned around to reveal a square pad of gauze. "Look underneath," she said. "But don't wreck the bandage. I have to keep it on." She stood still as he lifted the tape. "When it's all healed," she said, "I want you to do me a favour. I want a couple of pictures. So I can see what it looks like when I'm not all twisted around."

As he replaced the bandage, Jon said — "I'm proud of you. You're making progress."

Comparing this party to the one for Peter's play was like comparing people who inhale to those who fake it.

The man lashed to the wall was hurting for real. He hung from iron cuffs, whimpering lightly as the person wielding the whip — a woman in a clear plastic dress and tall red boots — stood by and smoked a cigarillo. There were welts on his back and the backs of his thighs, as well as tiny dots of blood.

"I don't know about this," said Indigo.

"It's okay, just relax. The thing you have to remember is that everyone here has a choice. Nobody's forced into anything. This is what they want. And they can stop any time."

The party was in a mansion accustomed to parties, on the outskirts of a wealthy neighbourhood, west of downtown. It had heavy drapes and polished floors, and nothing personal. Downstairs, it might have been a gallery, if it weren't so dimly lit. Most of the walls had been removed, creating one expansive room, broken only with pillars and screens. The only art on the walls was human.

In this setting, Indigo looked conservative. Even the mass of cleavage pushed into public by her dress seemed ordinary — practically sedate — among so many near-naked people.

She was intrigued by the wardrobe more than any specific, sexual acts. The woman in a pink plastic bikini and matching platform shoes. Cock rings. The rubber dress so tight that its owner must have had to coat herself in oil to slide it on. The chainmail skirt with nothing on top and just as little underneath. Studded harnesses. Spiked collars. Metal. Rubber. Leather. Latex. Plastic. Fishnet. Skin.

The occasional silk or satin.

As her gaze extended down the room, she saw that there were people on a stage, performing in a beam of light. It took her time to make sense of the scene, to realize that what she was looking at was someone in a leather hood, gagged with a ball — a man — tied to a prayer bench, while another man stood behind him, intent on inserting a large and frightening dildo.

"I'm serious. I really don't know if I like this," said Indigo, not sure if she wanted to leave or get a closer look. "If I'm going to stay I need a drink." She smiled. "A stiff one. But after that, we'll see. I'm not making any promises. Okay?"

Jon put his hand on the small of her back to guide her forward through the crowd. "Whatever you say. Come on, the bar's over here. What do you want?"

"Something refreshing. Vodka with cranberry juice if they have it, and lots of ice. I feel like I've been sucking cotton balls."

When they each had drinks, Jon led her into a corner. From behind his pendant, he unhinged a miniature spoon and gave them both another hit of coke. Indigo found that after that her fear was gone, replaced by curiosity. It all seemed so complicated, to have to go to such extremes. Not to mention the expense, what with all the toys and clothes.

As she considered the effort it would take to be involved on a regular basis, a woman walked by swinging what appeared to be a machine gun with a giant rubber penis on the end — although, in fact, it looked more like a corn on the cob. Indigo smiled in spite of herself, incredulous. *And what do you think you're going to do with that thing?* She wasn't sure she wanted to know.

With her mood improved, Indigo held Jon's hand and kissed it, went to whisper something in his ear and brushed her lips against his face. She was starting to feel light-headed — not drunk, exactly, she was too alert for that. And speedy. But the ideas jumping into her head and out of her mouth felt fluid. There was hardness around her — pain and humiliation, willingly served and consumed — but the edges of her thoughts were soft. She'd been invited underground to peer at someone else's version — and, for the moment, cloaked in her own euphoric haze, it made her interesting. Or so she thought.

She followed Jon part way down the room, where they stood against the wall, watching the scenery. The music had become a sort of blaring electronica, which meant that, in order to talk, words had to be deposited directly into ears.

"Now there's an amazon," said Indigo, gesturing at a woman walking by.

Jon yelled — "You work it, girl" — then laughed and turned to Indigo. "That's Dana." The creature screamed, gripped him in her giant arms and kissed him hard. Indigo looked away.

"I haven't seen you in forever. Jesus Jon, you look good enough to eat." Dana was solid — over six feet tall, with jet black hair cut close and an edge that seemed at odds with her outfit. She wore a short silk dress that could have been lingerie, the colour of faded lilacs, with delicate straps across her broad, muscular back. Introductions were made, briefly, and Indigo found herself standing apart as they talked.

On stage, a slave was being strapped to the top of a table, and her ankles bound in stirrups. The machine gun lay on the floor.

Indigo leaned into Jon — "Listen, this is starting to look like a trip to the gynecologist. I'm going to find the washroom, I think it's upstairs. Don't go anywhere, okay? I'll be back in a bit." She went to leave, then said — "Oh wait, I need my lipstick." It was in Jon's pocket so she wouldn't need a purse.

"Hang on a sec." Jon said something to Dana that made them both laugh, then turned to Indigo, put the coke in her hand and shouted — "Here. Take this. Dana wants a line. She'll show you where the can is. I'll be here."

Upstairs, rooms led into rooms led into rooms — each furnished in its own distinctive way, with custom chairs or rubber mats, and brightly coloured couches stretched with vinyl. Dana pulled her through a maze of portable fantasies, each carried out in its own small square of space. Every so often, a cluster of people would shift so that some wandered off, others were added and a few became part of the show. Sadomasochism, up close and interactive.

The washroom door was closed, so they leaned against the wall beside it. "Vamp?" asked Dana, pointing to Indigo's wine-coloured nail polish.

"No. Dubonnet."

"I like Dubonnet. With 7-up."

"Sounds sweet. In England, if you want a spritzer it's wine and 7-up."

The washroom door opened, spilling out a man and woman dressed in matching leather thongs and nothing else.

Dana locked the door behind them. "So how do you know Jon?"

"We met at a party," said Indigo, handing Dana the packet of coke. "Here you better do this." She adjusted her breasts in the mirror, then smiled — "We go to the same school. I'm what they call a mature student. What about you?"

"We go back," said Dana. "I used to be his muse. That's what he said once, but we were high so probably not. I just like how it sounds. I've been called a lot of things, never that. It was because I brought him here. He said it gave him a whole new way of thinking." She did a hit and passed the spoon to Indigo. "You're lovely."

"Not for me, I just did one," said Indigo, taking the packet. "It's the dress. Jon helped me pick it out. Said I should be outrageous. For a change. But thanks. You look nice too."

In what seemed like a single motion, Dana bent forward, covering Indigo's mouth with her own as she unzipped her dress and put her hands on Indigo's hips. Dana was a wall of silk and flesh.

For the briefest of moments, Indigo was aware that her brain had stalled. She didn't know what to do so she didn't do anything. She felt like an observer — to the point that she imagined herself sitting to the side, sketching their single, fused profile. And then she opened her mouth allowing Dana's tongue inside, conscious of the workings of her mind as it tried to label each sensation, each emotion — hoping she wasn't so far gone that she'd forget.

Physically, there didn't seem to be much difference. She'd known men whose mouths were soft, some that were hard, depending on the circumstance. This was soft and hard at once — demanding but still somehow generous.

The emotions were harder to grip. There was confusion mixed with excitement, which turned all-too-quickly to regret. She felt out of control, anxious and then self-conscious. "Listen," she said, turning her head to the side. "Listen, Dana. I'm straight. No offence, but I'm not into this."

"Hey girlfriend, don't give me that. Sure you are." Dana pressed her hands on Indigo's breasts. "It's the straight-girl fantasy. Overpowered by gorgeous lesbian. Pretend I insisted — blame it on me and enjoy yourself. I know you're hot as hell. You might as well admit it."

"I don't care if I am or not," said Indigo. She was trapped against the counter. "I don't want to. Seriously, I don't." Even as she said the words she wasn't sure; she sounded defensive.

"Jon thinks you do. Consider it a gift from him."

Indigo froze. "He knows about this?"

"It was his idea. What's the problem? He wants you to have a good time. And that'd be me — one of the all-time greats. Come on, baby. Aren't you curious? I don't bite. Well I do, but I won't. Why not just relax and have some fun?"

Taken by surprise, Indigo's first reaction was to defer, to accept the decision and the fact that it was made without her, see what happened next. They kissed again and she felt Dana's hand slide down between her legs.

The trouble was she couldn't seem to think, to decide if this was good or bad, or beyond those kind of judgements. She liked Jon and trusted his intentions, or thought she did. And he wanted her to do this. She should be grateful that he was going out of his way to broaden her own, meagre horizons.

"Stop," she said. "I'm not kidding. Get off me."

"Listen baby, chill. Jon said —"

"I don't care what Jon said. And I don't have to chill. You chill. Get the fuck off me." She pulled herself away and faced the mirror, zipping her dress under Dana's scornful gaze. They watched each other in the glass, both apparently waiting, until Dana leaned forward, smoothed Indigo's hair behind her ears and said something so banal and obvious that Indigo let out a small, involuntary laugh. "You're gonna regret this."

"I don't think so." There was nothing else to say.

With Dana gone, Indigo stared at her own reflection. There was something in her face, something she couldn't read — in the glow of her eyes and cheeks — as though her innermost thoughts were beyond her.

It might have been exhilaration.

She gave herself a coy smile, wondering which part of the scene had boosted her most — having a woman find her attractive, the taste of female lips or telling Dana to go fuck herself and, by extension, Jon.

Then again, it might have been as basic as arousal, although she didn't want to think so. She didn't want to be the kind of person who'd refuse a ride simply because of pre-conceived ideas or her own, randomly imposed limitations. If that was the case, she thought, I'm a knee-jerk kind of girl, sitting in the dark of my own closed mind. Out loud, she said — "That's good. I'll have to remember to use that."

She sat down to pee and, somehow in the process, noticed her own, absurd train of thought. If she didn't want to grope a stranger in the bathroom, she didn't have to. She wasn't repressed, necessarily. The flush was indignation.

Before she left, Indigo fussed with her hair and put on lipstick, changed her mind and did a hit. I am cute when I'm angry, she thought, remembering an argument she had with Sam, once upon a time in a land far away, that ended in sex.

What an odd place to feel nostalgic.

On the way downstairs she realized that the words getting ready in her head were old and tired, like something from a bad sitcom. *Who do you think you are? Don't you ever do anything like that again. What the hell on earth were you thinking?* But when she got there he was gone.

Her inclination was to leave, but that was silly. He was here somewhere, probably looking for her. She stood on her toes to get a better view and spotted Dana, sitting on the edge of the stage with a slave between her legs.

The crowd was no longer purely fetish. There were men from the leather bars, with their jaunty leather caps and furry chests. And people from the clubs. Urban couples, pumped from the steam of the dance floor. Here to push the night to its final, licentious conclusion.

Some debauchery before bed, dear?

Why yes, thank you. Don't mind if I do.

On the dance floor, Indigo saw a man lick his partner's armpit.

Reeling from the scene with Dana, she no longer felt intrigued or entertained. (Or so she told herself in irritation.) The show that continued around her had become, if not exactly common, then familiar — endless and therefore exhausting. After what seemed like very a long night, titillation was harder to come by. She wasn't angry any more, just anxious — to find him and be somewhere else.

The room felt suddenly small and she pushed against it.

As she snaked around the people on the stairs, she wondered why he hadn't waited. He'd been so full of adoration — said he wanted theirs to be a grand passion, something to remember. At the time, it sounded romantic. But now, pressing her way through the bodies, it sounded young. And temporary. And of course, it was.

Still, there was something troubling about a man who spoke of love while discarding any pretense of forever. She wasn't used to that much honesty. Not even with herself.

When she finally found him, he was sitting on a shiny red couch with a woman in his lap, naked and straddled around him so her breasts were in his face. He took his hand off her thigh to wave. "Indigo, come here. I want you to —"

But she was gone, set in motion by the shock. She shouldered herself through the crowd and down the stairs, to the front of the coat check, then as fast as she could out the door. Clasping the folds of her coat around her, she ran to the corner in search of a cab, then stopped — Jon had her money in his pants.

It was late, but she had to call Sam. She wanted to hear his voice, wanted to see their car pull up, get inside, close the door behind her. So what if he called her a bitch? She wanted to go with him wherever he wanted to take her.

She called collect, hoping he wasn't asleep.

It rang once. "Hello?"

"This is the operator. I have a collect call from your wife. Do you accept the charges?"

"Yes of course. Indigo? What's wrong, are you all right?"

"I'm fine, just stranded. Listen, I'm glad you're awake. I know it's late, but can you come and get me? Please. I'm in the west end." Her voice was high in the back of her throat.

"Hang on." Indigo heard a woman's muffled voice, then Sam's. He sighed. "Indigo? Look, if you really need me I'll come. But can't you take a cab?"

"Oh my God, Sam — I didn't realize. I'm sorry for calling so late. I'll talk to you soon, okay? It's fine, I'm fine. You're right. I'll take a cab."

A rush of prickly heat made her head feel light and dizzy and she leaned against the booth. Sam had a date. It was late. He was probably having sex. Right now. She thought she was going to faint and closed her eyes, regretting — what? — everything and nothing, whatever brought her here, to this particular state of distress, this part of town, through the smeared plastic doors of this phone booth. Indigo stood with her hand on her chest, feeling the beat on the palm of her hand, calmed by the hollow sound of breathing. She felt a dull pain in her heart; or maybe it was something else — her ego disguised as her heart. For the first time, she wished she was home with Sam, protected from herself.

There were quarters in the jar beside the bed — enough to get her home, she thought, as she pushed out of the doors, sniffling.

At the corner, she heard a shout and turned. Jon was jogging toward her, doing his jacket up as he ran, exhaling clouds of steam. When he was close enough to touch her arm, he said — "You shouldn't have left."

"Can I have my money?"

"Indigo, don't be that way. Come on, what have you done with Helen?"

"Oh for crying out loud, just give me my money. Please."

"Indigo. Listen to me. Listen. If you aren't comfortable with something, we can talk about it. But it's only flesh. It's not important."

"Whatever." She was looking past him down the street.

"Look, you and I have something special, right?" He paused, but she didn't answer. "Right. A fledgling relationship. And it makes sense that we have to nurture and feed this relationship — by experiencing things apart, and then using those things to keep us entertained as a couple. All I'm suggesting is a way to minimize the dull bits. Indigo, you're smart. I think you know it's only sex. What we have is much more important. Do you understand what I'm saying?"

"Of course I understand, I do speak English. But I don't have to agree, just because it works for you. Maybe I'm not like that."

"That's okay, this is a new thing for you. You'll come around, I know you will. And until then we'll take it slow. Now come on, let's go back to my place. My nuts are ice cubes."

There was desolation in the way she abandoned herself to Jon — just a hint at first, buried under the chemical hope and enthusiasm. It was there in the way she thought of Sam as they talked and did more lines. And later, in the first grey light of the morning, in the way she followed Jon's lead as he took off her dress and pulled her in front of the mirror, put his hands on her shoulders, kissed her mouth and pushed her down. The despair came when she lay down to sleep and couldn't — obsessed with the details, haunted by the movement of the clock.

Seventeen

The bleakness was a dark purply brown, almost puce. It came in waves, like nausea, surging outward from her body, through cracks in the beige plastic blinds and into the world. The day was brown, all cement and mud and sky that might have been falling. Indigo's mood was black.

It had been almost nine by the time she fell into a jittery, fitful sleep. Sam had made her restless, entering her dreams, thrusting and moaning and laughing. Why was he laughing? The woman in the dream was faceless, unknown with one exception: she was everything Indigo wasn't. Whatever that meant. Probably blond. Stable. Devoted to more than herself.

It was barely noon and everything hurt. Indigo lay huddled at the edge of Jon's bed, cold, stuffed up and annoyed by the sound of his breathing. She imagined her face tinged with green. Not a happy green, not the green of grass or buds or Jell-O. More like mould or rotting flesh. Palliative green. Ocean green, from the point of view of someone drowning.

To herself, Indigo whispered — "Fuck positive thinking," then smiled, perversely proud of her gift for morbid thoughts, which seemed to increase with lack of sleep. She slipped out of bed and winced at the pain in her temples, gathered her clothes and quickly put them on, hid beneath her coat and fled.

Outside, the air scraped at her lungs as she walked, head slung low, while shards of light and noise assaulted her senses. The zip of her dress was like an icy metal chain, pressed along the length of her stomach. She longed for aspirin and a cup of tea, the comfort of her mother's house.

She struck a deal with herself to resist all cabs for at least six blocks. Six was her favourite number, chosen in her late teens because it was sacred to the goddess Aphrodite, and because the Christian church called six the number of sin. And this was her penance, clicking down the street in heels, depressed and shivering. As she walked, she abused herself by imagining details — the look on Sam's face as he led his date upstairs, what he would have said, where he might have put his hands. This morning, he'd have made her toast with cheese or scrambled eggs, shared between the sheets.

That woman is having my sex, thought Indigo. In my bed, with my husband. And all I can do is nothing. The urge to swear was overwhelming, but she took it as part of the punishment. She coughed and felt her nasal passage burn, hid her face in her lapel, and succumbed to a small flood of self-pity — until she noticed how pathetic she was and stopped.

Out loud, she said — "All right. That's enough."

In fact, she could *do* any number of things, if she could only decide what it was she wanted. But that would mean thinking about Sam and her marriage, or the end of it, in a concrete, rational way, and making choices. She resisted that above all else, at least for now, because she didn't trust her judgement; there was something about her state that seemed erratic, even to her.

Emotionally, it was as though someone she didn't know very well had called from the corner, say a business associate or better, a lover she had to impress. He'd be there in fifteen minutes, which was fine, except that her house was a disaster. There was no time to clean, so she piled the crisis into a closet, shut the door and ignored it while she entertained. The mess was in there, waiting for her to face it — by taking everything out and deciding its rightful order or, and the thought did cross her mind, simply sealing it off with drywall. Either way, it was an awesome task, one she was happy to avoid.

Still, the downside was a sense of unfinished business where Sam was concerned. A consistent, low-grade desire for this person who was there and suddenly wasn't, as though he'd been amputated from her life. And now the sickening throb of jealousy, deep in her chest.

Nancy was waiting at the door, rubbing at Indigo's legs, happy to see her.

Indigo picked up the phone. The tone said there were messages. Probably Jon, wanting to know why she left so early, why she didn't wake him up. And Sam, making sure she got home okay. Good old Sam. She'd get them in a minute.

"SIDNEY —" She checked the closet. Damn. Now she'd have to go looking for the cat. Again. He'd done this once before, about a year ago; Indigo had helped her mother search, calling his name, stapling posters to telephone poles and hoarding. Three days later he swaggered up the walk, tired and hungry, with matted hair and a deep scratch in his nose, quite pleased with himself, or so it seemed to them.

Indigo changed into tights and a sweater, hung the dress out of sight and heaved a sigh so deep she had to lean against the wall. It was good to be home.

"SIDNEY —" Standing on the porch, she wondered if he was smart enough to be doing it on purpose, as an act of revenge. What if he was sitting across the street somewhere, hidden by bushes, watching her with that amused, superior look? She was getting paranoid.

A cup of tea and then, if he's still not home, I'll go for a walk, she thought. But he'll be home by then.

In the kitchen, she said — "Hey Nancy, where's Sid? Where's the boy? Is he upstairs someplace? Did I let him out?" She put some food on their plates and the plates on the floor, and then some water on the stove.

God, she was tired. "I'm too old for this," she said, opening the fridge and staring inside, hungry but cautious, protective of her hollow stomach. Maybe some toast. Start slow. She picked up the phone to see who called.

Sam was first. It must have been early. "Just making sure you got home okay, so call me back. I'm a little worried, I guess, but you're probably fine, I'm sure you're fine. That was weird last night. I'm tempted to come over there, but I won't. What's the point? If you're not home, you're not home — right? I don't want to wait on the steps. So call me ... as soon as you get this, okay? I'll be here."

Nicole was next. "Indigo. You missed a great party, but I'm not calling to rub it in or make you feel guilty or anything. Well, maybe I am, but not only that. I have an idea. I want to meet this boy of yours. Let's do dinner. Your place. Thursday or Friday. Saturday's out, Spider's got a gig. We'll invite Tim and his honey. And I might help you cook if you're nice, but I doubt it. You know me ... So what did you do last night? Better be good to blow me off like that. Just kidding. Anyhow, I'm here all day. Recuperating. You should have been there. We didn't get home till, like, five or something. I don't know. Whatever. Talk to you."

And then the Humane Society, asking her to call. They had Sidney.

Indigo's chest tightened. She dialled, pressed "1" for English, then the extension number, tapped the pads of her fingers on the counter as she waited.

"This is Laura."

"Hi, it's Indigo Blackwell calling. I understand you have my cat? Sidney? Tabby, black and grey with a brown stomach. You left a message?"

"I'm sorry Mrs. Blackwell, but your cat's in pretty bad shape."

Indigo sucked in her breath and swallowed. "Oh my god, what happened?" Her voice was thin and choked, but it wasn't until she hung up that Indigo caved. A moan twisted out of her throat. "This is my fault," she said, sliding down and wrapping her arms around her knees. "I did this. Oh Nancy, what have I done to the boy?" She rocked her spine against the cupboard door. This wasn't happening. Why didn't she notice him leave? Because the lights were off. Because she wanted to hide from the kids. This was her fault. Sidney was almost dead because of her. She almost killed her mother's cat.

Indigo sat on the floor, dazed, until the kettle whined and the phone began to ring.

"Hello?" She sounded small.

"Indigo. What's going on? What's the matter?" It was Jon.

"Sidney almost died."

"Who?"

"Sidney. The cat ... my mother's cat." The words started to pour. "He must have got out when I left and now he's almost dead. Crawled under the hood of a car. To get warm, I guess. He should have been inside. It was freezing. They found him on the road, poor baby. All burnt and oily. Who knows how long he lay there, in pain, all by himself ... what he must have been thinking ... how afraid he must have been ... in the dark, in a strange neighbourhood. I wasn't there to help him or hold him. Take him to the vet. I didn't let him out ... I'd never let him out all night. I would have come back. He should have been here in the house with ... safe ..." She was crying too hard to continue.

"Indigo, it's okay. It's only a cat. It's not the —"

"Stop. Shut up. JUST SHUT UP. Don't say that. I can't believe you'd say that." The infusion of anger gave her voice a rising, hysterical quality that made her think of crazy women out of control, screeching tires. "It's not okay. Nothing's okay. It's not okay at all. I love that cat and he almost died. My mother loves him and he almost died. She trusted me to look after him and he almost died. Do you see the pattern here? It's not ... nothing's ..." She took a deep breath. "I have to go."

"You want me to come over?"

"No."

"Fine. Call me later. I want to talk to you, so don't forget. Later." The phone went dead and she stood, ear pressed to the silence as she made her tea, wondering what to say to Sam.

She didn't have wait. The phone rang almost as soon as she replaced it in its cradle. "Indigo. You're home. Are you okay? That's dumb, of course you are, you're there. What was that about last night? Where were you?"

"I'm fine, it doesn't matter. Sorry I called so late."

"You sound funny. What's the matter?"

She spoke slowly, each word heavy in her mouth. "Sidney's at the Humane Society. It's bad, but he's going to make it. So they say."

"Indigo, that's awful. What happened?"

"It doesn't matter, he's alive. I'll tell you later, okay? Some other time?" And then — "I don't know what I'm gonna say to Alice. This is all my fault."

"It's not your fault. I don't care what happened, I know it's not your fault. It's nobody's fault. You know that Indigo. It was an accident. Don't be so hard on yourself, your mother can handle it. These things happen. You want to come over here? I have hot chocolate."

"No. I have to stay with Nancy. I'm going to lie down for a bit. I didn't get much sleep. But thanks. Really, I mean it."

"All right. Call me if you change your mind. I'll be —"

"Can I ask you something?"

"Sure. What do you want to know?"

"It's none of my business, but —" She stopped. "Nothing, never mind. I should let you go."

Curled fetal on the couch, anxiety aimed at her homework, Sam and Jon, remorse at the cat, Indigo made a decision. She'd allow herself the day to wallow, then get over it; she'd get off her ass and do some work tomorrow.

By the time she had another conscious thought, the light had been drained from the room. The day was gone and she was hungry. Less shattered than before.

The phone had been ringing in her dream, but the house was quiet. Nancy was warm at the back of her knees.

Indigo lay still, listening to the clock in the kitchen, a passing car, the whine of the world in the distance. Nancy stood up and stretched, then climbed over Indigo's legs and sniffed at the breath coming out of her nose. "I'm still alive, cat. Come on, you hungry? Want some tuna? We'll share. I could handle that."

While they were eating, someone called but didn't leave a message, hung up and called again. Or it could have been somebody else. Indigo didn't know and didn't care. The roar in her brain was as much as she could stand. Conflicting waves of thought that sloshed between her ears and foamed behind her eyes. It was hard enough to listen to herself, to stay intact as she relived the night before, examined it whole then picked it apart; as she mentally beat herself about the head for failing Sidney, for making a fool of herself at the party, for calling Sam.

She looked at the phone as it rang, the waves reaching out like a pair of hands — hands that might have held her shoulders, pulled her close and stroked her cheek, or wrapped themselves around her neck and squeezed. It was as though contact with another person, anyone, would ruin her composure, push her down into the wreck she was this afternoon, dazed and crumpled, arms folded over her face.

She thought of the party, how it made her claustrophobic. And afraid. Afraid that after all she'd given up, this new reality she'd been so desperate to create, this ostensibly thrilling existence, was actually based on false assumptions; that after all the wanting, all the talking, she lacked the courage to be wild.

Or was it the interest?

Okay, so she tried some drugs, experienced an altered point of view. A start perhaps, hardly revolutionary. Given the chance for something truly new she fled — although, in fairness, she did loosen up at Jon's, let him slap her ass. He'd even left a bite mark on her shoulder.

At the time, Indigo couldn't help feeling self-conscious, as though there was something innately silly in what she was doing. Like when Jon ordered her onto her knees and she nervously giggled. And wasn't it peculiar that sexual submission should be seen as subversive or a test of one's limits or at the very least exciting, when a truly submissive woman, outside of a sexual context, is — for all but the most insecure and parochial males — inherently dull?

As she sat at the kitchen table, Indigo realized that for the first time in weeks she was eager to work, intrigued by what she was making. So she lit a fire, unplugged the phone and began to sand her silver box. The idea was to start with coarse sandpaper, then go finer and finer until there were no scratches left on the surface. But, since she was sanding the piece by hand, Indigo knew that a pristine finish was more than she could hope for. In on time would have to do.

By midnight, her brain had delivered a concept — or the beginning of one, anyway — which could turn out to be either funny and good or awful, or something in between. Her video would be an exposé on the plight of the Queen of the Pixies.

She imagined an older, chubby man in drag — a silver dress with pearls and silver pumps, wand and tiara, the hair on his legs matted under sheer silver hose.

The concept began with a single fact: the Queen is frustrated. Or, as she says, at the end of her bits. It grew from there.

Apparently, pixies oversee dancing, in much the same way as the tooth fairy gathers teeth. They're in charge. Always have been, except that pixies spend most of their lives invisible, and they're modest by nature, so they don't get a lot of press.

Indigo imagined the Queen suspended in the air, waving her wand, holding a small silver purse with meaty fingers. It's supposed to look as though she's levitating, except that the wires are obvious.

The Queen is nostalgic. She misses the days of dancing around the maypole, Victorian parlour dancing, ballroom dancing — although she concedes that ballroom dancing is making something of a comeback. But in any case, that's not why she made herself apparent. She's here because the world is going to hell in a handbag. Her words. The pixies are running amok, hanging out in nightclubs, refusing to leave London, New York, Los Angeles and now even Toronto. Half of them are strung out on pixie dust. Something must be done.

The Queen fancies herself media savvy. She's embarked on a North American tour to raise awareness, first among the press, then opinion leaders, club and dance hall owners, the public and, finally, the errant little pukes themselves.

That was as far as Indigo got with the story, but it was enough to make her hopeful. Cautiously optimistic. She could start on the script tomorrow, begin the search for a chubby (preferably hairy) man with a sense of fashion.

Indigo had just turned off the lights when the doorbell rang.

"Who's there?" She could see the top of Jon's head through the glass.

"It's me, open up."

She opened the door an inch. "What are you doing here? It's a bit late to just pop by, don't you think?"

He shrugged. "You didn't answer the phone. I said I wanted to talk to you."

"No offence, but I'm not in the mood. I'm tired. Pretty bummed. It's late. I'll call you tomorrow."

"Indigo, let me in. Please. I'm sorry about the cat." And then — "I like cats, really I do. I'm sorry. Come on, let me in. I'm freezing."

She stared at him for a moment, then stepped back, hugging her arms to her chest. "You want some tea?" She turned on the living room light and stood, waiting. Jon sat down.

"Got anything else? Some wine maybe?" His voice took on a

musical, teasing quality. "I have a surprise for you, something to wake you up."

"What do you mean?"

Smiling, he held a small clear bag pinched between his thumb and finger, then shook it back and forth like someone else might ring a bell. "I got us some —"

"Not for me," she said, repulsed by the thought of inflicting more drugs on her weary brain and limbs. "Not a chance."

What appalled her the most was the fact that she found this toxic young man on her couch so damned appealing. The more potential he had to destroy the more attractive he became. God, she was so predictable. "Look," she said, finally, feigning a level of maturity beyond her current sense. "You're a popular guy, I'm sure you can find someone else to party with. I'm not into this at all. I've been a mess all day because of that stuff. I don't know how you can stand to do it again so soon — or afford it, for that matter, but I guess that's none of my business. If you don't mind though, I think you should go." As she spoke, she sat beside him, then slowly slid her hand in his. She hoped he wouldn't leave.

"Don't get so uptight. If you don't want to do it, we won't — no problem. I thought you'd want to, that's all. It doesn't have to be an issue. It's not like we have to or anything, just because it's there. I'll have some tea, then we'll go to bed. You got a TV up there? I didn't notice."

"Who says you're invited?"

"Oh come on, don't be mean." He kissed the palm of her hand. "You want me to stay, admit it."

After uncomplicated sex, free from design or engineering, Indigo said — "My friend Nicole wants to meet you. Well, technically you met at Tim's party, but she wants to *meet you* meet you." They were propped against the pillows, Jon displayed unselfconsciously, Indigo under the covers, watching television.

"Which one's Nicole?" he asked, speeding past a half a dozen channels.

"Blond, gorgeous, tall. Works for COOL-TV. We're looking at Thursday or Friday, if that's okay with you. I'll cook. It'll be Nicole and Spider, Tim and Darcey, you and me."

"Dinner with your friends, that's serious."

"Not really. What does that mean, don't you want to come?"

"Of course I'll come, don't be stupid. Friday."

She stared at his profile for a moment, then said — "What did you want to talk to me about?" In the flickering white light his skin had a smooth, ghostly quality, almost iridescent. His half-hard penis lounged against his thigh.

"Nothing really." He clicked the remote, then paused. A woman paced, naked, ranting at her lover in Italian. "I wanted to make sure we were cool, that's all. The party was pretty intense. Plus later. You know." As he said the last few words he rolled toward her, ran his finger down her arm. "Ever watch porn?"

"Sure. A few times."

"Like it?"

"It was okay, I guess. Nothing special. Why?"

"Just curious. Getting to know you better, that's all. No reason."

In the morning, Indigo got up to pee then crawled back into bed, falling asleep with her cheek against Jon's spine. When she woke, her hands were bound above her head. "What's going on?" She could feel her insides start to jump.

"Nothing you don't want."

Indigo yanked at the binding, then twisted up to see what it was: one of her stockings, tied through and around her wrists, over the curved metal rung of the headboard, knotted again and again. "What is it with the male fucking species? You don't know what I want. How would you know?" She took a breath and closed her eyes, tried to still the frenzy in her chest. When she was able to speak calmly, she said — "How did you get so arrogant? I mean, I know you're young, but this is too much. I can't believe it ... you ... what makes you ..." She stopped and tried again. "Jon, listen to me. Let me go. Now. I mean it. Untie me."

Grinning, he reached out and, with an exaggerated show of suspense, peeled the covers off her body. His hands hovered over her breasts and down her sides as he kneeled, clearly excited.

"Jon, please. I can't stand this, I'm claustrophobic."

"Then relax," he said. "I'm not going to hurt you, you know that. God, you're so beautiful." Against her will, Indigo began warming to his mouth. As he pressed himself between her legs, he said — "And I guess you don't like this either."

"That isn't the point." She kept her face turned away, refusing to engage, preserving her anger. "You're a jerk, has anyone ever told you that?"

"All the time. But it's what you asked for, you'll see. The other night." He patted her thigh as he jumped off the bed and said — "Wait here" — then ran downstairs.

He came back with a camera.

Indigo had an urge to laugh, but out of alarm as opposed to amusement. It was sort of like the urge she'd had years ago, to jump out of the boat miles from shore, when she spotted a shark off the coast of California. More than just a little inappropriate. She tried to keep from grinning wildly. "Jon, listen to me. If you take a picture of me like this, I will never speak to you again. I'm serious."

"Oh Indigo, don't be so melodramatic. You said you wanted a shot of the tattoo, so I brought my camera. I know what I'm doing. It's not like I'm going to show anybody. I'll make sure it's flattering. I promise."

"I can't believe you'd do this," she said, her voice now barely a whisper. "My taste in men really sucks."

Jon stood above her on the bed and aimed the camera. "Let's get a shot of the front first," he said. "You'll see, it'll be nice. You look so pretty."

In one swift move, Indigo put her weight on her left leg and kicked as high as she could with the right, almost connecting with the camera before Jon swung it out of reach. He laughed. "Feisty, this morning, are we? All right, all right, let's get this done. Here, I know what you want." Putting the camera down, he flipped her over. "You don't want to look at me. See, I'm not so dumb. I can read the signs."

Surprisingly, he removed the bandage gently. "That's an amazing piece of work," he said. "Tattoo's nice too." She heard the camera click three or four times as he kneeled between her thighs, and then — "Ever had it here?" He pressed his hand in the crack of her ass. "Where's that wet stuff?"

"Don't even think about it." With her face in the pillow, it was hard to hear the fear. "You said you wouldn't hurt me. Jon, you promised."

"I don't know Indigo. You've got such a beautiful little ass, how can I resist? I bet it's virgin territory." Her entire body tensed as he inserted the end of his finger, then stopped. "I just thought of something. Indigo, you never said you loved me. I mean, I told you, but you never said it to me. I think now's a good time, don't you?"

"What are you talking about, we hardly know each other. Now get the fuck away from me."

"Is that any way to talk?" He pushed it in a little further, then stopped and pulled it out. "You know, I don't think you understand what I'm saying."

She heard fumbling, felt his fingers wet and cold with gel, then a bolt of pain as he pushed in the tip of his penis. "I love you, is that what you want me to say?" She was screaming now, and starting to sob. "I love you, do you hear me? I love you. Now leave me alone, please."

The moment she started to cry, Jon pulled himself away and rolled her on her back. "Indigo, I'm sorry. I was just fooling around. I didn't mean to upset you. It's just a game, I thought you liked it. I thought you wanted to try new things, just the two of us. I'd never do anything to hurt you. Please, baby — don't cry, I didn't mean it, I'm sorry." He held her face in both his hands and kissed her eyes and then her cheeks and then her mouth. "Say something, Indigo. Say you forgive me. You've got to know I'd never —"

As he groped for the knots she responded, wrapping her legs around his back. "Wait," she said. "Finish."

He shook his head. "You don't —"

"It's all right, I want to. Really. It's okay. Like this though, face to face."

As she lay beneath the quietly heaving Jon, she imagined what they looked like from above. She remembered something her grandmother said, years ago, when she was dying and afraid. "We're all such pathetic little creatures." Straining against the pull of chafing wrists, Indigo thought she agreed.

Eighteen

When it was over, Indigo kept her back to Jon, found her robe and tied it tight around her. "Let me have a quick shower. Then I'll make something to eat." Her voice was soft. There were light pink creases on her wrists.

She'd wanted him to say something, to apologize and keep right on apologizing while she threw him out of the house. She wanted the look on her face to be a smirk as she tossed off some pithy remark that made him ridiculous. She wanted to sneer with revulsion, beg him to stay. She cleared her throat but then, afraid, said nothing. Behind her, the chink of his belt as he put on his pants.

In the shower she cried. And when she came out he was gone, a note in his place on the bed — *Indigo. Forgot I have to be somewhere. Remember I love you.*

Why did it seem like a threat?

He didn't call that day or the next and the week disintegrated into a series of progressively needy messages on his answering machine, each one followed by regret. She didn't have the number for his pager and, among the many excuses she tried bouncing off her own dwindling pride, she suggested that maybe he hadn't been home. He didn't return her calls but, feeling what she described (to herself) as perversely optimistic, she went ahead with plans for the dinner party; she phoned Tim and Nicole, bought groceries, left yet another message.

"Hi. It's me again. I know you're busy but I need to confirm Friday night. Everyone's coming at eight. So call if there's a problem. Otherwise I guess I'll see you then. Okay? Hope you're having a good day."

As she hung up she thought, I'm such a jerk.

It was good to keep busy. That's what she told herself, that it took her mind off men. Deprived of sleep, she had the sensation of floating, unable to think whole thoughts and yet consumed by the pieces. But if the downside was a distracted, some might say flaky demeanour, the upside was a restless, happily productive week.

She worked on her freelance assignment — picked up the research, wrote an outline, spent the promised cash. Her silver box was handed in on time, flawed but in her own opinion gorgeous. She finished a long, rambling essay on the question *When is it propaganda?*, gave some thought to her script and convinced the burliest guy in her class to be Queen for a day. Her art history exam was less successful — she'd be lucky if she squeaked a pass — but she told herself it didn't matter. Why waste energy on things she couldn't change?

During spare moments, Indigo plucked her eyebrows obsessively thin.

And conceived elaborate plans to run into Jon by chance, but never did.

Sam of course she saw. Of course, because she'd spent several concentrated hours letting herself stew in embarrassment over the call, fixated on the woman she now thought of as his girlfriend. Indigo had come to the admittedly impractical conclusion that she had to file for divorce, sell the house and probably leave town without ever coming face to face with Sam again. He'd get on with his life, marry his yellow-haired amazon — who would not only support him in his quest for the bestselling novel, she'd also pay for a nanny after popping out two fair children, a boy and a girl, neither of whom would ever cry.

For her part Indigo hoped she'd fade to that soft-focus place in his memory, where she'd be wistfully conjured up on the rare occasions that he and the new Mrs. Blackwell argued. (It would be unrealistic to think they'd never fight.)

She had it all figured out.

And then he called, sounding kind and sympathetic.

And she said yes, she'd love him to be there when she picked up Sidney. "That's nice of you to offer. I appreciate it."

After that it got weird — or as she said to Nicole, "oh so very polite." The first words out of his mouth could have come from his father. "Supposed to snow later." He was standing on the porch but looking away from the door at the sky. "Weather channel said twenty centimetres. Maybe more. Hard to know."

In the car she thought of a hundred things to say, ignored them all. Stole glances at his profile.

Sam talked hockey. He was playing again, late at night with some guys from university. First time out he lost his dinner in the bleachers.

"It's a great way to get in shape," he said. "If I survive."

Later, with the drugged and bandaged Sidney close beside her, Indigo tried to translate the experience into something she could understand. She stared at the metal bird. If anything, the afternoon had been notable for absence. There were none of the questions she expected. No recrimination, talk of divorce, ultimatum. Only the smallest, most cordial conversation.

One more time, she thought, with feeling.

Indigo turned to check for snow and saw that Sam was there, half an hour later. Still in front of the house. Sitting in the car, hunched forward, leaning his forehead on the steering wheel. She didn't move, just kept watching through the window.

After a while, he lifted his head and drove away.

Jon appeared at nine on Friday night. Everyone else was there and Indigo had just admitted the obvious — she didn't know if he was coming — while suggesting excuses that no one believed.

Conversation stopped when the doorbell rang. "That must be him," she said, forcing a smile, wondering if sweaty hands implied relief or disappointment. Nicole was watching her face with a combination of what appeared to be pity and support; she meant well even if it did seem condescending, and Indigo thought it was sweet.

"Hey, you came."

"Of course I came." Walking past her into the hall, he handed her a bouquet of pale carnations wrapped in plastic. "But thanks for the long neurotic messages."

He was smiling and she thought it was a joke, decided to take it as one. It seemed like the wrong time to press her irritation.

Inside, Jon shook hands around the room. Indigo watched. He was perfect, like the night she met him: assured, soft-spoken, vaguely formal. There was something crisp about him, the way his white, seemingly bloodless skin was framed with dark hair and black clothes, even his shiny black shoes. There was no need to be nervous, she thought, hiding behind a sip of wine, exposed.

After that an awkward silence. Indigo's fleeting impression was that it descended on her guests like poison gas, but she thought she was probably overreacting. Jon took a seat on the couch beside Darcey. Tim coughed. Spider opened his mouth to say something, then changed his mind.

"Do you want —" Indigo started at the same time as Nicole, who stared with open curiosity, then said — "Indigo says you're a genius."

Indigo groaned. "Let me at least get him a drink before you start with things like that."

Jon said — "So I've been told."

"What kind of work do you do?" asked Darcey.

"Different things. Painting mostly. Sculpture. Video." He accepted some wine. "It's not as noble as it sounds. I'm easily bored." He raised his glass. "Salute."

Leaning back in his chair, Spider looked doubtful. "Do you show anywhere?" he asked. "I know you're a student, but is there a chance we've seen your work?"

"Not yet," said Jon. "I've had some interest, don't bother with it much. I've sold a few pieces, you know, word of mouth. I'm in no hurry."

"Really? Why's that," said Indigo. "I thought you'd be eager to get out there, show them all how good you are."

"You thought wrong," he said, still holding Spider's gaze. And then, his voice less hard — "I've agreed to do a show next year, but that's just a favour to someone I know. My mother, actually. She's got a friend who owns a gallery, some old rich broad. Wants to show me off. I couldn't refuse. Not while I'm a kept man."

"I thought your mother died," said Indigo.

"She did, this is my aunt. But she's like a mother. Supports me like a mother."

"You don't want people to see your work?" asked Tim. "If it was me, I'd be plastered all over the place."

"Why? The more you want them the less they want you. It's the way of the world. Trick is to do great work that's different, put it out there just enough to get them thinking about you, then tell them all to go screw themselves. TV helps if you can swing it." He put his drink on the table and fixed his gaze on Indigo. "If it works, they'll be climbing all over themselves to wipe my butt with hundred dollar bills." He shrugged. "Whatever."

"Are you really that wonderful?" Spider's tone was lightly sarcastic.

"I know I'm supposed to be modest, but why? I'm good, through no fault of my own. I mean I work like a fiend, but so do a lot of really lousy artists. Anyway, that's no guarantee. There's some pretty minor talent out there getting some major recognition. They have the luck and the audacity, and they get in everyone's face. Unfortunately, the flipside is that some truly gifted people never get anywhere. Tough. Talent ain't enough. There's a lot more to it than that." He leaned forward. "You gotta have a strategy. You gotta make it happen."

"What about you, Indigo?" It was Nicole.

"What's that?" She was staring at Jon, embarrassed by his edge but also riveted. "Oh, I don't know. I'm no genius, that's for sure. But whether I end up good or mediocre, who knows. I hope I'm good, but I'll tell you one thing — I haven't been working hard enough. This semester seems to be getting away from me already. I don't know why."

"You've had a lot on your mind," said Tim.

"I guess."

When the food was on the table, Indigo walked back down the hall and into the living room, looked at the faces turned toward her and said — "Okay, dinner's ready. It's penne with chicken and snow peas and sun-dried tomato pesto."

If she heard correctly, Nicole had just asked Jon if he considered himself promiscuous, to which he replied — "Only when I get a chance." Nobody laughed and she wondered what he'd told them.

"Smells great," said Darcey, breaking the silence as they descended on the long wooden table. "I grow my own basil in the summer. You'll have to let me know if you want some."

"I do," said Spider.

"Spider made the pesto," said Nicole.

"And the herb bread," said Indigo. "But I warmed it up, and we all know that's the hardest part."

"I brought dessert," said Jon.

Indigo, sensing what he meant, leaned into his ear and whispered, "Don't say it, not if it's what I think it is." Then louder, as she lit the candles — "So Spider, what are you up to these days?" She passed the bread to Jon. "Spider's the drummer for Cringe."

"I know, I saw the show at the Opera House. What do you call a guy who hangs out with musicians?" He smiled, nodding in anticipation. "A drummer." Everyone stopped what they were doing and Jon, folding his arms in front of his chest, said — "Seriously. You guys are good overall, but your guitar player sucks. You should replace him. He's gonna keep you down."

Spider rested his fork on his plate. "Can't agree with you there, man. But if that's your opinion, you're entitled to it. Funny how it is though, when you're in the public eye people think they have the right to be insulting. I'm sure you'll find that out."

"Oh, I've taken plenty of criticism."

"I bet you have," said Spider.

"And I'll get more."

"I have no doubt."

"And I'll tell them all to mind their own fucking business, they don't know what they're talking about."

Everyone froze and looked at Spider, who lowered his fork, then shook his head and laughed. "You probably will too, you son-of-a-bitch. Tim, would you please pass the pepper?"

The mood around the table seemed to lighten, but sitting next to Jon, Indigo felt him stiffen at the words son-of-a-bitch. He was flexing the muscles in his jaw, glaring at Spider. She handed him the large bowl of pasta, then said — "Darcey. I hear you just got back from California."

He put the bowl in the middle of the table.

"I've been back a while," she said. "But it was great. I was supposed to go for a week and stayed a month.

"L.A.?" asked Nicole.

"East of there, in the desert. It's a retreat. I've been there before, it's unbelievably beautiful, owned by some friends of mine."

"Sort of like a spa?" asked Indigo.

"More rustic. They offer workshops and seminars, plus they bring in different people. Healers, nutritionists, that kind of thing. The hiking's incredible."

"Were you there for something specific?" asked Indigo.

"I was learning reiki. It's a type of —"

"I have a friend who's into that," said Jon. "She made me this." He touched his pendant, but Darcey was busy putting salad in Tim's bowl, then her own, and no one answered. He filled his glass with wine.

"Aren't you eating?" asked Indigo.

"I'm not hungry." He pushed his chair back from the table. "Excuse me."

When they heard him lock the bathroom door, Nicole said — "Talk about intense."

"He's not usually like this," said Indigo. "But I hate to say it — you're going to think I'm nuts — I find it sort of appealing. In a weird way. I think you've got to expect outrageous things from artists, especially good ones. Make allowances. They're not like everyone else, they think different. He really is an amazing talent."

"You romanticize everything," said Tim. "You always have. And I'm sure he's more than happy to let you buy into that whole eccentric genius trip. He can be as brooding as he wants and you don't say a word. We'd all like that." He put his arm around Darcey and squeezed her shoulder. "Except me. I want to be as sweet as pie to my honey all the time."

After dinner they stayed at the table. Indigo and Tim cleared the plates while Jon told a story about giving away his only coat in what was then the Soviet Union.

"It must have been twenty below and all she had on was this thin wool jacket," he said. "I remember it was all frayed at the collar. My father was there on business, so I knew he'd buy me another one. We were going to Paris in a day or so. But you should have seen the look on this girl's face, like she couldn't believe her goddamn eyes. They can't get stuff like that over there — this was an expensive leather coat — even if they have the money, which I'm sure she didn't. The ruble's a joke, and there's nothing to buy anyway."

Indigo couldn't help noticing that he'd chosen a story that showcased his own generosity, travel, wealth. She wondered if he did it on purpose, which would mean that he actually cared what people thought. Since he'd come back into the room he seemed more animated; Indigo thought she knew why.

As she rinsed the plates and put them in the dishwasher, Tim leaned beside her. "So you really like this guy?" His voice was low, and further absorbed by the water.

"Sure. Why, don't you?"

Tim looked past her into the dining room. "It isn't that. He's all right. Interesting in a pretentious kind of way. I didn't think he'd be the sort of guy you'd like, that's all. I thought you preferred them a bit more front and centre. This guy seems pretty full of himself. But hey, what do I know? Don't listen to me."

"When do I ever?"

"Oh, that's nice."

"I'm kidding. Besides, it's not like I want to marry him. I like him in the same way that I like putting my hand over a hot flame, see how close I can go without getting burnt." He looked skeptical, so she said — "Relax, I'm having fun. Don't all women secretly want men that are bad for them? And Jon's not even that bad, a little wild, but I like it. I've never really done wild."

"Speaking of marriage, how's —"

"He's fine. Dating up a storm. Haven't you seen him?"

"So it's really over?"

"Corpse city."

"You think I should call him, say hello or something? Maybe go for a beer?"

"That'd be nice, whatever. Just don't tell me what he's up to. I don't want to know. But get the details. Just in case." She put her hand on the tap to turn it off, then paused. "Listen, I want to ask you something. Jon's into coke. Not all the time. You know, every now and then. But I think he brought some. Would you be into something like that?"

"Sure. But Darcey won't, no way. She's a your-body-is-your-temple kind of girl. And I bet Spider's the same, so Nicole won't either. What do you think?"

"Same as you. I'm going to ask him not to say anything."

As she turned the water off, Nicole came in with the placemats. "What are you two whispering about?"

Tim put his arm around her and Indigo batted her eyes. "Nothing you won't hear later." Then walking into the dining room — "Anybody want coffee?"

"I have something better," said Jon.

"Wait —" Indigo tried to jump in, but he continued. "Anybody want a line?" Indigo winced and looked at Tim, who shrugged. Spider and Darcey looked at Jon and then each other. Nicole looked surprised but vaguely amused.

"I don't think they do," said Indigo, sliding into her chair as Darcey said — "You guys do what you want, it doesn't bother me. I like a little toke from time to time, but that's about it. Coke's too hard on the system."

"What about you?" He was holding Spider's stare.

"I stopped doing shit like that years ago."

"Of course you did. Anyone else?"

"Go ahead if you want to do some, don't let me stop you." Darcey was looking at Tim, who said — "No, that's okay. I don't think so, not if you're not."

"Don't be ridiculous, I'm not your mother. Do what you want."

"Okay then, I'll do one if Indigo will."

"You sound like you're in high school," said Darcey. She ripped a piece off her napkin, rolled it into a ball between her fingers, then dropped it on the table.

Grinning, Jon pulled a small plastic bag from his pocket. "What about you, Nicole?"

"No thanks. The last time I did that stuff I cornered some poor guy, had him practically pinned to the wall while I told him my secrets. I hate it when I do that." She looked like she wanted to laugh, and Indigo finally said — "What's so funny?"

"We are." Nicole poured herself another glass of wine. "Don't mind me, silly duck. I'm just having fun. And this new man of yours, he's like a stick in the spokes. Can't help it, I think it's hilarious. Not that I think he's good for you or anything. No offence."

"None taken," said Jon.

"That's why you like him," said Nicole. "He knows how to make us all twitch, you included." She giggled and Spider surprised them all by taking her hand and kissing it. "You're so bad, do you know that?" He looked at Jon across the table. "She has a way of stating the obvious. And to tell you the truth, I don't care what you put up your nose. It's not like I've never done it. What do you say we just relax and enjoy the rest of the night, each to his own vices."

"Well, it won't be as much fun," said Jon. "But if that's what you want, let's all be polite and *get along*."

The last two words were slick with a sort of joking sarcasm and Indigo, who'd been looking for the subtext, felt as though Jon had somehow staged the whole event — beginning with the scene in bed, her anxious week and then the fact that she couldn't ask him about it in front of anyone, which meant that by the time they were alone any anger she'd felt would have dulled; even the impression he made on her friends, and the way he chose Spider for a bit of verbal sparring, then tried to shake them up, especially her, by putting the drugs on the table.

And if she chose to dwell on it, which she wouldn't until it was over, she'd begin well before the scene in bed, at the moment they met — from the moment a kinder, gentler Jon found his way inside her head and, like a pretty weed, he grew.

It seemed suddenly possible, even probable, that he treated his life as he would a piece of art, something to create for his own pleasure, amusement, intrigue; something to manipulate, simply because he found he had the talent. He'd even alluded to it, she thought, when he said he was easily bored.

By the time several bottles of wine had been opened and drunk, the party had moved to the living room. Spider and Jon talked music and art. Nicole and Indigo talked over each other. Tim tried to get a word in. They only quiet one was Darcey, who sat curled at the end of the couch, listening, speaking when spoken to, relinquishing small tense smiles as necessary.

Beside her on the end table, was a growing mound of napkin balls, but when Tim asked what the matter was, all she said was — "Nothing, I'm fine, just a little tired, nothing serious."

And when he tried again later — "No I don't want to leave. Stop worrying."

And then, finally — "No thanks, I've had enough wine. Maybe some tea though. That would be nice. Thank you." Knowing the kitchen as well as his own, he made her tea.

When, mid-conversation, Jon dumped another pile of powder on the coffee table, Nicole said — "Okay, that's it you guys. I want to do one too." She kissed Spider's shoulder. "Don't get all uptight, it's just one line. And I'm only doing it because I know you disapprove. I want to see if you'll still love me in the morning."

Indigo said — "Better watch out Spider, I've seen this mood before and it's frightening. Imagine someone who says exactly what they think all the time."

"That's not true," said Nicole, hugging Spider's back as he chose another CD and put it on. "Well, maybe it is." She giggled. "What the hell, let's be bad for a change. You gonna do one with me?"

Still in the grip of her arms, Spider turned to face her. He attempted a stern look but couldn't pull it off and grinned. "I guess if you put it that way —" He looked at Jon. "That stuff any good?"

At the respectable stroke of midnight, Darcey stood up and threw the tiny balls of paper in the fire. "I'm calling a cab," she said to Tim. "Why don't you stay. I'm just going home to sleep. I'm tired."

"You don't mind?"

"Actually, I think we're going to leave too," said Nicole. "Thanks sweetie. It's been a slice."

When she'd said the last of her many goodbyes, Indigo drifted back inside to the living room, numb and, for the moment, happy. Jon was on the phone.

He raised his finger to his lips. "Messages." When he hung up, he said — "I gotta go."

"You're leaving?"

"Have to. I promised I'd meet someone. You want to come?"

"Where to?" she asked. "Not that place again."

Jon pulled out his wallet, then turned away to look inside. He seemed distracted. "What? No, nothing like that. A club, then maybe a boozecan. Maybe. If he's not at the club. It's Peter. He said he's with some friends." She looked skeptical, so he said — "Come on, come for an hour. What are you going to do here, talk to the cats?"

Their destination turned out to be Safari, an expansive new club with zebra walls and leopard seats, constellations of light on the ceiling. Under the bleating silver strobes she spotted an elephant, probably fibreglass, cornered by the untamed urban crowd and, off to the side, a giraffe. On the dance floor: animal prints, writhing to a steady jungle beat.

Outside, the doorman had shaken Jon's hand as he pulled aside the heavy velvet rope to let them pass; the line of hopefuls glared and stamped their feet.

By the time she checked their coats he'd walked ahead, cutting a path which just as quickly closed behind him. He turned to make sure she was coming and, when he saw that she was, kept moving. When she got to the bar he was there.

"Why don't you get us both a drink," he said, handing her a twenty dollar bill. "Gin and tonic, lots of lime. I'll be right back."

And now Indigo stood at the end of the bar, holding both their drinks, feeling conspicuous. She decided not to wait and began making her way through the press of beautiful people, giving the men who caught her eye flirtatious glances. It's that bravado thing again, she thought, happy to discover a trait that suited the setting.

She spotted Peter first — still relatively far away — in the glow of a staircase. Jon was on his left, almost hidden by the woman wrapped around him.

The trio turned and went upstairs.

Indigo put on her best awkward smile and followed. At the top of the stairs was a door and then a lounge, walls painted in a primitive artscape, cartoon-like animals peering out from tall, whimsical grass.

"Here you are," she said, attempting brightness but sounding like an over-excited soprano. By the time Jon disengaged himself and took his drink, her smile was gone.

"More to the point, here *you* are," said Peter. "Jon said you didn't come but I knew you did. I must be psychic. Indigo, this is Lily. I'm sure Jon's told you about her."

Lily, who was short and voluptuous, with a full red mouth and hair dyed in chunks of yellow and orange, said — "I can see by the look on her face he hasn't." She was at least 35, maybe 40. Her clothes were black except for a grey, leopard print scarf around her neck.

Jon said — "You told me she wouldn't be here."

"I couldn't stop her," said Peter, clearly enjoying the scene. "Once she found out I was meeting you, well, she's like a truck. You know that. You of all people."

Indigo said — "He used the name in a story. Once. It's nice to meet you."

Lily looked her up and down and then stepped closer, staring in her face. "How do you know? That it's nice to meet me."

"I don't. I was being polite. I don't even know who you are."

"I'm the one who almost got away. But now I'm back — at his request, I might add." She jerked her head in Jon's direction. "What do you think of that?"

"Don't start," he said, accepting some folded money from Peter and handing him a small square packet. "Lily's a friend of mine, sort of an old mentor —"

"Bastard. I'm not old, you're a kid. Just a scrawny little fucked-up kid."

"She's also a mean drunk, don't mind her. Come on, let's —"

"*Don't mind me*," said Lily, thoughtfully. "Now there's some wishful thinking, telling one girlfriend not to mind the other girlfriend. I know all about you, Miss I'm-looking-for-kicks-Indigo — or is that Mrs. — and by the way I'm not drunk or mean. It's just my natural, sparkling personality." She cocked her head to one side in a way that Indigo thought looked ridiculous. "You're Jon's new pet project, the earnest one, who makes up for it in malleability. I must say you look good, I'll give you that. Oh, and I'm not possessive either. I think that's wise with boys like Jon, don't you?"

It was one of those indelible moments, the kind people play again and again in their heads, turning them upside down and sideways, wishing they'd said this or that. Indigo had been having a lot of those lately, more than her share, she thought, wishing someone else would say something, give her time to think.

They were watching her eyes, waiting, and in the split second she had to make a choice, only one thing seemed certain: they couldn't be allowed to know she was wounded. Call it instinct, but she tilted her head in an unexpected parody, smiled and said — "Yes."

Peter snorted and started to laugh. "Is that all you're going to say? Indigo, you really are adorable. Can't I have you next?"

For his part, Jon stood by impassively, offering nothing — no denial or apology, no reassuring words. If anything, he seemed to find it entertaining.

"Well," said Lily. "Isn't this civilized. So Jon, you naughty boy, are you giving us a line or what? We'll go to the bathroom together, just us girls."

"You go," said Indigo. "I've had enough. I'm out of here."

"I'll take you home," said Jon.

"No. You stay, it's Friday night. I'm sure you have drugs to deal, although I don't know why you bother, if your mother's so rich — I mean your aunt."

"Is that what he told you?" asked Lily. "And you believed him. That's precious. What else did he say? I don't suppose he mentioned the part about living all his life in a box in a subdivision. I can sum it up in two words: fake wood panelling. His mother died when he was young and his father has terrible taste. Sells vacuum cleaners —"

"Now you're going to upset her," said Jon. "You know he sells cars."

"Poor Jon. When I found him, he was, dare I say the word, typical. A suburban teenager. Boring. With no imagination, which is hard to believe for someone so artistic. He liked to sit in his rec room, listening to heavy metal, sketching rock bands. Never went anywhere, except Florida once. And it was March break, so it doesn't count as travel. No, he'd never tell you that. It's much too ordinary. And we all know that's a sin." She stroked his cheek. "I'll say this for him though, the boy learns fast."

A few minutes later, as Indigo did up her coat and thanked the doorman, it occurred to her that she must have had a lot to drink. She wasn't even that upset.

Nineteen

It was December by the time they strung him up and shot him in the park. His name was Kim but people called him Bruno — because he looked like a Bruno, and because he acted like a Kim which made it fun to call him Bruno. The famed gentle giant. More than two hundred pounds of sweetness, stuffed in a too-tight silver gown. Or at least that's what they called it.

After exhausting any hope of finding an actual dress that big and silver in the vintage stores, which was all she could afford, Indigo tried a costume rental company, where she lucked into the whoppingest, shiniest bodysuit she'd ever seen. (It was still too small and gave him cleavage by the mounds.) She bought drapery fabric for the skirt, from a factory outlet, and a band of lamé for the waist and over the shoulder.

Completing the queenly look — a tiara and long white gloves with chunky coloured rings on top. Five o'clock shadow spread across his pallid skin, made pastier in the light of fuchsia lips. He'd even allowed her to paint his beloved Doc Martens, silver like the moon, the orb of dancing couples; the colour of disco balls.

Hoisting him up had been a challenge. There were five on the team, each directing their own video, working as actors and crew for the others, conspiring to overcome technical hurdles, such as making Bruno fly.

Concealed beneath the lamé was a harness, discovered much to Indigo's glee at an army supply store. Attached to the harness — a long metal cord, and to that a metal bar.

Standing on a ladder, Bruno tossed the bar over a branch carefully chosen for its wide dependability, then descended to the second step. Carol and Indigo held his legs. Diego and Stanley each held a side of the bar, pulling it further and further back until the cord lifted Bruno's immense shape up and away from the ladder.

"You okay Bruno?" asked Indigo.

"I can fly!"

"What about you guys?"

"No worries," said Diego. "Light as a brick."

"Okay, pull him higher. Yeah — there, that's it."

It wasn't especially cold but it was wet. A layer of snow stuck to the ground and their bootprints turned to slush. They'd brought a folding table to put things on and keep them dry: thermoses of coffee and juice, extra videotapes and a blanket for Bruno (who insisted he was fine), plus a tarp in case it snowed.

Indigo tested different angles while he got the hang of his role, learned how to steady himself as much as that was possible, improvised a jig.

"Carol, you want to get the boom?" Indigo had signed out the long, pole microphone, less for the sound than for the camp. She wanted to see it in the frame, hovering. "Okay Bruno, whenever you're ready."

They were planning to repeat the interview twice — once from the ground and once from the top of the ladder, then again at another location and, finally, in front of a blue screen so she could superimpose the Queen on other footage. Like a dance contest from the '50s, with couples falling asleep mid-step, dropping to the floor. It shouldn't be too hard to find an old musical, she thought, or people twisting in the streets, but a royal ball — that might be more than she could hope for.

She was considering a macramé bag of camera tricks, retro-style, like dividing the screen into squares and swirling the picture. And interviews with men and women on the street, unrehearsed. What do people really think of pixies?

Most of all, she wanted options.

"Wait," said Bruno. "Where's my wand?" He put his hands on his hips. "I am the Queen and I demand satisfaction. Where is my star on a stick?"

Indigo handed him the wand. "My most humble apologies, oh mighty one." And then — "All right, let's do this."

The dancing metaphor had proven fairly awkward. But it had been her first creative spark and she'd become quite attached to it. So instead of letting go she half-heartedly scanned her thoughts for something better and, when she didn't find it lurking in her mind, said to herself — "That's how it is," — and bullied a script into shape. "Next time," she insisted, "I'll refuse the first three ideas on principle."

That said, the details needed work and she spent a great deal of time on the couch/in bed/walking to school, considering the plight of the Queen and her pixies.

That and her own.

Sam and Jon had both been working on her, in their way. And she wasn't proud of the fact, but she was softening. In both directions. Even though she didn't say so. She was too busy to act on it, too withdrawn from anything social.

That and she liked the attention.

To her credit (which she duly noted), she also questioned her sanity for giving either any thought. There was Jon: arrogant, dangerous, possibly drug addicted and almost certainly a liar. And then there was Sam: not quite so arrogant or dangerous, but a better liar than she used to think.

From Jon there were apologies, accompanied by denials and compliments and the conviction that they weren't finished with each other yet, they still had things to go through.

From Sam, a crescendo of pleas for the state of their union —
that sacred bond she now testily referred to by its first initial —
and how it deserved an effort in return, something more. And
then, if it still didn't work, all right, they tried their best. In other
words guilt, coated with charm.

Listening to Sam one day, she thought it was too bad she
didn't have a class on product design. He wanted to stop by
later, give her the draft of his book. Her opinion meant a lot, he
said. And it occurred to her that someone ought to make a
perfume called Indifference. The bottle would be square,
impenetrable, the imposing shape of rejection. It wouldn't smell
like anything at all.

She told Sam she couldn't read it right away, not for a week at
least, maybe two. "So drop it off whenever." He slipped it
through the door while she was out that afternoon, in a brown
manila envelope.

She left it on a shelf, unopened.

Instead of a monologue, she decided on a mini-documentary. The
beginning would be a series of white stick cartoons on black,
showing the pixie organization in the same way that a football
coach might show a play, circling key players, using arrows and
heavy white lines. A stick version of the Queen, in all her bulging
glory, would be drawn sitting in a throne at the top of a pyramid,
under the headline QUEEN = BOSS. In the bottom corner, one
of the lowlier pixies would be shoving another, who'd stick his
tongue out.

For the voice over, Indigo wanted to mimic the kind of hushed
reverence normally reserved for golf and wildlife. "For thousands
of years, pixies have roamed the earth, invisible, benevolent, their
only joy coming from the joy they bring to others ..."

To make a long story a little less long, things have changed in
pixie-land. And the Queen is not amused.

Once upon a time, there was order. They numbered in the
thousands, lived in clouds above the forest. As a rite of passage,
each pixie — upon reaching the age of 16 — spent six years in
the world, putting humans in the mood to dance.

It used to be that pixies were glad to go where they were told
and even gladder to return, six years later, still 16 but wiser and
with aching feet.

It used to be that when the pixies came back, they married,

had little pixies and lived happily until the age of 36, when they disappeared in a shower of sparkles, only to be born again six years hence.

"But all that's gone to hell in a handbag," said the Queen. "They don't want to stay where they're told, so they leave people standing in lines on the dance floor, repeating the same ridiculous steps over and over. I'm sure they think they're clever, but I wouldn't know because half of them don't come back. Not ever. They hang out in clubs past their allotted date of departure, which means they start to age at six times the usual rate. And they know perfectly well what that means: no little pixies for them. But if what I've heard is true, some are even relieved. Can you imagine such a thing?"

Acting as the interviewer, Indigo said — "Majesty, what do you think might be the cause of this dissent?"

"Pixie envy, of course." Bruno jabbed his wand in the air. "Kids today are full of it. Pixies assigned to some tiny mountain village know all about the nightclubs and the mansions with clover-shaped swimming pools, parties that last three days with movie stars and heaps of pixie dust."

His voice dropped to a hiss — "All that sex" — then boomed with indignation. "What do you expect? They think it sounds glamorous. They feel resentful, as though they're missing all the fun. So they flit away and crash the parties, which is a breeze when you're invisible, and — poof — that's it. Ashes to ashes, another one bites the dust."

For background, Indigo had amassed footage of waltzing and the jitterbug and line dancing. And she'd wrangled permission to shoot in the Palais Royale, a dance hall built in the '20s, with a wooden stage and slatted floors, a verandah looking over the lake.

In the cavernous hall, the Queen had walked toward her as she glided backwards, shooting. "Pixies today are spoiled," said Bruno. "They want too much. They think they can go against their destiny. If you're out there, listen carefully. You're fooling yourself, but you can't fool me. What you're looking for doesn't exist. I know these things. That's why I'm Queen."

Twenty

When Indigo answered the door, Tim was sitting on the snow encrusted railing of the porch, leaning his head against the wall. "She says I'm a child."

"You are a child," said Indigo. "It's like, a hundred below and you won't even do your coat up. Do you not own gloves?"

Tim giggled and almost fell, but caught himself. "Fuck it's cold."

"Are you coming in or what?"

"What." He tucked his hands under his arms inside his coat.

Indigo watched him for a moment, then said — "Have it your way." She started to close the door.

"Wait," he said. "Don't leave. I need you. I need a hot toddy. Do you love me? Will you make me a toddy? Without the water and lemon. And don't bother to heat it. Whiskey's fine."

Indigo took his outstretched hand and pulled him up. "Nope. We're out of booze. Tough luck."

A few minutes later, he sat slumped on the couch with his feet on the table. "She doesn't like me any more." There was a hole in one of his socks.

"Don't you want to take your coat off?"

"I love this woman, Indigo, what am I going to do?"

"Seriously? You love —"

"I never told her, not that it'd make a difference. She wants a grown man, damn it, I'm a grown man. What does she need a grown-up for anyway? Maturity's overrated. Boring. Who needs it? I don't know what I'm going to do, Indigo you have to help me, why don't you call her, no you can't do that, she'd know I was here —"

"Tim. TIM. You want some coffee?"

"Beer."

"I don't have any beer, you don't need any beer."

"Beer."

"You're a maniac."

"I brought you a present." He pulled a bag out of his pocket and handed her a pair of dark green plastic glasses. "They're good for the soul. I don't have a soul and everyone knows you gotta have soul." His head, which had been sinking closer and closer to his chest, popped up like a marionette. "So what about that beer?"

She put them on and looked toward the lamp. "These are cool," she said. "Thanks, sweetie."

"They're chakra glasses. Green's the heart. I bought them for Darcey. Sign in the store said, what the fuck did it say?" He closed his eyes for what seemed like a long time and she thought he might have passed out, but then he said — "Forgiveness. Did I mention she dumped me?"

"I figured." Indigo wondered what she always wondered in situations like this, if it was one particular thing or a combination of all things that decided Tim's fate. She'd have to get the sober details later.

"Compassion. That was another one. And love. Unconditional

fucking love. That green's really got the groove on. One helluva fucking colour."

"Don't you want to give them to her anyway, sort of a parting gesture?"

"I tried, she wouldn't take them. They have other colours, you can exchange them if you want." He sniffed and wiped his nose on the side of his hand. "They were supposed to make her love me. Didn't work. She wouldn't put them on. They have indigo — those'd be good for you." He made a fist and tapped the centre of his forehead. "Right there. That's the third eye chakra, whatever that means. What did the sign say? Inspiration. Imagination. I can't remember what else. Oh yeah, concentration. Magic glasses."

"Maybe I will trade them in. I could use some inspiration, all things considered. God knows I'm sick of love. Then I could focus on my work and do wonderful things and that'd be enough. All day I've been thinking, what if I really am terrible? Or not even terrible? Bland. Nothing. Blah." She put the glasses on the table. "What if everything I ever try to say is crap? What if —"

"You should have seen the way she looked at me, like she couldn't believe she'd ever let me touch her." Tim, who had slid further into his jacket, sat ripping his nails with his teeth, staring ahead. "She wouldn't even let me in."

"I don't know what to say." Indigo took his hand away from his mouth and held it. "Give it some time, then call her. Maybe she'll change her mind, maybe she won't. I'm the last person to be dishing out advice on love. But since you ask, it stinks. Now come on, it's time for dinner. Why don't I make us something to eat?"

"I don't want to eat."

"Don't be stubborn, you're chewing on your own fingers. I'll make grilled cheese, you love grilled cheese."

In a sudden burst of momentum, Tim stood up, noticed his shoes beside the couch and sat back down. "I gotta go, I'm late."

"Late for what?"

"Just late."

"Then why don't I call you a cab? You don't have your bike do you?"

"I'm a cab. Naw, the walk'll do me good." At the door, he hugged her for a long time, and kissed her hair. "I love you, Indigo."

"I love you too, sweetie. You know that."

"No, I mean it. You're the best."

"Then do me a favour — don't drink any more, okay? Take it easy. You can come back later if you want, we'll have a sleepover. If you want to talk or don't want to talk, it's up to you." As he cut across the driveway, she called after him — "And don't forget to eat something. Or you're gonna feel like shit."

He half turned — "Yes mother, I'll be good" — then turned back and missed the curb and almost fell. "Just kidding," he yelled. "Anything for your amusement."

Twenty-one

The first blow cracked the plastic. Nicole was sitting on the floor, leaning against the tub, gripping the hammer in her clenched right fist. Indigo sat in the doorway. "Abort is such an ugly word," said Nicole. She smashed the disk against the brown ceramic tile, again. "Not like *having* a baby. *Giving* birth. They both sound so benign, don't you think? Like they don't involve blood and all that tearing. And stretch marks. And pain. Big pain. And then at the end of all that, a baby. What the hell am I going to do with a baby?"

She pressed her palms to both cheeks. "This can't be happening."

With the next strike, a pill flew sideways under the cabinet. "Go ahead and run," she sniffed. "It won't do any good. Ninety-nine percent effective. Who makes these things, the Pope? I'm gonna smash every last one of you to powder."

Indigo reached onto the counter for the stick, then sat staring at it with her head against the jamb, willing the blue stripe back to pink, ignoring the fact that this was Nicole's third pregnancy test, that all three brands confirmed the obvious.

She felt like throwing up in sympathy.

"Did you really not miss any? Not even one?"

"I don't know, maybe one or two. I was here, the pills were home. I couldn't help it. I put them in my purse after that, but I guess it was too late." Nicole sighed. "It's all that talk about having babies. This is Spider's fault. He jinxed me."

"He's not even going to be upset, is he?"

"No. He'll probably be happy, knowing him. Not that the timing's great. But I can see him now, bobbing up and down like a goddamn puppy. Telling me we'll find a way, that goddamn love will find a way. He's going to be smiling too, I know it. And then I'll have no choice. I'm gonna have to push his stupid face in."

Nicole had called that morning, clearly after a great deal of thought, to inform Indigo that — "Life is mocking us."

And Indigo, who felt weak and grey herself and had, in fact, been fetal on the couch, agreed. "But I suppose you're referring to something in particular?"

"You won't believe the day I'm having," said Nicole. "I got that fucking job."

"Gee, that's terrible Nic. Let's see — New York ... theatre ... music ... money ... parties ... scads of men. You must be so disappointed. I like that word. Scads. Don't —"

"I threw up. Again. At the Concert Hall. That's every night this week. Like biological stupid clockwork. Couldn't even make it backstage, had to lunge into the can, past all those women. I could tell they knew."

"Knew what?"

"Pay attention, Indigo. I'm pregnant."

Indigo, who was still horizontal on the couch, sat up. "No way."

"Way. Fucking way." Nicole was quiet for a moment, then

said — "What are you doing home? I was calling to swear at your machine."

"Cold. Nothing serious."

"Me too. The flu, can you stand it? On top of everything. I feel like shit. Hey, you want some chicken soup? Spider made the best soup, with veggies from the garden. He froze them in the summer."

"Of course he did," said Indigo.

Nicole's voice softened. "Come over, please. I need you. I'm at his place — he's not here, he's rehearsing. Come and let me rant."

Indigo hauled herself upstairs to dress, and called a taxi.

Nicole had a lot on her mind. That's what Indigo told herself anyway, her excuse for holding back on details. For one thing, she was skipping school. And when she said she had a cold, she lied; it was a hangover — she was just as wrecked, but it was strictly self-induced. The night before, when Tim wouldn't stay and she couldn't find Nicole, she did what she'd been trying not to do. She called Jon. She wouldn't have said so, but she felt like getting high.

"Hey," she'd said.

"I knew you'd come around."

"What are you doing?"

"Working."

"You feel like company?"

"If you want. Bring something to drink."

"You alone?"

"Would I tell you to come if I wasn't?"

"I don't know, probably."

"I'm alone," he said, and then hung up.

Putting on makeup, she pretended she was inventing a character based on herself, more or less. Make believe. But as she changed into someone more revealing — with blacker clothes and redder lips — she accused herself of treachery. She felt like a prisoner who'd escaped and then gone back to flirt with the guards. This can only lead to trouble, she thought, putting a bottle of wine in a bag. It's not too late to cancel.

"I won't be long," she told the cats. "I promise."

And then, almost immediately, she'd been pulled into what she later called the undertow; later that night, when she couldn't sleep and tried to drown her gloomy thoughts in clumsy metaphors. It's not that she couldn't swim at all. She'd simply overestimated her abilities, got caught in Jon-the-riptide. Dangerous waters.

The bull's-eye on his door was painted over, replaced by the black silhouette of a woman. She knocked on the head and when he yelled "It's open," turned the fist.

Inside, the room was cool and fumy. Dark, with the exception of the farthest corner, where Jon stood lit behind an easel, prodding a vast canvas with a long slim brush. The windows behind him were open.

"There's a corkscrew in the drawer," he said, not moving.

As she poured them each a glass, her eyes grew accustomed to the shadows. Against the wall — another painting of the silhouette, standing in a window, arms outstretched, from the perspective of the ground below. When she realized it was her she smiled, flattered at first and then relieved that it was tasteful.

She stood beyond the easel, not sure whether to talk or what to say. "Can I see what you're doing?" she tried.

He didn't look up or nod or respond in any way so she took it as a yes and moved behind him. "Oh my God, I'm naked." On his easel — a portrait of her, bound like Jesus to the cross, but with studded leather cuffs. She was larger than life, attached to an outdoor billboard, high above a busy downtown street.

It was no silhouette.

"You're nude," he said. "It's called *The New Religion*. Like it?"

"No, I don't like it. It looks exactly like me. You're not going to show anyone."

Jon spoke directly into her face, so close that she could taste his sour breath. "Stop ... being ... so ... up ... tight." And then, spreading his arms in the gesture of a preacher — "Think of it as a celebration. Of the body. Your body." He paused. "You do this every time. Do you know that? Do you have a clue? Whenever you're faced with something just a bit out of the ordinary. And I've got to tell you Indigo, it's getting tired. Why the —"

"All right," she said, stepping back. "All right. I'm sorry. It's a shock. That's all. You caught me by surprise." This is a bad sign, she thought. I'm apologizing. He's the jerk and I'm apologizing. I shouldn't have called, shouldn't have come. I should try to find my spine. She almost smiled as the words came out of her mouth — "I must have left it in my other purse."

"What's that?"

"Nothing. My brain," she said, knowing he'd take it wrong.

"I'm glad you —"

"No. I mean for coming here. I must be an idiot."

And then he was laughing and wiping his hands with a cloth and she didn't understand. "You're very cute," he said. "Don't get mad, you are. Peter's right. Oh come on, let's not fight. Let me make it up to you. You want a line?"

She nodded. "I want to buy some and go home. How much does it cost?"

"I'm sure we can work something out, but don't leave yet. I'm sorry I upset you. That wasn't my intention. Honest. You're the last person in the world I want to hurt." He took her hands and kissed them gently. "At least I paint a flattering picture, did you see those breasts? Don't I get something for that?"

When they were sitting on the couch, she said — "You're not the person I thought you were."

"No one ever is."

"Yeah, but with you it's more extreme. You do it on purpose."

He thought about it for a moment, then said — "I think it's an honest way to live. We all distort ourselves, Indigo. We all lie. Most people won't admit it, or they don't even notice." He handed her a straw and held the mirror.

"You lie," she said, leaning forward to inhale.

"I invent my own story."

"Why?"

"Because it amuses me. I'm not going to apologize. I enjoy being myself, which is more than I can say for you, most of the time. People bore me. But the way they react to me — now that's entertainment. I love to make them squirm. I'm good at it."

"You're a total narcissist."

"And that surprises you? Don't kid yourself, we're each the lead in our own production. Who in this culture isn't narcissistic? I can tell you, the list is small and you're not on it. I don't see you feeding the hungry. Oh sure, maybe you drop off a tin or two from time to time. At Christmas. But that's about you and your guilt. I don't see you dedicating your life to humanity. What's your main concern? Let's see. How to be happy. How to spice things up. How to have more fun. Not exactly Mother Theresa." He stopped to do his line, then sniffed and wiped his nose with the side of his finger. "Hey, don't feel bad. From what I hear, Mother Theresa wasn't exactly Mother Theresa."

Fits Like a Rubber Dress 263

"Watch who you criticize, she's gonna be a saint. Besides, she's closer than most. Closer than us."

"Sure," said Jon. "If you like that brand."

Indigo thought for a moment, then said — "People aren't as bad as you make out. And you know something else? I bet the older you get, the more you'll see that. I bet you'll become less cynical. Funny it used to be the other way around. Cynicism grew on people, now it fades. One hopes."

"What are you saying, we're all essentially good? There is a God? Smoking doesn't kill you?"

"I think most people are good. Not all good. Nobody's all good. But we're not all manipulative little shits —"

"Oh, so it's just me then."

"Of course we look at things from our own perspectives. Blame it on physiology, we look out from our bodies, that's the way it is. But if everyone was as ungenerous as you think they are —"

"Indigo, I love when you're naive. Take your shirt off. Please."

"Don't be ridiculous. I'm not having sex with you."

Jon stood up and sighed. "If you're going to be that way about it ... Another glass of wine?"

"I don't know." He was standing above her, waiting. "Sure. Why not. What the hell."

As she got up to follow, he turned and grabbed her black wool shirt and ripped it open. Just like in the movies. And then she was back on the couch, underneath him, smothered by his open mouth and heavy limbs.

"It wasn't a lot to ask."

Jon used her shoulders to push himself up, then left her sprawled on her back on the couch while he went to get the wine. "I've missed you so much," he said. "Besides, I know you like it rough."

"I'm taking one of these," said Indigo, putting a packet of coke in her pocket. "And I don't like it rough. How much do I owe you?" She didn't even try to close her shirt.

"Sure you do. I've been there, remember? Who's hiding the truth now?"

"Think what you want. How's that? I'm not going to play any more."

"You know you'll be back." His face was strangely quiet.

"Want to bet?" She took two twenties from her purse.

"Keep your money," said Jon. "My treat. It's not like I'll never see you again. That party? You say you hated it, but I know you didn't. You were mesmerized."

"You don't know anything," she said, aware that she was about to tell him — if not a lie, then only half the truth. "Because if you did, you'd know it's the clothes. I like the clothes, what can I say? It's really quite simple."

What she didn't tell him — had no intention of telling him — was that she had in fact spent a great deal of time trying to decide what she thought about the party. She might not have wanted to watch the gynecological exam, but she couldn't help but appreciate a place that discarded any pretense.

What she didn't tell him — had no intention of telling him — was that her fantasies had started to feature leather and submission, other women. He'd be cocky if he knew, think it made his point. He'd never believe that she liked them where they were, in her head, as fantasies. They were exciting precisely because they went further than she ever would. Or wanted to.

She'd have liked to go again, without Jon, but knew she wouldn't. This bothered her. More than she thought it should. Which provoked several days of self-inflicted torment on the subject. Why wouldn't she go again? Maybe what she'd always thought of as her exhibitionistic impulse, wasn't. Maybe she was all just talk. At one point it occurred to her that maybe she was being judgemental; she fretted over that for a while, until she realized that the person she was judging was herself. If anything she felt like an impostor. Watching when she wanted to neither smack nor be smacked seemed to somehow impose on their privacy. Then again, privacy didn't exactly seem like an issue. Maybe voyeurs were welcome, if not as kindred spirits, then at least as sympathizers. Or maybe — and this was the reason she feared — the reality had somehow let her down. The drugs, the sex, the clothes. She'd expected them to satisfy the part of herself that thought of herself as boring, if only for a moment. They hadn't. Maybe she should try again.

Indigo stopped with her hand on the door. "I used to think you had a secret," she said. "Some kind of key to happiness. I don't know why. You're as much of a mess as anyone. I'd guess more."

As she waited for the elevator, Jon yelled from down the hall — "You have primitive ideas of what a relationship should be, Mrs. Blackwell. And they don't suit you. Wake up and taste the flesh. You'll find it tastes an awful lot like me." He slammed the door.

On her way home, she thought of the portrait on the easel. She had visions of a different exit. One where she picked up a wide brush and covered her body in thick red paint. Or threw a tin of blue. Or took a knife and slashed her face right off the canvas. Of course, he might have liked that.

If she chose to admit the truth — even to herself, which she did not — she'd have to acknowledge that she might have liked the drama, more than she wanted.

Indigo locked the door behind her, resigned to the fact that the picture might appear at school, on a wall or in a hallway.

Oh well, she thought, throwing her coat on the banister and sitting on the stairs to pull her boots off. It'll add to my mythology.

There was a moment when she thought she wouldn't do the coke. She had a busy day ahead, an early class. She'd already noticed that anything gained she had to pay for in the morning. She needed her mind. And she was alone, which made it somehow more depraved. And more exciting.

Which led to the excuses. She'd stay up late and be creative. Figure out her life and write it down. The class could be sacrificed. It would be good for her to think, see things from another point of view.

By three, the rest of the world slept and she was pacing. It was horrible alone, not at first but now that she was wired. She wanted to talk, and someone to listen. And she wanted to stop doing lines, kept telling herself that each small hit was the last, until it was gone. And then her problems started. She paced upstairs and down, almost calling Jon for more, but not, wanting more than anything not to have done this. Or to do it forever. Never come down, never face anything ever again. Never again, she swore, what must have been a hundred times. The palms of her hands and feet were sweating.

At least, when she finally managed to crash, her house was spotless.

When Nicole called, it had been to leave a message.

It was early afternoon. Indigo lay on the couch, awake and in pain, with her arm across her eyes.

"Life is mocking us," announced Nicole. And Indigo agreed.

At the door, Nicole said — "You look like hell."

"Thanks, so do you. Holy cow, this place is gorgeous."

It was nothing like Indigo had pictured. She'd expected less — something unassuming and comfortable, which it was, but in a worn, thrown-together way, which it wasn't at all. The front door opened into a large living and dining room, with high ceilings and Persian rugs and hardwood floors, stained green. A billowy couch offset a slim Italian chair. The stereo sat on a carved Malaysian sideboard. The walls were the colour of dark, volcanic sand.

Later, when they were eating soup, Indigo said — "So when are you going to tell him?"

Nicole pushed her bowl away. "And I'd want to do that why?"

"Finish your soup, it's good for your virility." And then — "Sorry. You're not going to tell him?"

"No, I mean yes. I guess I'll have to." She rested her chin in her hand. "When I know what I'm doing, which I don't yet, so keep your mouth shut. But you know, I've been thinking about this and I have a theory."

"What's that?" asked Indigo.

"Whoever masterminded this whole deal decided that pregnancy had to be awful — and really really long — so at the end of it, when you've got this squawking little thing that keeps you up all night and spits on all your suede, it's better. By then anything's better, you're so desperate to pop the thing. What do you think?"

"There's got to be someone we can lobby. And while we're at it, let's get him to make them smaller, like the size of an egg. A hen's egg — we don't want him misunderstanding and making it a pterodactyl egg or something. And here's one, he should make that time of the month that time of the year. 'Cause you know it's gotta be a man. If women got to choose, *they'd* be having the babies. Or quarterly. Even that'd be —"

"What am I going to do, Indigo? I've wanted this job, like forever."

"Does it have to be one or the other?"

"What do you think?" She stood up and poured the rest of her soup down the sink. "Of course it's one or the other. It's not a family channel. You think they're going to have me waddling around, doing the scene in maternity sequins? Breast-feeding backstage?"

"So you're going to turn it down?"

"And what, say no? I think I'll just stay here? Be a mom? Wallow in bodily fluids? That's what mothers do, isn't it?"

"It's good that you're looking at the bright —"

"Hang on." Nicole turned around, surrendering her guts to the sink, then running the tap while she leaned on the counter. "I have to go home. I'm supposed to work tonight."

"There's not a hope. Why, what's going on?"

"*Nixon*. The musical. It's opening night." She sunk into her chair and put her head down. "I don't want to leave him. There, I said it. I must be in a weakened state. How can I even think that? How could I stay for a man? That's just dumb."

"You could stay for the baby," said Indigo.

"Don't say that. It's not a baby yet."

When Nicole called later, she said — "I want you to know I tried. Not to spill my guts. Literally or otherwise. I must have been delirious." Her voice echoed deep in her chest.

"You sound worse," said Indigo. "What happened? Tell me."

The way she explained it, Spider wanted to make sure she had something to eat before *Nixon*, so he made an early dinner which she managed to get down, then ran to the bathroom and tossed. When she came out, he put his hand on her head and cheek — "He's very maternal" — and said she wasn't going anywhere.

"That was it," said Nicole, "the moment that led to my downfall." Figuring the right time would never present itself, she'd already mentioned the job — while he was cooking. "He didn't even flinch," she said. "He congratulated me, can you believe this man? Said he knew it all along, they'd be crazy not to take me."

"So he wasn't even mad?"

"Nope. Used the word disappointed. Just like a dad would. Said he didn't exactly love the idea of me living in a whole other country. But get this — he said we'd find a way to work it out. That's exactly what he told me. That I've worked hard and he was happy for me."

"Is he for real?"

"Apparently. But listen, after I lost it in the can, he puts me to bed, right? And brings me Neocitron. I never could handle that stuff."

"Sounds ominous."

"Yep. So there I am, all hot and sleepy. And against my better judgement, which I must have hurled with everything else, I find myself telling him that I haven't accepted the job. I said I should, that I might, but I'm having second thoughts. Is that not the stupidist thing you ever heard?"

"No."

"Who asked you? Okay. So picture this. We're lying in bed and he's holding me in those arms of his, you've seen those arms, pushing my hair out of my face, kissing my forehead. I opened my mouth for a sip and wham — *I'm pregnant.* Two little words flopping all over the bed."

Indigo winced. "Ouch. What did he say?"

"Nothing at first. Then he asked if I was serious, and I told him no, it was all a big fat joke. So then he smiles, just like I said he would, and says 'Whadya know,' which irritates the hell out of me, of course, and now I'm wishing I kept my big mouth shut. And then he says, 'I thought you were on the pill,' which pushes me right over the goddamn edge."

Indigo couldn't help laughing. "So you ranted for a while, what else?"

"You think you're smart, don't you? Okay. I ranted for a while. And he tells me that he wants me to have it, but it's my choice. And he wants to marry me, to which I say a great big whopping *I don't think so.* And he's so calm and supportive that I just want to smack him." She paused. "And then I started to cry. End of story."

"No, not end of story. How did you leave it?"

"Well, I never did make it to work. I'm still at his place. Someone else'll have to cover *Nixon.*"

When the phone rang again, Indigo picked it up and said — "Hello Nicole" — because Nicole always was a bored and sullen patient, and because she needed to bitch and didn't want to aim it all at Spider. That's what friends were for.

It wasn't Nicole.

"Is this Alice Keating?"

"No, it's her daughter."

"Oh, I see. Indigo. It's you I'm looking for. This is such an old number, I didn't think —" She hesitated. "It's Mrs. Keeler, dear. Tim Keeler's mother."

Twenty-two

The morning was cold but offensively cheerful. The man on the radio told everyone to bundle up and get outside, enjoy the sun, smile at passers-by. "Be happy if it kills you," he said. "It's only December. There are dreary days ahead."

Indigo wasn't listening.

She wasn't doing anything, just sitting on the couch with her coat already on, waiting for Sam to come and take her to the funeral. Normally she railed against the morning. Not today. Sleep was either fleeting or a nightmare. And so she stayed awake, immersed in details. Her brain demanded details.

His bicycle would have been covered in a light layer of snow. Tim never minded riding in the dark or the wet. He thought of himself as a cowboy, undaunted by the elements, unafraid, unfettered. Only when the real snow came would he leave his bike at home, when there were mounds of ice or vast lakes of slush in every gutter. Only then would he concede.

She imagined him looking at his watch.

Seven o'clock — some of the boys might be at Babel. She knew he'd gone to Babel; he'd been seen. He wanted a drink. Something to get Darcey out of his head, put him out of his mind. He would have argued with himself. She was only one girl. No, that's wrong. Indigo was always after him for that. She was a woman. The one who didn't want him.

It would have been snowing harder by the time he left the bar after waiting, alone, for an hour. Waiting and drinking, staring at his hands around the glass. Just as well, he might have thought. After that many drinks, the desire for company might have evolved into a need for oblivion. From there he went to the liquor store — the police had filled her in on that — where he bought Russian vodka. Stolichnaya.

Outside she imagined him throwing the bag away, pushing the bottle deep into the inside pocket of his coat. "Onward," he might have said, raising his hand in mock salute. It was part of his schtick.

At the corner of Dupont and Bathurst, Tim pulled over to the curb. This was fact. The driver of the truck said that when he pulled up beside him, Tim had been putting on his gloves. So he'd probably ridden for blocks, but only just noticed that his hands were pink and aching.

The light turned green and Tim stood on the pedals, propelling himself forward as the truck to his left turned right. Another fact.

People always say it happens fast and maybe that was true. Maybe there really was no time to react or think as he fell against and under huge black wheels, sliding sideways, still gripping his bike. But maybe he also had a sense of the gradual unfolding of events.

It was here that Indigo tried to stop her brain. Without success.

Late at night, this is how she lived it: In his ears, the garbled roar of music playing backwards. He watches his arms as they try to protect him, but he isn't sure if he sees his leg twist horribly back or only feels it. He's conscious of the smell of oil, of wetness, something sharp pressed into his ribs. It's like the dream he had of being folded into smaller and smaller squares and every time a limb escapes a hand reaches out from the sky and shoves it back. He's only partially conscious of fear.

When the doorbell rang, she stood like someone wrecked, with only the essential motion. She felt as though her head was lined with cotton batten; her shoulders weighed her movements, made her slow. And then he was talking. "Are you all right, you're pale? I should have stayed. Did you sleep at all? Did you eat? Here. Please, you really should have something." He pulled a banana out of his coat, peeled half and put it in her hand.

"I'm not a child," she said, taking a bite, grateful for the care and feeding.

Sam had been the first person she called, when the pressure in her chest made breathing hard and short and painful, when she was wild with emotion, ranting through sobs — while her brain still fought to refuse the information.

He'd been there right away and stayed two days, helping to absorb the shock, insisting she eat, putting (as opposed to taking) her to bed. He held her while she cried and ran her baths, went to the store for pills to make her sleep. A willing chauffeur, he helped her suffer Mrs. Keeler and the details — all those lousy details — that go along with death.

She hadn't been to school in almost a week, although she'd spoken to her teachers. She'd spoken to everyone. As a favour to Mrs. Keeler, she'd gone through Tim's address book, broken the news over and over again until her insides turned to glue. How he'd been riding his bike in the snow, how the truck had sucked him in, how the cars behind honked frantically and finally cut the driver off to make him stop. How he died on the side of the road.

She didn't mention the drinking unless she was asked. Or the fact that he might have survived if a certain glass bottle hadn't been over his heart, under his coat. If they read it in the paper, fine.

Darcey was the worst — the way her body jackknifed forward, the pain that tore at her face. Indigo had shown up at her house, afraid to call ahead. "Hey," she said, keeping her tone as neutral as possible. "Can I come in?"

Scanning the porch, Darcey said — "Indigo. What are you doing here? Where's Tim? I can't believe he sent you." She looked annoyed, until she saw the way Indigo's mouth curled down at the ends, and the red around her eyes. "What is it, what's wrong? Tell me."

As far as Indigo could gather, Tim had been drunk all afternoon. He was drunk when he got to her house. And he was drunk hours before, when he stood pounding on the door at Darcey's.

At first she wouldn't answer. "We'd said everything there was to say. And he was hammered. You saw how hammered he was. Yelling like a fool." When she finally opened the door, he was standing on the porch holding his bicycle. "I told him to go home, he didn't even have the sense to do his coat up. And he was standing there just kind of weaving, all unsteady. I told him he should leave his bike, he could pick it up later. It was snowing."

"Of course that'd be too sensible," said Indigo. They were sitting on the floor in Darcey's living room, holding cushions in their laps.

"He said he knew I cared, which for some reason incensed me. I told him he didn't know squat. So he pulls this bag out of his pocket, starts trying to tell me what a wonderful guy he is —" She stopped, pressing her fingers on her eyelids.

"Chakra glasses. I know. Forgiveness." She put her hand on Darcey's back. "Listen, you don't have to do this."

"It's all right." Darcey took a breath, exhaling slowly. "He went to take the glasses out and his bike fell. Made this huge crashing sound as it hit the porch. And he just stared at, like he was trying to figure out how it got there. Then he gives me this stupid grin and says — 'My horse is sick. Can't we come in.' It was a funny thing to say when you think about it. I wish I laughed."

They sat at the front of the chapel: Darcey, Indigo and Sam, Nicole and Spider, shoulder to shoulder, overwhelmed, waiting for the epilogue.

Indigo stood and walked forward, spreading her hands on the polished wood of Tim's closed coffin. She couldn't believe he was in there, found it hard to comprehend. Tim Keeler's coffin. Three words that should not have been allowed to go together. Not yet, she thought. Not now. Not before — what?

She'd heard it more than once already and it pissed her off, perhaps unreasonably. "He died before his time." Come on, she thought. I mean, what kind of jellied pap is that? Sickness aside, was there really a point at which she could have said — "Okay, his time's up, Take him now"? Unless he got so old that all he did was lie down or sit, in relative health but with a body good for nothing else but waiting, which has to be rare, which means that most of us will die before our time. She wondered what it was, exactly, about that particular line that comforted people. Was it because they were so afraid of death that a person who died before he withered enough to let everyone around him grow used to the fact that death was indeed the only place to go, had to be seen as distinct from them? When people say — "He died before his time," she thought, what they really mean is — "I don't have to relate to this in terms of myself, or my family, or my best friend. This was a freak occurrence." There are no bounds to the human capacity for self delusion.

Indigo stared at the photograph, black and white in a cold silver frame.

Tim smiled back.

He was behind the bar at Vox and he was psyched. It had been his second day on the job. He'd never wanted much he had to work for, resisted making plans, said he refused to spend his present in the future. But he was thinking that he might like to own a bar one day, maybe on a beach. Nicole, who at the time lived across the street, went home to get her camera, to mark the momentous occasion. Indigo made a toast. "Don't try to deny it," she said. "You have a goal. We're both witnesses. Cheers to you. Make it someplace nice for us to visit, like Tahiti."

Indigo turned to the guests. Tim's people gathered in a room, she thought, so many people. Were they really here to say goodbye, as though a trace of his life still clung to the body — as though he might be somewhere near the ceiling, watching? Then again, who was she to say he wasn't? Didn't everyone fantasize about going to their own funeral, try to imagine who'd be there, which stories they'd tell? (It occurred to her, as she processed the image, that even here her mind sought the unoriginal, the cliché that made it all somehow familiar. Perhaps especially here.)

If anything, it seemed more like a declaration, proof that he'd been loved or liked by many, evidence of conversations had, life lived, spread out in rows along the pews in matching black. Each one counts.

Indigo thought of her mother, imagined her consumed by jungle, deep in concentration, reflecting on the way points of light sneak through the canopy. She hadn't called in more than a week, didn't know any of this. She was spared a little longer, spared the formal images — the dichotomy of flowers on a casket.

This was the kind of situation that cried out for a mother, made Indigo grieve for the one she had, prematurely, as though she was never coming back now that Indigo had proven she could live without her.

She faced the coffin, rested her fist on the cool polished wood.

Dead at 30. It seemed unreasonable, but what did reason ever have to do with death? Or for that matter, life? That we have control is our illusion, she thought. All roads lead to Rome.

Tim had asked what she thought about God. Maybe in a subtle way he knew. A premonition. Funny, she'd never thought of Tim as that instinctive.

She'd read somewhere that what people call the soul is actually an unseen force like microwaves or gravity, except that it carries forward memory. An appealing idea, but she couldn't help thinking it was all simply a case of our collective ego having grown way out of proportion to the inconsequential blip in time and space we occupy. The trouble was, she'd prefer to believe something else. She'd like to believe in something as opposed to nothing, even if there was nothing. A terrible thought occurred to her: she was an atheist. Pretending to be an agnostic. She really should try to be more positive.

Indigo felt Sam's hand on the back of her arm and wondered if funerals were, by their nature, as surreal as this one was to her. The juxtaposition of present and past, love and fear and anger, said and unsaid thoughts.

Tim's brother Matt stood beside his mother near the door. Mrs. Keeler, who veered between weepy and enraged, who had managed to stay consistently drunk for the past several days. Indigo had been at her house when Matt arrived the night before. The first thing he said was how hard it was to get away, that he had to be back in L.A. the following night. And then, as his mother lurched toward him — "Mother, I know you're upset, but please don't start. It's been a long day."

Indigo decided then to hate him, as a tiny gift to Tim.

Toward the end of the service, Nicole leaned closer to whisper in Indigo's ear — "Jon's here. At the back. There, with that theatre guy, what's-his-name, Peter."

As Indigo looked he nodded, almost imperceptibly, and waved. She turned away, imagined crawling into the coffin. Not because of Jon. He barely made an impact, good or bad, which felt like progress. It was everything else. She wanted to hide from her thoughts, disappear, hide from the world. She wanted to sleep.

On their way out, Sam stopped to see if Mrs. Keeler wanted them to come by later, while Indigo excused herself to find the washroom. Jon intercepted. "Indigo, I've been trying to reach you. I wanted to know how you were, see if I could do anything."

"I'm okay," she said. "Thanks. It's been a rough week. Darcey's really a mess. I guess we all are. That's Sam. Over —"

"I see you're still speaking to this asshole," said Peter, stepping closer. "Even after Lily. Can't tell you how much fun I had that night, she's quite a trip. Too bad you had to leave. She said she liked you. Any friend of —"

"Shut the hell up," said Jon.

Ignoring him, Peter let his eyes wander down and up Indigo's long black dress, then sighed. "So he really does exist, this phantom husband of yours. I must say I'm disappointed." He went to put his arm around her, then changed his mind and touched her shoulder. "I still think I'm a better choice. Much better looking."

He said it softly, almost kindly, as though by maintaining some of his normal lusty humour, he could distract her from the pain of having best friends die.

She wiped her eyes with the balled up tissue in her fist. "I should go. I'll see you guys —"

"You coming to the wake?" asked Jon. "It's tonight at Vox."

"I know. It depends how I feel. Maybe."

"You have to," said Peter. "I hear he wanted a big party. Something truly spectacular. And he wanted us to put a pinch of his ashes in everyone's drinks all night."

"That's gross," said Indigo. "He did not. You're lying."

"So what do you think he would have wanted?" asked Jon.

"More time."

"Besides that."

"Well, a party. I agree with that. Lots of drunk people going on about how great he was. So I guess I'll come. I can do that. I should. But I think he'd want to be scattered someplace. Somewhere exotic, like Tahiti."

"I'm there," said Peter. "When do we leave?"

"I'll have to get back to you on that. Mrs. Keeler has this antique urn thing she's planning to put him in. She wants to keep him on her mantel." Indigo put her hand over her mouth to hide a yawn. "Excuse me. Can you believe it? Poor Tim. I mean, we're talking about a guy who left home to get away from his mother. Don't get me wrong, he loved her and everything. But he'd freak if he thought he'd end up in a pot in her living room." As she looked back at Mrs. Keeler, Sam caught her eye and smiled. "I'm going to try and talk to her, see if I can save him. I'm not sure why, but I think it's important. I think he'd like Tahiti."

When it was over, Indigo sat in the car, slouched against the window. "I'm going to go home, try to catch a snooze," she said. "You coming to the wake?"

Sam put his hand on her knee. "Here's the deal. You look like hell and you need something good to eat. So we're going home, to my place. You're going to sleep. I'll make an early dinner. Then if you want I'll drive you home to change and then to Vox. I don't know if I'll come. I have some things to do."

She didn't have the strength to resist, even if she wanted to — which she somehow thought she should but didn't. It felt good to have his attention, reassuring. She put her hand on top of his and closed her eyes.

Maybe she'd punished them both for long enough. He was sorry, said he loved her more than anything. (Don't they all say that? It must be in the manual.) He said he loved her.

As she softened, her inner voice began to doubt her outer story. She questioned her own motives, asked whether leaving Sam didn't have more to do with being single than it had to do with his experiment. (Is that what I'm calling it now, she thought, an experiment? What a joke.)

She refused to listen, insisted that moving out had been the only choice. She rubbed her forehead, thinking — Okay, I'm feeling nostalgic. Nothing wrong with that. But it's not like I have amnesia. Sam acted like a jerk. And it started way before he took it out of his pants for some guy. What do you say to that?

Her demons took another tack. All right. You needed time and now you've had it. But is it possible that the next logical step is back? Maybe (and this didn't seem like as big a maybe as it used to), she and Sam had learned something — or as the how-to-be-a-better-me books say, grown as people. Maybe they were stronger now as individuals, which would make them new and improved as a pair. It might have been a great big shot of vitamin B to the butt of their marriage.

Then again, she did tend to rationalize and he had been kind when she was broken. Her resistance was low. Her oldest friend was ash, and maybe bits of bone and teeth, and she was fearful of the world. Sam held the illusion of safety.

When he'd parked the car, he said — "It's none of my business, but that guy you were talking to, the one in the leather jacket, is he the one you're seeing?"

"Not any more. How'd you know?" As she opened the door, she turned to face him. "Never mind, it doesn't matter. We're friends. Or I think we might be. Eventually. We'll see how it goes." She got out and walked ahead, eyes down, jacket open to the wind, oblivious.

Inside, the surprise caught in her throat.

The living room was changed. The walls had gone from white to slate. The couch was under the window. There were oversized, brightly coloured cushions on the floor, an arrangement of beige and blue dried flowers, plus a beaten silver bowl.

"What's the matter? Don't you like it?"

"Sure, it isn't that," she said. The tears that had teetered on the brink now fell in streams from swollen eyes. "It doesn't have anything to do with that. Looks great. It's just that I can't believe he's gone."

Sam put his arm around her shoulders. "I know, sweetie. I know. Can I get you something?"

She shook her head. "Everything's a mess," she said. "I hate this."

"I know you do."

Sniffing loudly, Indigo stepped out of her shoes and into the living room. "I think I need a nap."

"No, go on up to bed. You can use my robe if you want, it's behind the bathroom door. It's clean."

"You coming?"

"Maybe in a while. Try to get some rest."

On the stairs, she paused in the light of the window, noticing that the dead plant on the sill had been replaced with a very-much-alive pot of irises.

She was almost afraid to look in the bedroom.

As she passed Sam's office, she saw that it was clean — but otherwise the same. Nothing that excluded her, she thought, any more than usual. Nothing she couldn't come home to. At the closed bedroom door she stopped. In her mind she saw Tim, leaning back on the bed, ankles crossed, his face absurdly painted.

Her cheeks felt hot as she opened the door.

The room was almost as she'd left it, except that he'd taken down their wedding photo and put in its place a poster for Bitter Campari. And it was neater, without any clothes flung over the chair.

Indigo tossed her purse on the bed and went to get the robe. "Don't get all weird," she said, quietly, distracting herself with small talk. "You don't believe in ghosts. And even if you did, it's way too soon. I'm sure these things take time. And he wouldn't look for you here anyway. If he's coming at all, he'll come to the house. But he won't because he knows you'll give him shit. He'll wait a while. He hates it when you're mad."

In the bathroom, she hung her dress on the back of the door and slipped inside the robe. Reluctantly, she leaned toward the mirror. Her eyes were red and swollen, as expected, cheeks pale, lips a darker pink than normal. Who cares, she thought. I look like shit. So what.

As she went to wash her face, Indigo's eyes fell down to the counter, onto a pair of chunky clip-on earrings, gold with green glass stones.

They didn't register at first. But even when they did, nothing. No tears. No self-pity. No regret. No flutter in her gut. It was possible that part of the pain she felt was jealousy, hard to know for sure. It had been there for days, gripping her skin from the inside. If it chose to divvy itself up differently, take some away from Tim and give it to Sam — well, frankly, it was all the same to her.

Indigo held the earrings in her hand. They were heavy and ugly and her initial thought was to flush them down the toilet. Instead she put them on and tucked her hair behind her ears.

I do look upset, she conceded. On another day that would be a clue.

Out loud, she said — "And so the power shifts." She was thinking that until this moment, she'd had the advantage. Sam wanted resolution. This or that, black and white, married or divorced. She preferred things open-ended. Now she'd have to make an effort, if that's what she wanted. Now she'd have to choose.

She stood straighter and tried to imagine who she'd be if she wore these earrings. Somebody corporate, maybe a lawyer. Real estate agent? Receptionist? Someone who smokes. Probably tall, she thought, with helium breasts. A tiny waist and long, shapely legs. Barrister Barbie. Garters under pin-striped skirts. They were too flashy for an accountant, but she was probably buying into some old and withered stereotype.

Okay, so I'm making assumptions, she thought, finally, putting the earrings on the counter. And I guess I am a little green. But think about it. He left them here on purpose, to let me know my time is up.

BEEEEP. *And the winner is — ugly earring woman.*

BEEEEP. *Sign these. You lose.*

Okay Mrs. Blackwell, you're free to go.

In the bedroom, she pulled the curtains open wide. Lately, when her eyes were closed, she was conscious of the darkness in her body, of the blood that poured, the organs in her chest pulsing — or quivering — whatever it was that organs did. She wanted to sleep in the light.

She lay on her side of the bed, wondering if madness grew from grief.

Why didn't she know if Tim was happy, overall? They used to tell each other everything. They used to ask. She'd better ask Nicole — although Nicole was fairly vocal; she wanted the moon and now, potentially, its child. And Sam. What did Sam need to make him happy? She always asked herself, although she rarely had short answers. That and they tended to change.

Where marriage was concerned, she knew that if she had to write it down, she'd seem confused. But that would deny the moments of absolute clarity she had on either side of the subject. She preferred to think of it as torn.

It was only lately, since the accident, that she'd begun to look fondly at the folds, even wistfully, mostly late at night. A cloistered life of sorts, it had appeal as a place that she could hide in comfort. Sam still had appeal.

The rest of the time, she had trouble seeing herself committed — to the man, or to what Jon derisively called the institution. It seemed like a place to hide and not be found.

More often than not, she liked to think of herself alone (the unthinkable), working in metal, writing, humming to the radio, wearing flimsy cotton dresses, silver bangles on her wrists. She'd been working on what she called her short-term love theory. There was no denying that she wanted love, or something that resembled love: passion among great friends. (Maybe that was the definition she'd been looking for.) But maybe, just maybe, there was something to having shorter-term things (it demanded a better word than relationships) with lovely, intelligent men who'd nonetheless make injudicious husbands.

She suspected there were many.

She'd seen a film set in Greece, so now she dreamed of turquoise water. She'd have a whitewashed house on a hill, looking out to the Mediterranean. It was actually a new version of an old fantasy: Santa Fe, adobe house, sprawling land (different movie). But the sea held more appeal.

She'd have waves of visitors. Friends. Ex-lovers. Friends of her lovers. Weighty conversation. Houseboys. She'd paint her toenails blue as sky, walk barefoot on the sand and rock, drink cold pink Zinfandel from crystal flutes.

Of course, the inherent problem with the short-term love theory is where to draw the line and end it. If it's rocking along quite happily, how do you say — *Okay, that's it then. See you in Greece*. Pluses and minuses to everything.

She hated that.

When she woke, it was to the tune of ice cubes hitting glass. Sam was beside her on the bed, sipping scotch. "How long did I sleep?"

"A couple hours. You hungry?"

"Starved. Who's the woman?"

"What woman?"

"The one you're having sex with."

Sam smiled. "Don't beat around bush or anything. Say what you mean."

"Life's short." She waited. "You don't want to tell me?"

"I'm not having sex with anyone."

"Don't give me that. I saw the earrings. Just like you wanted."

"What are you talking about?"

"In the bathroom. Those awful green things. I know you wanted me to see them. And it's not like I don't understand. You —"

"Indigo, don't you think you're being just a teeny bit self-centred? Everything doesn't revolve around you. We went to a show. She came from work, changed into a pair of jeans. That's all. She forgot them. We're not sleeping together. We've only gone out a couple times."

"Sure. Whatever you say. Look, it's no big deal. We're not together any more. I'm curious, that's all. Who is she?"

"Someone who works for the magazine. Lorraine. Lorraine DeLorenzo. No one important. No, that's not fair. She's nice. I like her. Why, you jealous?"

"What if I am? It's normal. Not that it matters."

"It doesn't have to be this way."

Indigo made a show of clamping her eyes shut and pulling the covers over her face.

"All right," he said. "All right, I get the point. Don't think about it now. In a few days, when you're feeling better. Then we should talk. Come on, let's eat." He pulled the blanket off her head. "I made vegetarian chili."

She opened her eyes. "When did you go vegetarian?"

"Never. When did you become so nosy?"

Indigo smiled. "Nicole says it's part of my charm. I want to know everything. Then mostly I forget and ask again. It's a genetic thing."

By all accounts, it was a wild goodbye.

It started gravely. Condolences in reverent tones, gentle tears. They blew his picture up and hung it on the wall. Stories flowed along with drinks. Friends embraced. Ex-girlfriends met, compared, spoke fondly.

Indigo sat at the end of the bar, under the weight of all those times she sat at the bar, talking to Tim.

As people came, she traded sympathies. But there seemed to be a time lag, an extra second or two between words said and understood. She watched their mouths move, nodded encouragement, apologized for strange behaviour. She felt removed, as though an invisible shield kept her apart. "I'm not all here," she said, and people understood. "It's funny. My ears are acting up. I know it's noisy, but it's all kind of numb. I feel like I'm under water."

She sipped her drink and watched people through the distance of the mirror, trying to imagine how they'd go, how old they'd be allowed to get.

Of say, a hundred in the room, she tried to guess how many'd make the papers. The owner of Vox liked to skydive; that could be dramatic. And she supposed someone might be shot. On the other side of the world, she thought, there are people who stand in front of government buildings, soak themselves in gasoline and strike a match, just to make a point. Out in a blaze of glory. Or anyway, a blaze of something.

By the time Jon arrived, the crowd had already consumed trays and trays of purple Jell-O shooters on the house. One of Tim's friends, yet another skinny twentysomething with close-cropped hair and pants that defied gravity, stood on a chair, heaving toasts above the noise. "Cheers to a fucking great guy," he yelled, raising his beer. "We'll miss you, mate."

As Jon slipped in beside her, Indigo said — "If you had to die, how would you want to go?"

"With a bang." He motioned for a beer. "And I do. Have to die. Hate to be the one to tell you, so do you."

"Funny," she said, tapping her swizzle stick against the bar. "I was just wondering about that. The big bang theory. Do you think it counts if you get news coverage and if it does — why? And for what, posterity? Who gives a shit? You're dead. But if that is the case, I suppose CNN would be worth more than, say, an article buried in the back of the paper."

"Good point," said Jon. He was leaning sideways on the bar, practically on top of her. "I'll have to remember to die alone. A plane crash would totally defeat the purpose. Lots of coverage. None about me. Maybe a hostage thing. In a television studio. Live. And it should last a while. To build suspense. Like all day and into prime time."

"So we're talking gunshot."

"Not necessarily. To kill me, he — or no a she, then we'd go international for sure — should have a really big bomb. So big they'd have to evacuate blocks and blocks of the city. She'd be doing it as some kind of biting comment on the state of the art world, so that who I am is relevant, not to mention newsworthy. And, of course, I'll be famous. So they'll know all about me. And everything I've done will double, no quadruple in price." He paid for his beer and took a sip. "But get this, before she hits the detonator, she'll spike me with a great big shot of heroin. You know, to ease the pain."

"Sounds nasty."

"Of course." He smiled. "How do you want to go? And don't say at a ripe old age, in your sleep. Not if I've taught you anything."

"Well, if it's not an option — I'd like one of those instant deaths they're always talking about. 'And in other news, the oldest woman in the world died instantly today.' Spontaneous combustion."

"Don't you want time to prepare, collect your thoughts?"

"Life is the process of learning how to die. Socrates. Or something like that." She looked at the glass in her hand, half empty. "I have time," she said. "What do you think I'm doing?"

"Okay, fair enough." Leaning past her, he yelled — "Hey Margaret, how's it going?" — then waved at a woman down the bar; she was pale and slim, with vivid red hair and a brown velour dress, tight and to her ankles. The woman half-turned, saw who it was and looked away.

"So where's your other half?" he asked, unbothered.

"I don't have another half, this is it. But if you're talking about Sam, I came alone. He had things to do. And Nicole has the flu. And Darcey couldn't face it. She feels pretty awful, like it's her fault or something, which is nuts. I was going to go over, but she wants to be alone."

"You look like you could use some perking up."

"What does that mean?"

"Nothing. I just thought you might want a little pick-me —"

"I don't want anything that's going to keep me awake. Ever again. I don't want euphoric, I want sleep. I want oblivion. Anyway, drugs depress me. Now these —" She held her glass by the stem. "Can you believe I'm nearly thirty years old and this is my first martini? Well, strictly speaking it's my third. But the others have all kind of blended into this one." She poured the last few drops in her mouth and crunched the ice. "Whatever. I'm out of here."

As she stood up off the stool, Jon grabbed her hand and held it. "Don't leave yet. I have something to show you. At home. I was hoping you'd come."

"You've used that line before," she said. "And you know what? Whatever it is, I don't want to see it. Give me a call some time. We'll grab a coffee."

"Peter's right. You are mad about Lily."

"No, it isn't that." She leaned against the stool and picked up the swizzle stick. "If you really want to know, I was making a mess of a soldering job the other day, a silver band for my thumb, and I realized that I don't need you to save me. Not from the boredom or anything else. No offence. I mean you're interesting, but you're not that interesting. And I'm not even close to being in love with you, which means I don't have to take your crap." As she smiled, the crease above her brow softened. "And you want to know what else?"

"I don't think so."

"I clued into the fact that this whole school thing is exactly what I need to get my head straight. I can't tell you how liberating that is. I've been wasting time." Indigo broke the stick in half and dropped the pieces in her glass. "Oh, and one more thing — you don't love me. Never did. Don't think I don't know that." She lifted her coat from the back of the stool. "But you know, I appreciate the gesture."

By now Jon was smirking. "I know what this is about," he said. "You're going back to your husband."

Indigo shook her head and sighed, raising her eyebrows at the same time in a look she hoped said pity. "You're too much. Listen carefully. I don't want to come over. I'm not angry and I'm not running back to Sam. It's just that you're a lot of work and I need that energy. I have things to do." In other words, she lied.

At that moment, as Indigo put on her coat, she believed that her life was about to turn back on itself. She had a few days of independence left, then she and Sam would talk, make up, make a mess of his room with all her things. She left the bar confident that, this time, she'd insist on equal footing. Things would be different. She'd kept him waiting long enough.

Outside, the night had warmed since she was sober. The air felt smooth on her face and even the lights of the cars seemed gentle and subdued; the traffic sounded far away, muted by the ringing in her ears.

The sex was bound to be fantastic, she thought, forgetting that although it used to be good, once upon a time, she never would have used the word fantastic. Not even at its best.

Standing on the sidewalk, Indigo decided that the sadness wasn't gone but it was lighter. She took a pen and scrap of paper from her purse and wrote — BUY MARTINI GLASSES, then sagged against the cold brick wall of Vox.

At the corner, a hot dog vendor pulled the hood of his parka close around his head, tongs in mitted hand. He shared the hungry late night crowd with the lone hardy busker, the man with the saxophone, leaning down the wall, playing *Stardust*.

At home, Indigo left a trail of clothing up the stairs, ending with her bra beside the bed. That was it for several hours, until the pounding on her brain woke her up. And then she couldn't sleep. She rummaged in the drawer for aspirin, drank some juice, reconsidered her opinion of martinis. Washed her face and brushed her teeth. Lay in the dark. Then gave up and made some lemon tea, got back into bed with Sam's first draft. She wouldn't have said so, but she thought it might act like a sedative. She was wrong.

It only took a few chapters to realize that the gay best friend had been promoted from minor to major character. Gus (the protagonist) was still a mobster's son, still married and still being blackmailed by his sister. He no longer had children. And surprise surprise: in chapter four, his wife — a woman who just happened to quit a career in advertising to go to film school — came home early on a cloudy afternoon, and found him on the receiving end of a rather energetic blowjob. (So now she knew.)

Of course, the scene took place in the kitchen.

And, of course, she got it all on video.

Leaning forward as she read, Indigo couldn't decide whether to laugh or wake Sam up and give him hell. Or both. He had more nerve than she'd given him credit for; the man was bold — and clearly shameless. And to think, she almost used it in her video. The real performance. Except that she thought it might betray his trust. She'd been loyal to a bond of marriage so obscure it existed in her mind.

She read the scene again.

In her initial shock it had seemed almost funny, the idea that he'd recycle a moment so potentially embarrassing. But the closer she looked, the more angry she became. The wife was a vain, self-centred bitch. So horrible to live with that his homosexual tendencies, once effectively suppressed, flowed freely (not to mention often).

When she found them together, she kept the camera rolling as she walked calmly over, grabbed a handful of the man's hair and yanked his head back hard, out of her husband's lap. And then, hurling obscenities, she went to the refrigerator, opened the door and let fly the contents. Jars of pickles and jam, garlic black bean sauce, even a half-full can of apple juice. Still sneering, she turned to the crisper, keeping up an assault of tasteless remarks as they fled the barrage of cucumbers, carrots and zucchini — followed by a slab of bacon.

Fits Like a Rubber Dress   287

To describe her, Sam used the phrase "physically beautiful." But — and this was the push that sent her skidding over the edge — he made her blond.

Twenty-three

In spite of her own apocalyptic expectations, Indigo did not look old age in the face on her thirtieth birthday; she didn't obsessively check for wrinkles, the effects of gravity or stray white hairs, didn't gaze soulfully into the eyes of her decline. Sure, she spent a few bucks on a cream guaranteed to give her the skin of a ten-year-old, and a contraption that promised firm, rippling abs in a day and a half. But her heart wasn't in it. She couldn't seem to muster the angst.

In fact, it wasn't old age on her mind but the alternative.

A few weeks after the funeral, she had what she called a minor epiphany — "Unless that's an oxymoron," she said to Nicole, "in which case, I'll go with revelation." She'd been sitting in the dark when it happened, watching a TV couple abducted by TV aliens. Huddled in a corner of the couch, she was overcome with the realization — no, the absolute certainty — that nothing mattered. In the perspective of the earth's puny place in the universe, nothing that happened here mattered in any big (or even mediocre) way. And most important, her own personal life and death — the subject of such extended ego-anxiety — was immaterial.

It was such a relief to know.

"I wouldn't call that minor," said Nicole.

"Technically I think it is, because I've been sort of leading up to it. You know, because of Tim. I've been telling myself that when you're dead you're dead. You're too far gone to care, you know what I mean? You're not going miss anything."

"Yeah," said Nicole. "It's not like you sit around watching your friends have all the fun."

"Or grieving for yourself."

"Unless you're a ghost."

"Which has got to be rare," said Indigo. "So what's there to be afraid of? It's all in our heads."

Unfortunately (because Indigo did so like things settled), she later had what she called an inverted epiphany. (She didn't like the word regression.) Deep one night, she found herself awake and shaking, practically numb with fear of death. Her hands and feet were cold, her heart was beating out of its mind and all she wanted was to hide under some psychological bed until her time was up. "My God," she said to herself. "We're all going to die."

Indigo pulled the covers up to her chin.

And then she smiled, a small knowing smile, and a heaviness descended on her limbs. "Okay," she whispered. "You're over the top. We can deal with this. We understand over the top."

In the shadows on the ceiling were the days that stretched ahead, concealed by time that hadn't come. Days that would matter while they mattered, in their own ephemeral way to the people who lived them. Life for the sake of itself, she thought, strangely comforted. Swept into the past like a sand mandala.

When she finally drifted off she dreamed of monks in orange robes. And heaven.

Indigo's birthday was far enough into spring that the snow was usually gone. It was something she relied on — the accepted natural course — and in those rare years when white had refused to relinquish its hold she took it as a sign. That this year's birthday brought a final gasping storm wasn't completely unexpected. The sleet that whipped the windows of her new apartment as she lay in bed being 30 was, in her mind, just one more example of assumptions gone to hell.

Months before, as she rounded the corner of the new year, she'd had the gall to envision yet another new beginning, this one tidier and free from complications — with enough dough for a fabulous flat with a garden, tulips in the dirt — went so far as to count on it.

Her mother had blown through the door in January, tanned and happy with the work she'd done in Bali, eager to turn the ideas that spilled from her sketchbook into canvases — and the third floor into a studio. "But honey, there's no pressure to leave," she said. "It's your room. You can stay as long as you want."

Or longer.

Like all good loose ends, Indigo assumed that the sale of the house could be tied up quickly. She and Sam would split the money, then say goodbye in a good-natured, some might say intimate manner, the way couples are supposed to when they still claim to like each other's company.

She'd been angry at first, about the violence he'd seen in her face and described in his book, her no longer private rage. But when it came right down to the yelling, there'd been less than she thought to say.

"What if people find out it's true?" she asked.

"What if they do, who cares? It'll make me interesting."

"You sound like me."

"Then maybe I've learned something."

He was being too congenial and she hesitated. "What about the wife? You think I'm like that? You think I'm a total bitch?"

"Indigo, she's supposed to be a bitch. She's fiction. My blond bitch goddess. I did it on purpose, to draw a nice fat line between real and unreal. I couldn't have made her like you, could I?"

When he grinned she knew he thought he'd won. And more than just the argument. Sam thought his strategy of pushing here and nudging there, holding on then pulling back had won her over. "Besides," he said, "any resemblance to actual persons, living or dead, is purely coincidental. It'll be right up front."

Indigo said — "I'm filing for divorce."

The smile hung on his mouth a moment too long, while his eyes turned to alarm. "I don't —" He stopped and tried again. "I thought ... I don't get it, why?"

She shrugged. "I want to be alone."

To which he snapped — "Don't be stupid. Nobody wants to be alone."

"Don't call me stupid."

It took some back and forth — attempts at persuasion mostly, some recrimination — but eventually they settled down to details. They opened a litre bottle of wine, sat on opposite sides of the couch. He chose the bed, she wanted the old wood table in the kitchen. He picked the computer, she the Persian rug. Him the desk, her the armoire. They divided dishes into sets, wandered (slightly impaired) through photos, books and music.

Sam swore she'd never find anyone else who loved her like he did.

She said she'd take her chances. "I don't respond to threats."

He said he was sorry if it sounded that way, it wasn't his intention. He wondered, as they finished the last of the wine, if she wouldn't like to go upstairs. "You know, once more for the road?"

She thanked him anyway. "As much as I'd like to," she said, "it's probably not a good idea. And I'm trying to stick to those."

What followed was the steady erosion of Indigo's best laid plans. Did the real estate agent actually laugh when they mentioned the price they hoped to get, or only grin in disbelief? "Holy smokes, where've you guys been? The market's in the crapper." He used the tip of his pen to pick his teeth. "Cut a third right off the bat." They planted a sign on the lawn and divided the duties; smiled as couple after couple opened closet doors, twisted taps, mewed apologetic thank-yous as they left.

At the first promise of an offer, they sat on the same opposite sides of the couch, waiting. "This might be it," said Sam. "The first day of the rest of your life."

Indigo made a face. "Great, be sure to use that on the book tour." And then — "I'm sorry, that wasn't nice." When he still looked wounded, she said — "You know what? Forget the other day. I'm game if you are. One for the road?"

She led him upstairs but even that had changed. She no longer needed validation — not from him — and discovered that without that need, there was no sense of urgency. No real desire. In its place she found nostalgia, and a kind of permeating sadness. This is nice, she told herself, looking over his shoulder at the titles of books on the shelf. Of course it's nice. Taking the lead, she tried sitting on top and facing away, arching and letting her hair fall down her back. She was imagining his point of view, of her spine and the motion of her ass above him, when he suddenly gasped — "Christ, Indigo. What the hell have you done?"

She hadn't mentioned her tattoo.

On the morning of her birthday, snow hurled to the earth in great watery clumps that melted when they hit the ground. Under the covers Indigo stretched, first to one side, as far as her back would allow, and then the other. She glanced through the window at the falling sky, then curled and closed her eyes.

In her dream she was lying in bed, curled, watching the snow. When she woke, she wasn't sure if she'd been sleeping.

She'd expected to wake up feeling doomed, and her first reaction was to wonder why she didn't. It had to be some newly gained maturity. Here she was, no longer in her 20s — technically no longer young, although she did tend to put stock in that whole state of mind thing — and her mood was damn near perky. She had the urge to call her mother.

With a final yawn, she got up and put some water on the stove.

It wasn't the place she had in mind. There was no deck or little garden. No fireplace. No bedroom. Just three square rooms above the Bridal Barn. Converted office space with fluorescent lights and decent hardwood floors. (She and Sam had yet to sell the house, which meant that Indigo hovered somewhere close to broke.)

Still naked, she folded her bed into the couch, made tea and stood to the side of the window. The world was shades of grey. Umbrellas, slanted to the wind. Cement. The boy sitting in the doorway, head down, his bare hand open and extended. Inside, her flat was like a shadow. Muted blue. Indigo shivered but stayed where she was. With her hands hot around the cup, she felt happy.

There was a time when she drank orange pekoe. Every morning. Without variation. She considered the monotony penance for her own rebellious thoughts, which she never acted on but fretted over nonetheless. (In hindsight, she rather liked the irony.) For all her thirsting, she'd been afraid of her creeping lack of satisfaction.

Of what that meant. As much as she fantasized — and yes, she admitted it, obsessed — she used to be afraid of where she'd end if she started making changes. That seemed like a very long time ago. Now she lusted after motion. Monumental change or minuscule, it didn't matter. She discovered that it got her high to change her apartment, mind, plans. Company forward, lunge. Now she drank anything but orange pekoe.

When Nicole buzzed, Indigo slipped into tights and a sweater and ran down the narrow front stairs to let her in. "Hey," she said. "I'm nervous. You've done this before, right?"

"Don't worry, I'm practically a hairdresser." Nicole handed her an Easter lily wrapped in yellow foil. "I can't believe it. Thirty. Are you ever old."

"And you're getting thick around the middle. We all have our crosses."

"Oh sure, make fun of the pregnant lady. That's very nice."

Since Christmas, Nicole and Spider had been negotiating what Nicole called this kid thing. She turned down the job in New York and agreed to move into his house in her seventh month. In return for being the mother of his child, she received several rather expensive items of clothing, plus a *fabulous* white gold band inlaid with diamonds — which she was not obligated to wear on her left hand. In addition to the gifts, the obnoxiously excited Spider agreed not to even think the word marriage for at least one year after their own tiny, screaming human entered the world. "And one more thing," she said.

"Name it," said Spider, more to her belly than to her.

"If the kid wrecks the girls I want new ones."

"Only if it's safe. None of that silicone shit."

"Deal." She kissed his forehead.

Describing the scene to Indigo, Nicole said — "This kid thing ain't half bad. Did I mention we're getting a nanny?" They were in the kitchen, Nicole mixing the bleach in a plastic bowl while Indigo watched. "This stuff reeks," said Nicole. "Go jump in the shower."

Indigo ignored her. "What's it like? I mean, being pregnant. Do you feel okay? Are you nauseous? Does it move around in there?"

"I never felt better," said Nicole. She was standing with her back against the counter, leaning. And then — "All right, that's not exactly true. But I can't believe how much energy I have. I was dead the first three months. Sick like a dog on peyote. Now I want to go dancing. Except that I get really cranky. Without any warning. It's scary, let me tell you. Spider hides. Or he tries to humour me, which makes it worse. And I can't stand the smell of smoke. Or meat. I think I'm having a vegetarian." She put the bowl down and rested her hands across her stomach. "Okay, let's talk about something else now. This is the only conversation I ever seem to have. And unlike me, it's getting thin. Now go wet your hair. Let's do this."

As she sat waiting for her father, Indigo wondered if her new vivid do would provoke his disapproval. She was at a table for two by the window and, although her back was to the door, she faced a mirror. The seat had been chosen on purpose, because it let her watch the room — and his arrival — from a distance.

Anxiety twisted in her stomach. Not because she feared his criticism, or even because she hated the way their conversations always degenerated. Those were the pat reasons, held on to and polished for years, but never the entire truth.

Since before Christmas, an uncomfortable thought had been living in Indigo's mind. It occurred to her that she wanted to provoke his disapproval. She wanted to provoke him. It was something she did well. But as much as she liked to expose his pretensions, as much as she liked him in the role of evil dad, she knew it was only a caricature. And frankly, what she thought of as this late-breaking flash of insight made her squirm.

There was something else as well. They were different enough as people to want different things in life — in her life. That was fine, even expected. He was the father; he had as much right to an opinion as she had not to listen. But Indigo was beginning to suspect she enjoyed making decisions that would make him think he failed. Failed with her. Failed her. She didn't make the decisions to spite him, exactly, but she was kind of tickled when they did.

Indigo picked at a piece of bread. She hadn't seen him since Christmas, when they actually tried to have a conversation — defined later by Indigo as an exchange as opposed to a barrage of thoughts — much like adults would.

In its usual way, that well-mannered, chestnuts in the fire thing had begun to unravel early. They'd been in the living room, Indigo filling a garbage bag with wrapping, Richard in his favourite chair drinking coffee laced with booze. The twins were in a corner, sprawled in matching grey sweats, surrounded by disks and manuals, and identical laptop computers. They could hear Charlotte in the kitchen making breakfast.

"Aren't you going to call Sam?" asked her father. "At least wish the man a merry Christmas."

"No, he's with his family."

Richard's eyes followed her movements as she bent to retrieve a stray piece of ribbon. "It's damn hard work, marriage. Not for the weak."

"Yes," she said. "I mean no, I guess it isn't. For the weak." Indigo was in fact being obtuse. The only thing she told her father was that she and Sam had separated. The reason, she had said, was private.

He regarded her coolly, then sighed. "You're a very foolish girl. Do you hear me? Very foolish." When she didn't respond he continued. "I'll tell you why. First you throw away a bloody decent career, now a damn good marriage. Do you not see how spoiled you're being? Can you not stick anything out? It's a harsh world. Lose sight of that at your peril." As he put them down, his empty cup and saucer clattered. "You want to know what I think? I think you should march upstairs right now and call your husband, and do whatever you need to do to patch things up. Was there another woman?" He paused. "I can understand why you wouldn't want to discuss it. But even things like that can be forgiven. If you're willing."

Indigo shook her head. "There was no other woman."

At first, when she thought she might go back to Sam, she was afraid her dad would be all weirded out if he knew the gory details. That he'd never let it go. Then afterwards, she didn't feel like getting into it. Why upset him, she thought, knowing damn well she didn't care. It occurred to her now that some twisted part of her brain enjoyed her father's sniping. She liked to get him riled.

He was still watching as she tied the garbage bag and sat in a chair near the boys. "For Christ's sake, Indigo. Do you have to be so goddamn stubborn? Life isn't all milk and honey, sweetheart. It's hard work."

The more he watched, the more angry he seemed to become. "So what are they teaching you at film school? How to make dippy little art house crap that nobody sees?" He laughed. "How to live on the backs of taxpayers?"

"That's not funny dad." It was one of the twins.

"Right," said Indigo. "That's it. In the den." And then, standing up — "I'm sorry, that didn't come out right." She made her voice soft and musical. "Can I speak to you please? In private."

In the den, Richard picked up the framed photo of him with his arm around the Premier (who Indigo thought looked decidedly put upon). "What? Am I getting to you? Don't like to hear the truth, is that it?"

"I don't know how to put this delicately," she said, wanting in fact to be as indelicate as possible. "I walked in on Sam getting a blowjob from a man."

Her father's eyes shot open. "No," he said. "I don't believe it." He let the picture fall to his lap.

"Believe it," said Indigo. "It happened in September. Got it all on tape."

"You did not."

"Yep I did."

"That rotten bastard."

As she told him the story his face grew increasingly pinched. "I always knew there was something not quite right about him. Do you have a lawyer? You're going to need a good lawyer. I'd give you the name of mine but your mother's is better."

"That's what she said."

"She would," said Richard, allowing a grin. "You did the right thing sweetheart. You should have told me sooner."

"While we're here there's something else," she said.

"I know, and I'm sorry. It's just that I want what's best for you, you know that. You really should have told me."

"That's no excuse. You should know better. Fuck dad, you're a psychiatrist. You're supposed to know how to —"

"Watch your —"

"Listen to what I'm telling you." She measured her words out slowly. "You may not behave that way. I won't accept surly. Not any more. Not from you or anyone. Do you understand? I won't allow it. Go be a brute with somebody else."

"Indigo, you don't —"

"Just wait a minute. It's not all your fault. I'd love to say it is but it isn't." She took a breath. "Here's the thing. I think I kind of enjoy pissing you off. Don't ask me why but I do. So I'll try to revise my side of things as well." She sighed. "Okay, I'm done. There's no reason to talk this thing to death. Are we cool?"

It took him a moment to spot her. "Would you look at that," he said. "My combustible daughter's a redhead, how appropriate. I'm kidding. No really, it suits you." Her long curly hair was the colour of copper, bleached with chunky blond highlights. "Here, this is for you. Happy birthday." He handed her an envelope, then said to the waiter — "Chardonnay. A bottle of your best."

Inside was a cheque. Enough for six months rent and more. "I've decided to help you," he said. "You can pay me back later, when you're a bigshot Hollywood director. I'll let you take me to the Oscars."

Twenty-four

The most significant thing about Indigo's thirtieth birthday was that it felt decidedly insignificant. She examined the details, turned them over and poked them with a stick to see if they revealed any hiding neuroses.

She had coloured her hair. In a pinch that could be considered a response to fading youth. (That or a response to boring hair.) She drank what seemed like vats of wine with her father over lunch. They chatted. They laughed. *They didn't want to leave.* It was clearly suggestive of something.

Afterwards, fuelled by wine, she did some shopping. Bought some lingerie — an iridescent blue-green bra, matching g-string. And a dress she'd have to return because she'd wake up the following morning wondering what the hell she'd ever been thinking. (It was orange.) She went home and took a nap. Slipped on the bra and panty, danced wildly around the room for a while. Couldn't help noticing how much she enjoyed being there alone. Put it out of her mind. Drank real champagne with her mother and her mother's boyfriend over dinner. Opened presents.

Brian give her an IOU for a free session of therapy. "Psycho or massage," he said. "It's up to you."

That's what made her notice. Her response seemed excessively sane. This would never do. How could she expect to create interesting work if she couldn't even conjure up a phobic response to her thirtieth damn birthday?

When she said goodbye, Alice kissed her forehead. "It's not even ten o'clock, honey. Don't you want to hang around for a while?"

"No, I'm kind of tired. Actually, I still haven't unpacked my jewellery stuff. I thought I might do that. Or go to bed and do it in the morning. I have a lot of work to do between now and the end of the term."

"When's that?" asked Brian.

"A couple weeks. But I'm taking classes most of the summer. Another video workshop, then drawing — which I need desperately — then metal sculpture."

"Talk about keen," he said. "How'd you do with that video, anyway? The one about the fairies."

"Pixies. Okay, I guess. It passed."

When they discussed it, her teacher used the words fine, amusing in parts, competent. The concept, script, camera work, effects: all adequate. He didn't know her well, he said, but it seemed like less than she could do. Ordinary, despite her obvious attempts to be bizarre. It didn't have substance. Felt linear. And literal. As though she didn't challenge herself to go beyond her own fixed thoughts.

"Next time," he said, "why don't you try something that doesn't feel as comfortable, doesn't come as easy. Forget the jokes. Experiment. Challenge your basic assumptions. Force yourself to think differently. Think like an artist."

Chastened, she submerged herself in experimental video from the last two decades. Kept telling herself that video art is not television; it doesn't have to entertain. Narrative structure is optional. It doesn't have to be pleasant, or even interesting in the conventional ways that most people think of as interesting. It need not have a conclusion — but if it does, it doesn't have to explain what it is.

There was a video of a house, shot in real time from across the street. For thirty-seven minutes nothing happened. Indigo tried to find the significance. Did the number 37 mean something? Was it a comment on the loss of stillness in everyday life, or the need for patience? Was it about meditation? Should it make her think of the homeless? Or was the point to challenge her, the viewer, give her time to rest on the question — what is art?

Feeling guilty, Indigo fast-forwarded through most of it.

At first she told herself that her personality was ill-suited to too much visual quiet. Even with her growing taste for solitude, she was too anxious a person to simply focus on an object. (She made a note to take up yoga.) But as she conceived and rejected ideas, she began to think that her problem was really control. She wanted to force people to perceive her work a certain way, by making it as obvious as possible.

At home, Indigo found herself sitting in the window, attracted by the changing human landscape. She decided sleep could wait.

It was no longer snowing as she headed west on Queen, inconspicuous in monotones — slim black pants, fitted shirt and leather jacket. The crowd that had seemed so thick beneath her window, thinned as she walked against it until, eventually, there were only scattered people on the sidewalk. At Niagara she spotted the club she'd been hearing about, the one with no sign but a crush of bodies, dancing where they stood, chatting loud above the music.

At the bar, she asked for beer.

On another night, it might have been frightening to be alone in a space with so much conversation. She might have felt awkward, as though everyone else knew everyone else. The subdued orange light might have seemed to exclude instead of invite her.

But tonight — tonight she was brave.

Or maybe that's not true.

It only seems brave, she thought, in the way that a widow seems brave. Friends who don't know what to say always say — "You've been so courageous," when really, what choice did she have?

Indigo stood at the edge of the bar, watching faces as they passed and the screen above the bottles, silent music videos. A man squeezed in beside her. "Same again," he said, handing the bartender his empty bottle of beer.

He glanced sideways at Indigo — "How's it going?"

She smiled. "Fabulous. You?" He had light brown skin with hazel eyes, and straight black hair to his shoulders. She thought he was lovely.

"Fabulous, huh?" He shifted slightly toward her. "Sure, why not. Fabulous. We're all fabulous." When he'd paid for his beer, he said — "I'm Julian."

"Indigo."

"What's that?"

She leaned closer. "My name. It's Indigo."

"I never met an Indigo before." His gaze was intent and disconcerting and her own eyes darted to the crowd. "Are you waiting for someone?" he asked.

"Will you think it's weird if I'm not?"

He shook his head.

"Then it's settled. I'm alone,"

"Then you don't mind company?"

Indigo felt a sudden twinge of arousal. "That I don't."

"Great. The night's not a wash," he said. "So tell me, who is Indigo?"

She paused, thinking she might prefer to keep her details to herself. "You first."

"Okay." As he looked her up and down, he took a breath and let it go slowly. "Okay, how's this? Indigo is a charming and hopefully single redhead in her 20s, with beautiful teeth and what appears to be a smudge of lipstick on her forehead." He reached out and erased it with his thumb.

"I meant you," she said, blushing. "Who is Julian?"

"Ah, well that's different. Julian's *faaabulous*. He's a brilliant architect, still toiling away in the basement. Not for long, of course, but I'm sure you could tell that just by looking at him." He tapped his finger on his perfect cheekbone. "Let's see. He's the nicest guy you'd ever want to meet, handsome, 28 and, as luck would have it, single." He took a swallow of beer. "Your turn."

"All right," she said. "Indigo's a student. Film and video. Likes it. She's unattached, recently, likes that too. She lives down the street. And I guess she's a little bagged. It's been a long day."

Feeling the pressure of his body next to hers, not touching, she wondered what he'd think of Greece.

"That's it?" he asked. "Nothing else?"

"Oh, and it's her birthday. She's 30. Isn't that enough?"

Acknowledgements

Many thanks to my mother, Mary Ann Girod, and my father, Robin Ward, for a lifetime of support and encouragement; Robert Bouvier, for patience, advice and faith during what must surely have felt like a lifetime; Timothy Findley and Bill Whitehead, for guidance and many acts of kindness; Barry Callaghan, for publishing chapters; Russell Smith, for advice and introductions; Anne McDermid, for her skill and generosity; Marc Côté, for thoughtful editing and real champagne; Kirk Howard, for reasons that are obvious; Lynn Susan and Sarah Strange, for their example; Rebecca Timmons, for inspiration and sheer enthusiasm; Dona Noga and Lisa Murphy, for letting me talk it through; Margaret and Gerry Lukane, and Marco and Michelle Willis, for encouragement and countless invitations; Andrée Bernard and David Day, for too many things to list; Raven and Daemon at Urban Primitive, for letting me watch; Marsha Stonehouse, for stories and pictures; Denise and Nancy at Headstrong, for hiding the truth; the Ontario College of Art and Design; and the Humber School for Writers.

An excerpt of this book was published in *Exile*.